Cedric

Cedric

Footprints in the Sand

BF STEBBING

Inspired by a True Story

XULON ELITE

Xulon Press Elite
555 Winderley Pl, Suite 225
Maitland, FL 32751
407.339.4217
www.xulonpress.com

For information:
How Great Thou ART Publications
P.O. Box 48, McFarlan, NC 28102
www.howgreatthouart.com

Cover by: Carolyn Wisniewski

Paperback ISBN-13: 978-1-66288-916-5
Ebook ISBN-13: 978-1-66288-917-2

"A dog is the only thing on earth that loves you more than he loves himself."

Josh Billings

Summary

A shipwrecked Newfoundland dog finds his way to a small village on the English coast during the Victorian Era and rescues twenty-three people from other shipwrecks. Based on a true story.

Contents

Part III

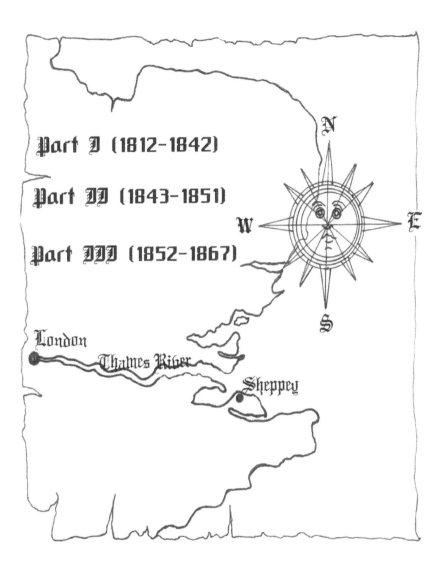

Part I (1812-1842)

Part II (1843-1851)

Part III (1852-1867)

London

Thames River

Sheppey

𝕯𝖊𝖉𝖎𝖈𝖆𝖙𝖊𝖉 𝖙𝖔

Rachel and Faith, two young ladies
who added life to the story.
My artist-friend Carolyn Wisniewski.
My endearing wife, Saundra –
the source of my inspiration.
Dale Bryson, my workhorse, without whom this story
would have never been told.
And my loyal dog, Hohty, who taught me much about
the ways of Cedric.

Preface

With the ebb and flow of the North Atlantic, the mighty Thames River inevitably makes its way to the heart of England. Quite often, the waters are calm, providing a safe voyage to and from the ports of London. Unfortunately, the weather in the British Isles is quite capricious and can quickly turn. Through the never-ending tempests, many a weary ship has been taken asunder.

This maritime cemetery has also laid hold on countless naval ships. Britain has always been a warring nation and vulnerable to invasion. The ancient Romans were one of the first to invade this Celtic land, followed through the centuries by Dutch, Spanish, and French armies and the sacking of villages by Vikings. Yet it was not always the brutal storms or the smoke of battle that brought so many vessels to their demise but rather the foreboding sandbanks that lay in wait beneath the shallows, a centuries-old graveyard of shattered ships and dead men's bones where more than seven hundred ships now lay at rest on the bottom of the channel. To anyone giving an attentive ear, the villagers would tell a tale or two, pointing out where certain vessels had gone down and directing the eye to skeletal remains of masts and hauls still clinging to the sandbars. Some would go on to boast of treasures salvaged along the shore.

Sheppey was one of a handful of villages on the coast, nestled but a stone's throw away from the estuary. Surviving countless years of storms and hardship, its inhabitants were as tempered as the windswept beach, their cottages stitched together like old burlaps. As one heads inland, the geography changes from a rugged coastline to undulating hills with sheep and woodlands. Many of the men in Sheppey worked this land, toiling upon the good earth with knobbed fingers day after day and managing to put a few sixpences in the till. In time, their legs and strength would give way, and they would no longer be able to travel the road that provided their livelihood. Some chose to make their living at sea, but the winters were long and the boats were scarce. The women were more fortunate as the sheep upon the hillsides were a saving grace, providing yarn to knit socks and mitts to be shipped to London along with the fishermen's cod. The villagers were uneducated and tight-lipped and with no inheritance coming or going.

The war machine would take its share of young men with insatiable demands. Likewise, the young women followed a similar path, venturing to London to seek a better way of life. One could say they left for selfish gain when, in truth, it was merely an act of self-preservation. However, a handful of persistent souls would remain. Holding fast to their tattered cottages, they married, had children, and continued scraping out a living. Sadly, the church cemetery would be filled with little mounds and tiny crosses as newborns quickly died from sickness or disease. Freezing winters and starvation also took their toll. And so, Sheppey's childbearing generations had all but washed out to sea. The remnant of aging villagers was in dire need of a younger generation—the cooing of an infant, a prancing toddler, or a youthful smile. Through it all, the village flew its tattered flag, symbolizing not glory but perseverance.

The early 1800s brought a brighter note upon the gray horizon as the wheels of British conquests continued to churn.

One could say the catalyst for the Industrial Revolution was Napoleon's defeat at Waterloo. Shortly after that, Victoria would wear the crown. Thus began the glorious Victorian Era. Like the shining star over Bethlehem, her coronation brought hope to the commoners. Queen Victoria was of good character, endowed with faith in God and a deep compassion for her people. Throughout her reign, Great Britain would become as prosperous as in the time of Solomon.

As sterling as the era may have been, it is difficult to conceive of the abject poverty that dwelled within the darker enclaves of London. Caught upon the millstone of mass production, the slums had become a starving state within the state. Other troubling concerns were weighing upon the monarch, such as the exploitation of child labor, recent military defeats, and mumblings of discontent within their far-reaching colonies.

In time, that glowing star of hope diminished. Even during their darkest hour, the Sheppians remained stalwart, chin up, gazing upon the brooding sky and sighing, "God save the Queen." The villagers grasped at straws, the most recent of which was a businessman who ventured into Sheppey with a purse full of crowns, intending to establish a business. Was there prosperity on the horizon? Momentarily coming to life, they took hope in the possibility of steady work and food on the table. Unfortunately, like the morning mist, it quickly faded away; the man departed and never returned. Resigning themselves to the simple fact that this was their fate in life, they continued to mutter, "God save the Queen.

Through the heavy clouds of such despair, there was another distant star. And though life had all but been snuffed out by the merciless vicissitudes of life, it would eventually make its way through many a tempest and begin to glow brightly upon Sheppey. But that would take time.

Part I
(1812–1842)

"If you will observe, it doesn't take a man of giant mold to make a giant shadow on the wall; and he who in our daily sight seems but a figure mean and small, outlined in fame's illusive light, may stalk a silhouette sublime, across the canvas of time." John Townsend Trowbridge

....

Chapter 1

A Tale to Tell

As patrons make their way through the Tate Museum, strolling past a vast display of Turner and Gainsborough masterpieces, they arrive within other spacious rooms with works from the Victorian Era: paintings redolent of the chivalrous days of yore along with the colorful prose of the Pre-Raphaelites.

Amid this collection is a rather large painting of a Newfoundland dog. Set within a backdrop of sea and gulls, he stares at the viewer with a rosy-pink tongue. The picture allows one's imagination to wander. *Who is he? And what is he doing here*? The title does offer a clue: *Bob, A Distinguished Member of the Humane Society*. It was painted in the early 1800s by the English master Sir Edwin Henry Landseer.

Delving through the archives, we obtain more insight. The dog had been a survivor of a shipwreck on the Thames River. He had drifted to the docks of a village and made the pier his home for the remainder of his life. Throughout the ensuing years, this remarkable creature would dive into the tumultuous waters and rescue twenty-three souls from other shipwrecks.

So, let us commence from here, filling in many blanks with our creative touch. The name of our noble creature will be *Cedric*. We will begin by following his footprints in the sand as he somberly makes his way into the coastal village of Sheppey, next to the estuary of the Thames.

....

Chapter 2

The Lone Survivor

T he *HMS Britannia* was built to be invincible. A double-masted brig of the Royal Navy, resplendent with white sails and tight halyards, she boasted twenty cannons and a crew of one hundred. Sleek and fast, she sailed the seas like a gull upon the sky.

One fine morning in 1839, the vessel prepared to leave port with a host of distinguished emissaries, flags, and banners flapping in the Norwegian breeze. Slowly, the valiant ship departed, and passengers waved a warm farewell as they set out on their voyage to London. It started well enough with calm seas and a hearty wind. However, being late autumn, it was a tentative season for storms.

By the second day, a tempest had swept down from the north, bringing strong winds and torrid rain upon the ship. Ensnared within a whirlwind, the *HMS Britannia* groaned hopelessly as towering waves hammered it broadside. The main mast crashed to the deck, and the ship began listing, passengers being swept overboard. Lanterns smashed and shattered within its haul, the tenacious winds muffling the sounds of agony and weeping. Beaten and battered, the remaining mast, entangled in sails and halyards, collapsed into the sea. Like stunned prey, the ship gave a final sigh and sank, leaving an empty void. Throughout the nocturnal hours, wreckage washed ashore: personal items, lifeless bodies, and shattered remnants of the vessel–along with one solitary survivor.

Chapter 3

𝔄 𝔖𝔬𝔪𝔟𝔢𝔯 𝔐𝔬𝔯𝔫

At the first pale light of dawn, a dog slowly rose from the sand. A light rain was falling. Battered and with matted fur, he meandered around debris and bodies, searching for his master. Pausing, with waves lapping against his paws, he looked out to sea and then, having no sense of direction, listlessly lumbered down the shoreline, a trail of footprints in his wake. In the distance was the hazy silhouette of a village.

Several fishermen were tending to their boats as the dog passed by. Downcast and with slow steps, he headed to an old pier and cautiously made his way over the warped planks to the end. The dog lay down in exhaustion, his eyes fixed on the sea.

Possibly, a seagull had been the town crier. In actuality, a villager had seen the ship in distress during the storm. By late morning, everyone knew of the tragedy, peering across the channel and searching for signs of the shipwreck. Word was that a dog had wandered into the village. Straining, they could vaguely see some foreign creature's shape at the pier's extremity.

There was one other who had noticed the dog stagger into Sheppey. Pinky was a mainstay at the Wayfarer Inn–a permanent resident and a lookout, so to speak. From the tavern window, he studied the dog and believed a vessel had gone down.

Retrieving his coat and cap and buttoning up, steadied by a cane, he limped north searching for signs; his one good leg was as strong as any man's. The carnage became evident with flotsam, trinkets, splintered beams, and bodies washing in and out of the surf. Limping around the wreckage, he returned to the Inn, taking a moment to study that creature on the pier again. He thought it best to let him be, at least for now, and headed inside.

Staring into the vacant North Atlantic, the dog remained motionless throughout the day. How could he make sense of everything that happened? Where was his master? He thought of his home in the mountains. They called him Mats. His master was his best friend. There were children. He loved to romp through the meadows with them during the warm summer days and swim in the lake. There was a pretty woman. She had a kind heart, always tenderly caring for him, brushing his thick coat, and giving him special treats.

He remembered the day well. His master had put on his leash and led him to the docks. Groomed for the occasion, he was proud to be by his master's side. There were large ships with tall masts and people everywhere. They passed by crowds of strange faces, many pausing to admire how big and handsome he was, leaning over and patting him on the head and praising him for being such a good boy. They then boarded a vessel. Soon afterward, it pulled up anchor and set sail, seagulls merrily following in its wake. Mats loved the water, especially this vast sea, the likes of which he had never seen before.

The next afternoon, as the ship made its way across the channel, his master took him topside and reclined in a lounge chair, Mats comfortably resting by his side, enjoying the loving hand that caressed him. Drifting into a beautiful bliss, they were lulled to sleep.

And then a stirring. Mats lifted his head. The sea became rough, the sky heavy with clouds. The wind howled like a wolf as large waves beat against the ship, rocking it within deep swirls. Someone began bellowing commands, people dashing back and forth, many falling on the slippery deck. The main mast came crashing down. Caught in dismay, he was separated from his master. People were screaming and crying out to God. The ship listed to one side. A horrific wave battered it broadside, and many passengers were swept overboard, including Mats, the churning sea all but taking him down. Thrashing furiously, people all around clinging to anything to stay afloat. He paddled in circles. Where was his master?

He saw him in the distance, splashing and crying out for help. Fervently pressing on, Mats finally pulled alongside, his master desperately wrapping an arm around his broad shoulders. Having no bearings, Mats paddled with the current. His master became heavier, the body lifeless, and then let go, drifting away face down. Mats fought against the waves to reach him. Finally clenching his shirt in his jaws, he pushed on. However, exhaustion and the weight of his master's body took their toll, and he released him, a large wave becoming the great divide and sweeping him out of sight. Mats frantically continued to search for him until his strength was gone. The sea then had its way, pushing him to shore. Exhausted, he lay down in the sand. That's all he remembered.

He remained on the pier, somber and motionless as dusk turned into the nocturnal hour. The sea had calmed, and the rain ebbed. He could hear the surf pleasantly breaking against the pilings, swaying the structure with its rhythm. A single light flickered from a window on shore and then went out. All was dark as he closed his eyes.

....

Chapter 4

The Pier

Pinky arose before daybreak, lit the lanterns, and started a fire in the hearth. He sensed the dog had remained on the pier overnight and would give the morning time to stretch its light across the sea. Preparing a pot of tea, he sat by the window and waited as a crimson blush spanned the horizon.

The storm had been brief but deadly, doing its damage and moving inland. Putting on his coat, Pinky made his way to the pier. Pressing on, he plodded over and around the precarious planks. Through the openings, he could see the surf pushing against the pilings.

The dog's head remained on its paws. As Pinky drew closer, he raised his eyebrows and meekly flapped his tail. Pinky gave him a hearty pat. The dog's heavy coat was soiled and matted but had fine markings. "Been thru it, 'ave yer? Wager y'ave ah tale 'er two ter tell in 'at big ol' 'ead of yers?" Bracing himself on the cane, he encouraged the dog to follow. As they slowly made their way to the Inn, villagers peered from their windows at the unlikely pair.

Jarvis and Bertie, the owners of the Inn, immediately embraced the dog. Bending down, they consoled him with heartfelt words and tender strokes. Jarvis gave him a good rubdown, manifesting a handsome coat. Dogs were a rarity in the village, especially one of such good breeding.

Pinky hobbled to the kitchen to prepare a large bowl of mutton stew, tossing in a hearty portion of odds and ends as Bertie brushed his fur.

Though famished, the dog ate like a true gentleman, taking his time and occasionally looking at them with a thankful glance. Wiping his hands on his apron, Pinky said, "Ee's ah beaut. A pup 'ee is. Big an' strong. An' wit no name." Groping around its neck, he unbuckled a collar of fine leather. There was the faded imprint of a name tag. Presumably, it had perished at sea. He bent down and looked the dog square in the eye. "Yer might be high falut'n, but yer the salt've the earth." Rising and considering for a moment, he said: "Yer jes like an ol' seafar'r ah once knew. Name be Cedric. Ah fight'r 'ee was, an' a big 'eart. 'At's wat we'll call yer– Cedric." Though the name was alien to the dog, he would respond to it, sensing these were good people and he was so alone. Comforted, he ambled over to the hearth and fell asleep, remaining in a deep slumber throughout the evening and into the night.

Early the following day, Pinky made his way down the stairs. There were still embers glowing in the hearth as he started a fire. Cedric remained half-asleep, slightly opening his eyes and giving a few tail flops. After a pat on his head, Pinky went to the kitchen to prepare a pot of tea. Returning and taking his seat by the window, he watched as the stars peacefully began to flicker out one by one.

A low whimper pierced the silence. Cedric was by his side, wagging his tail. Knowingly, Pinky limped over to the door, and the dog departed into the early hour, vaguely making his way to the end of the pier and coming to rest.

....

Chapter 5

The Fish House

Sheppey was one of a string of remote villages sprinkled across the coast of the British Isles; tucked between the craggy rocks and vast beach, a row of worn cottages extended from north to south. A church was resting upon a small hill on the southern end, with the cross on its chapel more like a battered weathervane. The path then meandered into the woods and open countryside, proceeding northwest to London.

At the northern end of the village was the Inn and a fish house, with a barren beach extending to where the North Atlantic clashed with the Thames. A tributary of the river meandered around the northeastern side of Sheppey, creating a cove, its port of entry since the early days of Briton. Out to sea was evidence of half-sunken vessels lodged against the sandbars. Villagers often said if one listened carefully, the ships would tell their tales in the wind.

With a demand for fresh cod, the fish house was a secure business. Weather permitting, the boats would make their way out of the cove, past the surf each morning, and return at dusk, packing their catch and shipping it to London, the only exception being a cod or two purchased by a villager with a sixpence to spare. The fish house was as weather-beaten as its boats, both having prevailed through many storms. However, the pier was more tentative, its pilings vulnerable to the unforgiving waves as it swayed precariously during rough weather.

Observing it on blustery days, the fishermen would nod their heads, knowing its days were numbered.

....

"Cherish your visions. Cherish your ideals; cherish the music that stirs in your heart... for, if you remain true to them, your world will at last be built." James Allen

....

Chapter 6

A Quixotic Soul

J arvis Merriweather was a dreamer, his daydreaming path beginning at a young age. As a boy, he thought of the days of yore, the Knights of the Round Table and St. George slaying the dragon. As a young man, Jarvis enlisted in the service of King George III. With a fervent sense of duty for God, king, and country, he dreamed of the chivalry still embedded within his heart. Brash and zealous, Jarvis thought he was invincible and was more than prepared to fight for the cause (whatever that may be). Quickly promoted, Major Merriweather was given a command in the British Heavy Dragoons and tested in battle time and again, for which he would receive a fair share of medallions upon his chest.

The gallant warrior made his final charge during the Battle of Salamanca in 1812. Orders were given to attack a line of French troops entrenched upon a hillside. Mounted, with sword pointed heavenward, he gave the command to advance. Onward they went through a breast of golden meadows as the trumpets blew. A maelstrom of bullets and cannonade then commenced with its deadly symphony. Charging through the smoke and hell of battle, the dragoons fell to the left and right. Upon cresting the hill, Major Merriweather was struck by a bullet in the abdomen. Off he fell, his horse charging on without him. The British were victorious that day, but at a heavy cost. More than half the regiment lay wounded or dead. The major was taken from the battlefield and shipped to a hospital on the British mainland.

Most veterans say that romance and war make for strange bedfellows, the battlefield often laying such frailty as love to ash. However, there are exceptions to every rule, and Major Merriweather would be one of those more fortunate souls, being struck by Cupid's arrow while recovering.

During the early nineteenth century, caring for wounded soldiers was considered as base as digging ditches, especially for ladies of leisure. Mopping floors and laundering were suitable only for those of the lowest degree. Nor would a woman of society conceive of the indignity of changing bloody bandages, festered wounds, and bedpans.

Bertie was of a different sort, both in status and heart. Though of a lower class, she deemed changing bandages and bedpans a higher calling. Young, vibrant, and Christ-bearing, Bertie saw such labors as nothing less than compassion. And she desired to do whatever was needed for these young brave men, whether mopping floors or tending to their wounded bodies.

Like many of the young women in Sheppey, she too had set out for London. Yet Bertie was not in search of a husband or a better way of life but to find work in a hospital and care for these countless men who had sacrificed so much. Upon arriving, she traveled the maze of red tape and made her inquiries. Sensing her merit, a head surgeon believed such compassion could heal souls and broken bodies and put Bertie to work.

Foremost, she desired to tend to the wounds of the heart. Many patients, infirmed beyond repair, had been abandoned by friends and family with no hope for a future. Between caring for wounds and bloodied bandages, she began spoon-feeding their faith in a loving God, letting them know there was much hope, for life always held its purpose.

While making her rounds through the battle's aftermath, she came to the bedside of Major Jarvis Merriweather. Who knows how many subtle glances it would take before love beckoned?

Within the cultural hierarchy of British society, Jarvis and Bertie were a mismatch; his newfound affinity for a peasant girl would go against the grain of the aristocracy. Born and raised on a regal estate, Jarvis had lost his mother while still a child, and his father, the venerable Brigadier General Thomas Merriweather, took him under his wing and reared him among society's best. Thus, the announcement of his son's marriage was most grievous, as much a disgrace as a child born out of wedlock.

However, Jarvis remained undaunted. He had established a new set of principles on the battlefield and would draw his line, standing firm with his romantic resolve, the battle scars and medals so rightly earned, giving him the liberty to do as he pleased. Furthermore, while wounded on the battlefield and near death, he had offered a fervent petition to the Almighty: *Save me, and I will serve you for the rest of my life.* And it was this newfound faith that invariably directed his heart to Bertie. Major Merriweather's mind and heart still overflowed with the dreams he held during his youthful years, and this love for Bertie overflowed with his purest ideals.

The major departed from the hospital in the winter of 1813. The wedding was set for the early days of spring. The ceremony was held in the little church atop the hill in Sheppey, with only a few close friends and relatives attending, one of whom was Jarvis's father. The old general had softened, consenting to the wedding, arriving in his military best, and bestowing a generous sum of crowns upon the newlyweds. Though Jarvis was overjoyed to see his father, he remained ever the purist and refused the gift, determined to make life on his terms.

The couple remained in the village, moving into the cottage of Bertie's parents. Cobwebbed, dusty, and in disrepair, it was their honeymoon suite. Bertie's beloved father had recently passed away, and her mother had fallen ill. There was no such thing as savings, and like everyone else in Sheppey, the newlyweds found themselves one step above destitution. Nevertheless, Jarvis remained enthusiastic, rolling up his sleeves and aspiring to put the abode in proper order. Opening the window, stoking the fire, cleaning deep pockets of soot, and repairing cupboards and chairs were but part of this newfound ideal, for he was determined to make the best of circumstances no matter what the hand of fate might bring.

Yet the heavy clouds of oppression looming over Sheppey would, in time, all but snuff out the candle of his diligence and high hopes. Breaking away from the entangled web, he would stand outside in the evening hour and face the sea. Taking a deep breath and heavy with thought, he would again lay hold of his imaginary sword and raise it undaunted toward heaven. For Jarvis was nothing less than Don Quixote, and these present-day discouragements were nothing more than a handful of windmills for him to conquer.

....

Chapter 7

Laying a Foundation

A nd let us not lose sight that Bertie's compassion was entwined within the major's aspirations. As a young girl, she saw the good in every villager and, through those youthful years, continually tended to their needs. Now, after several seasons, she would return to Sheppey. This time, she was not alone, as the hand of God had placed an enthusiastic husband by her side. It would not take long before they had a dream, a vision, sailing somewhere beyond the flight of the gulls and the windward clouds, for they saw an Inn, a resort on the coast that would bring tourists down from the city. And would not prosperity then flow throughout the village? Most assuredly, Sheppey had its romantic whims with the open sea, meandering seagulls, and the steady flow of vessels sailing by.

Jarvis's father passed away a year after the wedding, leaving his son as the sole beneficiary of the entire estate. This time, such generosity would not go for naught, for the attrition of life within the village was taking its toll, settling his somewhat whimsical soul within the stark reality around him. Still, after taking an ample portion of the inheritance, he dispersed the rest among extended family members and, foregoing the estate, he and Bertie decided to remain in the village. However, with such financial stability, they gazed upon that illusory star, envisioning the birthing of their Inn as a reality.

The foundation was laid in the spring of 1815. The Inn was not only constructed with toil and sweat but also prayer. A three-story building, securely framed, it could withstand any gale that blew in from the northeast. Save for the church, it was the only structure in the village without a thatched roof. There were twelve rooms in all, decorated with Bertie's articulate touch. The windows facing the sea gave lodgers a view of the sunrise and the seagulls passing by. Bertie envisioned a tea shop near the lobby. However, such a dream was too far-reaching for the times, and a tavern would have to suffice. There was a kitchen, a simple menu, and a limited variety of ales and spirits. The final touch was a hand-painted sign of a three-masted ship hanging over the entrance, *The Wayfarer Inn*.

Unfortunately, no sooner had the ribbon been cut than an emptiness seeped in. Was it not part of the misery that beset Sheppey? Oh, the villagers attended the grand opening all right, with its ample drinks and dainties. But as was their nature, they then turned their heels toward home and ne'er returned. Before the Merriweathers could blink an eye, dust had settled in the rooms, and the bell for service in the lobby lay silent. Beset with a dearth of patrons, the menu quickly spiraled down to a few meager selections. The villagers were not epicures, nor was there a desire to dine out and part with even a farthing. Those few who did hap into the tavern to taste the ware scoffed, *'Tis better ta eat me grub at 'ome*. Like the cobwebs within the rooms, the vacant tables only added to the despair of Jarvis and Bertie.

By the end of the initial season, the dispirited couple could be found standing outside facing the North Atlantic again. With a sigh, they sensed their dream had been swept away like the other glimmers of hope that happed upon the village. Spiraling down, they began asking the brutally honest question: Who would want *to vacation in this place anyway? It leads to nowhere, and the winters are merciless. The only form of entertainment is the gulls, if one can call them that. And the coast is as barren as Sheppey's womb.* With overlying grief, their hope sank into an empty well. Speaking of which, Bertie suffered a miscarriage. A second child died at birth the following year.

When the day was done and the ledger tallied, the libations would keep the Inn afloat. The fishermen, as constant as the gales, straggled in at the end of the day and took a perch. They were the most industrious lot in Sheppey, with a handful of coins in their pockets. Like old pelicans, some would find a secluded corner to self-indulge. The more convivial sorts gathered at tables, freely offering their opinions on worldly matters before emptying themselves of any dialogue and staring silently at the walls. Late in the evening, as the lanterns were snuffed, they would stagger to their cottages, humming a merry tune, and stumble into bed. Upon rising the following day, they would go about their labors on the sea and invariably return to their perches for the evening hour. It was the old proverbial snare, as not a one had the desire to abstain from their elixir, only paying the price the following day with a heavy head and a larger hole in their pockets. Could it not be said, *Watch the six pennies, and the crowns will take care of themselves.* And so, as the fishermen netted the fish, the tavern netted the fishermen.

One must take a moment to consider this dilemma for the Merriweathers as their conscience had to weigh the merit of selling liberations with the integrity of their faith. Alas, seeing Jarvis had invested everything in the business, they realized there was no other way than to compromise. Though neither imbibed, serving pints and quarts was the reasoning that had to prevail to keep their doors open.

Many an evening as they stood outside staring upon the dreary sky, they could faintly hear the hushed whisper of God within the wind: *Pay attention, Jarvis and Bertie. An extraordinary set of events is about to happen, and good tidings will come through countless storms. I will then come knocking at your door with many soaked and weary survivors from the sea. For indeed there is room in your Inn. And that sign, swaying upon the rusty hinges could read,* The Good Samaritan. *Be patient, for your rooms will soon be dusted and filled. And by the way, all those wretched souls will be delivered to you by an extraordinary creature.*

....

Chapter 8

𝔎𝔢𝔱𝔠𝔥

―――

Winter drew nigh. By dawn, the sea and sky merged into an ominous gray. The Wayfarer Inn's sign swayed recklessly in the brisk winds, and the gulls had taken flight. Pinky continued to study Cedric as he stoically remained on the end of the pier.

At one time, Pinky was a handsome man. Rugged and convivial, he invested his younger years in adventure and countless military engagements. Reflecting on the glorious past, not a day passed without thinking of his horse, Ketch. Named after a sleek vessel that sailed the seas, he had been undaunted through many a charge in the heat of battle. Ketch was invincible, and they were inseparable.

He remembered the day well. It was during the Battle of Salamanca. Charging against a battery of French artillery, horse, and rider went down in a fusillade of cannon shot, Pinky tumbling over his noble steed. Ketch lay motionless, bleeding, and with short, heavy pants, his eyes wide and frantic, imploring his master to do something. There was no other choice but to put Ketch out of his misery. It was the only time that Pinky wept. It would also be the end of Pinky's military career. When the smoke cleared, he received a severe wound to his left leg and the loss of an eye. And so, as quickly as a cannon shot, he lost his best friend and career. Strange–with the passing of the years, it was as vivid as yesterday. All humanity has regrets–for Pinky, it was leaving Ketch on the battlefield without an honorable burial.

Turning his focus to Cedric, the storm intensified, waves surging against the shoreline and hammering the pier. Pinky still couldn't figure out why he remained out there. There had to be more to it than missing his master. He had taken the dog under his wing, each morning calling him to the tavern for a meal and then spending an hour or so in silent conversation by the hearth. Something about Cedric reminded him of Ketch. It was that look in his eyes. On pleasant days, they would go to the beach where ol' Cedie boy would come to life, frolicking in the surf and chasing sandpipers.

Pinky continued to drift, reflecting on his countless travels across the high seas and the ebb and flow of people that had washed in and out of his life. As he looked out on his small portion of the world, he found himself content, the peace and solitude proving to be the best portion of his life. The wind had picked up, waves now sending a spray over Cedric. He could not help but think how that solitary figure was so much like himself.

Ironically, Pinky had served in the same regiment as Major Merriweather, fought in the same battle, attacked the same French battery, and was wounded on the same hill, though in different units. It would not be until Bertie introduced them in the hospital that they became comrades.

After a long recovery, Pinky made his way down the coast to attend the wedding. For the occasion, he donned a patch over his eye. His wound had left a dark cavity and an overhanging pink eyelid. A fellow veteran bestowed upon him the name *Pinky*, a title he carried along with a smile.

After the wedding, Jarvis implored him to remain and assist in the construction of the Inn. Handicapped, pegged leg, patch and all, he proved to be Jarvis's right-hand man. However, more than his good friend's persuasion, the barren beach and rustic village convinced him to stay.

It had been many years since the Inn had opened, and Pinky was as permanent a fixture as the creaking sign out front. His hair and stubble were graying, and considering his physical idiosyncrasies, one could easily take him for a beached pirate from the Barbary Coast. Yet, perchance, if patience had its way, his smile and that one good eye, along with his many tales, would sway the most critical heart.

Pinky remained faithful to his dear friend and his good wife as the Wayfarer Inn sank into deeper despair. Managing odds and ends such as cleaning, maintenance, working the kitchen (if ever the occasion), and serving libations during the evening hours were part of his daily routine. On rare occasions when a sojourner would spend the night, he would even hobble up the stairs to the room and tidy up. His stipend was meager, though well compensated with meals, an occasional pint of ale, and a roof over his head. *Who could complain?*

The wind began to beat upon the coast with all its fury. Cedric raised his head, focused on something out in the swirling gray, deep in the abyss. And then there it was, a crippled vessel bobbing in and out of the waves. Cedric rose, his face like flint against the wind. He paused, and then, as quick as a blink from Pinky's good eye, he dove into the sea. Immersed in the violent tempest, he fervently pressed on, the current pushing against him as waves crashed over his head.

A torrential rain beat against the window, and everything merged into one. Pinky wiped the glass, squinted and strained, occasionally catching a glimpse of Cedric's head bobbing in and out of the sea. There was another fleck of the vessel, and everything faded into the whirlwind.

Churning with a fury, Cedric began passing debris and bodies. He could hear the vague sounds of weeping and pleas for help and saw survivors holding on to flotsam in the distance. They were scattered and drifting. Pushing on, bodies floating head down with shattered remnants of the vessel strewn across the sea. Arriving where the ship had gone down, the bowsprit still tipped the waves. The cries for help had dissipated. Treading water and searching, a solitary figure was clinging to a plank.

Paddling with a fury, Cedric pulled alongside. The man was barely afloat, all but unconscious, gasping and coughing. He gathered whatever strength remained and lunged forward, desperately wrapping an arm around the dog's broad neck and feebly struggling to paddle with the other. It was a cumbersome burden, weighing Cedric down as his large paws struggled to paddle onward. As fate would have it, a favorable current pushed them inland. Reaching the shoreline, the man let go and crawled to shore. Sprawled out, his face pressed against the sand, he expended the last of his energy and passed out.

Cedric stood over the body. It was impossible to drag him to the village, so he waited. Then, lying down, he shielded the man against the elements as best he could. The day was closing fast, and the rain continued to fall.

....

"I have uttered what I did not understand, things too won-derful for me, which I did not know." Job 42:3 NKJV

....

Chapter 9

𝕭𝖔𝖘𝖚𝖓 𝕭𝖑𝖚𝖙𝖍𝖊𝖗𝖘

P inky limped outside, the rain stinging his eyes. He looked north for any signs of Cedric or the vessel. Dusk was merging with the heavy sky. Buttoning up, he made his way up the coast, Jarvis running out to accompany him. As bodies washed ashore, they recognized the uniform of the British Navy. Then, in the blurred distance, an image appeared. *Was it ol' Cedie boy?* Pinky pitched his cane in the sand as they quickened their pace. *Aye, 'tis 'im all right.* He was standing over a body, wagging his tail. His fur was soaked.

The man was lifeless, a sailor of the British navy. His flesh was as white as a whale's bone, and his body pressed into the sand like a sea-shell, the tide lapping over his lower body. Then, a slight stirring. They quickly raised him to his feet as he slowly became conscious. Wrapping his arms around their shoulders, they made their way to the Inn, Pinky bracing one side with his cane. For all practical purposes, the Wayfarer Inn was the only place in the village where a weary soul could mend.

A blazing hearth greeted them as they struggled through the doorway. Bertie retrieved an armload of blankets, and after the men had undressed the seaman, they bundled him up and laid him down on two tables pulled together. He returned to unconsciousness. Save for the lanterns and hearth, the evening was pitched in darkness and silence.

Numb and still in shock, the seaman finally sighed and opened his eyes, only his scruffy head protruding from the blankets. He was gently raised and placed in a chair by the hearth, Jarvis handing him a glass of hot rum. The blanket fell as he extended an arm, a faded tattoo on his forearm. A smile surfaced on his unshaven face as he took a sip. Though rail-thin, he seemed strong of sinew. Pinky made his way to the kitchen and returned with a bowl of hot mutton stew. The seaman remained more attentive to the rum. Coming to life, he began recollecting it all with abbreviated thoughts.

Oscar Bluthers was his name, a bosun aboard the ill-fated *HMS Prince Edward*. A gale off the coast of Africa had given the ship a good beating. "Crippled we were, limp'n our way ta port'n London. An' 'en the storm, worse 'an the first. Ah collaps'n topsail crushed the Capt'n. Tak'n on water, list'n, ready to capsize." The bosun went on to mutter that all the officers were killed or swept overboard. "Sink'n fast. Foun' meself 'n command. Gave orders ta 'Band'n ship!'" Most of the other men had perished by the time he leaped overboard. There was a deep moment of silence. Raising his head, he blurted out, "Bles't ta be 'live." With that, he drooped over, and all fell silent once again. That was enough for one day. Jarvis and Bertie half-carried him to a room on the first floor where he would sleep throughout the evening and late into the following morning.

Word of the shipwreck sinking reached the grocer's ear early the next day. Mrs. Filmore, the proprietor's wife, was the hub of news coming and going throughout the village. Bertie had stopped in at the break of day for staples and told her of the disaster, mentioning that a seaman was the lone survivor–a Bosun Bluthers of the Royal Navy. She went on to say that, quite miraculously, he had been rescued by that dog on the pier and concluded by mentioning that the good sailor would be sharing his story in the tavern that evening, and everyone was invited. Shortly after that, the word was heralded to one and all.

Though shipwrecks were expected off the coast, the sinking of the *HMS Prince Edward* held a most peculiar note with the details of this seaman's miraculous rescue. The villagers soon concluded, "Ne'er a tale 'ad been told in all 'ese years!" And could they not add it was just as stupendous as the sinking of the Spanish Armada? Throughout the day, curious eyes peered out upon the pier. The dog looked quite noble, poised as Lord Nelson himself.

Late in the afternoon, Pinky went out and called him. It was time to tidy him up for the evening presentation. Cedric immediately perked his head and arose. Pinky marveled at how he had so quickly responded to his new name. He also admired how such a large dog could gingerly make his way across the warped planks.

....

Chapter 10

"An' 'ere ah 'ees!"

———

By early afternoon, Bosun Bluthers was his old self again, full of vim and vigor. The hearth had dried his uniform, and he looked presentable. Cedric, too, was groomed for the occasion. The stage was now set for the event, and the seaman was ready to tell his epoch tale.

The villagers began trickling in at twilight. Lanterns were lit, and the hearth glowed. Entertainment such as this was a true rarity in Sheppey. Cedric rested nonchalantly by the fire. Several guests meandered over and, bending down as best they could, gave him a tender pat and rasped, "Ee's ah good boy." Looking up with his large innocent eyes, Cedric flapped his tail with a warm reply.

The fishermen were the last to arrive, lining the far wall as all the tables were taken. Roger Osborne, a true rarity among the villagers, had discreetly nudged between them. Excitement was in the air, and on such an occasion, it was not a time to pinch pennies. Reaching merrily into pockets and purses, everyone celebrated with a pint or two, and hearts and bones were soon coddled.

When all were served and settled, Bosun Bluthers took the floor. With a broad smile, he looked out upon the packed house, believing everyone had come to see him. "Like ta call meself 'Bos'n Firs' Class Osc'r Bluthers." Puffing out his chest, he added, "No such thing as 'Firs' Class,' but ah was as good as 'ere was. Not a midshipm'n, mind yer, but

27

next bes' thing. Work'd me way up from swabb'n decks ta bos'n's mate, ta bos'n." He then went on to tell them of the fate of the *HMS Prince Edward* and that last fateful evening off the coast. "Storm 'it us close ta shore, but couldn't see ah thing. Nev'r seen such a gale! Me mates van-ish'd like 'at!" The bosun snapped his fingers. "Capt'n been crushed an' waves 'ad swept the other offic'rs ov'r the bulw'rks." He added that the rest of the crew leaped into the sea as the ship began to sink.

"Noth'n left but splinter'd masts an' dead man's bones. Ah cries out, 'Band'n ship! An' o'er the side ah went. Moan'n an' groan'n all roun'. An' 'en noth'n! Me mates all gone. 'Bout ta go under meself. Grabbed 'old've somethin' an' 'eld on fer dear life. Ol' man death rattl'n 'is chain, the deep sea tugg'n at me bones. Said me ten 'ail Marys." With added drama, the bosun pressed his hands together and looked up at the ceiling, "Oh, 'ave mercy on me, dear Lord! 'Ave mercy on me!"

He continued by saying how nearly blind from seawater and bone weary, he was ready to let go. "B'tween the devil an' the deep blue sea 'ah was. Then, lo an' behold, see's ah large furry 'ead come bobb'n t'wards me. Can't b'lieve me eyes! Pulls 'long side an jes looks at me–no choice but ta grab 'im 'round 'ees big 'ol neck. An' off 'ee goes, paddlin' wit all 'is might. Waves crash'n over me. Can't see noth'n. Thinks ah'm a goner. 'O, Lord, 'ave mercy on me!'"

Jarvis handed the bosun a glass of rum. Pausing to take a swig, he wiped his mouth with a sleeve and smiled. Looking over at Cedric, who seemed to be following his every word, he said, "Reach'n shore, passed out like a dead man. Cedie boy 'ere, 'ats what ol' Pinky calls 'im, stayed by me side, 'ee did." Taking another gulp of rum, Bosun Bluthers opened his arms wide, "An' 'ere ah 'ees. As 'live as Jesus!'" Perked by the libation and prouder than a peacock, he took a seat. *Enough said.* For it had only taken a few moments for his audience to mumble, *Should call 'imself 'Blabber'n Bluthers.'*

Pinky rose and came to the forefront. The villagers were acquainted with him only at a long arm's length, watching him hobble in and out of the Inn or making his way to the grocer's. And that was as close as they wanted to get. Pinky paused, looking out at the dour faces. His smile broadened, knowing it would only take a moment to cocker their hearts. After all these years, this would be his formal introduction to the villagers.

A master at the pause, he continued to wait. He slowly began to lure them in, his voice coarse but resonant. His tone was sincere, as if speaking from the heart. He told of that first rainy morning when the dog had wandered into the village and how the wretched creature spent the night on the old pier. Early the following day, Pinky persuaded him to come to the Inn, where he was cleaned and fed. That was when he gave him the name Cedric, and he and ol' Cedie boy had been best friends ever since. Pinky then told of his noble steed, Ketch, who had faithfully carried him into many a battle against Napoleon. Cedric proved to be just as gallant during that terrible storm when he saw this noble creature dive into the sea and swim toward the shipwreck. All eyes remained fixed on Pinky, absorbing his every word; only the crackle of the fire was heard during the pauses. Pinky ended by saying he knew the heart of ol' Cedie boy and that he had arrived in the village not only to rescue souls from the sea but for the good of every soul in Sheppey. "'Ees 'eart's as pure as gold." Taking a seat, Cedric came to his side and licked his hand.

Though the bosun's story had been entertaining, Pinky's was more passionate and heart-to-heart. If truth be told, the villagers would rate his presentation the best they had ever heard. Many a feeble hand raised a glass to toast, a glow upon their faces as Pinky gave a slight nod. All eyes fell on Cedric, that estranged dog who had mysteriously found his way into their village.

The evening was dark. Many villagers made their way over to give Cedric a pat on the head and a few kind words; some even turned to Pinky and offered a slight smile of approval. Then, donning their coats and hats, they departed into the late hour.

A naval vessel sailed down the Thames in a few days and docked in the cove. Officials entered the lobby of the Inn, requested a block of rooms, and began surveying the aftermath of the shipwreck, rummaging through the debris and retrieving bodies that had washed ashore. In the evenings, they indulged in libations and Pinky's mutton stew. Before departing, an official handed Jarvis one hundred pounds, a token of appreciation from the British government for the care of the bosun, along with their lodging (which they thoroughly enjoyed). They then proceeded to take Bosun Bluthers to port in London. Jarvis and Bertie stood outside, beaming with joy as they waved farewell. Pinky observed from the tavern window, occasionally glancing at Cedric, who had returned to the pier. And all returned to normal.

In the solitude, Pinky made his way over to a beam near the front door. Taking out his knife, he carved a solitary notch, signifying the rescue of Bosun Bluthers. Reflecting, he wondered how many more there would be.

"The road that stretches before the feet of man is a challenge to his heart long before it tests the strength of his legs."

St. Thomas

....

Chapter 11

The news of the sinking of the *HMS Prince Edward* finally reached the good pastor and his wife, the last cottage to the south end of Sheppey. It went without saying that any nonsensical gossip stopped at the door post of Pastor Theo and Mildred, who quickly disengaged from whimsical hearsay or imaginings. However, news of a shipwreck was always troubling and heartfelt, and this one even more so. The talk of the town was that the dog that had wandered onto the pier had rescued a sailor. Could there be an element of truth in it all? Mildred always found the grocer's commentaries to be a good source for the facts. Seeing such, she made it her intention to visit the grocer and divide asunder nonsense from the truth.

On a raw morning, the pastor's wife made her way north to purchase staples but, more so, to receive an earful from the proprietor's wife, Mrs. Filmore. She was middle-aged, rotund, and literally full of herself and immediately set to task with the latest headlines. Mildred was attentive, packing her ware and quite awed as the story unraveled, occasionally interjecting with a reflective, "I see." She became all the more intrigued when Mrs. Filmore mentioned that the dog leaped from the pier during the height of the storm and swam to the sinking ship to rescue that drowning sailor. "If you look out on the pier, you can still see that fine creature. Pinky calls him Cedric. The Inn hosted the village the evening after the storm, and the sailor told it all." Mildred and her husband would never patronize a place that sold libations, and she hesitated to believe every jot and tittle of this far-fetched tale. (Mrs. Filmore did tend to be swept away with enthusiasm and a stretch of exaggeration.) Thanking her, she departed with her basketful of staples and a significant question mark still looming over her head. It is simply too much to pack into a practical mind.

The shop offered a closer view of the pier, and she could clearly see the image of that dog. Heading south, she continued looking over her shoulder and considering it all. As she passed, a small gathering of villagers chitchatted like barn swallows. Leaning an ear in their direction, she picked up quips and tidbits with the wind, "'Tis true! That is true, indeed. And, Cedie, 'ee saved 'at ol' bloke, 'ee did." Mildred's curiosity was beginning to get the best of her.

Several days passed and the days were becoming brutally cold. All the while, Mildred's reasoning evolved, finally muttering, "If it is true, then the poor dog needs a home." She then prepared to take the journey farther north to the pier.

Mildred poked her head outside early in the morning to test the elements. Greeted by a freezing wind, she quickly closed the door with a shiver, settled in, and prepared a tea, waiting and hoping for the wind to die down. Half-past, she opened the door again. It had waned a bit, encouraging her to launch into the day. Without disturbing her sleeping husband, she put on her coat, wrapped a scarf around her neck, tucked her head in a woolly, and proceeded on her venture, carrying a parcel of food and a length of rope.

The village slowly awakened, chimneys merrily releasing smoke into the winter sky. The sun passed through a veil of clouds, offering a faint sentiment of warmth. Fishermen occasionally passed by, giving her stoic nods as they headed to the fish house. Mildred humored herself;

ne'er a one ever set foot in the church, not even during the worst of storms. She knew full well the tavern was their chapel.

Pausing near the grocer's to catch her breath, Mr. Filmore stood out front and surmised the day. Framed in the doorway, a white apron accentuating his rotund body, he manifested an opulence unbeknownst to the rest of Sheppey. The portly face, along with an aloof air, confirmed as much. A pair of glasses perched upon a stubby nose and a balding head completed the image. Mildred noted that he too, could use a little church.

Observing the tether in her hand, he perceived her intention and pointed a forefinger toward the pier. Squinting and teary-eyed from the wind, the dog was still there, poised in the same position. Catching a second wind, she nodded and continued on her way, the wind blustery enough to keep her head low. Her teeth began chattering, and her bones chilled as the warmth of home dissipated. Too old for this, she mused as she continued to totter along.

The fish house marked the end of her journey with the pier, jutting out into the sea. There was no way she would dare to venture across that decrepit thing. Sitting on a crate, she studied the dog at a distance. The sun was now more merciful, spreading its golden light upon the sea. She admired the liveliness of the seagulls sailing over the channel, saying under her breath, "That's the spirit, my little songbirds!"

"Morn'n, Mus Millie." A rugged-looking man approached. Sammy was the mainstay of the fish house, living in a small hut to the rear. Weathered by the sea, his body was tempered, and he was healthy-looking in a raw sense. Underneath the scruff was an unpolished handsomeness.

"Good morning, Sammy."

It was a rare occasion for him to see her this far north. Seeing the parcel and rope, he asked, "What's 'is? Find yerself a pup, did yer?"

"Haven't yet made the poor creature's acquaintance. He's certainly the talk of the town."

"A good'n, 'ee is, Miss Millie. Got a lot of pup in 'im. Don't think 'ees a day over two years." Sammy asked if she intended to take him home and added, "Somethin's call'n 'im from the sea. Perched 'ere a fortnight. Not mov'n a hair, 'cept fer feed'n." Knowing she couldn't make it across the pier, he offered his assistance: "I'll fetch 'im fer yer."

"Oh, thank you, Sammy. Here–take the tether."

Over the years, his time at sea had given him a sprightly nimbleness. Well-versed in the pier, he knew its many snares like the back of his hand. Nor was he the intimidated sort. Mildred watched with admiration as he made his way across the planks. It was an incredible feat to her, all but imagining the structure swaying beneath him. As Sammy drew closer, the dog arose and wagged his tail. Sammy tied the rope around his neck, and the dog followed along.

Mildred leaned over to introduce herself. They were all but eye to eye as she patted his head. To her amazement, the dog was quite large. His shoulders were like those of a plow horse. Though he had similar traits, she thought he resembled a friendly bear. White areas dappled his otherwise black, furry head with dark markings extending between the eyes and encircling his nose. The only splash of color was his tongue freely lapping the air. Staring into that innocent face, she said, "My, you're a grand one." He raised his eyebrows, giving a melancholy look that could melt a stone. Mildred unwrapped the cloth and gave him a meal.

Sammy watched. "We've been tossing 'im some bits late in the day." Mildred waited while Cedric ate. The sun ascended with a burst of warmth, making the time pleasant. After he finished, she took hold of the tether, "Come along, Cedric, or whatever they call you, I'm taking you home." Looking at her with those deep brown eyes and trusting her kind and gentle spirit, he wagged his tail and obliged.

Sammy watched the odd pair saunter away, Cedric rising past her midsection. He hollered, "Yer can take'm 'ome, Millie, but 'eel be back! The sea be call'n 'im!" She gave a slight nod and a little wave with the back of her hand as she made her way south. Though the wind remained brisk, it was mercifully behind her.

There were several stops along the way, taking the opportunity to catch her breath and showcase the new member of her family. Several villagers awkwardly exited their cottages to look closely at Sheppey's newfound hero and bestow adoring pats on his head. More than gracious, Cedric offered a few licks and several wags of his tail to one and all.

Mildred approached the cottage of Gertrude and Agnes. Though none of the houses offered a welcome mat, it was less inviting than the rest–cold, shuttered, and still. Gertrude stood at the front door, Agnes behind her in the shadow. Sheppey had its share of recluses, pessimists, spinsters, and godless souls, but Gertrude and Agnes were the consummation of them all. Dressed in black, they offered the world a sinister greeting. Gertrude grimaced, her face contorted at the sight of Mildred and the dog. Mildred, well versed in their brooding, greeted them softly and kindly.

Gertrude smirked. "I see we've 'nother mouth ta feed in 'is wretched place! Where 'd ya find 'at beast?"

"His name is Cedric, Miss Gertie. Lovely sort, isn't he? He was on that ship that went down in late October–rescued that seaman from a shipwreck. The poor creature seems so stranded and alone. I'm bringing him home."

"I know all 'bout 'im. Keep 'im 'way from 'ere! Don't want 'im sniff'n 'round and discharg'n 'is goods on me property. I'll give 'im a whack 'eel nev'r ferget!" She held up a broom in a threatening manner.

Mildred kept her distance but remained pleasant. "The good Lord bless thee, Miss Gertie," and pulling on the rope, departed.

Another peculiar villager was standing by his door. Surnamed 'the professor,' Roger Osborne was the only educated resident in the village. His cottage was nestled on a slight hill just to the north side of the church and next to Mildred's. Roger was pleasant enough, not as musty as the other villagers or battered by life's vicissitudes. An intellectual sort, he was somewhat removed and left his neighbors with little to banter about. To him, such solitude was what he cherished most. His only companion was his little dog, Otto. Roger was industrious, investing the wee morning hours in writing, a candle burning in his window. At sunrise, it would be snuffed and his workday completed. At this time, the villagers could see him standing by his door, staring out to sea and taking in the brisk air with a pipe in hand. Like a Swiss clock, rain or shine, he was always there at that hour.

Observing the dog, he immediately conjectured it to be the hero of Sheppey. Pulling at his pipe, he wondered who was leading whom.

"Good morning, Roger." Mildred stopped. In the blink of an eye, Otto scampered out and jubilantly scurried around the large foreign creature. Cedric backed up and stood motionless, not knowing how to handle such an overwhelming greeting. Roger was amused, deducing he shared a similar social tendency. Tapping his pipe, he inquired as to what, perchance, she was going to do with such a fine specimen.

"My dear Cedric–that's what they call him–now has a family. Coming home to live with the mister and missus. Needs a wee bit of cleaning up and some tender loving care."

Roger gave it a moment's consideration and then told her the dog was a fine breed, worthy of a pretty sum of crowns. A Newfoundland was noted for its size and strength and purported to be an excellent swimmer. Fishermen have used them as workhorses, hauling nets to shore and occasionally even boats.

"Don't tell that to the fishermen," Mildred jested. Though she was intrigued by Roger's wealth of knowledge, more pressing concerns were at hand. Eventually, there would be time to glean more from his insight. Energized and with a second wind, she thanked him and gently took Cedric in tow.

Pastor Theo was also standing by his door, basking in a touch of warmth. However, he was not there for a breath of fresh air, being perplexed as to the whereabouts of his wife. It was not like her to be absent in the morning, especially for such an inordinate amount of time. She did mention her intention to venture north and see that dog for herself.

Relieved to see her talking with Roger, he still questioned why she had brought the creature home. As she approached, he mused, "What do we have here?"

"Just bringing home a wayward son."

"I see." Knowing her intention, he pondered what the future might hold with such a behemoth in their small abode. Most assuredly, it would eat them out of house and home. Sighing and sending up the wisp of prayer, he thought, why couldn't she have brought home a little dog like Otto?

Returning to reality, he moved aside and opened the door wide as his good wife herded in her *lost lamb*. Watching him enter, he had as much grace as a flock of sheep, bumping into everything before settling down next to the hearth.

During the warmth of midday, Mildred took Cedric outside to bathe him. Drying him off and brushing him down, she led him back into the cottage for a meal. That evening, she escorted him outside for the night, settling him down inside the picket fence and saying a little prayer before retiring. Closing the gate, she was comforted, knowing his thick coat would keep him warm on such a cold night. Clean and fed, Cedric rested his head on his paws and nodded off. The night air was brisk, the stars all but frosted, as a full moon sailed in and out of a pillowy sky.

Early the following day, Mildred peeked out the door. Looking around the side of the cottage, she noticed the gate was ajar. Far up the beach, she could only imagine Cedric returning to the pier.

....

"Love is like wildflowers; it's often found in the most unlikely places." Ralph Waldo Emerson

....

Chapter 12

𝔉𝔩𝔬𝔴𝔢𝔯𝔰 𝔬𝔣 𝔖𝔥𝔢𝔭𝔭𝔢𝔶

B irds and flowers are some of the sweetest accents of nature. Strewn throughout the earth with flecks of color and song, they are the final touches on earth's masterpiece. Possibly, it takes the passing of years or the eyes of a child to appreciate such unheralded gifts fully. Subtly, they work together, for a bird has the unique trait of carrying digested seeds to other parts of the land and discharging them, taking root, budding, and blossoming into flowers. However, upon harsher and more barren lands, such as the shores of Sheppey, seeds will not take root, as sand and rock are not fertile soil for flowers. Nor does one find a songbird within these coastal areas, just sandpipers and seagulls.

Let us now introduce two unique seeds that would grace the land of Sheppey. These two orphaned girls would arrive, but not from the droppings of passing birds. In due season, they would take root, sprout, and blossom.

The pair of siblings had spent their younger years on the outskirts of London. Unfortunately, their father met with an untimely death, and for the next several years their mother did her best to make ends meet, doing whatever menial jobs would come her way. Invariably, it took its toll. Debilitated and grief-stricken, she fell ill and bedridden.

Though the girls tended to her and managed the household as best they could, the jar of coins in the pantry was soon empty. In desperation, the mother, barely able to hold a quill, wrote to a distant relative, imploring her to show compassion and take the girls.

Nora vaguely remembered her cousin. They had lived worlds apart and were distant relatives. However, sensing the dire need, she put everything aside, hitched her horse to the wagon, and traveled the rugged terrain to the city. A fortnight after her arrival, the mother passed away. After tending to the burial proceedings and other affairs, Nora packed the girls' belongings and returned to Sheppey.

It was the first time the girls had ever seen the countryside, and they found the ride picturesque with the lush tones of early summer. Basking in the warmth and the fresh air, they remained silent throughout the long ride, bewildered and heartbroken.

Rachel Thomson was born in 1825, shortly after the death of King George III. It was also a year when the Industrial Revolution was in full throttle. Ironically, as throngs of migrants were heading to London, the young sisters were departing. Faith, one year the younger, was born just before the Parliament abolished slavery. 1826 was also a year noted for being the end of the Irish famine (sadly, only one of many). Rachel was fourteen, and Faith was thirteen. Coincidentally, they arrived in Sheppey the same season as Cedric; he to the pier, and they to the west side of the village.

The ride gave Nora time to consider this transition, which would alter the course of all three lives. Country life would be good for the girls, a wholesome place to mend their souls. Hopefully, in time, they would love it as much as she did, and the many chores that needed to be done would build character. Then again, they would be good company, especially during the long winter months. It had been a long season of solitude, and she was now endowed with a little family.

The country road meandered south by southeast. Late in the day, it reached a stretch of rolling hills and woodlands. Nora pointed out her cottage. It stood on a far-off hill redolent with sheep, a country mile from the village.

Nora and her husband laid claim to the land years ago. Having removed themselves from metropolitan life, their desire was the ambiance and peace of nature. It was remote, idyllic, and nestled near the coast. Unfortunately, Nora's husband passed away in the prime of his life. Educated, industrious, and an excellent craftsman, he had left the home in good order. Now middle-aged and having a substantial inheritance, she was secure for the remainder of her days.

With time and experience, Nora could handle everything on her own, from raising sheep to cutting firewood. She had a wholesome beauty as natural as her gardens, the flowerbeds becoming her extended family. She enjoyed putting her hands in the good earth and observing the wonderful process of seeds coming to fruition. If a traveler were to wander past her cottage on a summer's day, her gardens could be perceived as some of the most resplendent in all the British Isles.

Throughout the ensuing days, Nora continued putting the pieces together, prioritizing the girls' education. Nora was educated and well-versed in life through travel, reading, nature, and her faith and intended to broaden their knowledge with an introduction to Latin, science, and arithmetic. Her first love, though, was nature. And, whenever the days were pleasant, she planned on guiding them along the creek, pointing out myriad natural artifacts and nurturing an appreciation for the quiet ambiance. There was also a desire to instruct them in intangibles such as discipline, respect, and an attitude of thankfulness.

For Rachel, the highlight of her education was Nora's library, a collection of books Nora's husband had acquired throughout the years. Faith and Rachel were both voracious readers, and during the colder months, they would read when time afforded. Rachel gravitated to the art books redolent with their black-and-white illustrations of works by the masters. Curling up by the window that faced the distant sea, she gleaned from Renaissance, French, and Dutch masters and continually copied pictures of etchings by Rembrandt and Durer. Faith proved to be more like Nora in her love for nature and animals.

Nora also had the ambition to teach them the basic fundamentals of drawing. However, this was a dilemma as Rachel's abilities far exceeded hers. However, her young student considered art secondary to her new responsibilities. Nevertheless, Nora insisted it be a priority to continue developing her God-given talent.

On occasion, Nora hitched Mr. Wilson to the wagon to take the girls to the village. He lodged in a separate area of the sheepfold and could often be seen accompanying the sheep on the hillside. Not a workhorse, his duties were relatively light, and Nora was relieved to find him dependable during the long journey to London.

Nora was an anomaly in Sheppey. The villagers kept to their own, remaining base and ignorant of the ways of the world. However, they were attracted to her, for Nora manifested an inner peace and a natural charm that were alien to them. The sparkle in her hazel eyes added a consoling touch, and she greeted everyone sincerely and with an amiable smile.

In time, Nora allowed the girls to venture into Sheppey independently. Young and energetic, the hike would give them an introduction to the village, and she always encouraged Rachel to take along her art materials. Such ventures never made it past the grocer's. There was subject matter everywhere for Rachel to draw, and Faith, a natural ambassador of goodwill, warmly talked with everyone along the way. Though the villagers were detached, Faith had a delightful way of penetrating their barriers. In the meantime, Rachel would wander aside and discreetly take out her materials to draw odds and ends, such as a battered bucket, a withered plant, a window of one of the cottages, or various gestures of the villagers. The old inhabitants quietly observed her with curious glances. Though giving the impression of indifference, they were intrigued. All the while, her little sister rambled on. Thus, the introduction of the girls had been made. There were now two flowers in Sheppey, and no one could deny their fragrance or beauty.

And so, in that fateful year of '39, the girls and Cedric arrived, the former by land and the latter by sea. The following year would mark the marriage of Queen Victoria to Prince Albert.

....

"If a man does not keep pace with his companions, perhaps it is because he hears a different drummer. Let him step to the music which he hears, however measured or far away."
Henry David Thoreau

....

Chapter 13

A Peculiar Acquaintance

P inky could always be found by the tavern window in the early morning, waiting for the break of day and thinking. He thought about that extraordinary rescue of the seaman and how it seemed to have resurrected the entire village. *Cantank'rous souls 'ey was.* A stretch of cool pastels spread across the sky, casting a faint light upon the pier. And there was ol' Cedie boy, a beacon of light in more ways than one.

The news of the sinking of the *HMS Prince Edward* invariably made its way past the home of Theo and Mildred through the woodlands and over the hills to the doorpost of Nora's cottage. The girls immediately pleaded to see this dog. Acquiescing, Nora finally allowed them to hitch Mr. Wilson as the day was dreary and they were of age. She again encouraged Rachel to carry her drawing materials and hopefully sketch this extraordinary creature.

The girls set out the following day. The hour was brisk, the trees barren against a somber sky, though their enthusiasm curtailed the cold. And could this now be considered their maiden venture to Sheppey? Though they had hiked to town several times and gone to the grocers with Nora, it would be the first time with Mr. Wilson, who naturally made the ride pleasant. They were also traveling all the way north to the far end of the village.

The cottages were shuttered as they passed by; save for the smoke ascending from the chimneys, all was still. In the distance, they could see the dog on the pier.

Arriving near the Wayfarer Inn, they tied Mr. Wilson to a post. Proceeding to the pier, they called out to the dog. However, it was to no avail, as he remained focused on the sea. They tentatively began making their way across the pier.

Pinky saw them pull up. How peculiar; in all his years in Sheppey, nothing ever changed. Now, all but overnight, Cedric had made his way into the village, then that miraculous rescue, and now these two young ladies arrived out of nowhere. He watched with amusement as they hopped and skipped across the precarious pier. Cedric turned. Flapping his tail, he slowly made his way toward them. One of the girls leaned over and gave him a pat on the head. She seemed to be talking to him. He wagged his tail more vigorously.

Pinky decided to introduce himself. Putting on his jacket, he grabbed his cane and proceeded out the door. The air was brisk. He then limped his way across the pier, proving to be quite adroit for having only one good leg. The girls were impervious, remaining focused on the dog. One of them had taken out a pad and pencil and seemed to be drawing Cedric. The other was holding down the edge of the paper, stroking him with her other hand.

They then noticed this peculiar man coming their way, a cane in one hand and doing a strange thump and hobble over and around the warped planks. The wind was blowing through his hair, and there was a broad grin on his face. At first, they were intimidated but were put at ease when the dog began wagging his tail. Pinky paused a few steps from them. Hands on a cane, he presented himself with a slight tip of his cap and a smile. Rachel awkwardly returned to her drawing. Except for the sound of the surf, all remained quiet.

Rachel had situated herself to one side of Cedric and faced the sea, drawing the dog's profile and noting several seagulls in the background. Working quickly, her sketch was completed with various details and dark accents. Pinky drew closer. She had captured his penetrating eyes. Bending over, he gave Cedric a hearty pat. "Ee's a good'n, 'ee is. Best'ove friends we 'ees." Cedric raised his head, flapping his tail more enthusiastically. Pinky stood and braced himself, "First ta see 'im com ta town. Name be Cedric. Calls 'im 'Cedie Boy.' Luv ta share a pint or two wit 'im an' 'ear 'is tales. Ah, but 'ees not a drinker." The voice was course but tender, and the girls were at ease.

"Pinky's me name. Wus a' stow'way 'bout yer age. Spanish galleon head'd fer the Cape. Capt'n discover'd me tuck'd 'way an' put me ta work." He struck an extraordinary pose with the patch and windswept hair. Rachel thought he would make for an excellent drawing. For now, she put her materials aside and continued to follow his tales, which seemed as inconceivable as this dog's rescue of a sailor.

Thus, the introduction of Pinky to these young flowers and the beginning of countless stories spun throughout the tomes of his wanderings. Between the lines, the girls would discover a treasure of parables. In an odd way, he balanced the scales of Nora's maternal tutelage–her faith and integrity on the one hand and Pinky's worldly perspective on the other, similar to the scales of biblical scriptures and Greek mythology.

After concluding his adventures on the high seas, Pinky told them his residence was at the Inn, a permanent fixture. The girls inquired if they could visit from time to time. Rachel added she could possibly even draw him. To which he warmly consented. The wind began blowing with more force, and a deep cold settled in as the sun buried itself beneath the clouds. The girls gave Cedric a loving embrace and bid Pinky farewell until the next time. Boarding the wagon, they turned and waved goodbye and headed south. Seeing Pinky with Cedric left a lasting impression.

After all his years of isolation within the village, Pinky had finally come upon a precious pair of souls to share the treasures of his tales with. Like Faith, he was the convivial sort, never letting a soul pass by without a warm greeting, making an attempt to share his amiability with one and all. Invariably, the response by the Sheppians was always a deafening silence with an air of indignation. *Stranger 'ee 'ees an' ah stranger 'ee'l always be.* Their quick consensus was that he was nothing more than a patch-eyed, peg-legged alien and not one of them. And that grin and all his jabbering convinced them that he was jes' clammor'n fer 'ttention. Set like stones within their own miserable lot, ne'er a smile was ever extended.

Alas, Pinky found himself content to remain within his own little world, and let them be. Seemingly a silent line had been drawn. However, on that evening with Bosun Bluthers, they saw him in a different light. Now, they would often bestow a slight nod of approval while remaining at arm's length. However, on this blustery day, a warmth had been kindled in old Pinky's heart, even a new stride within his hobble, as he returned to the Inn.

....

Chapter 14

A Pair of Gargoyles

Like moles in a dark hole, Agnes and Gertrude surfaced only on rare occasions. One had to be quick to notice as such foreboding creatures came and went like a vapor and were as silent as the grave. Roger amusingly labeled them *a living pair of gargoyles*.

On one frigid day, one could have the misfortune of seeing them briskly traversing the muddied path on their way to the grocer's. Leaning into the headwind, baskets pressed against their bosoms, they were impervious to the world around them. Tight as clams, their eyes never wandered. Attired in black, they were as sinister looking on the outside as within the recesses of their hearts. Their black scarves and broad-brimmed hats framed a pair of bestial noses protruding from the dark cavities.

As fate would have it, Faith and Rachel were heading south, guiding Mr. Wilson homeward as the opposing siblings had their first encounter. Suddenly, a gust of wind blew the hat off Agnes's head and was quickly swept away. Faith, filled with jubilant energy, leaped from the wagon and scampered after it. Laying hold of the hat, she approached the bare-headed woman. Exposed like an old tortoise out of its shell, the woman's flesh was as pasty and pale as the underbelly of a fish. The top of her head was balding, scraggly black hair entwined in a gray mix, with liver spots dappling the waning hairline. Her mouth hung half-open, framed between thin lips, revealing several snaggled teeth and the sliver of a purplish tongue. A variety of moles dappled her chin. Yet it was the beady eyes that all but paralyzed its prey. Faith muttered, "My goodness!" Frozen like a defenseless rodent, she held out the hat. As rapidly as a snake bite, the old woman snatched it. (Faith even imagined a hiss.) Agnes quickly covered her head and strapped it down. The foreboding pair then abruptly went their way.

The day remained cold and gray. However, neither the weather nor this inopportune encounter would deter the joy of Faith and Rachel as they passed by the remaining cottages and headed into the woodlands. Youth has warm blood to kindle the heart that age can only envy. Before the evening had settled in, they had befriended the hero of Sheppey and sketched him, made the acquaintance of Pinky, and had the misfortune of meeting Miss Agnes and Miss Gertrude, the latter of which was enough to stretch the limits of darkness and light. An eventful day indeed.

···

"Behold, I was brought forth in iniquity, and in sin did my mother conceive me." Psalm 51:5 ESV

....

Chapter 15

Peering through the Cracks

I t goes without saying that there were many unanswerable questions pertaining to Cedric's past. And one could say there were just as many missing links within the lives of Agnes and Gertrude, ominous question marks looming over their past.

Ironically, their cottage was situated in the middle of Sheppey, though far removed from the center of attention. Situated between the church and the tavern (neither of which they frequented), their abode was shut tight as a coffin, the doorpost all but bearing the stigma of a quarantine. As far as the villagers were concerned, it was a dark hole, and there was no desire to meddle any further. A pox be on ye! The irony was that this pair of outcast cronies had an uncanny way of knitting the villagers together, giving them a place to point their fingers and cast their stones, nothing less than a projection of their own miserable souls.

Agnes and Gertrude managed to discover recent events by pressing a curious ear anywhere they could. And, most assuredly, the gossip line wired from cottage to cottage circumvented their dwellings. Sometimes, it was plucked while packing their ware in the grocers while Mrs. Filmore filled the ears of other patrons. But the tidbits were few and far between. Like lizards beneath a rock, most morsels were gathered by peering through the cracks of their shuttered window and making their own deductions.

There was one other source as Sammy begrudgingly assisted in placating their insatiable curiosity. It was common knowledge that he was the only vestige of their family fishbone. Sammy had been somewhat removed, spending his years living behind the fish house and making his living from the sea. Occasionally, he would make his way down and bring them a parcel of cod or split and stack firewood. Though Sammy was few of words, the sisters were masters at the pry, and invariably, he would blurt out a reply with a brevity of words, sometimes with nothing more than a grunt or a nod of his head. Through such badgering, along with all the other piecemeal information they gathered, Agnes and Gertrude could weave together the events of the shipwreck and that strange dog from all the blather running rampant throughout the village.

Let us now take a moment to delve into the past of Agnes and Gertrude and try to answer some of those questions that loomed over their dark past. If ever the scripture held true, they were birthed in iniquity, and a generational curse would follow them throughout their lives. Rumors said that once they had manifested the sweet fragrance of youth as children. (One of the more vintaged Sheppians attested to as much.) It was common knowledge that neither married. *Who'd be in 'eir right mind ta wed 'em?* Some ventured to say there had been a romance way back when (which was quickly blotted out as ludicrous). The villagers admitted that there was a vague recollection of them being orphaned and a brother raising them.

Truth be told (if anyone cared), Agnes and Gertrude bore the brunt of a harrowing childhood, dwelling under the same roof with a father uglier in heart than old Beelzebub himself. Unfortunately, within the channels of life, his dark nature would be handed down to the next generation, and any semblance of innocence would be corrupted.

Neither Agnes nor Gertrude ever set foot outside the village. Disconnected from life, their only gesture to the world around them was of utter contempt. Eyes remained forward, and hearts waxed cold, as dead as the bones on the bottom of the sea.

....

"There is no worse evil than a bad woman." Euripides

....

Chapter 16

"Scoot!"

The early days of winter settled in, the days cold and trying. And it would be many months before this dismal season would give its last lingering groan and lumber over the hills, taking along its gloom and countless storms. However, there were a few merciful days within such somberness, a benevolent sun briefly making its way out of the clouds, temporally drying the muddy path.

Cedric took his leisure on such a day, basking on the pier in a soft, consoling breeze. Awakening from a pleasant slumber, he rose and made his way to the Inn. Pinky was waiting by the door with a morning meal and returned inside after a few hearty pats and gentle discourse.

It had been many moons since Cedric first wandered into the village and entered the villagers' hearts. They admired how he had braved the tempests and remained steadfast on the pier even during the most brutal nights. And that rescue of the seaman still left them in awe. Cedric was now a living monument and as much a fixture in Sheppey as the old pier. It should be noted that almost everyone adored him, but there are always exceptions to the rule.

Cedric decided to head south to visit Mildred. It had been a long time, and he missed her pampering ways. Passing by the row of cottages, his loving eyes and wagging tail greeted everyone. The villagers responded in kind with words of praise and often pats on his head. Even Mrs. Filmore made her way out and bestowed her approbations. Cedric would politely pause, giving everyone all the time they desired.

Continuing on his way, he approached the cottage of Agnes and Gertrude, the latter standing by the door sweeping dust into the air. Seeing him, she stopped and grimaced, though Cedric offered her a few friendly wags. Gertrude was not one to be swayed, knowing full well his manipulations. Wagging his tail and giving her that innocent look was simply a way of begging for food. With a sweeping movement of the broom, she shrieked, "Go 'way, yer mis'r'ble mut!" Cedric's ears immediately drooped. "Get!" She shouted as if casting a curse. Making another sweeping gesture, "Shoo! No place fer yer 'ere!" Cedric lowered his head and hurried away, his tail between his legs.

Mildred was removed from the incident, tending to her yard. Nor could she hear the curses flung in the wind. Looking up, she saw him coming and raised her arms jovially as if the prodigal son was returning, "Ol' Cedie boy!" His tail began wagging, though his head remained slightly bowed. Drawing near, she leaned over and tenderly stroked him, "Something troubling you, my dear boy?" He would never share what had happened even if he could as he tenderly licked her hand and lifted his eyes.

Cedric remained at the cottage throughout the day. Millie cleaned him up, brushed his coat in the sun's warmth, and fed him a hearty meal before settling him down near the hearth. Theo observed the reunion with a touch of irony, knowing the importance of practicing hospitality, as the Good Book says. As dusk settled in, she escorted Cedric outside to the fenced area, well aware that his home was always under the stars.

He nestled beneath an open sky, the stars sparkling as a lazy moon floated across the vast blue. He drifted, thinking of a time long past: his kind master, the mountains, the lake, and frolicking with the children– the best of memories–and slowly faded off to sleep.

The weather in Sheppey was as erratic as the sea. And, though a touch of grace had warmed the day, all was about to change. Heavy clouds covered the stars, and it became dark. The wind stirred. Cedric lifted his head, sensing the urgency.

Dawn made a waning appearance upon an ominous sky. Mildred peeked outside. It was bitterly cold. The gate was ajar. There was no sign of Cedric. Squinting her eyes and looking north, she could only imagine he had returned to the pier. With a quick shiver, she closed the door. Too early in the year for this, she muttered. Or was it? For one never knew the fickled ebb and flow of the weather. Tried and tested, she knew better than to be optimistic. Shuttering the window, she prepared for the worst.

Chapter 17

"Somethin's a com'n..."

S ammy stood in front of the fish house, looking out to sea. A swirl of heavy umber clouds and an agitated sea would soon bring the impending storm. Other fishermen began arriving. Knowing the signs well, there would be no launching of the boats. For that matter, they would not be working on their nets or any other maintenance. Quickly strapping everything down, they headed for their cottages. Sammy was left alone. The tide was swelling, waves pounding the pier. Cedric remained immovable. A solitary gull haphazardly flew overhead, crying out a warning and fading into the gray.

Pinky also studied the storm, the wind seeping through the window with an eerie sound. Cedric, all but in the eye of the storm, was intensely focused on something. Pinky watched him stand, freeze momentarily, and dive into the sea. A heavy rain began falling, and everything became a blur.

The *Bonnie Lassie* would take the full brunt of the storm. As quick as a bolt of lightning, her rudder was shattered, and the ship became as helpless as a fawn within the jaws of a lion. Spent and with no sense of direction, it rammed against a shoal. Planks groaned, halyards loosened, and the sails flapped recklessly. A wave crashed over the hull, severing the vessel in two, the aft drifting away and sinking. The fore remained afloat, taking on water and hopelessly bobbing to and fro before succumbing to the sea. A lone mast hovered above the waves as a solemn memorial.

Far past the sight of Pinky's good eye, Cedric had seen the vessel and took the leap. As he reached the telltale mast, lifeless bodies and wreckage formed a wreath around where it had gone down. There were no signs of life. And then a woman could be seen desperately hanging onto something and gasping for air. Cedric paddled furiously toward her.

Half-immersed in the deep swirls, her silver hair was wet and scraggly, her face gaunt and lifeless. Cedric pulled alongside. Releasing the flotsam, she began to sink. Cedric nudged her. She surfaced, gasping and coughing. Coming to her senses, she frantically lunged toward him, seizing his collar for dear life. Cedric labored past the debris and through the waves as he made his way to shore.

···

"What world lies beyond that stormy sea I do not know, but every ocean has a distant shore and I shall reach it."

Cesare Pavese

....

Chapter 18

A Diamond in the Rough

Hollering out to Jarvis, Pinky put his best foot forward and braved the elements as he made his way out the door. This much he knew: a vessel had gone down. Why else would ol' Cedie boy have leaped from the pier? Fending against the wind, he struggled northward. Blurred by rain and the heavy gray, he made out the image of Cedric in the distance, motionless, hovering over something. Plodding around scattered crates, chests, planks, and bodies, he was losing energy. Pitching his cane in the sand, he drew closer. Cedric wagged his tail. It was evident he was by the side of a body strewn on the beach. Struggling to draw closer, it was the lifeless figure of an older woman. Leaning over, Pinky took hold of her wrist, "Aye, she's still 'live." Lifting her as best he could, he staggered toward the Inn. Jarvis soon came alongside and carried her the rest of the way.

Bertie was outside anxiously waiting, shivering and praying, her hair and apron flapping in the wind. She saw the vague image of a small huddle approaching. With more clarity, Jarvis was carrying a body, Cedric and Pinky by his side. Hurrying inside, she pulled tables together and gathered blankets. The door soon pushed open, the wind howling, as Jarvis made his way over and gently placed the frail woman on the bedded tables. Her flesh was lifeless and cold. Bertie checked her pulse, "Thank God–she's still alive. Quick! We need to undress her and wrap her in blankets." Jarvis headed up the stairs to retrieve blankets and a robe as Bertie undressed the distraught woman discreetly. Pinky looked away.

"Oh, my," Bertie said softly. A diamond necklace was draped around the woman's neck, and her dress was of the finest quality. It didn't matter, for Jarvis and Bertie meted compassion equally to all. Placing her in the robe, Bertie laid her down and covered her with blankets as Pinky and Jarvis began rubbing her hands and feet.

All fell silent. Cedric was resting nearby and attentive. Minutes passed like hours. Finally, a blush of color surfaced. Slowly opening her eyes, the woman remained motionless. Then, a startled expression. Her lips quivered as she began recollecting the nightmare. Jarvis prepared a glass of hot rum as Pinky stoked the fire. They gently raised her, placing her in a chair beside the hearth.

She struggled to put it into words. Her name was Lady Bradshaw. She and her husband were emissaries of the Crown, living in Bombay and returning to London on the *Bonnie Lassie*. The voyage was long, though pleasant. Then, the storm. She looked over at Cedric. "There he is... the one who miraculously saved my life." She drifted occasionally, muttering and recounting it in piecemeal, and finished with a soft sigh. Bertie politely inquired if she would share her story with the villagers. With a wane smile, she consented. Soon, she was escorted to a room where she slept until late the following morning.

The next day, word spread throughout the village that another ship had gone down, and another extraordinary tale was to be revealed. And it was all to be told by the sole survivor the evening after next at the tavern. My, my, the villagers never had such entertainment. And she was a baroness at that! Naturally, Mrs. Filmore would be the maypole from which all news flowed, excitedly filling her patrons' ears with all the details of Cedric's remarkable feat as they wondered how anything could be more impressive than the rescue of Bosun Bluthers.

The headlines were of such monumental proportion that even the ears of Pastor Theo and Mildred were perked. After giving the invitation some thought, they once again prudently refrained, the news passing them by and inexorably going through the woods and tapping at Nora's door. Though of the same sentiment as the good pastor and his wife, Nora saw the invitation in a different light. She would make an exception to hear this remarkable story of a baroness and the heroics of this fantastic dog. Could it not also prove to be an enriching experience for the girls? Nora persuaded Rachel to bring along her art materials.

....

Chapter 19

A Classic Countenance

Lady Bradshaw prolonged her stay. Slowly regaining her strength, she enjoyed the simple ambiance of the Inn and sent word to London for her coachman to make the journey with clothing and other necessities. The carriage arrived promptly the following morning, the villagers standing in awe as it passed by. Never before had such royal aplomb made its way across their muddied path.

The Inn's livery was moribund, dormant, and dusty through the many vacuous years. With Pinky's aid, the coachman did his best in unhitching and tending to the team of horses. Jarvis assisted in carrying the large chest into the lobby and up the stairs to the room of Lady Bradshaw.

Nora and the girls arrived in the late afternoon. The lanterns were lit, and the fire glowed. All was still. Sammy had gathered various items from the *Bonnie Lassie* that were displayed in the lobby. Intrigued by the artifacts, Rachel took out her sketchbook and began drawing. Cedric was resting by the hearth and rose to greet them. Brushed and groomed for the occasion, he gave Nora an impressive introduction- quite a remarkable creature, large and genteel. After several pats and praise, she and Faith proceeded into the tavern, selecting a table near where they surmised the baroness would be making her presentation.

Bertie approached. Nora remembered her from years past when she had attended the church. They had always thought highly of each other;

however, with Bertie's marriage and the responsibilities of the Inn, they had drifted. After a pleasant conversation, Nora ordered a pot of tea.

Rachel joined the table and shared her drawings. Nora admired her ability to see a touch of beauty in everything. The girls began conversing in whispers. Nora looked around the tavern, musing upon its quaintness. It reminded her of a tea shop she had frequented in London.

A distinguished woman entered and seated herself directly in front of them. There was no denying who she was. Eloquently dressed, it seemed inconceivable that this was the same wretched soul who had been shipwrecked in the storm. Cedric came to her side, and she gently began stroking his head. Rachel was inspired by her regal appearance and discreetly pulled out her materials and started a sketch. Lady Bradshaw, being astute, sensed what she was doing.

Nora found it an opportune time to make her acquaintance. Rising, she approached and welcomed her to Sheppey, saying how grieved they were over the loss of her husband and the suffering she had endured. After introducing the girls, she asked if she could read a relevant scripture. The baroness graciously consented. Opening her Bible, Nora read from the book of Jonah. Listening attentively, Lady Bradshaw politely asked if she could borrow it for the evening.

The day was fading as Jarvis walked around the tavern, lighting the remaining lanterns and stoking the fire as the villagers began to stagger in. The baroness observed they were humble, bowed with age, and dressed in pauper clothes. That is, save for Mr. and Mrs. Filmore, who made their presence known in fine attire. Unfortunately, they were late arrivals and obliged to take one of the remaining tables to the rear. Lady Bradshaw felt peculiarly out of sorts but gradually began gracefully acknowledging everyone with a pleasant smile and a slight nod. The fishermen, working late, were the last to enter, once again lining the far wall.

Six pennies started rolling across the tables, and pints and quarts began to flow, everyone quickly thawing out and enjoying the festivity. Jarvis and Bertie were elated, another one of those rare moments.

Hopefully, there would be a full till at the end of the evening to balance the ledger.

Bejeweled, discreet in demeanor, and unpretentious, it was easy for everyone to see that the baroness was the antithesis of the crass ways of Bosun Bluthers. She had quickly taken note of Pinky's personality and, having no desire to make a show of herself, requested that he tell the tragic tale of the *Bonnie Lassie*. The Merriweathers wholeheartedly agreed, knowing no one could tell a tale like Pinky.

Jarvis stuffed the hearth as everyone settled in. Pinky took his position to the side of the seated baroness. Cedric was poised by her other side, and the coachman standing slightly behind. Cedric kept his head forward, staring peacefully at the audience, his tongue lapping the air. The lanterns and hearth cast a warm glow upon the setting. Nora was reminded of a painting by Velasquez.

Pinky waited, building the suspense. Though the villagers had made his acquaintance with that emotional presentation during the evening with Bosun Bluthers, he was now about to enrich that initial introduction. With a slight bow towards the baroness, he commenced. It was theater at its best–at least for Sheppey.

Speaking slowly and with masterful pauses, Pinky lured them in as he unraveled the sinking of the *Bonnie Lassie*. Raising his voice, he spoke of the powerful wave that hammered the vessel broadside and the many passengers swept overboard. One of whom was the baroness's husband, the honorable Chester Bradshaw. The villagers leaned in, hanging on to his every word, imagining the howling wind, the rough seas, and the agonizing cries for help. On and on he went, his words lingering within well-placed intervals, captivating even Mr. and Mrs. Filmore and the fishermen.

He directed his audience's attention to Cedric. "Ol' Cedie boy sees it all 'an takes 'is dive. Then noth'n. I makes me way north ta where it 'ad gone asund'r. An' lo, 'ere 'ee be." Pinky looked over at the baroness, "Lay'n on the beach, the missus soaked ta the bone. Giv'n up fer dead.

But Cedie's tell'n me she's 'live. Gently lift'd 'er. An' 'ere comes ol' Jarvis runn'n to me aid."

Pinky looked out upon the villagers. No one stirred, not even the blink of an eye. He had masterfully accomplished his purpose. Posting himself against his cane, he then gave a slight bow and took a seat. His presentation merited a standing ovation. However, the guests, spent in years, could no longer muster such energy and simply slowly bobbed their heads along with a feeble clapping of their hands.

Lady Bradshaw requested a final word. All fell respectfully silent. Opening the Bible, she said, "I would now like to read from the second chapter of Jonah." Her voice was soft, her presence refined and gracious. Quite a contrast to Pinky. "I will also add my own sentiments, making it more relevant to what I had experienced." She began: "Then Jonah prayed unto the Lord... He cried out by reason of his affliction... For Thou hast cast me into the deep, in the midst of the seas and the floods... All Thy billows and Thy waves passed over me. The waters compassed me about... closed me round about my head... I am cast out of Your sight." Looking up, she meekly added her own thoughts: "Out of the belly of utter hell, I too was desperate. With no hope I cried out to God." Her lips quivered. The silence deepened. She closed her eyes. Haunting memories returned, and tears whelmed. How could she ever put it into words? "When my soul fainted, I remembered God, and He heard my prayer."

Many villagers were leaning in, cupping their ears. The hearth highlighted her tears as she closed the Bible. "I was so alone... Everyone else had perished... My dear husband gone. The sea was dark and terribly frightening. I was losing strength. No longer able to hold on... sinking... ready to die. Then an angel arrived with only a breath of life left in my body." She looked at Cedric who responded by tenderly placing his head in her lap. "I have so much to be thankful for. After all my years of leisure and luxury, I have finally realized that there is a loving God who reached down and saved me from utter hell. He used this fine creature as my guardian angel. It goes far beyond anything I can comprehend and a debt I can never repay, surpassing all the silver and gold of my estate. Thank you, gentle souls, for coming this evening. May you be as touched by God as I have been." All was still, heads slightly bowed, and then a stirring as everyone slowly rose to depart. Many nodded humbly while others approached Cedric to bestow a tender pat and a few words of praise.

Rachel approached the baroness and presented the portrait. Versed in the fine arts, Lady Bradshaw knew it was done by a gifted hand. She had captured her very soul, even the sadness in her eyes. Rachel handed her another drawing. "I thought you might like to have this too." It was a quick study of Cedric. She had focused on his large, furry head and eyes. The baroness cherished both and thanked her. She thanked Nora for revealing the passage in Jonah and inquired if she could hold on to her Bible for several more days, mentioning that she had decided to prolong her stay. It would also be nice to see them again before her departure. Nora warmly agreed and bid her farewell, agreeing to visit in the morning.

After everyone had departed, Lady Bradshaw released her valet for the evening and remained in the peace and solitude of the tavern. The fire was consoling, and the ambiance quaint. Cedric returned to the hearth and dozed off. She reflected on the miraculous rescue. Images of the nightmare returned, which were quickly released. How could she ever comprehend that God had heard her cry and responded by sending this dog? She settled her eyes on the drawings.

Pinky approached. In his own peculiar way, there was a coarse charm. "Why waste ah fine even'n, me lady? Join me in ah glass've sherry?"

Considering, she smiled and obliged. "Why not?" For her, life had most assuredly changed. Merrily making a turn, he awkwardly made his way to the bar. Returning, she was amused at how he masterfully balanced the two glasses in one hand, using his cane in the other as a ballast.

The odd pair settled in. Pinky began telling the history of the Inn, saying he was one of the first to see ol' Cedie boy arrive on the dreary day after the sinking of the *Britannia*. How extraordinary, she thought! Listening to him was like an excerpt from a piece of classic literature. The hour passed pleasantly. Finishing her sherry, she bid him a good evening and retired.

It was late evening. The tavern returned to its silence. Cedric headed to the door and whimpered. Pinky rose and released him into the night. Closing the door, he took out his knife and approached the beam. With only the light of a lantern, he carved another mark alongside that of Bosun Bluthers.

....

Chapter 20

"If only she'd've stayed..."

A vessel sailed down from London to take a tally of the sinking of the *Bonnie Lassie*, retrieving the dead, etcetera; the crew and officials lodging at the Inn. Throughout the ensuing days, they busied themselves on the coastline along with the reams of paperwork. Before departing, they paid a handsome fee for their stay and set sail from the cove, leaving the sole survivor behind at her request.

During the reprieve, Lady Bradshaw was experiencing a mysterious transformation. How peculiar, appreciating simple things in life, breathing in the fresh sea air, admiring the beauty of the seagulls, and the peace. A more worthy cause had arisen within her heart, and everything was discreetly changing. In the past, her benevolence had been ostentatious and impersonal–token gestures toward humanity. However, she was beginning to believe her lavish treasures were now to serve a purer purpose.

Nora and the girls visited daily, always calling Cedric from the pier. They found the baroness to be neither pretentious nor condescending. Quite often, she mentioned God. And her love for Cedric was evident. One morning she expressed a desire to take him home and treat him with the royalty he so well deserved. Nora quickly redressed the request, stating that the villagers would be heartbroken as he was the only endearing thing in their lives. Lady Bradshaw agreed.

On the morning of her departure, the baroness received a final visit. Sitting by the window and enjoying tea, they spent a quiet moment looking out upon the vibrant sea. She again praised Rachel for the excellent drawings and mentioned that since it was impossible to take Cedric home, the next best thing was this delightful portrayal.

The coachman approached and handed Lady Bradshaw several small purses. The first, containing six coins, was given to Rachel, insisting she take them for her artwork. She mentioned the coins were somewhat of a rarity and had been part of her husband's collection. She then presented Nora with a small bag containing a generous amount of crowns, requesting it be given to the Merriweathers after she departed for their gracious hospitality. The final purse, filled with half-crowns, was also handed to Nora, imploring her to distribute them equally among the people.

The villagers knew she was leaving well in advance and lined the muddied path, waving as if the Queen herself was passing by. When the coach faded in the distance, an old woman muttered with a sigh of remorse, "If only she'd've stayed..." A forlorn sense then lingered, for they had hoped the wings of such prosperity would have spread throughout the village. Oh, the frailty of life within the village of Sheppey. Keep your eyes heavenward, a hushed voice said in the heavenlies. Did not Lady Bradshaw tell you of My mercy? And, lo, embedded deep within the clouds of your despair, you will see the faint glimmer of another star soon to shine its light past all your dark and dismal years.

....

"Heavy blizzards start as gentle snowflakes." Mark Helprin

....

Chapter 21

The Blizzard of '41

Invariably, winter was always too long, too bleak, and too harsh. Such a cruel season was not one for keeping its word, no matter what was marked on the calendar. Is not the adage that *March comes in like a lion and leaves like a lamb*? Most assuredly, as Sheppey faced the North Atlantic and the Siberian winds, such an adage was truer visa-versa. And so, the old brute tarried, intruding upon early spring and bringing a bitter cold that froze every soul's bone and marrow.

Sammy stood on the shoreline studying the signs. First, a heavy gray covered the sky. All lay still save for the smoke emanating from the chimneys. A few snowflakes began to fall. Returning to his hut, he stoked the stove. By mid-morning, the village was covered in white.

One cottage presented itself colder and more isolated than the rest, all but framed in icicles. An attentive eye would observe there was no smoke coming from the chimney. Drawing closer and glimpsing through the cracks, a pair of aging spinsters were bundled up and shivering. For Agnes and Gertrude had used the last of the firewood in the middle of the night, and a bone-chilling cold had seeped in undeterred.

Against her sister's pleas, Gertrude decided to venture out in search of help. Putting her coat over a swathing of clothing, she placed a woolly on her head, strapped the black-rimmed hat around it, and made her way into the tundra.

A blinding blizzard greeted her, stinging her eyes. She immediately became bewildered, staggering in knee-deep drifts. Wandering aimlessly, turning in circles, she stumbled and fell, lying motionless. Her breath ascended in short pants, her eyelids covered with a light dusting, and her black attire was quickly layered in white. The wind whipped around her, creating a grave-like mound. Gertrude had all but vanished.

The snow, in all its various shades of white, also covered the pier and Cedric. He rose, shook it off his heavy coat, and crossed the planks. Breakfast was waiting. There was no hurry, though, for he loved the cold as much as a warm meal. He caught a glimpse of a figure falling in the snow. Rambling through the drifts, he was soon by its side. There was the scent of that woman who had been so cruel.

Gertrude looked up, vaguely making out the large creature hovering above her. She knew it was him. His eyes were soft and caring. Gently nudging her, he settled beside her to keep her warm and fend against the wind. Between snowflakes and tears, she whispered, "Oh, God–forgive me."

Who knows how long the snow continued to cover her? The old woman's mind and body were becoming numb, her thoughts befuddled. Yet there was comfort in having this dog by her side. *Strange how he was so forgiving.* It was a compassion she had never known. Not that she deserved it, knowing full well that the bitterness she had meted out to the world deserved no kindness.

In the storm's blur, she sensed God's hand upon her. It was a touch as pure as the wind-driven snow, and the distorted ugliness so long lodged within her heart began to dissipate. It was a touch that could even melt the ice.

The snow came down with a blinding force. Gertrude had been away from the cottage a long time. Alone and fearful, Agnes would be the next to brave the elements. Bundling up, she made her way into the blizzard and was immediately overwhelmed. Pausing and squinting, she followed the cottages northward, trudging toward the Inn.

....

Chapter 22

A Black Speck upon the White

———

Pinky marveled at the silent beauty as he watched Cedric make his way through the drifts and went to prepare his meal. However, by the time he opened the door, Cedric was nowhere to be seen, only the vast snowscape and the suggestion of his footprints fading in the white. Something was foreboding. Bundling up and braving the elements, he followed the tracks as best as possible. A dark figure was seen in the distance coming his way. *A woman?* Picking up his pace, he came to her side. She collapsed in his arms. *It was Agnes!* She gasped for breath and told him her sister was lost somewhere out there. Jarvis came alongside. Wrapping an arm around her, he assisted her to the Inn. Pinky remained, his eye scanning the heavy blanket of snow. Cupping his mouth, he called out, "Cedie boy!" Immediately, a mound of snow erupted, and Cedric came plodding toward him. Pausing, he implored Pinky to follow, and then, turning, he trudged back to where he had surfaced. Pitching his cane, he pushed onward. Pinky could vaguely see a patch of black in the snow. *It was Gertrude.* Reaching down and brushing away the snow, she was all but frozen. Jarvis returned, and they quickly raised her from the white tomb.

Bertie had pulled the tables together. Agnes assisted in preparing the bedding, hoping beyond hope they would return with her sister. The door blew open as Jarvis entered, cradling Gertrude in his arms,

Pinky by his side; Cedric followed with a snow trail behind them. Agnes assisted in undressing her sister and wrapping her in warm blankets. Bertie wiped Gertrude's face with a warm cloth, gently brushing her hair and comforting her with whispered prayers. Gertrude was gaunt and lifeless, as pale as marble. Agnes rubbed her feet vigorously as Jarvis stoked the hearth to vibrant life. They then waited. It was that tentative and fragile moment between life and death. And who knew which way the hand of fate would go? All the while, the blizzard raged.

Gertrude blinked. *A miracle!* Her eyes began moving from side to side, trying to comprehend where she was. She saw Agnes. A sigh. Her flesh was returning to warmer tones. Cedric came to her side and licked her hand. She groaned. Her soul, too, was thawing, and she was defenseless against such compassion. Especially from this dog. *Why did he continue to show such love?* No one interrupted.

Jarvis and Pinky gently raised her, situating her frail body in a chair closer to the hearth. The glow from the fire revealed how far removed from beauty she was, her features grossly distorted. Pinky handed her a bowl of hot mutton stew. "Yer forch'nate ta be 'live, Mus Gertie. An' icicle, yer was." A waned smile surfaced. It was the first time anyone had ever seen her smile. Cedric licked her hand again. A tear came to her eye as she said, "Gift from God, 'ee is." For that matter, nor had anyone ever heard her mention God before. Agnes spoon-fed her the stew, and then they laid her down again.

The rescue of Miss Gertrude would be far more meaningful in the grand scheme of things than simply retrieving a haggard woman from the blizzard. For, like Christ, Miss Gertrude had risen from the tomb. And behold–everything had become new. The ball and chain of darkness and the plague which had burdened her all those years was gone.

Later in the morning, Pinky returned to the window. Snow framed the corners of the panes. Everything upon the coast had merged into one: the sea, sky, and shoreline blending into a pristine white. The pier was a long mound of snow, standing motionless upon the frozen sea.

The snow descended throughout the day. By late afternoon, it had faded into soft flurries dancing in the wind. Jarvis had gone to the fish house to tell Sammy about his cousin. They then headed to her cottage with armloads of firewood, starting and stoking the stove until the embers were glowing. By the end of the day, the cottage had thawed and warmed. Sammy went to the Inn, covered Gertrude in blankets, and cradled her in his arms as Agnes followed along.

Evening added a soft gray to the white. Pinky made his way to the beam and carved another notch. However, it was placed to the side of the others–a reminder that Gertrude's rescue had come during the blizzard of '41 and not from the sea.

....

Chapter 23

The Metamorphosis

The first warm days of spring arrived like a long-awaited sigh. Save for patches of snow in the shadows; there were no telltale signs of the blizzard as the sun broke through the clouds. Its benevolent warmth coddled both hearts and bones. The entire village had awakened, busying itself with the knocking down of any remaining icicles and doing its best to meander around the puddles.

Gertrude healed without a touch of frostbite. Strange, she found herself embracing springtime. Something new and alive seemed to be in the air. Naive to the ways of God, she knew she had been supernaturally spared from death and was overjoyed to be alive. But there was something else as Agnes soon followed her on this strange and wonderful path. Her transformation was more gradual, from day to day, as she studied the changes in her sister until the hour came when she, too, experienced the merciful hand of God. With childlike steps, the siblings, like a pair of golden butterflies, had come out of their cocoons.

One of the first signs of change was that their shutters were pulled aside, and on warmer days, the window was opened. At times, the villagers would see them piddling around out of doors–and without those dreaded hoods! However, Mrs. Filmore was the first to see them barefaced. And close up at that. "Oh, what a sight!" She told of a sparkle in Gertrude's eyes and even the suggestion of a smile. Truly headlines in its own right. Alas, everyone begrudgingly had to admit, '*Ey'ed changed ah mite.*

There was an even more extraordinary note, an exclamation mark on this supernatural transition. On a pleasant Sunday morning, the peering eyes of neighbors happened upon Agnes and Gertrude making their way down the muddied path to church! But that wasn't all. They were strolling along in colorful dresses and flowery bonnets! And there was more. A smile could be seen on their craggy faces if one looked closely. Gasping, hands clasped to heads, their neighbors exclaimed, "What's 'ees world com'n to!"

Throughout the week, the sisters had searched for something to wear. Delving deep within an old, musty chest, they finally salvaged a pair of dresses. Quite pleased to find they still fit, they even discovered a couple of crinkled bonnets. After dressing and looking at each other quite amazed, they set forth into the world.

The air was fresh and alive, seagulls sailing above them like a heavenly confetti. Even the old church bell rang with a note of purity. Critical eyes followed them the entire way, straining in disbelief, mindsets as fixed as barnacles upon a sunken boat. *Ne'er 'n all me years!*

The sisters tentatively entered the church, humbly and silently taking a seat in the rear pew. Neither had ever entered a church before, sung a hymn, heard a sermon, or, for that matter, ever read a verse in the Bible.

As coincidence would have it, it would also be Thomas' first Sunday at the podium. There had been no special turnout, just the same handful of dedicated souls. However, he did observe the pair of elderly women who discreetly took a seat in a far pew. Mrs. Filmore had shared with him the astonishing transformation of Agnes and Gertrude, and it had to be them. Mildred was seated in the front pew. Looking at the young pastor, she confirmed it with a broad smile, silently gesturing with her mouth and emphasizing each word while pointing a forefinger to her breast in their direction. *That's Gertrude and Agnes!* His heart stirred. To him, there could not have been a better welcome. Putting his notes aside, Thomas changed his message and preached on the tender mercies of God. Throughout the service, he noticed their heads were bowed.

After the sermon, the young pastor headed to the door to bid farewell and God's blessings to the handful of parishioners. He spent extra time with Agnes and Gertrude, mentioning he would like to visit them sometime.

The conversion of Gertrude and Agnes continued to bear its fruit. In time, their cottage became opened to the world, the light shining forth both from within and without. The ice had melted in more ways than one.

....

Chapter 24

"God's bless'ns to yer."

The road had finally dried, and the morning air was pleasant, presenting an opportune time for Nora to make a long-overdue trip to the grocer and invariably receive an earful from Mrs. Filmore on the recent happenings. Nora had been quite taken aback to see Agnes and Gertrude in church and would be the last to receive the details of Gertrude's fantastic rescue.

The loquacious Mrs. Filmore told it all. "Miss Gertrude was all but given up for lost. Frozen to the bone and covered in a mound of snow for only God knows how long. And then Cedric, our hero, comes trudging along to the rescue! Jarvis and Pinky soon followed and carried her to the Inn. Would you believe, not a touch of frostbite on her body? Then, the other day, she and Agnes came in without those dreaded hoods! Glory be! Seeing them bareheaded was shocking enough, but then, as they departed, Miss Gertrude said, God's bless'ns to you. Imagine that!" Nora smiled as she packed her goods, knowing it was nothing less than a spiritual transformation, something quite alien to most of the villagers.

Returning home and putting away the groceries, she turned to the girls. "Possibly it's time to pay Miss Agnes and Miss Gertrude a visit? You could take Cedric along. They would like that very much. And I'm sure those precious souls could use some help around their home." She returned from the other room with several pairs of woolen socks she had darned. "You could take these along as a gift. And possibly even a potted plant for their window sill."

The girls considered such a dismal proposal. After the horrific encounter on that windy day, *Who in their right mind would want to enter their cottage*? Though there were mixed emotions, they had seen them in church. And, well, they certainly looked different. There was also the thought of spending time with Cedric and visiting Pinky. Resigned to the fact that Nora knew best, they begrudgingly acquiesced.

The following morning, Mr. Wilson was hitched to the wagon, and the girls proceeded to Sheppey with gifts in hand. The sun graciously bestowed its warmth upon the day as daffodils blossomed and green buds tipped the branches of the trees. The fresh scent of spring was in the air. Arriving on the coast, they first set their hearts on visiting Cedric.

Reaching the pier, Faith called out to him. Cedric immediately rose and excitedly pranced around the warped planks, soon by their side. After a wealth of pats and praises for another incredible rescue, Faith encouraged him to follow along. Pinky was standing in front of the Inn and invited them to share a pot of tea. Cedric made his way to the hearth.

Pinky filled them in throughout the hour with all the dramatics of Miss Gertrude's rescue. A miracle it was. The old crone had changed in the blink of an eye, even taking off that dreaded hood. And Agnes, too. They say they had even become friendly of late. Leaning closer, "Ice 'ad melt'd off the ol' tarts."

The girls were captivated and much relieved. Rachel's thoughts drifted, studying Pinky's extraordinary face. When he had finished, she inquired if she could draw him. To which he wholeheartedly agreed. Making plans for the following Saturday, they bid him farewell. It was late morning when the girls headed southward, Cedric merrily following behind the wagon.

The cottage window was open, a gentle breeze lapping the curtains. Faith tied Mr. Wilson to a post and gathered the gifts. They then proceeded to the door. Rachel looked at her sister and took a deep breath. Tapping on the door, they waited.

A shuffle could be heard. The door slowly opened. Gertrude, slightly bent, greeted them with a smile, only broadening when she saw Cedric. Leaning over, she gave him a gentle pat. "An' angel, 'ee 'is." She then gestured for them to come in.

The cottage was musty but peaceful, a soft light entering from the window. Taking a seat at a small table, Miss Gertrude tenderly called Cedric to her side, stroking his coat and thanking them for bringing him along. Leaning over, she kissed his head and whispered, "O Cedie... fergive me." He stared at her with his large brown eyes as if there was nothing to forgive. Not to impose on the moment, the girls waited patiently. It was the first time they had seen the sisters close up, and they marveled at how their faces had softened. Handing a pair of woolen socks to each of the sisters, Miss Gertrude held hers up. Admiring the handiwork, she commented they would have done her well during the blizzard. Rachel mentioned her grandmother knitted them. Faith also gave them the potted plant Agnes placed by the window. Faith told them how good it was to have seen them in church. To which the sisters remained silent and rather meek.

Rachel's creative nature began to take its course once again, becoming intrigued with the face of Agnes. Not only had there been a miraculous change in her disposition, but she also saw a rare beauty and gentle touches in the features. *How uncanny to find her so inspiring.* Quite ambitious, Rachel politely asked if she could draw her. Miss Agnes was dumbstruck, beside herself and not knowing how to respond. Humbly placing a hand on her bosom, she muttered, "If yer like, Mus Rachel. No one ev'r asked fer such a thing."

Rachel pulled her chair slightly away from the table and retrieved her materials while studying her countenance. Miss Agnes straightened her posture and offered a wane smile. The angle was a profile and made her nose far too pronounced. An amusing note for the young artist, reminding her of a portrait done by Piero della Francesca in one of Nora's art books. She requested that Agnes turn slightly toward the light of the window, finding the front view more inspiring. She decided to use charcoal, though not as controlled as a pencil; it would produce a bold effect and quick results. Commencing with notations of the features, she began lightly blocking in the shaded areas.

The hour became one of pristine silence. The portrait was effortless. Cedric remained by the side of Gertrude, who tenderly stroked his head while observing her sister coming to life on the paper. Agnes remained motionless throughout the session, her eyes occasionally veering. Rachel sensed it was evolving on its own, stroke by stroke, revealing a mysterious beauty as if a veil had been lifted. *How could that raw, contorted face have softened so? Only God can create such beauty from ugliness.* Rachel's mind pleasantly drifted. The sisters reminded her of a pair of bowed sunflowers in that final phase of life; every stage of the sunflower held its beauty. Upon completion, the drawing was presented to Miss Agnes, who glowed, revealing more of that supernatural change.

Gertrude then began disclosing their past, which had remained shut tight to the world. Their mother was a kindhearted soul who had died when Agnes was a toddler. Their father was cruel, a miserable man who had only worsened after their mother's death. Distancing himself, he sat at the table and drank throughout the day. Soon, there wasn't a farthing left in the jar. The cottage became bare and dreadful.

Fortunately, an older brother, James, took his sisters under his wing. Like his mother, he had a good heart and did his best to help during those bleak years, working odd jobs on nearby farms. When their father breathed his last, the girls found themselves solely dependent on James. Barely a teenager, he was now the man of the house. Eventually, venturing to the ports of London, he obtained work on a merchant vessel and became a shrewd businessman. As the ship traveled to far-off countries, he learned the art of the trade, bartering English artifacts for silks, teas, and fine jewelry, which, in turn, he sold in London.

Tragically, their brother was killed at sea. Moroccan pirates had seized the vessel, taking its cargo and putting the ship's crew to the sword. It would take months for the girls to learn of his fate. "The well be dry 'gain," Miss Gertrude added remorsefully. "Livin' on bare bones." However, the brother had sealed a letter and told Sammy to give it to them if anything ever happened to him. One morning, Sammy delivered it. Opening the seal, the sisters fell to their knees with thankfulness, discovering that James had buried a small fortune near the cottage. A map had been included. His kind heart provided for them throughout the years, yet a deep-rooted bitterness would prevail. Possibly it was inherited from their father or the damage done during those early years. Whatever the case, the sisters became more sordid as the years passed, and James became a faded memory.

The visit surpassed anything the girls could have imagined. As dusk was nearing, they made ready to depart. Miss Gertrude said that Sammy would frame the picture, and they would put it in a very special place. Before leaving, the girls hugged them. Teary-eyed, Agnes, and Gertrude waved goodbye, watching Mr. Wilson make his way homeward. Cedric took his leave and returned to the pier.

The suspicious eyes of neighbors strained at the scenario, only imagining what was going on behind closed doors. Save for Sammy, the girls were the only ones to have ever ventured into that place, as to why, they would never know. All that was evident was a long embrace, everyone smiling and teary-eyed.

....

Chapter 25

Striking a Pose

Sheppey basked in the pleasantries of spring, and the first week of June presented itself as an ideal time for Faith and Rachel to return to the village. Deciding to hike, they departed at an early hour. Greeted by the solo notes of distant songbirds, a crescent moon, and a few stars were fading into the coming day, and it was still cool enough to see their breath ascending into the dawn. Rachel carried along her satchel of art materials for her session with Pinky. In the meantime, she searched for subject matter along the way, slowly building a portfolio of how she saw the world around her.

By the time they arrived on the coast, the village had awakened, windows and doors opened to greet the day with many villagers out and about. Faith, always amiable, greeted everyone with her innocent and ebullient nature, striking up conversations with anyone who would pause, which gave Rachel ample opportunities to sketch well-concealed treasures. However, within her quiet demeanor was the anticipation of doing Pinky's portrait. Pleased with the portrayals of the baroness and Agnes, she was enthusiastic about this new endeavor.

Reaching the pier, Faith immediately called out to Cedric, who rose and met her halfway. Falling to her knees, she wrapped her arms around him and spoke tenderly in his ear. Cedric's tail wagged in the mix. They then made their way to the beach. She had brought along a few pieces of bread for the occasion, tossing them into the air. The seagulls were quick to respond, hovering overhead, flapping their wings, and waiting to make a dive upon a morsel. Cedric gave playful chase before romping in and out of the surf and chasing sandpipers. Winded and laughing, Faith returned to Rachel, who was immersed in a sketch of one of the old fishing boats. They then proceeded to the Inn.

Pinky amusingly watched the scenario from the window and went to the door to invite them in. The conversation naturally became animated. The sun had its reign upon the day, and within the hour, Rachel inquired if it was a good time to draw his portrait. His smile broadened. She recommended going outdoors as there was little wind, and the weather proved ideal. The natural light and fresh air would make it all the more inspiring.

She chose the south side of the Inn to shield them from the breeze, placing Pinky in the indirect light with an intriguing backdrop of barrels, halyards, and wooden crates. Poised, with chest out, he stalwartly faced the sea.

That smile, permanently etched upon his countenance, along with the battered cap, a crop of untamed hair, and the patch over his eye, only enriched the image. Rachel had intended on doing a full-length portrait, top to bottom, cane and all. Upon further consideration, she decided to focus on just the face, which held more than its wealth of intrigue within the map of wrinkles and that penetrating good eye. Faith was by her side, patiently holding the paper at bay and following her sister's flurry of strokes, stroking Cedric with her other hand.

Pinky kept his eye set upon the channel, a sparkle reflecting the light from the sea. Rachel bemusingly thought it contained all the knowledge of the world. She made the patch less prominent, focusing on that eye and the eternal smile. Slowly, the drawing revealed his adventurous soul. She even captured a touch of his swagger. For a moment, it brought to mind the portrait of a smiling cavalier by Frans Hals. And so, at a very young age, the lovely Miss Rachel Thomson was finding a story to be told within every face. For that matter, even Cedric had a tale to tell within his large, furry head.

....

"Truth, like gold, is to be obtained not by growth, but by washing away from it all that is not gold." Leo Tolstoy

....

Chapter 26

Spanish Doubloons

M ildred awoke early. It was a fine morning, and she intended a similar venture north, having not seen Cedric since the blizzard and missing him dearly. Quite ambitious, she mused, *I have energy to burn. Especially on such a day as this!* Peeking her head out the door, she saw that the sun had already begun its ascension. Breathing in the morning air, *Yes, an ideal time to bring him home for a good meal and bed him down for the night.* Theo remained asleep as she quietly put on her hat and coat, and out the door she went, carrying along a parcel of food and a tether.

Reaching the Inn, she stopped to catch her breath and consider. Looking towards the pier, there was no sign of Cedric. She then saw him in the company of Pinky and the two girls.

Mildred approached the small gathering. *Quite touching.* It was peaceful and a rather unique setting. Though acquainted with Faith and Rachel from church, she had never seen them outdoors. Nora had mentioned Rachel was quite the artist, and she was impressed to see her diligently at work. Cedric came to her side, wagging his tail. Leaning over, she gave him a hearty pat. "Mats, he is. He's me boy." Cedric looked up and perked his ears.

Faith heard the comment, "Why did you call him that?"

"From the old country. Means 'a gift from God.' And so Mats 'tis is." Cedric wagged his tail more vigorously.

Rachel was adding the finishing touches to the drawing. Mildred peeked over her shoulder. Looking up at Pinky, she commented, "Well, you certainly made him dignified. Done him justice, you did. No wonder he's wearing that big grin." Giving him a stern look, "Now, mind your p's and q's, Mister Pinky–you have young ladies present."

"Ya knows me, Mus Millie. B'ave meself when ah 'as to."

"We're still saving a seat for you at church."

"Aft'r the storm blows een, Mus Millie. Aft'r the storm." It was the same response he always gave her. And though many a tempest had blown across the shore, Pinky was never to be seen upon a pew.

Rachel presented the drawing to him. Overjoyed, he told her he would always keep it close to his heart.

After Mildred had fed Cedric, she said, "Will be taking him home today. Needs some cleaning up and pampering." The girls were disappointed as they planned on taking him to visit the elderly sisters. However, seeing how Mildred adored him, they knew it was best. Pinky tied the tether around his neck, and the pastor's wife bid them a good day and headed on her merry way.

Pinky and the girls returned to the Inn. Sitting by the window and admiring the portrait, he pointed to the mantel, a space between two lanterns, "Place it 'ere, ah will."

Rachel took the opportunity to open her satchel. Retrieving a coin, she placed it in his hand. "I was wondering, Mr. Pinky, do you know anything about coins? It was given to me by Lady Bradshaw. She gave me several of them before departing. I mean, how much do you think it is worth?"

Studying it for a moment, he replied, "T'aint no farthing y'ave 'ere, lassie." Gently biting the corner with an eye tooth, he added, "Worth more 'an a pock't full've crowns." He then went on to disclose one of his endless tales. "Spent two years goin' 'round the world. Bonnie ol'

England ne're 'eard of such ports. At's 'ow ah found out 'bouts 'is 'ere coin." Holding it up and marveling, "Ol' Bonaparte 'en reared 'is head like a roar'n lion. Seys to meself, time ter fight fer God an' country, march'n ta battle wit Wellin'ton 'imself."

Puzzled, Rachel inquired, "Why did you bite the coin?"

Looking at her with that pensive eye and an imaginary wink behind the patch, he said, "Aye, 'tis a Spanish dub'loon yer 'ave 'ere." Nipping it again, "Rare for 'ese parts. No trump'ry 'ere, missy. Worth 'eets weight in gold." He coarsely laughed at his own wit, "I still don't understand. Why did you bite it?"

"Sometimes padded wit' weights. Stuffed with impur'ties, so ta say. Gold's soft'r, takes the bite 'an leaves 'eets mark." He showed her the mark and returned the coin.

"Oh..." Rachel replied sheepishly. Taking a moment to study her little treasure, she reached into the satchel again and placed another coin in his hand. "And what about this?"

"Now 'at 'ere's ah beauty." He lifted it up to the light. "'Tis ah soovereen. God save the Queen. Don't need ah bite. Worth ah pound've British sterl'n."

Rachel retrieved four more coins–two doubloons and two sovereigns–and placed them into Faith's hand. "These are for you. Promise to put them to good use." Faith was overwhelmed, gently cupping them and promising to use them well.

Jarvis and Bertie approached the table, curious to see the portrait. *It was Pinky all right.* They admired how such a young girl was able to capture his likeness. Jarvis said, "You have the mark of a little master."

Pinky interjected, "Want ter frame it. Bequeath'n it ter the Inn fer poster'tee."

Rachel retrieved the drawing of Cedric she had done when they first met. "Seeing how you have taken such good care of Cedric, I wanted you to have this, too."

The Merriweathers were impressed and very thankful, insisting on paying for the drawings. Rachel was awkward and hesitant. Bertie reminded her that a laborer was worthy of their pay. Jarvis then proposed a barter–a free dinner for them and Nora; to which they warmly consented.

It was early afternoon when the girls headed to the cottage of Gertrude and Agnes, their steps no longer tentative. Faith knocked and was soon greeted by Miss Agnes. Another close-up encounter, however, she was astonished to see that this was the same hissing reptile she had met on that windy day. Though her features were still contorted, a soft nature and a pleasant smile greeted her. *How could it even be possible that she was the same woman?*

They were invited in. Gertrude was seated at the table, and the girls took a seat. Miss Agnes pointed to her framed portrait on the far wall and became teary-eyed. Everyone remained quiet for a moment. A lively conversation then ensued. After an hour of pleasantries, the girls rose and bid them farewell, planning to visit again the following Saturday. Peering eyes continued to peek from neighboring cottages, absorbing as much as they could and having to fill in the rest.

Upon returning home, Faith enthusiastically told Nora that Rachel had sold the portrait of Pinky to the Merriweathers for three dinners. "Can we go? Please?"

Nora was once again obliging. Though dinner at the tavern would be a novelty, her prudent nature told her it was quite a distance to travel for a meal. And, most assuredly, she could prepare a much healthier one at home.

....

Chapter 27

Pinky's Mutton Stew

It was late afternoon. Though heavy with clouds, the day was warm, stirring the appetites of the girls as they hitched up the wagon and made their way to the village.

Arriving at the tavern, Faith directed them to the window table to keep an eye on Cedric. Glancing at the mantel, she said, "Look, Rachel–there's your pictures. They're beautiful!" Pinky had done them justice with frames. "I think they are your best drawings ever!"

Pinky made his way to the table, balancing a bowl of stew and a plate of thick slices of bread in his free hand. Faith sprang to his aid. He then returned to the kitchen to retrieve the rest of their meal.

When all were served, Nora bowed her head and said grace. Pinky was respectful but impervious. After a soft amen, he puffed out his chest, "Pinky's mutt'n stew, me ladies." Before tasting, Nora commented on how much the portrait resembled him.

"'Tis ol' Pinky 'aw right," and then added, 'Ow's the stew, ladies?"

Sampling a spoonful, Nora replied, "I must say, Mr. Pinky–it is quite good." She then added that it could hold its own with the finest of French cuisine. "Will you share your recipe?"

"Compl'mnt 'ndeed. No, mum–can't share. 'Tis a family secr't." Leaning over, he said, "Give yer a clue. Lots've mutton an' let it brew. Call me 'Pinky,' mum. No pretensions 'ere. Jes' ol' Pinky."

Nora let the barriers pleasantly fall. Though becoming acquainted with him the other evening at the tavern, this was a more personal introduction. The gruff voice and dubious appearance had initially given her the impression of some ruffian one might encounter in a dark alleyway in London. Going past the shell, though, she found him to be correct–there were no pretensions. Pinky was what he was.

"Not to pry into your personal life," she added, "but are you a Christian?"

Puffing out his chest once again, "'Ad me sword 'eld high fer God an' country."

"And we thank you for your service. The girls have told me all about your military exploits. However, I am inquiring about your heart, not your sword. In all these years, you have never attended our church."

"Guess ya could say, mum, 'ave an allurgy t' it. Bit too stuffy."

"Well, we hope you will make an exception to your rule one of these days. You could sit with us as our honored guest."

Pinky masterfully veered, weaving his way into one of his count-less tales. Nora was quite entertained, and it didn't take long to surmise that his stories were finely threaded somewhere between reality and a wandering imagination. She also discerned a good heart, even a touch of innocence within that crusty shell.

The delightful mutton stew and Pinky's company far surpassed what Nora had anticipated. After thanking him, she left a pound for his service, and they departed. The sky and sea had faded in the dusk with a light drizzle falling. However, they were all the merrier as they headed home.

....

"Let that night be bleak and joyless... Let the stars of the night disappear... Let it long for light but never see it..."

Job 3:7, 9 TLB

....

Chapter 28

A Troubled Soul

G reat Britain was now gloriously established upon the archives of history and the other great empires of the past. Holding high its valiant sword, it laid claim to possessions throughout the world's four corners, its prosperity overflowing. However, observing this shining blade with scrutiny, one would find its foibles. For the Victorian Era was a paradox. On its sharp cutting edge was wealth and might, while the other side was dull and chipped, the latter being the attrition of the abject poverty within its slums along with several abysmal military defeats. One such chink was the infamous Battle of Kabul.

The jewel of England's colonies was India. Ravishing its vast natural resources, the British parliament became greedy in protecting this prized possession. Believing Russia had ambitions to seize upon such treasures, an army of twenty-two thousand British and Indian troops was sent to Afghanistan to buffer India's border against an invasion. Unfortunately, Great Britain fell prey to its own fallibility as the expeditionary force would meet with utter defeat, not at the hands of the Russians but by the sword of warring Afghan tribes and a freezing winter.

There were several engagements. In the initial battle near the city of Kabul, the British army was victorious. A second battle, however, met with defeat. In January 1842, the remnant of the army retreated through a mountain pass, hoping to reach a southern fort in Jalalabad. In all, 4,500 soldiers of the 44th Foot, an Indian brigade, and 12,000 family members and servants began the harrowing journey through the treacherous pass. Unfortunately, they soon fell prey to the freezing cold and the vengeful sword of 30,000 Afghans waiting in ambush. After the last shot was fired, the entire British force had perished, strewn across the frozen pass as far as the eye could see.

When the devastating news reached Great Britain, the nation's heart sank to one of its lowest points. There was one faint glimmer of hope, a token of valor they could claim as a lone officer crawled out of the mountains and staggered into Jalalabad.

Wounded and frostbitten, Lieutenant Sumpter suffered from severe trauma and a head wound and would require many months in a hospital. The hellish nightmares did not thaw, and the doctors let him be, knowing time could be the best healer. Unfortunately, orders were rushed through from the British embassy to ship him home. He was to be honored by the Queen. Foregoing medical persuasion, the orders were emphatic. *He was still part of the British Army, and military protocol would have its way. Chin up, chest out, and bite the bullet.* Such a motto overruled the medical staff, and they acquiesced, shipping him home on the next vessel.

The *HMS Ballantyne*, overloaded with wounded soldiers from various battles, departed from India in late summer. Though it would take many months to reach the English Channel, the journey was graced with clear skies and calm seas. That is, until reaching the coast of England, when a vicious tempest quickly took hold of the ship and sent it to the bottom of the sea. The vicissitudes of nature would not discriminate on this day, taking no pity on hundreds of Great Britain's best, all maimed for God, Queen, and country.

Queen Victoria was distraught beyond measure. Her empire was in dire need of something to once again hold high its valiant sword. Through such despair, there was another glimmer of hope. As extraordinary as it may seem, the same young officer who had survived the massacre in Afghanistan was also the only survivor of the *HMS Ballantyne*. Bringing him home and honoring him became all the more urgent, hopefully restoring a sense of glory to her people.

There was another silver lining in this mix. Rumor had it that the officer was rescued from the sinking vessel by a dog and his invitation to the palace began to take on greater proportions. However, the Queen would keep the tale of this mysterious dog close to her bosom, at least for now.

....

Chapter 29

And finally it came

The coast of Sheppey remained relatively calm after the baroness's departure. One tempered season rolled into another. Save for the blizzard and a few thunderstorms that stirred upon the sea; no ship had gone down or snared upon the bars. The villagers knew full well they were not destined for everlasting peace, and another tempest would invariably soon make its way across the channel.

It was mid-autumn in the year 1842. The sky darkened. A strong wind began to blow against the coast. Battening down anything that could be swept away, the Sheppians retreated to their cottages, boarded their windows, lit their lanterns, and waited as the rain began to fall.

Pinky focused on the brooding sea. By late afternoon, high tide had strengthened with powerful waves pounding the pier. Through the rain and fading light, he could see Cedric. He then caught the glint of a sail in the whirlwind. Another glimpse, the vessel was leaning heavily, its sails flapping helplessly. Cedric rose. Before Pinky could blink his eye, he leaped from the pier, all but immersed in the sea.

Though the storm had beaten the vessel into submission, it would be a sandbar that sounded the death knell. Leaning precariously on the shoal, the ship rocked and swayed, defenseless against the ravaging sea. Hammered by one wave after another, many were swept overboard. It continued to list, a shattered mast tipping the sea like a giant oar. Like the jaws of a lion when finished with its prey, the vessel was released from the bar. Staggering helplessly, it began to sink. Knee deep in water, the call went out to abandon ship. The remaining men on the troop carrier, crippled and maimed, had no choice but to take the leap.

Lieutenant Sumpter remained on board, tending to those too weak to fend for themselves. Taking hold of a man on crutches, he urged him to go over the side. Without hesitation, the brave soldier complied. And then another, with bandaged head and an arm in a sling, followed the order and went over the side. The deck was nearly void of life as the lieutenant frantically muttered, *Who else*? A blind man groped in his direction. Taking hold of him, the officer leaped into the sea. As soon as they hit the water, the man was swept away.

Desperately clinging to flotsam, Lieutenant Sumpter drifted within the heavy swirls. Finding himself alone once again, he grieved that none of those good men were still alive. The mountains flashed before him, the harrowing pass and the dead, everything becoming inextricably entangled. Darkness was consuming the sea, the solitude haunting. More than from utter exhaustion, he was grief-stricken and defeated, ready to let go. He then saw a strange creature churning his way out of the abyss.

....

Chapter 30

The Lieutenant

Like the ark after the storm, the villagers opened their portals to take inventory. The wind had waned, and the sea was calm as the last drops of rain dripped from their tattered roofs. With no discrimination, the tempest had meted out its fair share of damage and departed. Fortunately, the roofs had held. The bowsprit of the *HMS Ballantyne* still protruded from the sea, pointing heavenward.

By evening, the muddied path was a thoroughfare, villagers making their way around the large puddles and picking up debris. Glancing up into the gray sky, they paid their token of homage to the Almighty, muttering feeble prayers and thankful to have survived. Some commented it was the worst storm in memory. But who was to say, as memory has a tendency to befuddle things? Storms are storms and fade with time. To everyone's amazement, the old pier was still standing. *But where was Cedric?*

Lieutenant Sumpter lay unconscious on the beach. The cry of a passing gull stirred his senses. There was something pressing against his side. Staggering to his feet, it was a dog. He remembered grabbing hold of him. The creature also rose and wagged his tail. *Friendly.* Moving a few steps down the beach, the dog turned. *Was he suggesting to follow?* The officer looked around. The beach was strewn with debris and broken bodies. *Where was he?* It all came back to him as they slowly made their way along the shoreline. The sea was placid, the lulling waves consoling, as if nothing had happened. A village could be seen in the distance.

Pinky was standing outside, scanning the beach and hoping for any sign of Cedric. A solitary figure vaguely appeared in the distance. *Was that Cedric by his side?* Grabbing hold of his cane, he quickly hobbled out to meet them.

Closer... *He's wearing the uniform of the Queen's service. An officer?* Cedric became excited, wagging his tail as he drew closer. Shivering, the man collapsed in Pinky's arms. Strapping an arm around his shoulder, Pinky struggled his way south. Jarvis then came to his aid.

Entering the tavern, the men laid him on tables Bertie had placed together. His lips were blue, his flesh pale as the winter sky. Bertie quickly unbuttoned his tunic. Jarvis took off his boots and began rubbing his feet. Pinky placed the wet uniform near the hearth and bundled him in blankets. Bertie gently wiped his face, pulling back his blond hair, thinking, *How handsome.* Covering him up, they waited.

In time, he came to his senses. He whispered, "Thank God." Bertie gently raised him and spoon-fed him the warm stew. He began recollecting: "Transporting wounded troops from India... then the storm... vessel was devastated... everyone abandoned ship... helping the wounded... sinking fast." A long pause, a blank look in his eyes. "Had to jump overboard... waves crashing over me... debris and dead men everywhere... Alone, so alone..." He then drifted into unconsciousness. Jarvis and Bertie assisted him up the stairs to a room where he slept soundly into the night.

....

Chapter 31

Painful Recollections

Lieutenant Sumpter awoke late in the morning. Bertie had quietly placed his dry uniform in the room, making him quite presentable as he descended the stairs. Pinky was seated by the window. Greeting the young officer, he amiably invited him to pull up a chair and share a pot of tea. He looked rested. One would never have known save for that distant look in his eyes. After a few moments of casual conversation, Pinky pointed to the pier. "At's where ol' Cedie boy sees yer goin' down. Lept in, an' saved yer life." The officer struggled to comprehend it all.

Jarvis and Bertie joined in, amazed to see his remarkable recovery. How he had fended against the sea and the freezing cold was beyond their comprehension. Somewhat hesitant, Bertie asked if he would share his story with the villagers; most assuredly, it would be an inspiration to everyone. There was a moment of silence. His eyes were downcast as he muttered, "No." Respectful of his sentiments, she let it be.

Jarvis said he and Pinky had served in the British army and inquired about his regiment. "The 44th Foot. That is before it was annihilated." This, too was a quandary, as they wondered what other painful recollections there were.

Removed from military protocol, he began unraveling everything with painful introspection. Congested with insurmountable nightmares, it had to be released. He told them he was the sole survivor of an expedition force of 22,000 sent to Afghanistan from India, the victory and defeat in Kabul, and the retreat through the mountains. The Afghans were tenacious warriors, and the British fought valiantly. Freezing and outnumbered, they stoically held off the enemy time and again. However, the relentless attacks of 30,000 guerrillas and the cold eventually took their toll, with frozen bodies and animals strewn as far as the eye could see.

Along with a dozen other men, he managed to escape on horseback. They were cut down one by one- save for him and his beleaguered horse. The latter died of fatigue after carrying him through the pass. Starving, cold, and bleeding from a head wound, the young officer all but crawled to the fort in Jalalabad.

Continuing, more in a whisper, "If only they had let me remain in the hospital..." Orders were sent to release him as soon as possible to set sail for London and be honored by the Queen. He muttered, "I'm no hero." Truth be known, Lieutenant Sumpter thought himself a coward. "I should have died with the rest of them..."

He then disclosed the events of the sinking of the *HMS Ballantyne*. Stalling, he recollected the horror of it all, barely able to utter his leap overboard. There was no mention of the blind soldier.

The sea proved to be as sinister as the ice-covered mountains. Clinging to debris and floating aimlessly, all the other men were dead. Life was fading fast. He wanted to die... Then this thing appeared, surging toward him out of the storm and making its way next to his body. "Something was consoling in that creature's eyes. I lunged out and took hold. Then all became a blur..." Looking over at Cedric, he smiled. "There he is, rank and file among the best."

It had been decades since Pinky's last battle. Though he had witnessed many a tragic sight with innumerable tales to tell, everything paled in comparison with what was told by Lieutenant Sumpter.

....

Chapter 32

A Subtle Glance

Two days passed after the storm before news of the sinking of the *HMS Ballantyne* reached Nora's cottage. Hitching Mr. Wilson, the girls climbed aboard, and Nora headed to the village. Naturally, Mrs. Filmore would tell them all the details.

Yes, another ship had sunk. It was transporting wounded troops home from India. You can still see its tip over the waves if you look out to sea. Poor souls, wounded soldiers, many had washed to shore. There was one survivor, a young British officer. Mrs. Filmore became more excited as she continued, telling of Cedric's unbelievable rescue. *The next morning, Pinky and Jarvis saw him on the beach by the side of that wretched survivor and carried him to the Inn. Strange... they say he was also the only survivor of a terrible military battle in Afghanistan.*

Faith and Rachel listened attentively. Looking at Nora with imploring eyes, they hoped to visit the Inn, see this man for themselves, and congratulate Cedric. With a gracious nod, Nora consented, knowing it would prove to be another one of those rare experiences.

Upon entering the Inn, they immediately spotted the young man in his military uniform. Seated by the window with Pinky and the Merriweathers, Cedric was by his side, wagging his tail as they entered. After a cordial nod, Nora directed the girls to a table near the hearth.

Pinky rose and approached, offering his amiable salutation. "What're yer ladies 'ave?"

"A pot of tea will be fine, Pinky." Nora then added in a hushed tone, "Who is that young man?"

"'Ee's 'im, mum. Only surviv'r, ee is. Ship went down an' ol' Cedie boy swam out an' saved 'im.'"

The officer looked their way, his eyes meeting Rachel's before she could turn. "Bring 'em ov'r, if yer like. Ee'd be delight'd ta meet yer."

Nora hesitated. However, before she could respond, Pinky hobbled away, soon returning with the young officer, Cedric, by his side. Faith leaned over and whispered loving words in Cedric's ear; his tail wagged as if understanding. After an introduction, Pinky made his way to the kitchen.

The man remained quiet. Nora thought it was a combination of awkwardness and military protocol. There was a deep sadness in his eyes. The girls were less perceptive, thinking he presented himself quite valiantly. Pinky awkwardly placed the tea and cups on the table and returned to the Merriweathers.

Nora said, "We heard about the tragedy of the *HMS Ballantyne*. We are so sorry. The channel can sometimes be quite cruel, especially during the winter season. Sadly, many ships have met such a fate."

"We were caught unawares, ma'am. Don't know what did us in, the storm or the sandbar." He turned to Rachel. "Mr. Pinky mentioned you are the young lady who did his portrait." Looking over at the mantel, he added, "That's also a fine portrayal of Cedric." Rachel remained quiet. He began letting down his guard, relieved to be in good company and temporarily removed from the haunting memories. "At one time art had been my aspiration–that is, before going into the military."

The conversation continued with pleasantries. However, Nora did not want to detain him from the Merriweathers and prepared to leave. She inquired if he would like to come to their cottage for lunch before his departure. They could come to town to give him a ride if he liked. Much obliged and thankful, he insisted on walking. Plans were made for the following day. She gave him directions, recommending that he arrive early to make a day of it. They then left and boarded the wagon. The lieutenant returned to his seat by the window. Rachel glanced in. Their eyes met inadvertently. So much was said in that vulnerable moment.

It was mid-December–the raw edge of winter had settled upon the coast. The waning sun looked like a silver coin within a thin veil of clouds. Chimneys let out their smoke in unison as several gulls sailed over the sea.

....

*"The human heart is like a ship on a stormy sea driven about
by winds blowing from all four corners of heaven."*
                                                    Martin Luther

....

Chapter 33

An Honored Guest

Lieutenant Sumpter lay awake. Sleepless hours. Haunting images...
Staring at the ceiling, that frozen pass and the never-ending trail
of death entangled with the sinking of the *HMS Ballantyne*. The blind
soldier haunted him most. *Would it ever go away*? He remained lifeless,
waiting for the relief of daylight.

With the first silver tint of dawn, he dressed and headed down the
stairs. Jarvis had given him clothes the previous evening, and everything seemed to fit. The lanterns were lit. Pinky was stoking the hearth.
Turning, he smiled and nodded, recognizing Jarvis's clothes. The young
officer took a seat near the window. Pinky made his way to the kitchen
and returned with a pot of tea. Placing it on the table, he respectfully
let him be.

Sunrise awoke with a pale light. He could see Cedric at the extremity
of the pier. *Such an extraordinary creature. How did he ever manage to
swim to the ship and then bring me to shore*? It was still beyond his
comprehension.

The sea was calm, and daybreak was pleasant, adding to his anticipation of the visit. Finishing his tea, he bid Pinky a good day and headed

out into the morning air. The sky became an open slate of gentle blue, the salt air brisk and revitalizing. Fortunately, Jarvis had given him a heavy sweater.

Walking by the edge of the shoreline, the surf lapped in and out of his steps. Pausing, he turned and looked to the northeast. The bowsprit of the vessel was still silhouetted against the sky. He then set his thoughts on a home-cooked meal and the good company that awaited him as the surf played its soothing melody.

There was a nudge. Startled, he turned. Cedric was by his side, wagging his tail enthusiastically. The lieutenant bent over and rubbed his head. "It's good to see you, too, ol' boy." Continuing on his way, he was surprised to see Cedric following along.

Reaching the end of the village, he made note of the church and headed into the woodlands. Within the barren trees, a bird was singing a soft note. Cedric walked in stride, stopping along the way to sniff a myriad of new things, a remnant of crumpled leaves beneath their feet. A panorama of pastures and undulating hills then spread out before the young officer, reminiscent of his childhood.

Let's see... go past the meadows and the smaller hills. Then, to the right, atop a larger hill... a cottage and several trees. The instructions were clear, and after a stretch, he saw smoke coming from the chimney of a distant cottage—an *idyllic setting.* A sense of joy overtook him as he picked up his stride.

Faith was the first to greet him and was elated to see Cedric. "Did you bring him along for us?"

"Not really. He joined me on the beach. He's become my best companion these days and delightful company during the hike."

She escorted them inside. The cottage was of good proportion, more spacious than he surmised. There was a sense of calm in the home he had not felt for a long time, and he was grateful to enjoy a portion of life that had long since slipped away.

Rachel entered the room and greeted their guest but remained reserved. He felt vulnerable to her beauty. Nora approached and encouraged everyone to settle around the table as she prepared tea. Faith lit a candle and immediately filled the room with her animation, telling Lieutenant Sumpter that Mrs. Filmore had told them everything about Cedric saving his life. Rachel sat across from him, listening but with a quiet demeanor.

Nora was humored by his dress. "You look quite the gentleman, lieutenant. Where did you find such attire? I must say, though–we were quite fond of your military uniform." It was good to see him smile.

"My arrival to your quaint village was quite unexpected, and Mr. Merriweather was gracious enough to suit me up for the day. Though he is somewhat older, we seem to have the same proportions from top to bottom. I must say, even the shoes fit."

The conversation took a convivial course, with Faith leading the way with a flow of topics and questions. All the while Nora studied him. There was a touch of aristocracy and a natural charm, though tarnished with that deep sense of sorrow in his eyes. When the time seemed right, she inquired, "We know you have been through ordeals that cannot be imagined. Nor do we wish to pry into those travesties, as our time together is meant to be a blessing to you. However, could you share more about how this incredible dog rescued you?"

Looking down at Cedric and gently stroking his head, he muttered, "But if the while I think on thee, dear friend, all losses are restored, all sorrows end."

"That's Shakespeare!" Faith exclaimed. "Nora had us memorize one of his sonnets every week when we were girls. That's Sonnet thirty, I do believe. It's one of Rachel's favorites."

Lieutenant Sumpter slowly began baring his soul. Something was consoling in being with this little family, and it came out like a long overdue sigh. "We lost an entire army in the mountains of Afghanistan. I alone survived, all but crawling to a fort in Jalalabad. Recovering from my wounds, I was put on a troop carrier sailing for England. It was filled with casualties from various battles. Everyone was in good spirits, looking forward to going home. Then the storm, so close, we could see land. The ship became damaged beyond hope and tossed against a sandbar. Men were swept overboard. Then, just as quickly, we severed from the bar. The ship listed taking on water, and the order was given to abandon ship. So much upheaval and no one to man the lifeboats. And the wounded, most too weak or crippled to leap. Even if they did, they would never have survived. To my knowledge, I was the last man overboard." Again, no mention of the blind man.

"I held on to part of a mast... entangled in halyards. Faint cries of dying men around me. All fell silent, save for the storm. Desperately alone, ready to let go... Then, out of the tempest, comes this strange creature tenaciously making its way towards me. It looked like a bear. Drawing closer, it had friendly eyes, eyes I could trust. It nudged me as if suggesting it wanted to help. With no other choice, I desperately grabbed hold of him. There was a feeling of utter helplessness as the waves crashed over us. By the grace of God, we made it to shore.

"I regained consciousness on the beach. There he was, still beside me–a dog, large and gentle. I started crawling along the shoreline, cold and exhausted. He remained by my side, shielding me from the elements as best he could. I passed out again. Who knows for how long?"

Staring into the flicker of the candle, he continued more to himself, "Regained consciousness. The dog was still there. It took a few steps down the beach and turned, suggesting I follow. Struggling to my feet, I stumbled forward. There was a village in the distance. And then I see Mr. Pinky coming toward me. Jarvis was by his side. You know the rest."

Relieved, he settled back, more at peace than he had been in a long time. "Strange–I always had a feeling God was with me. Don't know why? My faith had been all but nonexistent for so many years. Too independent and self-willed. It was in the mountains when I first sensed His presence. There can be no denying that a divine hand carried me to Fort Jalalabad. Then the shipwreck. I still find it difficult to comprehend it all, that He sent a dog to save me. Only God knows why I was the only survivor in both those tragedies." He bowed his head and continued almost in a whisper, "They are trying to make a hero out of me, trying to salvage something from the defeat in Kabul and the shipwreck. There was nothing courageous in anything I did."

Nora added some insight. "You say you were the last one to abandon ship? Becoming familiar with you, I would say you were most likely assisting the maimed and weak to the very end. There were many on that mountain pass for whom you also did your very best. Please don't be so hard on yourself." Tenderly pressing his hand, she rose to prepare dinner. Faith immediately took over the conversation, venturing into more amiable topics.

The roasted lamb was the best in Lieutenant Sumpter's memory, culminating with pie and coffee. After an extended hour, Nora cleared the dishes and persuaded them to go outside for fresh air. Faith remained and assisted Nora as Rachel and the young officer departed.

Walking aimlessly, they wandered upon the hillside, Cedric accompanying them. They settled upon some rocks overlooking the distant sea, the late afternoon sun still giving a semblance of warmth as shadows began covering the land.

He reflected on the beauty of nature, plucking a withered thistle and studying its simplicity. "I have always cherished withered flowers. Their muted colors have their own beauty, don't you think?"

Rachel remained quiet, Cedric resting by her side and attentive.

"As I mentioned, your drawing of Mr. Pinky is quite good. And that of my friend here is excellent."

"Thank you."

"You somehow manage to put integrity in your work. That golden touch is such a rarity. Do you have any plans for the future?"

"Not really. It is but a hobby–though Nora encourages me. She believes I am quite talented. However, my purpose is to assist her as much as possible."

"You are being too modest. There must be aspirations hidden beneath your benevolence."

"Well, now that you mention it, I would love to learn how to paint. 'Tis but a dream, though."

"It's an exciting time to be in London. There are studios where you could learn from renowned masters. A thriving city and a place to build upon affluent patrons that believe in your ability."

"I lived there during my childhood, though in a poorer district. I don't remember much."

The conversation wandered in other directions. There were even moments of laughter. Winter's days were short, and the sun began taking its turn with longer stretches of shadows cutting across the land, the silhouette of Sheppey highlighted in a final burst of sunlight.

"We had better be going. It's cooling down and becoming late." He assisted Rachel to her feet. The walk to the cottage was quiet, though much thought was within their steps.

Faith had started a campfire and was seated on a stump poking at the embers. Cedric went to her side and rested. The fire was animated; a flurry of embers, like orange fireflies, ascended into a deep Prussian blue. The lieutenant sat on a log to the other side of Cedric. Rachel seated herself across from him, giving him the discreet opportunity to study her, the warm glow of the fire only accentuating her beauty. *She seems complete in so many ways–wholesome, pure... unblemished by the world.* Nora joined them.

Rachel finally spoke: "You mentioned you studied art?"

"Yes, I grew up as a student in the fine arts. Weaned on portraitures, you might say. Loved studying the Renaissance and Baroque masters. Spent a season under a Dutch master in Amsterdam. However, portraits became tedious as I soon realized I was not a Gainsborough, nor did I desire to be. Too free-spirited for commission work and those demands for perfection. Began focusing on nature, at which time the brushes were put aside for God, Queen, and country."

Staring into the fire, he followed a different note: "I find several things enrich the soul. Ironically, the sea allows my mind to wander into a world of its own, trying to comprehend the depths of life. Quite ironic, is it not? Life has its paradoxes... Is it not also an irony that I find inspiration in the mountains? Possibly one day..." Looking up into the depths of the sky: "The stars also hold their wonder. This can also be said of a campfire. Makes for the best of company, especially for a wandering soul." There was a smile. Rachel thought him all the more handsome. *If only he smiled more.*

"What about a dog?" Faith interjected.

"Oh, yes, of course. Clumsy of me." Another smile. "The hearth and a good dog go hand in hand." Leaning over and stroking Cedric, he softly added once again, *"But if the while I think on thee dear friend..."* Rachel was intrigued by how he repeated that verse.

The hour finally arrived to bid them farewell. The day could not have been more medicinal. Rising, he thanked them for their gracious hospitality. Nora offered a ride to the Inn. Politely declining, he said the walk would do him good, and he had Cedric for company. Before leaving, his eyes met Rachel's, a world contained within the moment. Though the day surpassed his highest expectations, so much was incomplete.

The sky remained open, a half-moon casting its light upon the path as he followed Cedric's lead. His thoughts remained on Rachel as the haunting past had been pleasantly intruded upon.

The following morning, Rachel wrote to Lady Bradshaw. They had been corresponding throughout the year. She told her about the young officer and how much they enjoyed his company. His name was Lieutenant Sumpter, and he was of good character. He had also been in a recent shipwreck and rescued by Cedric and was returning to London to be honored by the Queen. Hopefully, someday, she will have the opportunity to meet him. Rachel concluded by telling her how well Cedric was doing and added a small sketch of him and the lieutenant on the stationery. Both were done from memory.

....

Part II
(1843–1851)

"Heroism consists of hanging on one minute longer."
                                                    Norwegian Proverb

....

Chapter 34

To Visit the Queen

L ieutenant Sumpter arrived at the ports in London with much pomp
and ceremony. A large crowd waited at the docks as the vessel
pulled into the harbor, flags and banners blowing in the breeze and a
band playing. The young officer was presented with honors and overflowing accolades, given the George Medal, and promptly promoted
to captain.

The following day, draped with ribbons and metals and at his red-
breasted best, Captain Sumpter proceeded to Buckingham Palace, a
royal carpet all but rolled out before him. Queen Victoria was seated at
the head of a grand table, a long row of generals and parliamentarians
to either side. Crowned and bejeweled, she was more majestic than he
had imagined. Though once having had the opportunity to see her, it
was from a distance. He had thought that, perchance, there might have
been an intimate meeting, reflecting on the campfire and how ideal
that would have been. However, amidst the countless dignitaries, it was
quickly put aside.

Everyone settled in, becoming respectfully silent. The Queen then commenced: "Captain Sumpter, on behalf of everyone here today and the entire British Empire, we are most honored and blessed to have you among us... in the land of the living." The acoustics in the spacious room carried her voice with resonance. "You have gone through unimaginable travesties, and your heroism goes beyond measure, more than meriting the George Medal. There is no need to go into the details of the tragic engagement in Kabul. We are well aware of that. However, this second catastrophe, the unfortunate sinking of the *HMS Ballantyne* with the loss of so many of our fine young men, has proven to be another exemplary example of your bravery. And that is what we would like you to share with us now. It is known that you assisted the wounded as best you could before the vessel went down. And you were the last man to leap overboard. At which time, you found yourself alone in the depths of the sea, being the sole survivor once again. Is that not correct?"

"Yes, Your Majesty."

"And rumor has it you were rescued by a dog?"

"That is true, Your Majesty."

"Quite extraordinary. Would you care to tell us more about that?"

"There's not much to say. We were sailing to port, returning home from India and overloaded with wounded troops. Suddenly, we came head-on with a tempest and cast upon a sandbank near the coast, many men being swept overboard. The rest clung to the bulwarks as best they could. Waves continued crashing over the hull, taking more over the side. And then the ship was released from the bar. We were taking on water and sinking. I assisted the wounded as best I could. Finally, I went over the side and grabbed hold of some flotsam. Everyone had perished. That's all I remember."

"Is it not also true that you were the last to abandon ship and assisted the infirmed to the very end? And did you not leap from the ship holding on to a blind man?" *How did she know that?*

"Yes."

"Now, what about this dog?"

"It all became a blur. Wind, waves, rain; light was fading fast. The sea was cold. I became numb, all but incoherent." He told as best he could and concluded by stating the dog's name was Cedric and that he resided on an old pier in the small coastal village of Sheppey. They say it was not his first rescue at sea. Queen Victoria had heard many a tall tale throughout her reign. However, none as extraordinary as this. The officer seemed upright, sincere, and in control of his faculties, and she believed his every word. Nevertheless, the consensus of the dignitaries around the table was that it was nothing more than an entangled fable, a mix of trauma and delusions, fabrications woven within a troubled mind. *The poor man simply endured too much.*

The Queen gave Captain Sumpter a subtle nod of approval and mused, "I see..." She then rose. "We must meet this marvelous creature. During recent times, our nation has been in dire need of heroes, whether it be man or beast." With begrudging harmony, heads bobbed, followed by a muffled "Hear, hear." She then tapped upon a glass, and all rose to give their honored guest a royal ovation, to which he silently reiterated, "I'm no hero."

....

Chapter 35

The Bradshaw Estate

In the early summer of '43, a letter arrived for Rachel from Lady Bradshaw. It was a pleasant day, and taking a break from her studio, she sat outside under the elm and opened the envelope. The baroness began by mentioning the young officer. He had received many honors upon arriving and was reassigned to a unit near London. The baroness again mentioned how fond she was of her portrait and the drawing of Cedric that was given her during her stay at the Inn, the latter being framed and hanging in a special place. She would cherish another portrait of him, a painting in oils. Would she consider such? Knowing she was unskilled in painting, London would be an excellent place to study. She had made inquiries as to her admittance to the Royal Academy. Unfortunately, it still remained closed to the female gender. However, she was on good terms with one of the leading portrait painters in the metropolitan area, who had consented to take Rachel under his wing. The correspondence was finalized by extending an invitation to come to London and attend the workshop. She could reside at her estate and be provided a stipend to care for all the necessities.

Rachel took a deep breath. Her entire perspective on life changed with a few penned words. A whirlwind of thoughts. *Too much to comprehend. Was art truly her calling? Was she good enough to take on such a monumental proposal? Could she adjust to city life? Being separated from Faith? Nora also depended on her.* Yet beyond such heavy concerns, she realized it was a golden opportunity. *Would she not be able to spread her wings and embrace an entirely new dimension of life? Most assuredly, such an invitation would never come again. There was also the possibility of seeing him.*

Throughout the day, Rachel continued to struggle. She needed Nora's insight. Invariably, she would put everything to rest. Late in the afternoon, they sat at the table. Faith was also present. Rachel shared Lady Bradshaw's proposal with them, and Nora and Faith were immediately thrilled with the opportunity, wholeheartedly encouraging her to seize it. With much relief, Rachel agreed. The next morning, she responded to the baroness and accepted her generous offer.

A carriage from the Bradshaw estate arrived within a fortnight. After a long and emotional goodbye, Rachel entered the coach with a small bag of belongings. The coachman then headed west by north through the countryside. In ancient times, one would say, *All roads lead to Rome.* However, in this present day, all roads led to London, the jewel in the British Crown and one of the most glorious cities throughout Europe. And the young and lovely Miss Thomson was about to venture into its wonderful fold. She was eighteen years of age.

The day was in rhythm with the season, the sun having its full reign, basking the land in its warmth. Rachel found the scenery inspiring, vaguely remembering when she first came to Sheppey. Her heart stirred with emotions, her mind dancing from one thought to another, still uncertain but excited beyond measure. The ride was debilitating, the coach traversing over many a rough road–though of little concern to its passenger as she was soon to enter into a life far beyond anything she could imagine.

By late afternoon, the estate came into view. Though the ride was arduous, Rachel was overwhelmed with excitement. Leaning slightly from the window, the coach passed rows of manicured hedges and lush gardens. The coachman pulled the team of horses to a halt. A large fountain with spewing stone sculptures was centered before the residence.

The staff immediately came out and stood at attention, poised in immaculate black-and-white uniforms. A valet stepped forward and assisted Miss Thomson from the carriage. With humility, she stepped out. For the first time, she was self-conscious of her dress and aware of how unprepared she was for such an occasion.

Lady Bradshaw stood at the top of the steps. Distinguished and graceful, she greeted her guest warmly. The valet then escorted Rachel up a broad spiraling staircase to a room on the second floor. It had a delightful view of the sprawling estate. She then joined the baroness in a portico on the west wing. A light fare was served by two servants who tended to their every need. Rachel was finally at ease. Having the luxury to absorb the immaculate grounds and spend time with her gracious host, she sensed she had made a good decision.

The baroness studied the young lady. Her features were all but perfect: a delicate neckline, clear hazel eyes, and a slight olive tone to her skin. There was a sincere and gentle way about her. "I hope you like your room. It is on the east wing and will offer a delightful sunrise."

"Yes, I do." Rachel was too excited for words.

"It will be my pleasure to host you during your stay. I very much look forward to our time together. Your apprenticeship will start on Monday morning. However, it may be best for you to reside in Westminster throughout the week. I have a house there, which is much closer to Sir Wisham's studio. Then, if you so desire, you can return here on weekends. At which time I will attentively listen to the progress you are making." Rachel continued to take it all in, basking in the warmth of the afternoon and overwhelmed by the baroness's benevolence.

"One more thing... that dearly beloved British officer? It is easy to read between the lines in your letter that you are quite fond of him. I had the honor of meeting him at a recent ceremony and mentioned your arrival. To say the least, he became quite animated. I then inquired if he would like to join us for a luncheon."

It proved to be the exclamation mark on this new world that was now stretching out before her. Like a fairy tale going from a country cottage to a sprawling estate and learning to paint under a renowned master! This alone fulfilled a dream. However, it was the news of Captain Sumpter that consumed her emotions. And to think–she would hopefully now have the opportunity to know him better. *Was life supposed to overflow with such blessings*? Rachel responded with a smile, "I think a luncheon would be fine."

With that settled, the baroness realized Rachel's dress required immediate attention. Seeing that the young officer was soon to make his presence known, she insisted on something more appropriate for the occasion, "Though you are quite lovely as you are, my dear, it may be time for a change. Dress is quite significant in our society. Sadly, people will judge you, even rank you by such–though I am certain your beauty and demeanor will only enrich any changes I am going to suggest."

She then laid out her plans. "My coachman will take you to Piccadilly Circus tomorrow morning. I have invited Captain Sumpter for brunch the Sunday after next, and we are short on time. The shop is called *The Piccadilly Princess* and is located on the east side of Westminster, not far from where you will be residing. It is one of the finest dress shops in London. There will be other accessories that will be required. Mrs. Barthow will tend to you." She then added, "Rachel, I realize how awkward this may be, as you know nothing about this sort of thing. Mrs. Barthow will give you the very best guidance, even advising you on preferred fabrics and other garments. She will also make the purchases from the draper's shop, saving you time and alleviating the pressure of having to make such decisions. I feel quite confident with any recommendations she may offer. For now, select two summer dresses. Cotton is preferable. There will be more selections when we have time. You will be fitted for one dress first. We will make it an urgent request. Everything will go on my account." Rachel continued to be both thankful and awed.

....

119

Chapter 36

The Piccadilly Princess

Rachel was quite fond of the coach, marveling at the team of horses clopping through the heart of London. She was fascinated by the wide boulevards, monuments, picturesque parks, and well-dressed people passing by her window. *So far removed from the muddy path in Sheppey.*

The Piccadilly Princess was in the heart of Westminster, a lavish section of the city. Entering the shop, she was immediately intimidated by the vast array of dresses with all the frills and fluffs. *How could she be true to herself in making this transition? However, Lady Bradshaw's request would prevail, and there was no turning back.*

"You must be Miss Thomson?" Rachel turned to be greeted by an elderly woman. "I am Mrs. Barthow." She was refined and without pretension. Rachel liked her.

Warmly clasping her hand, she added, "You are just as lovely as Lady Bradshaw said. She forewarned me that this would be a new experience for you. Please don't be overwhelmed by it all. Styles change as quickly as the weather. Some of this apparel is already outdated. And to be perfectly honest, most of it would only detract from your natural beauty. We don't want to make a gaudy show of it, do we?" She smiled. "The baroness has recommended several dresses, one to be completed as soon as possible." Mrs. Barthow placed a finger to her chin. "Let's see... so we have decided to do away with the frivolity?" She guided Miss Thomson through the long aisles of apparel, still considering out loud, "Nor do we need a corset to tighten your waist." Leaning closer, she whispered, "Thank God. We certainly don't want to dress you in that pompous Polonaise style with all those bulbous hoops." Drawing closer, "Which only tends to give women a larger rump. To be honest, I think it's for old spinsters." Rachel liked her more. She then guided her to the latest fashions. "We'll also do away with these tedious layers of flounce and petticoats. Unfortunately, there are some guidelines you will need to abide by–accepted protocol, shall we say. However, we can stretch it for someone as delicate as you. Pulling out a white latticed dress, "I like this. It's called the Bertha style. A low neckline yet maintains modesty, designed especially for someone like you. We'll trim it with a lace flounce, don't you think?"

"Yes." Rachel was delighted with the choice and breathed a sigh of relief.

"Good. Then let's make some notes and measure for patterns." Jotting down information, Mrs. Barthow paused once again, returning a forefinger to her chin. "I do believe a soft egg white or light beige would be ideal for the season, naturally of the finest cotton and interwoven with a light latticed fabric. Do you agree?"

"Yes, that would be fine."

"Long sleeves are a must. Let's keep them somewhat transparent." Taking more notes, "If it is all right with you, I will select suitable shoes and gloves, along with stockings and appropriate undergarments."

Mrs. Barthow stood back, taking in Rachel's full stature. "Let's now consider a hat. The icing on the cake, is it not? I don't want to downplay your beauty by placing such lovely features in its shadow. Hats do that these days with the wide brims and all those frivolous flowers and plumes. Such a flashy bird's nest! One has a tendency to focus more on the top of the head than the individual beneath it." She considered... "We'll don you in a Poke bonnet. Though a little irregular, I believe it suits you perfectly." Gently placing one on Rachel's head and tying it around her chin, she stood back. "I think that will do just fine. Let's now proceed with your measurements."

Chapter 37

Prim and Proper

The following morning, the coachman came to deliver Rachel to her new residence. Before departing, the baroness mentioned that both the carriage and coachman were at her beck and call and to be used for weekend visits to the estate if she so desired.

It was a three-story white house with yellow trim, nestled in an exclusive area of Westminster. There was a lush park adjacent to the front. The coachman took her bag and escorted her in. The interior had high ceilings with a spiral staircase ascending to the second floor. Save for the coachman's quarters, she would have it all to herself. He directed her up the stairs. A large room, perhaps a study, immediately caught her attention with its long windows facing the park. It afforded excellent light and, with a little rearranging, would make an ideal studio. She chose an adjoining room for her bedroom.

Settling in, Rachel relaxed, enjoying the ambiance while attempting to organize her thoughts. One of her first objectives would be a painting for Lady Bradshaw. *Possibly a portrait? How else could she repay her?* Throughout the ensuing months, she would make a point to study her features and paint from memory. She would also do the painting of Cedric she so desired. *However, she would first have to learn how to paint. And who knew how long that would take? Hopefully, the paintings would be completed by autumn and presented to the baroness for her birthday.* Her mind wandered in other directions: creating the studio, imagining the first day in the workshop, soaking in her surroundings, and Captain Sumpter.

Monday awakened with a clear blue sky. The air was fresh and cool; lush greens filled the trees as she entered the coach. The team of horses proceeded to trot through the boulevards and over the newly constructed London Bridge. Rachel consumed it all–the wealth of monuments, the long rows of classical edifices, and the prim-and-proper Londoners coming and going.

Sir Wisham's studio was located on the outskirts of Peckham's lower-class district. He had chosen the second floor of a moribund industrial building for both his studio and workshops.

Rachel ascended the stairs. The room was a vast open space with large windows facing the front. There were several models dressed in vivid costumes with small clusters of students and easels around each. All but one window was covered, casting a soft light on the models. The students were immersed in their work. She was relieved to see some were young women. A low masculine voice broke the silence. Rachel presumed it was the instructor critiquing a student's work. She waited patiently.

Sir John Wisham was one of Great Britain's premier portrait artists. Cut out of the mold of Reynolds and Gainsborough, he had recently been knighted for his exemplary works. Lady Bradshaw had discovered him during his younger years. Requesting several commissions, she began promoting him within her circles. Word quickly spread, as did his fame. For this alone, John Wisham was indebted and welcomed Miss Thomson with open arms. It would be here where she would learn the semantics of grinding paints and oil painting methods like the masters.

The colorful dress of the models was inspiring, and though Rachel had brought along her satchel of drawing materials, she continued to wait. The maestro finally glanced up and noticed her. Approaching with a warm smile, he said, "You must be the aspiring artist I have heard so much about?" He had a full head of white hair, like the mane of a lion, and penetrating blue eyes. Several years past middle age, he was vibrant-looking with a sense of well-being.

"My name is Rachel, Sir Wisham. It is truly an honor to meet you."

"My pleasure indeed." He quickly added, "Pardon me, my dear, but I have to leave for a few moments. In the meantime, look around and see what the other students are doing. My studio is over there, on the far side. If you have drawing materials, please feel free to join in. Again, it is a pleasure." He then exited.

Left to her own, she meandered throughout the room, respectfully making her way around the easels. It reminded her of a symphony, everyone painting in harmony. The models were far enough apart to offer each student a desired angle. She marveled at the uniqueness and quality of each painting, especially the jewel-like application of transparent layers of color, one over another. The students remained focused, acknowledging her presence with slight nods or smiles. It was obvious they were accustomed to visitors. Finding one of the models most intriguing, Rachel retrieved her sketch pad and, positioning herself between several easels, began sketching. The artist within her immediately took over, everything around her becoming secondary.

The session ended when the maestro returned. The models departed for the day, and the students cleaned their areas. Leaving their paintings on the easels, they gathered in another part of the spacious interior to learn the semantics of mixing pigments. Sir Wisham requested one of the students to assist Miss Thomson.

At the end of the day, Rachel inquired as to where paints and other materials could be purchased. Upon leaving, tired but exhilarated, she directed her coachman to the shop. Early in the evening, she returned to her residence, fully aware of the demanding days that lay ahead. Her hours were to be precisely measured. After a brief rest, she began organizing the studio. Another new world. When time permitted, she would begin the paintings for Lady Bradshaw.

Chapter 38

The Luncheon

T hough the 19th century proclaimed Great Britain as one of the greatest empires in history archives, it still played second fiddle to the continent in the art world. For centuries, the ongoing flow of prodigious masterpieces had come from the mainland: the Italian Renaissance, the Baroque Period, the Golden Age of the Dutch Masters, the French Neo-Classical Period; the works of the great Spanish and Flemish artists, etcetera, etcetera. Yet, as England took its passage through the Victorian Era, it began to rise to the occasion. In short order, it would contend with the excellent works upon the continent.

To ascend to such aesthetic heights, workshops were established with protégés studying under the best British painters. The National Academy had also raised its standards as a prestigious art academy. However, art was still considered a man's profession, and admittance to various academies was for the male gender only. The workshops would thus prove to be especially beneficial for women. And so the stage was set for Miss Rachel Thomson's tutelage under the prestigious Sir Wisham.

During the initial days, she was quick to lose confidence, believing the other students were far more talented and questioning whether or not she had made the right decision. Fortunately, everyone was encouraging–such doubts were what they had all experienced. A new confidence was soon birthed, and by the end of the second week, she was prancing into the estate, sharing with the baroness all the details of what she had learned. Lady Bradshaw listened attentively and appreciated the enthusiasm.

The dress was completed, and the luncheon with Captain Sumpter was set for one o'clock the following day.

Early Sunday morning, a servant assisted in dressing Miss Thomson, proving to be another awkward experience for Rachel was more than capable in dressing herself. This would be another exception, as she obligingly remained as still as a manikin while the handmaid proceeded to layer her with garments. Patience and humility prevailed, and the entire procedure was completed within an hour and crowned with the bonnet. Moving to the side, the servant presented her in front of a full-length mirror. Standing in awe, Rachel appreciated the splendor and grace of the new image. And Mrs. Barthow was correct–the bonnet suited her well. After making her appearance known to a glowing Lady Bradshaw, they departed for St. Paul's Cathedral. The parks and boulevards were vibrant with life.

St. Paul's Cathedral appeared. Situated upon the highest hill in London, it looked over the entire city, all but proclaiming the glory of God. Drawing closer, she saw the architectural wonder, the likes of which she had never seen in Nora's art books. Then, again, all she had to compare it with was her little church in Sheppey. The interior proved even more magnificent with the stained glass windows and massive dome, its immense space difficult for her finite mind to comprehend. Taking a seat near the altar, Rachel found herself among the very best of British society. She reflected on her church in Sheppey and how meek those souls were.

The sermon was short, far different from Pastor Theo's longer and more personal messages. However, the priest was sincere, and his words left her with much to consider. After the service, Lady Bradshaw introduced her to some acquaintances, all of whom were elated to meet such a charming young lady.

Captain Sumpter arrived on horseback precisely at the hour. A valet escorted him to the portico. Presenting himself in his military best, he was once again struck by Rachel's beauty, stalling for a moment and losing sight of the formalities. After being seated and a few pleasantries, brunch was served. *How different.* He thought. *No longer under the stars or nestled by a campfire.* It also afforded a wonderful ambiance with the sprawling landscape and lush gardens. *However, the only thing that remained the same was her beauty.*

The baroness observed the pair from her own vantage point. There was something stirring in the air besides the soft breeze. She had an innate sentiment that they were made for each other. Interrupting the moment, she commented, "He looks quite dashing, doesn't he?"

"Captain Sumpter is a tribute to the British crown." Rachel meekly replied.

"If you're going to be a portraitist, my dear, it would be difficult to find a more noble countenance. Possibly something to consider?"

"It's such an irony." He noted. "I also pursued the fine arts and portraitures though losing interest after enlisting, and now find such a suggestion to be something I would welcome very much."

"Would you consent, Rachel?" The baroness inquired.

"Yes. It would be an honor."

"Well, then, why not set up a time and commence?"

"Possibly you could come by next Saturday? My studio is in Westminster. Sometime in the morning? Let's say, nine o'clock?"

"That would be fine."

The baroness glowed. Throughout the remainder of the luncheon, she mused upon the fact that she had done her part. *Now–give it time to see how it all plays out.*

*"Thou art a soul in bliss; but I am bound upon a wheel of fire,
that mine own tears do scald like molten lead."*
William Shakespeare

....

Chapter 39

𝕻ortrait of an 𝕺fficer

I t was a resplendent day. The city abounded with life as Captain Sumpter walked the long stretches of boulevards in the morning air. Parks were lush with colorful blossoms as horses merrily galloped by. All seemed to be smiling within his own little world. In a peculiar way, the walk was similar to the one he had taken in Sheppey–the anticipation of seeing her, with pleasant thoughts in each step. Arriving at the hour, he knocked on the door. An elderly valet greeted him.

"Good morning. I am here for a nine o'clock portrait sitting."

He entered as Rachel was descending the stairs. Once again, he was struck by her beauty. After exchanging a warm greeting, she directed him to the studio, the large room brightened by the light from the windows and a glimpse of the park. The room was cluttered with the tools of the trade, with drawings scattered about. The easel looked new, not yet christened with dapplings of paint. A palette and blank canvas were waiting. There was a lit candle on one of the sills. *Peaceful.* He would have cherished such a studio during his younger years.

"As you can see, I'm new at this," Rachel said a little nervously. "Your portrait may be somewhat premature as I am but a novice. God willing, I will do my best."

"I have faith in your abilities. Let's say I will be the face that launched a thousand portraits."

She smiled and requested he take a seat on a stool in front of the easel, positioning him so the light was on one side of his face. At times, her body brushed against his–*the wisp of an angel.*

Everything became quiet as she prepared her palette, the artist within her setting to task. She then did a quick preliminary drawing. Placing it aside, she laid in the composition on the canvas with a large brush and loose strokes. *She seemed to have learned a great deal in a short amount of time.*

He broke the silence, "You have such ambiance here. It can be as simple as that candle flickering on your windowsill. Whatever kindles the heart." His words faded.

Late in the morning, the session ended. Captain Sumpter stood and stretched as Rachel cleaned her brushes. Staring out at the park, he muttered, "Sad, in the midst of such beauty, there can also be notes of sorrow."

Seeming impervious, she continued to busy herself. His words weighed heavily upon her. *How could she ever comprehend the mental agony that followed him like a haunting shadow?* It was a tender moment. She had a desire to embrace him.

Captain Sumpter walked over to the easel and studied the work. Though laid in with a flurry of brushstrokes, it was done masterfully. Even in this initial stage, it revealed more integrity than anything he had ever done. She had focused on the eyes. *They look sad.*

Rachel escorted him to the door, mentioning she would be working on it whenever time permitted. There should be another session, possibly the following Saturday. She implored him to allow her coachman to return him to the base. Pleasantly refusing, he replied it was a fine day for a walk, and they bid each other farewell. Returning to her studio, she watched him proceed down the boulevard–a solitary figure in so many ways.

....

Chapter 40

An Unspoken Love

C aptain Sumpter found himself walking the same path as the previous Saturday, the sun coming forth again in all its splendor. Crowned in lush greens, the trees shimmered in the warm breeze, and the city basked in the golden light. Yet there were deep concerns within his steps. Granted, he was excited beyond measure to see her. And he thanked God that the thought of her permeated the heavy gloom like the sweet scent of spring. He found all the pure ideals of love in her, and there was the faint hope that they could possibly have a future together. However, he faced the stark reality that his emotional wounds would never heal; doubt weighed heavy when considering a future together. There was something else, though, even more foreboding. He had received orders his unit was shipping out. Another expeditionary force was being sent to Afghanistan, and this could conceivably be the last time he would ever see her. He felt vulnerable. The walls he constructed as a safeguard were eroding around her, and his true emotions could easily overtake him. Time and again, there was an impassioned notion to take her into his arms and tell her. He had written her a letter in case he faltered.

Arriving promptly at the appointed hour, the valet directed him to the studio. Preparing her palette, Rachel turned to greet him. *He looked regal in the morning light.* She quickly averted her attention, preparing for the session. Captain Sumpter walked around the room. The smell of oils brought back memories. He studied his portrait. *She had added details. The tones were excellent, especially in the highlighted areas. For someone just learning to paint, it was very good.*

Rachel requested he return to the stool and take the same position. Studying the pose, she drew closer and made adjustments. *A vulnerable moment. There was the impulse to embrace her.* It slipped away.

"Sir Wisham worked with me this week on flesh tones. I am also learning to paint with glazes. However, I didn't do as much as I intended. Let's add some more touches and hope for the best."

He now had the opportunity to observe her undeterred as she picked up a brush. Occasionally, she would glance up for various details and then return to the canvas. *Those eyes were so clear, a purity not corrupted by the world. Her beauty soft, all but perfected, like a Raphael Madonna.* There was a moment when their eyes met and hesitated, laying bare their souls. A nervous energy filled the room, their feelings awkwardly contained. It was one of those surreal moments when heaven and earth touched. One could easily imagine cherubs hovering above. No paint or brush could have done it justice, and another tender moment passed by.

The session was not as long as the previous week. She turned the easel around, apologizing that it was still unfinished. She would hopefully bring it to its conclusion in the coming weeks. The area around his head had been vignetted, scumbled with earth tones extending to the borders. He thought it complete, though revealing too much of his soul in those eyes.

"I tend to be critical of anything pertaining to me. However, I must say, you are doing a remarkable job." He then told her another British unit was being dispatched to Kabul and that the military had requested his services once again. He would be leaving immediately. The moment became somber. He added in an empty tone, "May I write?"

"I would like that very much." Rachel's words were broken. Trying to avoid his eyes, she focused on cleaning the brushes. He approached. She was afraid to face him for fear of a flood of tears.

"I have this for you." He handed her the letter. "I can express myself better with a pen." Captain Sumpter painfully had more clarity, able to separate reason from his emotions. *Possibly this was best.*

Trying to be cordial, they bid each other farewell. She remained in the studio as the valet escorted him to the door. She watched from the window as he made his way down the boulevard. It was all so incomplete. She studied the painting, as unfinished as their relationship. There was a deep, foreboding feeling. She had contained so much within her heart. The letter remained sealed. His words would be far too much for her to take in. Possibly, in time...

....

"One ship sails east, and another west. By the self-same winds that blow, 'tis the set of the sails, not the gales, that tell the way we go." Ella Wilcox

....

Chapter 41

Three Notches upon the Beam

M ore than a handful of seasons passed since Cedric made his way into the village, establishing himself upon the pier and the hearts of the Sheppians. His acclaim began with the sinking of the *HMS Prince Edward* and Bosun Bluthers' rescue, soon followed by the shipwreck of the *Bonnie Lassie* and the rescue of Lady Bradshaw. Then, there was the tragic sinking of the *HMS Ballantyne* and its lone survivor, Captain Sumpter. However, beyond these supernatural heroics, Cedric was about to accomplish an ever more extraordinary feat, far surpassing the finite comprehension of man.

Heading to port in London, the *Libertine* was overloaded with immigrants looking for work in the city's industrial heart. Some were returning home to families. Everyone was nervously pressed on deck as the storm pursued the ship like a hound from hell. "'Tis a mean one com'n, Cap'n!" the bosun shouted in his ear. The captain was at the helm and vaguely caught sight of land through the torrential rain, the wind whipping around him. For a moment, he considered a veer south-ward to escape the brunt of it. Over the years, he knew his adversary well. And, though the *Libertine* was three-masted and could hold true against the wind, trying to outrun it would prove futile. The passengers, huddled together, waiting, wet and anxious. He then bellowed, "Batten the hatches! All passengers below deck!" Immediately, the bosun went fore and aft, blowing his whistle as the vessel set course for the inlet. It proved to be of no avail as the vessel was quickly engulfed in the full force of the storm, its bow slapping down upon the unforgiving waves. Any sign of land had vanished.

Wave after wave pounded the *Libertine* like a battering ram, snapping the halyards with the sails flapping in reckless abandon. A large wave crashed upon the haul, flooding the compartments. The passengers frantically escaped through the hatches; many quickly washed out to sea. The main mast shattered, the bilge flooded, the ship keeled to one side and then went asunder.

Thus, the *Libertine,* sinking into the depths, would be one more of the countless ships that had met their fate off the coast of Sheppey. However, three unlikely souls would miraculously survive to tell the tale.

Chapter 42

The Threesome

The rain began late in the afternoon, soon to be followed by tenacious winds. By early evening, the storm hit the coast with all its fury. Through it all, Cedric remained undaunted on the pier, his eyes set somewhere out to sea. And then a vessel appears. Far off. Sinking. Rising to his feet, he leapt into the sea.

The *Libertine* had sunk by the time he made his way through the pounding waves, wreckage, and bodies. He sees a woman, nearly unconscious, clinging to something. Paddling with an indomitable determination, Cedric was soon by her side. Finding the strength, she desperately took hold of him, and he then made his way to shore. There was the vague cry of a girl in the distance.

Cedric pulled the woman inland past the surf and immediately charged into the waves, returning to the aftermath of the shipwreck. A boy was holding onto something, frightened and crying. Pulling alongside, he frantically took hold of Cedric's collar.

Heading inland, there was that cry of that girl again. Cedric caught sight of her. She had drifted farther away. He left the boy by the woman's side on the beach and surged into the waves again. Exhausted, he drew closer to the girl. Half-submerged within the swirls, she was desperately holding on to a barrel. Gasping for air, she lunged toward him and wrapped her arms around his shoulders, weeping hysterically. She would be the last passenger to survive the ill-fated *Libertine*.

Shocked, wet, and freezing, the threesome huddled together alone as Cedric ran down the beach. All but lifeless, the woman stared into space, the boy clinging to her side. The girl, teeth chattering, stood apart, watching the dog fade in the distance and hoping this was not their end. They waited and waited... She then saw him again–far off. He was returning, two men by his side!

The following morning, Bertie shared the details about the ship-wreck and the three survivors with Mrs. Filmore, who was flabber-gasted by such a tall tale. However, knowing the integrity of Bertie, it had to be true. Being the maypole of all hearsay in the village, she immediately broadcasted the unbelievable rescue to any and all who entered the shop, even telegraphing it to passersby along the muddied path. Curiosity and exclamation marks ruled the day, and it would not be long before villagers began making their way to the Inn to have a look-see. Cupping their eyes and pressing against the tavern window, they saw a woman and a boy wrapped in blankets and a scrawny young girl by their side. Bertie politely shooed them away, saying they needed time to mend. However, everyone was invited to come to the Inn the following evening to hear their remarkable story.

In the meantime, the rain had ebbed, and Cedric casually returned to his post. Throughout the day, villagers continued to gaze at him. If their aged bodies could, they would gladly have shuffled to the end of the pier to give him a hearty pat on the head. If nothing else, their raspy voices would have shouted across the windswept shore, exclaiming how proud they were of him. But those years were now behind them, leaving them in place and silent, though with coddled hearts and wane smiles.

Chapter 43

"'At's six, ol' boy."

———

The sky remained a steel gray and quickly darkened by early evening. A biting wind and freezing drizzle kept the villagers bowed low as they made their way around the puddles to the Inn, lanterns from the cottage windows faintly guiding their steps. Anticipating the entertainment that awaited them, not a soul seemed to mind. To them, it was comparable to the very best of London's theatres.

They stood in a queue outside, the sign swaying and creaking above the door as they proceeded to enter. Taking off their wet hats and coats, they settled in. Soon every chair was occupied. The hearth was robust as the shoddy gathering merrily dug deep for a few sixpence, and the pints and quarts began to flow. If truth be told, they would have paid an extra sixpence for admission.

Pinky's mutton stew was a delightful side note. On such a dreary evening as this, the Merriweathers offered it at a reasonable price, and not even the pauper's purse felt the pinch. Throughout the year, he had been adding to his recipe: a little of this and a little of that. The first sampling was offered to a fisherman who gave his gruff approval after tasting a spoonful. That was enough to keep Pinky meddling within the cauldron. However, it would be the culinary approval of Nora when he truly began stirring the stew with more enthusiasm. Before the entertainment commenced, the caldrons were bare-boned, and the spoons licked clean.

The threesome was seated near the hearth, Cedric nestled by the side of the distraught woman. Still wrapped in a blanket, her head continually bobbed back and forth in a catatonic state, the little boy remaining by her side. They say she had lost her entire family. No one knew his story. Then there was the girl who had clung to the barrel for dear life. It was perplexing to put her in the mix of such a tragedy with that ongoing smile and her lively green eyes.

The Merriweathers had requested Pinky to take the podium to be the lead-in for the young girl as she insisted on telling her own story. Relishing the moment, Pinky had stood by the door greeting the villagers as they entered. Though knowing ne'er a name, he treated them as honored guests.

He took his position next to the castaways. "Even'n. Good ta see yer smile'n faces." (One toothless smile was evident in the audience.) Looking over at Cedric, he said, "Ol' Cedie boy wanted ta stand 'is post t'night. Seys, 'Nay, yer be join'n us.' An' 'ere 'ee is." Cedric rose, wagging his tail and coming to his side as though on cue. (More smiles.) Pinky leaned over and gave him a hearty pat and began recounting how Cedric had drifted into town on that rainy morn several years past and then reminisced on the tragic tales of the *HMS Prince Edward*, the *Bonnie Lassie,* and the *HMS Ballantyne*, many a head bobbing and recollecting. Possibly, it was the libations or the anticipation of what was to come, but the crinkled smiles broadened. (Were they finally taking a liking to him?) Not a soul surmised what was to follow, as the young girl was not about to play second fiddle to anyone, not even Pinky. Stepping forward, he graciously bowed out and took a seat.

"Good evening. My name is Adaline." Her youthful smile added a new energy to the evening. She presented herself quite ladylike. Somewhere between cute and pretty, her auburn pigtails framing a freckled face. "As you know, I am one of the three survivors of the tragic sinking of the *Libertine*. Well, we had clear sailing as we departed from France. Everyone was most excited about coming to London. And, oh, we were so near the coast. We could actually see land! And then that terrible storm came upon us! Horrific waves jolted the vessel as quickly as a lightning bolt, and many of the dear passengers were cast into the sea. Poor souls... Wave after wave came crashing over the deck. Everyone was screaming and crying hysterically. The sails flapped helplessly. And then the main mast snapped, making a terrible crash and crushing more people.

"The *Libertine* drifted helplessly... Water began rushing in. Sinking fast. So frightening! Another mast came crashing down. The lifeboats were shattered. People started abandoning ship, leaping into the sea. I didn't want to go down with the ship, nor did I want to take that leap! The ship began leaning to one side, ready to tip over, our bodies pressed against the bulwarks, towering waves crashing over us. There was no other choice but to take that leap. But I can't swim! There was a petrified boy standing next to me. I quickly grabbed hold of him and, with a fervent prayer, tossed him overboard. Don't ask me how, but I also jumped into the sea! It was the scariest moment of my life. Splashing, coughing, and gasping for air, I tried to find something to hold on to. Clung to a barrel. People all around me crying and drowning."

She spurted it all out in one breath. Holding back tears, she looked out at her audience, every eye attentively fixed on her. Continuing in a low tone, "I was useless. Couldn't help anyone, not even myself. All I could do was pray, 'Help us, God!' My dress was soaked and pulling me down. My shoes were like lead weights. The water was cold! I was growing faint, barely able to hold on to that barrel. 'Dear Lord, help me!' The screaming and weeping around me stopped. Everyone had perished. At least, that's what I thought. I then saw a woman in the distance. She was holding on to something and drifting away. It was terribly sad."

Adaline looked over at Cedric. "And lo and behold, I see this wonderful creature chugging toward me. I thought I was seeing things! Didn't know what it was! He then veered away and swam to that poor woman! She barely had enough strength to take hold of him, and away they went. I yelled, 'No—wait for me! Come back!'"

Adaline took a moment to catch her breath. The villagers remained in awe. "In a way, I was glad to see them swim away to only God knows where. But what about *me*? I didn't want to drown! The water was extremely deep. It seemed like hours passed. I then saw him again, this time pressing furiously in my direction. Thank God!" She looked over at the little boy. "But he goes right past me and paddles towards that young lad, who was barely hanging on to something. In all the upheaval, I hadn't noticed that he was the same boy I had pushed over-board! And off they went.

"The waves began taking me asunder. Choking and coughing, I felt as if I had swallowed the entire ocean. Didn't have the strength to keep my head above water or to hold on to that barrel any longer. My prayers became feeble... slipping into the depths. Then I saw him again! This time he was definitely coming in my direction. I could now clearly see it was a dog! Paddling closer, he had loving eyes. No time to ask him what he was doing or where he had come from. Nor did I care. Taking a leap of faith, I grabbed hold of him with all my might. His fur was soaked. How wonderfully strange to feel so secure holding onto him." Cedric remained attentive to her every word, wagging his tail when their eyes met.

"Reaching land, I saw the boy standing next to the woman. They were shivering and soaked through and through. I could now see how large the dog was. Thank God, he was so big and strong. He made his way over to the boy and gave him a gentle nudge as if to say every-thing was going to be all right. And then he trotted down the beach! Oh, no—we were alone again. Teeth chattering and bewildered, we huddled together in the dreary twilight. I would have passed out from exhaustion, but I was too cold, and thanking God that my feet were on solid ground!

"We knew we were going to turn into icicles if help didn't come soon. Then, far down the beach, we saw two men and our furry friend coming toward us. I started jumping for joy." She looked over at Jarvis and Pinky. "They were carrying blankets and hurrying as fast as they could. Bundling us up, Mr. Pinky assisted the boy, and Mr. Jarvis carried the woman. I stumbled along as best I could, very happy to be alive and hoping and praying we would soon be warm." She clasped her hands and jubilantly concluded, "Thank God for this Inn and these good people. And, of course, our dearly beloved Cedric." She then curtsied and took a seat. The villagers gave a warm though feeble ovation, their smiles lighting up the room like candle flickers. A tear or two could be seen, highlighted by the hearth.

Everyone lingered as they rose to depart, several going over to the young girl and praising her for her courage. Others made their way to Cedric, giving him a pat and a few gentle words before making their way out into the night.

Bertie took the boy to a room and tucked him in while Jarvis carried the woman up the stairs to another room. Adaline remained, assisting with clearing the tables before ascending the stairs to a room on the third floor.

The tavern lay still save for Pinky. Making his way over to the beam, he took out his knife and carved three more notches. Contemplating... "'At's six, ol' boy." Studying them for a moment, he blew out the lanterns and went to bed.

The sky remained pale the next day as if mourning over the *Libertine's* sinking. However, the wind had abated, giving the gulls clear sailing over a placid sea. If one looked closely, the bow of the *Libertine* tipped the waves–another telltale headstone.

....

"To fill the hour–that is happiness." Ralph Waldo Emerson

....

Chapter 44

Like a Stray Kitten

A ship sailed down from London with its host of officials to survey the aftermath of the sinking of the *Libertine*. A semblance of relatives also arrived to retrieve the little boy and the bereaved woman. No one came for Adaline. Like a stray kitten, the Inn became her shelter. As God would have it, she had been placed on the right doorstep, the Merriweathers caring for her with open-armed compassion. Full of life and exuberance, the young girl was thankful to be alive and have a roof over her head.

Adaline's childhood was one of sorrow. Her large Irish family had scrimped and scraped from day to day, abject poverty being a way of life. Weaned within such disparaging years, her parents had instilled in her a thankful attitude for everything and anything the good Lord provided.

One of Adaline's gifts was a huge Irish heart and a sincere desire to reciprocate for any kindness that might come her way. Finding herself stranded in the Wayfarer Inn, she strapped an apron around her waist and began a thorough cleaning and dusting of the rooms, making her abundant energy available for anything else that needed to be don,; whether assisting Pinky in the kitchen or waiting on customers (if ever there were any). Nevertheless, there would be ample hours to do as she pleased within these days. Most of her time was spent with Cedric. There was a lot of girl in her and plenty of pup in him. They frolicked on the beach and walked along the coast on pleasant days. During the quiet hours of late afternoon, she could be found, pencil in hand, writing by the tavern window, for Adaline loved prose. And is not the heart of every Irishman that of a poet?

....

Chapter 45

Taking a Repose

Roger's dwelling was as much an anomaly within the row of cottages as that of Agnes and Gertrude. The austere beauty of the coast and the solitude were the main reasons he had moved to Sheppey. In an odd sort of way, it was like a monastic cell. On rare occasions, one could see him taking walks along the shoreline with his little furry companion. Then again, a villager or two would have a glimpse of him at the grocers. And, if one arose early enough, one would invariably see him standing by his door, smoking a pipe, and looking out to sea like clockwork, watching the sun tip the horizon. Seeing him as a round peg in the midst of square holes, or more like a smooth around hard rocks, the villagers let him be.

As of late, he was thinking about that dog. *Cedric, was it?* He had certainly made an impression on the villagers, putting a gust of wind in their sails, the likes of which he had never seen before. The morning was merciful, and he was motivated to take Otto for the long walk north and become better acquainted with that creature who had made his home on the pier.

It was late afternoon; the sounds of the surf and meandering gulls made for a pleasant trip as Otto excitedly weaved in and out of his feet and the lapping waves. They finally drew near the pier. Roger could see him posted at the extremity of the pier. Otto became excited as they drew closer, his barking muffled by the surf. Cedric remained indifferent, looking steadfastly to the northeast. Roger could see the remnants of several vessels above the whitecaps. Taking the various tales into consideration, he let his mind wander, musing as to how that creature could have accomplished such ineffable feats. *Leaping into the sea... swimming through those vicious storms... bringing survivors to shore? Extraordinary...*

The wind picked up, and the sun tucked itself within a bed of clouds. There was a deep chill in the air. Otto's fur was wet, his little body trembling. Seeing the Inn, Roger gave the tavern consideration. *Why not? A hot toddy would be good for the soul.*

The tables were vacant. Otto immediately scurried to the hearth and settled in, Roger sitting near the fire. A young girl approached.

"Good day, sir. My name is Adaline." She was donned in a white apron. Her bright green eyes and smile were as warm a welcome as the hearth. It was an innocent face, sprinkled with freckles and framed in auburn pigtails, more than enough to surmise she was Irish. She turned her attention to the little dog. "Oh, he's adorable! And I see he's found the perfect place. The day has become quite raw, you know."

"It is delightful to be here. My little friend's name is Otto. My name is Roger. Some call me the professor." He was casually dressed but far better attired than the other villagers. Several years beyond middle age, his hair was thinning. Her first impression was that he was quite distinguished and a man with much knowledge. He also seemed pleasant.

"Were you here the other evening when I told the tale of the sinking of the *Libertine*? I don't recollect seeing you."

"No. I don't make it out much. Mrs. Filmore mentioned that a girl had been stranded and was now residing at the Inn. I presume that is you? I did manage to indulge in the entertainment provided by Bosun Bluthers. However, that was before your untimely arrival. You were also rescued by Cedric, were you not?"

"Yes. He's my hero!"

"So–Cedric brought you to shore?"

"Oh, most assuredly!" Her face brightened. "Don't ask me how, but he swam through those gigantic waves, paddling like a steamboat. I was holding on to a wooden barrel, attempting to stay afloat. Did you ever try holding onto a barrel to keep from drowning? Almost everyone else had perished. Didn't know who or what this creature was or where he came from–but didn't have time to ask and frantically grabbed hold of him!"

"And that's the story?"

"No! Far from it. He rescued two others!"

"Fascinating..." Roger muttered.

"I've been a server here for a fortnight, and you're my first customer. As you can see, my apron is still pressed and clean. Only the fishermen come in, and I don't serve libations except to dinner guests. Would you like to try our house specialty today, Mr. Pinky's mutton stew?"

"Since it's a bit blustery, I believe I will. And bring a hot toddy too, if you would please."

Left to his thoughts, Roger continued in his attempt to put it all together. *That dog had to be incredibly strong... A miracle those survivors hadn't frozen...*

The girl returned with a bowl of stew and a hot toddy. "Your mutton stew, sir, expertly prepared by our sous chef, Mr. Pinky. There's his portrait over there on the wall, next to that of Cedric."

Tasting in a gentlemanly manner, he paused, "Quite good. Compliments to Mr. Pinky. Mrs. Filmore told me he is quite the chef."

"Oh, yes. And quite the talker, too, when he wants to be. Loquacious and dramatic with countless tales of his past and all the glorious adventures. I have come to revere the dear man and learned not to put anything past that one good eye of his. He's quite out of the ordinary–if there is such a thing in Sheppey."

"Mrs. Filmore spoke fondly of you, young lady. She mentioned you are an aspiring poet and that you had given her a poem for her birthday. Ireland and poetry–quite a combination. You are Irish, are you not? To now have you residing in Sheppey is quite a tribute to our little village."

"Well, yes, I am Irish to the bone. And yes, I did present Mrs. Filmore with a poem for her birthday, to which she gave me a big smile and a cookie. However, I am but a struggling poet, my pen not yet finding its wings." She veered, "I see you prefer a table by the hearth. The window table is a favorite for me and Mr. Pinky. Naturally, the hearth is good if you prefer the warmth as the cold tends to seep in through the glass, though the sea makes it all worthwhile." Continuing with a sigh and an endless flow of words, "I haven't truly made the acquaintance of anyone since my untimely arrival. That is, save for my presentation when the entire village came to the tavern. As you most likely know, they have a tendency to keep to themselves. However, they peek in the window from time to time. And then there's the fishermen. They come in for their pints of ale each evening. That's what they do in Ireland, too." She then inquired, "May I ask where may your cottage be?"

"To the south end, near the church."

"Do you attend?"

"No. My faith is in other things."

"Oh, what a pity. It seems there is little room in this life for anything save for God. Especially for someone like me–living through a potato famine and then being rescued from a sinking ship by a dog tends to make one stronger in their faith. Now that I have so much time, I often think of how glorious God's creation is. I have recently come to the conclusion that He is a poet! Can you imagine? His verse is everywhere. As of late, I have even observed that the sky, with all its variances of gray, is uniquely different from day to day. It is quite beautiful, like a series of paintings. In this alone, I can find my inspiration. You must see it too? Oh, the riches of God. The depth of His priceless treasures goes far beyond our finite minds."

Playing over the religious topic, Roger said, "The grocer went on to mention you are quite the one for chatter, also a rarity for these parts. That is, save for Mrs. Filmore and, of course, your Mr. Pinky. She went on to say you sometimes speak with a touch of prose."

"Oh, my! I'm quite honored. I wonder how she knew! Possibly, it was her birthday poem. If I may say so, you are quite out of the ordinary for these parts. May I be so bold as to inquire what you are doing here?"

"I write."

Adaline became as radiant as the morning sun. "That makes us kindred spirits! To find such a jewel upon these denuded shores! Within this austere exile, you must also be a contemplative?"

"Well, yes, you could say so." He found it ironic that he was beginning to enjoy the conversation.

"Then you most assuredly believe in God. The way of God takes much thought. My origin is Roman Catholic. The monasteries are filled with contemplatives. They think on God all day long."

He veered again. "Ah, Ireland... not only the land of the poets but also the home of the monastery. And so much misfortune. Tell me, Miss Adaline, how is it that so many great poets come from Ireland?"

"You are correct, sir! No heart flows with verse like that of an Irishman–or woman, for that matter. Save for Shakespeare, that is. My personal belief is that great literature comes from suffering. And, as you know, we have had our fair share."

"Beneath your cheerful guise, I sense the sorrow." For a moment, the animation abandoned her. He continued: "You are correct about Shakespeare, my dear–though one really doesn't know to what extent he suffered. However, we all go through our times of sorrow and suffering, some to a lesser degree than others. But who can really measure such a thing?" He looked into the glow of the embers: "Sometimes I think I have never *really* suffered."

"Maybe so. But there are exceptions to every rule." Her ebullience had returned. "God has possibly given you the gift of writing in spite of such. Not all literature was written with blood and tears. Have you ever read the Bible? Mrs. Merriweather lets me read hers. I read it every morning. It is quite fascinating. Did you know it is filled with prose? Solomon was quite the writer. In Ecclesiastes, he wrote, *'Tis better to go into the house of sorrow than the house of mirth.* I guess that is my inherited creed."

"To be honest, I have never given it much thought. A good friend gave me a classic volume many years ago. Needless to say, it remains dormant upon a shelf."

"Oh, 'tis something you would find most appealing, sir. However, it may take an effort as it can become rather tedious in the beginning and mind-boggling at times."

"As I have said, my dear Adaline, religion is not my forte." Though she was quite contrary and persistent, the conversation was stimulating. With only the chitchat of an occasional villager, the happed discourse of Mrs. Filmore, along with the coming and going of Mildred, most of his conversations were with Otto. He added more to himself, "*Thou, who dost all my worldly thoughts employ, though the pleasing source of all my earthy joy...*"

"Why, that's Mary Monck! She's Irish!"

"Tell me–do you find a difference in the writing styles of a man and woman?"

"Most assuredly!" she exclaimed. "All Irishmen know the frailty of life, like a blind person reading braille. However, the pen of a woman is more sensitive–if such a thing is possible."

"Personally, I prefer Thomas Moore: *Like the vase in which roses have once been distilled. You may break, you may ruin the vase if you will, but the scent of the roses will hang 'round.*"

The time for such conviviality was drawing to a close. It was late, and the sky had turned nocturnal. Before his departure, Adaline mentioned she would like to visit him sometime. "Oh, to have someone to talk to. Someone who understands."

The professor hesitated, telling her he worked late into the night and took naps throughout the afternoons. If his shutters were closed, he would be napping. However, any other time she would be welcomed. Paying the tab, he added several shillings for the service, to which she was extremely thankful. Putting on his jacket and wrapping a scarf around his neck, he took his hat and called for Otto, who quickly came to his side as they departed into the night.

Encumbered in the pitch of night, Roger's steps were ordered more by instinct. There was a slight stagger from the hot toddy. Fortunately, the muddied path had hardened, and some of the lanterns still glowed from windows, assisting in guiding him southward. Looking out toward the pier, it had disappeared into the dark. *That amazing creature...* He continued, *That young girl* had managed to jostle his rationale in a most lively way. *Such a creative mind... free-flowing with her own peculiar verse. She is earmarked for success, whatever form that may be. How had she found her way to the village? As unusual as the arrival of that dog.* A slight smile surfaced as he whispered, "*No man is an island, entire of itself...*"

···

Chapter 46

Verse

———

Though Adaline was nestled within the Wayfarer Inn, Jarvis and Bertie realized they could not give her the nurturing she needed. As of late, Bertie's health was failing, nor was there much for the young girl to do to fill her hours. The restaurant lay bare, the rooms remained unoccupied, and Pinky was always busy fixing things. Though time was well afforded for the young girl to stir up the prose within her heart, the days were vacuous. She needed a family and a friend her own age.

One morning, while visiting the grocer, Nora and Faith received all the details about the sinking of the *Libertine*; Mrs. Filmore concluded by saying, "Not one, nor two, but our beloved Cedric saved three souls! One is a young Irish girl about the same age as Faith. Well, a vessel sailed down to take those poor souls home. However, no one came for the girl, and she has remained quite alone at the Inn." Drawing closer, "I do believe Bertie has not been herself these days, and it's becoming too much for them to care for her." At that moment, Adaline walked in carrying a basket. No introduction was needed.

Nora instinctively liked her. *Who could not help but like that innocent face with those green eyes and radiant smile?* After several minutes of cordial introductions, her ebullience overflowed with animated run-on sentences. Nora sensed an immediate connection with Faith. *They could make wonderful friends...* Nora interrupted the ongoing chatter, inquiring as to how living at the Inn was going. She replied with a note of remorse, "Oh, fine." Quite impetuously, Nora asked if she would like to come live with them on a sheep farm. They could certainly use the help. To which Adaline became elated, responding that she would love such an opportunity. After completing their shopping, Nora and Faith rode her to the Inn to address Jarvis with their intentions.

The tavern was silent. Bertie was bedridden, and Jarvis was seated at a far table. Greeting them with a heavy somberness, he needed little persuasion to release Adaline into Nora's care. Turning to Adaline, Nora said, "Well, then, go gather your belongings. It's quite late in the day."

Adaline scampered up the stairs, quickly tidying her room and packing her meager belongings. She then bid a warm farewell to Mr. Pinky, who was busy repairing a window on the first floor, and gave a heartfelt embrace to Mr. Merriweather, tears of thankfulness streaming down her cheeks. He smiled meekly.

Crimped together on the wooden seat, Nora and the girls headed south. As they departed, Adaline looked out across the pier. Cupping her mouth, she yelled, "I love you, Cedie boy!"

Mr. Wilson could not have been more accommodating, trotting along at a pleasant pace and giving the girls ample time to become better acquainted. The wind dissipated as they traveled inland, and though the sky still carried its gloomy note, Nora thought this young lady's enthusiasm could brighten any day. During a lull in the conversation, she inquired as to what her plans might be when she came of age.

"I'm a poet." Adaline clasped her hands together, adding a touch of youthful drama. "At least that's what I aspire to be, how I love poetry! It all but flows through my veins. My mind is always wandering, searching for words–words that ring true to my heart. Though the day is gloomy, I see beauty around me, rain or shine."

"Such an aspiration is commendable. You will find a receptive audience for your endeavor throughout Great Britain. We have an attentive ear for poetry."

"Oh, yes! I don't deny that."

"Mrs. Filmore mentioned you did an excellent job helping the Merriweathers."

"Well, as you know, I drifted into their lives uninvited. Marooned these past several weeks, you might say. I did my very best to assist dear Mrs. Merriweather. She has been so kind to me. And I just had my birthday–fourteen years and two days old."

"We know how grateful you must be and that you will dearly miss them. Not to mention Cedric. However, the change should do you good. We live in a rather charming cottage. You can see it on that distant hill. It should inspire your writing. Faith's sister is also creative. As you most likely know, she did the drawings of Pinky and Cedric in the tavern and is now furthering her studies in London. With her gone, we will certainly appreciate your help."

"Oh, nothing shall please me more! I promise to repay you with all the sweat and labor that my frail body can expend. Nor will I babble on like this, which can be my tendency at times–especially when I'm excited."

Faith unhitched the horse when they arrived as Nora introduced Adaline to her new home. The cottage was peaceful and orderly. A pot-belly stove was to the far side, still bedded with glowing embers. A large window overlooked a vista of rolling hills. Sheppey and the sea could be seen in the distance. Many artifacts were calling for her attention. Of greater interest, though, was the bookshelf lining a far wall. Adaline drew closer as Nora and Faith busied themselves preparing dinner. There were books on literature, European history, and art, each seeming to complement the ambiance in the cottage. Her eyes settled on a book of Irish poetry. Time held still as she perused the pages, her heart absorbing every line.

It was only a matter of days before Adaline settled into the routine. The schedule with ongoing chores was the same, from sunrise to sunset. Waking before the break of day, the girls began by tending to the sheep. Though the winters were long and the days short, they quickly became fond of their time together, chatting away with abounding enthusiasm.

After breakfast, Nora granted them an hour to themselves. For Adaline, it was a special time to nestle by the window and the warmth of the stove. She saw verse upon the land, and her mind flowed with prose. *Who could ask for anything more?*

One morning, as the winter sun tucked itself behind heavy clouds with frost creating its little masterpieces upon the window, snowflakes began to fall like fluffy feathers. Soft and peaceful. It soon descended in a flurry, blending with the sheep and covering the land. She opened a book on Shakespeare. Every word rang true to her heart. Nora approached, requesting her assistance in the kitchen. Closing the book, she tidied up, a trail of thoughts lingering. Sheppey and the sea faded into the blur of white.

They attended the little church that first Sunday. The snow still covered the land as she watched her breath ascend throughout the ride. Memories of her childhood returned. She never had the luxury of traveling to church in a horse and wagon. She remembered the wet, penetrating chill, attending church barefoot, her hands and feet always dirty. The hills reminded her of Ballingarry, though Ireland's were more somber, the rocky land less forgiving. Nor were the hills in Ireland resplendent with sheep.

The bell in the belfry clanged a rusty welcoming as they pulled up. Adaline knew it was all part of her new world. Most likely, there would be a rather foreign doctrine from what she had become familiar with in the Catholic Church. However, she resigned to the simple fact that God could be found in any church. She noticed that Nora was carrying a Bible.

The walls inside were bare, a denuded wooden cross hanging behind the altar. *Where was the crucifix? The statues of the Blessed Virgin Mary and St. Joseph? The tabernacle and the stained-glass windows?* To her, art was a big part of God. What grieved her most was that the cross was bare. Seeing Jesus crucified in all his brokenness was always consoling and very personal.

Sitting on a wooden pew near the altar, they waited in silence. There was only a handful of people present. Her church was always filled, overflowing out the door. The pastor made his way to the podium. He was an older man with a pleasant smile. There were no vestments, just ordinary clothes like everyone else. He gave his small congregation a cheerful greeting. Everyone then stood, opened their hymn books, and began singing. Their voices were croaky and raspy–save for Nora, who carried the notes of a songbird. Adaline listened to the lyrics. They were beautiful and meaningful, like singing poetry. After several hymns, the pastor requested everyone to be seated.

He commenced with a soft voice, reading a verse from the book of Psalms. She liked his gentle spirit. He was humble and sincere. She also appreciated that he was reading from the Bible. Nora was following along in her own. The message was meaningful, giving her much to consider, and concluded with prayer. Nora introduced Adaline to a handful of people along with the pastor before heading home, two of whom were a very peculiar-looking pair of aging sisters, likable in an odd sort of way and rather removed. The bite of winter had thawed by late morning. The trees swayed in the wind as the sun meekly passed through the day.

And so, the transition from Inn to cottage was a dream come true. Adaline bonded with Faith like a sister; amidst the continual laughter was a pair of agreeable souls. And Nora proved to be the mother she had so long forgotten. All those troubled years were behind her.

....

"To serve is beautiful, but only if it is done with joy and a whole heart and a free mind." Pearl S. Buck

....

Chapter 47

𝕷𝖎𝖙𝖙𝖑𝖊 𝖂𝖔𝖔𝖑𝖎𝖊𝖘

Rachel's responsibilities were delegated to Adaline. Setting aside her creative whims, she devoted her time to the countless daily chores. She did, however, prove to be a different sort than Rachel. Still, her mind often remained in a creative cloud, and many bequeathed duties fell to the wayside or were done in a haphazard manner. It was a minor flaw to Nora as she remained focused on the girl's good qualities and her *joi du vie*, realizing life would be far less cheerful without her.

Adaline would also be taking over for Rachel with the ministry to Agnes and Gertrude. It had been nearly a year since they last visited, and Nora persisted they should continue, knowing the aging pair was in dire need of assistance and would enjoy the company. Faith told Adaline that it was the pair of elderly sisters she was introduced to in church. She also vividly described that terrible day when she first met them as Miss Agnes's hat blew off her head and how frightening she looked. But all that had changed. Adaline wilted, dreading the thought of even entering that musty old cottage. Though that horrific pair were indeed in church, this proposal had no enthusiasm. However, as tentative as she might be, she resolved to do her best for the sake of Nora.

It was a pleasant spring day as the girls commenced, inviting enough to go on foot. Arriving at the church, they headed up the beach, deciding to first go to the pier and call for Cedric, having missed him dearly during the long winter months. Upon arriving, Adaline called out. Cedric joyfully responded, prancing over the warped planks like a gazelle and wagging his tail fervently, greeting them with broad licks and an animated body. They then went to spend some time with Pinky.

There were no dead spaces in the conversation. There was so much to talk about in the brief interval of time afforded them, and after bidding him a fond farewell, they set out for the task at hand. Adaline recommended bringing Cedric along for the visit. Hopefully, he could prove a good ambassador and soften the edges in this rather dubious encounter. She was few of words as they headed south.

Faith knocked on the door. Gertrude slowly opened it and greeted them warmly. Adaline sighed, slightly more at ease, though Gertrude was far removed from any verse that stirred within her heart. Her face was contorted and, for lack of a better description, close up, and in the daylight, was uglier than anyone she had ever seen. However, the old woman's smile broadened when she cast her eyes on Cedric. Leaning over, she gave him a gentle pat as he tenderly licked her spindly fingers. Adaline breathed another sigh of relief. Things might not be as bad as she imagined.

They settled around the little table, Cedric coming to rest by Gertrude's side. Stroking his head, she said, "'Ee's ah gentl'm'n, 'ee ees." After a few pleasantries, the girls arose and proceeded to do various chores, proving awkward at times as Cedric consumed a disproportionate amount of space.

After an hour of cleaning cobwebs and musty corners, the girls prepared a meal with whatever was available. Gertrude humbly bowed her head and uttered a simple prayer, thanking God for the meal and bringing these two dear young ladies to help tend to their needs. And dear Cedric.

Adaline continued to soften, and her enthusiasm soon regenerated. The contortions in Miss Gertrude's features had somehow strangely begun to soften. During the meal, Adaline's zeal returning made an inquiry on a personal note. It did not take long for her to surmise that there was little life within the cottage. *To be perfectly honest, they lived in a state of apathy. There had to be more to life than sitting around and doing nothing, something constructive, working with their hands.* With her endearing Irish tone, she gently told them such idleness would only lead to despair and hopelessness and that any work they could apply themselves to would give them a sense of well-being and constructively fill their hours. There was a long moment of silence. With a slight nod, Gertrude said, "'Tis true." Adaline let it go from there. A seed had been planted. *Now, to consider what in the world they could possibly do.*

The girls bid them a good day while there was still light. Heading past the cottages, Adaline had an epiphany: *Why not have them make products for Nora's wool industry? She has a stable business from sheering her sheep and shipping the wool to London. And did she not mention there was a demand for woolen products, as the market for felting, especially little woolies of animals and dolls, was growing?*

Daylight faded, taking any semblance of warmth with it. The girls walked at a brisker pace. Nearing the turn in the woods, a young man approached on horseback. Riding closer, he offered a warm smile and inquired where the Wayfarer Inn might be. His dark hair was blowing in the wind, a black-rimmed hat holding it in place. Faith told him to continue straight up the path. Follow the cottages. There would be a pier jutting out into the sea. It was still light enough to see it. That is where he would find the Inn. With a tip of his hat, he proceeded on his way.

They began to speculate as to who the stranger was and why he had come to Sheppey. As they headed inland, the clouds dispersed, and the wind ebbed with stars settling upon the open sky and a full moon guiding them the rest of the way home. Before arriving at the cottage, Adaline said, "I will soon be leaving for Ireland." Faith did not respond.

It was late, and Nora was waiting anxiously. Adaline immediately began telling about their experience. Though she had been quite traumatic initially, the visit blossomed into something she could never have imagined. Nora was amused at how she had departed one way and returned another. Adaline then mentioned that Miss Gertrude and Miss Agnes could possibly make products for her business. Nora, always amused with her animated discourse and creative mind, listened patiently. The suggestion began taking on a clearer dimension. She realized, however, that the sisters would most likely not be up to such a task with poor eyesight and a lack of dexterity. She continued to allow the suggestion to settle and considered that *if they could manage, it would prove to be a good opportunity for them. They could possibly even learn to darn socks and sweaters.* Nora replied, "Let's take it one step at a time and see how they manage with a few simple woolies."

Throughout the ensuing weeks, she introduced the girls to the tools of the trade along with the step-by-step process of making the head of a rabbit and a small doll.

Within a month, Faith and Adaline could be seen carrying a bag of materials to town. Upon entering the cottage, Adaline immediately began excitedly telling them they would be making little woolies for Nora to sell in London with her other products. Though hesitant, Adaline enthusiastically continued to prod them on and accomplished her purpose.

After dinner, the girls tidied up and displayed the materials along with samples. Faith delegated the doll for Miss Agnes to do as her eyesight was most likely better and her fingers more nimble. The fluffy rabbit's head would be for Miss Gertrude. After an hour of instruction, they put them to task, patiently observing their every step.

Late in the afternoon, the finished products were displayed on the table. Adaline noticed proud expressions on the sisters' faces. It had all been worthwhile. She took a moment to study the portrait of Agnes hanging on the wall. Rachel had revealed a tenderness in the old woman.

A heartwarming conversation ensued, and then the girls prepared for home, taking the finished products along for Nora to see.

....

Chapter 48

A Thought Disclosed

T he man upon the horse was Thomas Payne, a nephew of Pastor
Theo and Mildred. He was cut from the same cloth as his uncle
and had arrived to replace the aging pastor in the pulpit. His uncle disclosed well in advance that the villagers' hearts were as cold as stone,
and their attitude was as bleak as the weather. Undeterred, the young
Thomas, fervent in his faith, knew his spiritual zeal and God would be
the wind within his sail.

There was another concern, though. For the old cottage behind the
church was to be his place of residence. To his chagrin, it looked as if it
had been there since the time of the Danes. The exterior was consumed
in thick brambles and entangled vines, making it difficult to cross the
porch and reach the door. The interior offered less hope, with deep
pockets of cobwebs and dilapidated furniture. Just the simple fact it
was in dire need of a thorough cleaning was overwhelming, thinking it
might be best to tear it down and start from scratch. Upon further consideration, the roof had weathered the years quite well, and the doors
and windows were sound. *And was it not pleasantly tucked away on the
far side of the church–affording peace and solitude?* One of the windows
overlooked a portion of the brook. *Possibly a good place to study during
the morning hour. And the interior was quite spacious.* Thomas resigned
himself to make a go of it.

The young pastor remained at the Inn a fortnight and then another. His room on the third floor proved pleasant. Here, too, was silence and solitude, along with a panoramic view of the sea and gulls sailing by. Seeing there was no comprehension of how long the renovations would take, he decided to let it all blow to the wind and enjoy his days as much as possible. Though a man of diligence, he would make an allowance to breathe in the hour and not succumb to the insurmountable frustration.

The first evening, he took the jaunt down the stairs to dine in the tavern. The tables were vacant, the lanterns lit, and the fire ablaze. *How odd–just for me.* The evening was raw and windblown, and the warmth of the hearth was inviting. Looking around… *Quaint and rustic.* He studied the drawings over the mantel. A rather odd-looking man doddered his way, an apron strapped around his waist with a cane bracing one side, smiling and nodding his head as his salutation. *Was that a smile or a grin?*

The greeting was coarse, though friendly. Introducing himself as Pinky, he proudly pointed to his picture over the mantel. *That was him all right.* Pinky went on to say it was drawn by a lovely young lass named Rachel. She and her sister were the most beautiful ladies ever to grace Sheppey. Thomas decided to treat himself to a glass of port and, naturally, be persuaded into having the house specialty. Pinky proclaimed it to be a good choice and did his one-step to the kitchen.

The stew was indeed an excellent choice, the port and the ambiance only added to the hour's enjoyment. Pinky lingered, telling of the shipwrecks and Cedric's heroics before telling tales of the Napoleonic Wars. It was either the port or the company, but Thomas joined in, stating he, too, served God and country during the Xhosa Wars. Though well-versed in Great Britain's battles, Pinky had never heard of such an engagement. Thomas went on to say it was a campaign in China and quickly channeled the conversation to God, believing the misfortunes of war was a good prelude to faith–to which the shutter over Pinky's good eye subtly came down, clearly evincing no interest in a sermon.

Several fishermen entered and afforded him the opportunity to limp away. *Quite an odd sort*, Thomas thought. *His heart will soften in time.*

Thomas took his initial step in establishing himself in Sheppey as, the first Sunday after his arrival, he proceeded to the podium of the little church. Theo and Mildred were settled in the front pew, thoroughly enjoying his passion and the fresh perspective he shared in his faith. Though a paltry congregation, Nora and the girls were a high note of encouragement, beaming like sunflowers as he preached. Mildred had mentioned to him the remarkable transformation of Agnes and Gertrude and told of their sordid past and that they had remarkably started coming to church. They were wearing flowery dresses, and she made a point to let Thomas know when they arrived as they took a seat in the far pew.

After the service, the young pastor went to the door to bid everyone Godspeed. The queue was minimal, affording extra time with this peculiar pair of sisters and saying he would like to pay them a visit soon.

Nora waited patiently to speak to him. Adaline had walked to the beach, and Faith waited by the door. Finally, when everyone departed, Nora had the opportunity to tell him how much she appreciated the sermon. She had liked him immediately. There was a spiritual maturity that went far past his years, and his passion was something dearly lacking in Sheppey. Not to slight Pastor Theo, as there was no denying he had served the village well. Nora mentioned his unique insight about the kingdom of God.

"Well, shouldn't it be so? Is it not my responsibility to share personal revelations? And does not the breadth and scope of our faith allow us such insight? We have a wonderful opportunity to seek God as much as we desire." His eyes caught Faith.

"Mildred mentioned that you intend to move into the old cottage?"

He laughed. "If ever I find a broom and pail and an infinite number of hours. It may be beyond my patience and ability. However, the Inn has been most accommodating. A home away from home, in a sense. And the Merriweathers have given me a most reasonable rate."

"Can we assist? Possibly, we could stop by tomorrow if the weather holds. We're pretty good at things like that." Faith kept an attentive ear throughout the conversation.

"You could say such assistance would be an answer to prayer."

"Well then, we will see you tomorrow. Adaline will remain at home to tend to the chores. Somewhere around nine? And we will provide the broom and pail."

The next day was overcast but pleasant enough for the ride. Thomas was waiting at the door, framed in brambles and brush. After tethering the horse, he introduced them to the work at hand. Immediately setting to the task, Nora and Faith were made for such a time as this. Thomas stood back and marveled, entertained and appreciative of their female industry. By late afternoon, the interior looked fit for living; even the potbelly stove seemed to sparkle. Nora had brought curtains, a table-cloth, and a potted plant for finishing touches. As they prepared to leave, he thanked them prolifically.

"There is still much to do," Nora said.

"Why don't I return tomorrow?" Faith added. "I'll bring lunch. Would that be okay?" Seeing Thomas was a man of integrity and all that still needed to be done, Nora acquiesced, also agreeing to leave the cleaning supplies.

Early the next day, Thomas descended the stairwell of the Inn with a new bounce. Not only was the cottage coming along, but something else was stirring. He sat by the window, journal in hand, and, as was his habit, considered the day and the things of God while the morning was still young.

Pinky limped over, served a pot of tea, and let him be as Thomas was already at work, quill in hand with a small bottle of ink to the side. Pinky had versed him in the dog's heroics, and he could be lost in that thought alone as he observed him on the pier. Putting the date to the top of a clean page, he sketched several seagulls along with a quick study of Cedric and then began to write.

Within the hour, the sun had ascended, making its bright mark on the morning. Thomas decided to pay the dog a visit, and the fresh air would do him good. *Why not even forego the horse and encourage Cedric to come along for the day?* Packing his satchel, he headed to the pier and called out. Ironically, Cedric immediately perked up and came his way. It was a warm greeting on both ends, and, with a little persuasion, Cedric followed along.

Some villagers were standing by their doors, beaming like the sun as Cedric passed by. Teetering out of their cottages, they slowly approached their hero to give him a tender pat and a few adoring words. Thomas mused with irony, knowing full well the greeting was not for him. Since his arrival, there had not been so much as a nod of their heads when he passed by. *It would be good to see such energy and joy in coming to church. Enough said. No one ever said it was going to be easy.*

Mildred was standing by her door, tending to some potted plants. Upon seeing them, she offered a jubilant salutation, "What brings you two this way? And why are you not on your horse?"

"Decided to hike and bring 'ol' Cedie boy' along. That's what Pinky calls him."

"Mats be his name. Dear me–look at the poor creature! He's all muddy and needs a good cleaning." She added, "No one else calls him that, but Mats is his name all right." Cedric wagged his tail.

"We're running a little late, Millie. In the meantime, give Theo our greetings.

"Why don't you come by tomorrow evening for dinner? And bring a few pieces of cod from the fish house."

Thomas nodded and continued on his way.

He arrived at the cottage before Faith and picked some daffodils near the brook. Holding them, he waited patiently near the porch, Cedric by his side.

Faith had decided to walk. As she passed through the line of woods, a basket in hand, Cedric rose to meet her. Thomas handed her the daffodils. "A small gift in appreciation for your assistance."

Faith had always cherished Nora's gardens, resplendent with their various blooms and blossoms. However, this was the first time anyone had ever handpicked flowers for her. As simple a gesture as it may have been, she thought it was the most beautiful bouquet she had ever seen. After a sincere thank you, they entered the cottage and began working.

Stopping at noonday, Thomas was more than satisfied with all that had been accomplished, and they proceeded to carry the lunch basket and a blanket to a patch of grass near the brook. Spreading the blanket, he laid down to rest, placing his hands behind his head and closing his eyes, the sun's warmth on his face. All was silent save for the gurgling brook. Cedric took the liberty to wade into the cool water. Voraciously lapping it up, he then shook the water from his heavy coat, everything being vigorously sprayed, giving them a good laugh before settling down in a patch of sunlight. Thomas closed his eyes again and began dozing.

Faith studied him. His face was dappled in the shifting shadows of the trees. His dark hair was shoulder-length. There was both a ruggedness and gentleness in his nature. To her, he was the most handsome man she had ever seen. *But what did she know?* She noticed a journal by his side.

"May I see this?"

Opening an eye, he said, "By all means."

Respectfully, she began to peruse the pages. They were filled with sketches and writing. *Rachel would like this very much.* She paused on a page dated the previous day. He had drawn a sketch of Pinky. *Quite different from Rachel's drawing, but very good.*

She turned the page. The ink seemed fresh. There was the notation of a few seagulls along the borders and a sketch of Cedric on the distant pier. The rest of the page was penned with thoughts.

Tuesday, June 18, 1850

The hour is mine. Tableside with a pot of tea, watching the sun herald the day. Faintly hear the cry of seagulls sailing over the sea. I can see Cedric is at his post. Yesterday was eventful. Much accomplished. Starting to have hope as things are now moving in a positive direction. Though the Inn has been quite accommodating, it will be good to have my own place. But it will take time, much time.

Faith will be returning this morning, and I am very grateful. She is bringing lunch, which will be a delightful break. Something is stirring... difficult to put into words. Never intended to feel like this, but my thoughts invariably drift her way. I would like to believe God's hand is upon such sentiments. Will wait and see. In the meantime, enjoying her company. As Saint Augustine said, "Love God and do what you will."

Thomas stirred his face now in the shade. She closed the journal and continued studying him. She would be the first thing he saw as he opened his eyes. The golden light of the sun framed her in a soft halo.

"Did you have a good rest?" "Yes." He would like to tell her of the beauty now before him.

She placed the journal by his side, "Thank you for allowing me into your world." She looked up past the trees, the sunlight brushing her face.

Thomas arose, and they prepared lunch, eating peacefully and tossing bits to Cedric. They then sat on a limb parallel to the brook. Their attention remained on Cedric, who, once again, immersed himself in the stream, lapping the water and submerging his body.

"He loves the water," Faith said. "It must be in his blood."

"I have been meaning to tell you how much I like your name. *Faith* seems so appropriate. Do you know why it was given to you?"

"Not really. I wasn't old enough. My parents died before I could ask that question."

The brook sparkled with sunlight and played its soothing melody. Faith nervously swayed her legs above it, tapping the water with a branch. As best she could reason, she was falling in love. *But how could she know? What's the difference between a whim and love anyway?* For that matter, *How many young men had passed her way in Sheppey? Yet what other explanation was there for this inexpressible feeling?* There was an impulse to take off her shoes, leap in the water, splash around like a little girl, and play with Cedric. However, her youthful emotions were kept at bay.

In many ways, Faith was the opposite of her sister. Though a pair of delicate flowers within the same vase, they had inherited different traits and were as different as a rose from an iris. Then again, how can one compare beauty with beauty? It was said that their father was as handsome as their mother was beautiful. He was tall and broad-shouldered with golden-brown hair. Rachel had her mother's hazel eyes and olive complexion. Faith had the same curved mouth as her mother, puckering up like a natural smile, along with the gentle slope of her nose. Though she was slight in stature, she had inherited her father's amber hair and brown eyes. She was in that transition, evolving from cuteness into the more refined features of womanhood.

Thomas had also been quietly observing her. She was the ideal of perfect beauty with a purity and innocence that only enriched her physical qualities. However, he respected more intangible traits such as integrity and a sense of trust–qualities that would never fade with time. Holding still within that moment, neither Thomas nor Faith was in a hurry to return to work.

....

Chapter 49

There is a time for everything

The inevitable took its course as the young pastor proposed to Faith. Theo was given the honor of joining them together in holy matrimony. Thomas would have it no other way, even if there were other clergy to choose from. Theo joyfully anticipated the ceremony, something that had been as far removed from the church as an infant's cry. The only wedding he had ever performed was that of Jarvis and Bertie. During the vast span of empty years, the bell only tolled for Sunday services and funerals.

The old pastor had been forlorn, downtrodden, more or less defeated after all those hopeless years, the villagers all but closing their shutters to God. To his chagrin, these stubborn souls only made their presence known in the church during brutal storms or burials. More times than not, as one was put asunder, he would look up into the bleak sky as the good earth was being shoveled over the coffin and say, "Ashes to ashes, dust to dust." Then, to himself, *Will there ever be any joy in Sheppey?*

His dear Mildred would have no part of his woe-is-me attitude, persistently nudging him along. *You've done a remarkable job, my dear. The wonderful seeds you've planted... standing firm in the faith no matter what winds have blown against you. And your fervent prayers, day and night, most assuredly have touched the heart of God, will have their way upon the hearts of these weary souls in time to come.*

Yes, yes. He would nod and, for a time, be appeased.

After much discussion, Thomas and Faith considered it best to put the wedding on hold until the autumn of '51. Most assuredly, it would give them time to become better acquainted and confirm God's hand was upon such a union. Furthermore, Thomas knew how much time and labor was still required to mend the cottage, and he wanted the honeymoon to be right. Thus, the church bell also waited patiently.

Within the span of time from the announcement to the tieing of the knot, two more vessels sunk along the coast: *The Sea Lurchin* and *The Dandy.* There would be three more souls rescued by Cedric and more notches upon the beam.

....

Chapter 50

The Vulnerability of it all

By late afternoon, Rachel was putting the finishing touches on the portrait of Lady Bradshaw. The workshop demanded most of her time during the summer, and it was a relief to know it would be completed for her birthday. Standing back, she considered it finished, though always with lingering thoughts. Granted, she had done it more or less from memory. *But was it good? Did it resemble her? Would she like it?* With a slight nod, she put the brush down and let it take its course. Sir Wisham was giving it a critique Monday morning. She would certainly know more about its merit at that time.

Rachel was also bringing the painting of Cedric to fruition. This, too, would be presented as a special gift. She had used a wealth of old sketches and, again, her memory to build upon the composition. And now, there he was, poised upon the pier, looking toward the viewer. The scene was bereft of color–his black-and-white coat with a blue-gray sky and sea and a few wispy clouds accented by distant seagulls. The focal point was the splash of red tongue and those penetrating eyes. Rachel caught a glimpse of the painting of Captain Sumpter against a far wall as a touch of morning light had settled upon it. *Strange–why did it still stir her heart?*

Sir Wisham gathered his apprentices in a semicircle, an easel with the portrait of Lady Bradshaw in the center. The maestro took a few steps back and reflected for a few moments. Rachel was to one side. Nervous. She was laying herself bare and vulnerable, knowing full well his critique would go far past any niceties.

He finally spoke. "Well, my dear, you have said it all." There was a sigh of relief. "It's remarkable the progress you have made in such a short time. Do you not agree?" He looked around at the other students, who nodded in accord. "Most of you have not met the honorable Lady Bradshaw. However, I, for one, can attest to the excellence of this portrayal. It breathes with life. Look at the eyes. It's as if Miss Thomson captured her very being. Who was it that said, *The eyes are the doorway to the soul*? Capturing the human soul upon a canvas is something that can not be taught. Remember: art's purpose is to be sublime, to touch the heart–something that Miss Thomson has masterfully accomplished." Rachel was consumed with emotions.

The young artist from Sheppey was proving to be a rarity, excelling beyond her measure of years–a natural and brilliant touch within each brushstroke. Like a shining star, she made the other celestials around her pale in comparison. Leonardo da Vinci once said, *Poor is the pupil who does not surpass his master*. Ironically, she was also beginning to sense how strange the world of an artist is: isolated and having to believe in oneself yet needing the approbation of others.

....

"I love walking in the rain because no one can see my tears."
Charlie Chaplin

....

Chapter 51

To Bury One's Heart

———

Rachel arrived at the estate by mid-morning. It was an autumn day, and the hour was raw. The baroness's seventieth birthday was to be a simple ceremony–no frills or throngs of congratulatory people. Tea would be served indoors.

Rachel began by telling her all she had learned throughout the week (foregoing the critique by Sir Wisham). She then mentioned Adaline and how Nora had grafted her into their little family. Faith had written to her countless times, telling all about her endearing friend. The family name was Brennen. They had been farmers near the village of Ballingarry in Ireland. The poor girl had been raised during a severe potato famine. Her father and uncle were members of the Young Ireland revolutionary group. Her family perished in the strife that followed, save for Adaline and an uncle. Taking her under his wing, they fled to France. After struggling for a year, they were returning to England, hopefully, to find work in the London factories. "As you most likely know, a storm hit off the coast and sunk the vessel. Her uncle perished, leaving her an orphan. My sister has shared many wonderful stories about her, and she has proved to be a hard worker and a delightful addition to the family."

The baroness then found the appropriate time to say, "I encountered Sir Wisham the other day. He mentioned that your paintings were far surpassing the other students' works. That is quite a compliment. Seeing such, I have let it be known there is a new up-and-coming artist in our midst. As you know, our society loves patronizing the art world, especially a rising star. With that being said, prepare yourself."

They eventually celebrated her birthday. There was no confetti, novelties, or a celebratory crown for simply blowing out another candle. The baroness was far past such adulations. And with this subtle spiritual transition, she found herself drifting farther away from the ornate world she once held dear. Many within her circle opined that old age and eccentricity had settled in.

After cutting the cake, Rachel gave a discreet nod to a valet, who approached the baroness from behind with her portrait in hand. Sensing his presence, she slowly turned. A soft emotion stirred within her. Then, a tear. Absorbing every aspect of the painting, she believed it more masterful than any portrait done by the hand of Sir Wisham. Though admiring its excellence, the baroness was too frail in years, too gracious and wise, to view it with any sense of vanity. Rachel nodded again, and another valet followed, bringing the painting of Cedric. *Yes, it was the Cedric she so vividly remembered.* Her lips quivered. The gifts lingered in thought and pleasant conversation.

"There *is* something else." Lady Bradshaw became somber. "Possibly, this is not the time for such. And it is unfortunate that I am to be the bearer of this. However, you should know. Our beloved Captain Sumpter was killed in battle."

Rachel's thoughts blurred.

"I received the message last evening." The baroness picked up the telegram and put on her glasses. *We regretfully inform you that Captain John Sumpter, an honorable officer of the 40th Foot, bravely fell in battle against Afghan tribal units near Ghazni, valiantly giving his life for God, Queen, and country.*

Placing the telegram down, she took off her glasses. "He had told his commanding officer if anything were to happen to him, he wanted you to be the first to know." She picked up another envelope. "This also arrived recently. It was addressed to me with a letter enclosed for you. He requested it to be given to you if anything..." There was a long moment of deep silence. "I always sensed something special between you two and cannot tell you how sorry I am."

Rachel bowed her head, tears whelming. Taking the letter, she politely excused herself and went to her room. A steady rain was falling. She had never opened the letter he had given her on that final day, for she sensed what sorrow and regrets would be in his words. She broke the seal and opened the letter given to her by Lady Bradshaw.

Dearest Rachel,

Words were never sufficient in expressing my feelings toward you. Even if I dared to be so bold as to say how much I love you, there was a premonition that it would only bring you grief in the end. Having to bury so many haunting memories, I sometimes feel as if I died with my comrades in the mountains; the coffin nailed tight during the shipwreck. Why should you be destined to share in these endless nightmares? War is so merciless.

Please know that the brief time we had together was the best chapter in my life. For that, I am most grateful. Our current situation is unpredictable. Indications are that we will soon be in an engagement with the enemy. No one knows what the future may hold. You deserve so much more.

Thank you for the best of memories.
Captain Sumpter

She went to the window. The rain was coming down hard. Seeing her image in the glass, the tears and rain merged into one.

Rachel returned to Westminster early Sunday morning. She needed time to be alone. The demands of preparing for the workshop and painting offered an escape, a world within a world, and a place to bury her soul.

....

Chapter 52

Into the Abyss

B y all measures, the year proved to be a contradiction for Rachel. Though the deep sorrow lingered, a new season presented itself in the world of art. Persuaded by Lady Bradshaw's endorsement, the cream of British society began to bestow its favor upon her. A flurry of requests came knocking at her door. *Lord So-and-So* or *the Honorable M.* desired a portrait by her hand. Alas, Miss Thomson put aside her heavy heart and commenced with one commission after another. With the demands and this new-birthed industry, there was no longer time to attend the workshops.

Though the commissions kept tapping at her door, there was an irony to it all as her zeal for doing the portraitures began to wane. Though the favor bestowed upon her bore its fruit with prestige and financial reward, the inspiration soon dissipated. For the young Miss Thomson realized that the emphasis within these portraits would not be dictated by her heart, but by the demands of her patrons, and glazing over wrinkles and any other imperfections was imperative.

Rachel was a purist. Never aspiring for either fame or fortune–ideals had always directed her path. To her, art was an innocent friend. Though this new-found fame had quickly spread, even reaching the continent, her heart abandoned its purpose. There was a condescending sense of control; some patrons even requested full-length portrayals.

At times, a baron desired to be portrayed mounted on his steed surrounded by his prized hunting dogs. There were requests for family portraits or paintings with symbolic portions of estates in the background. Most demanding, though, was their insistence on her coming to them. Genteel, by nature, Rachel obliged, bringing a portion of her studio with her. The only consolation was having the liberty to add the finishing touches to her studio.

With all its aplomb and garnishes, this new season drew to a conclusion by Miss Thomson's twenty-third year. Gently closing the door, she accepted no more commissions. There remained, however, the draining task of completing unfinished works. Stressed and depilated, she found it all but impossible to bring them to fruition. For how could she work without her heart upon the brushes? At times, while laboring over glazes or fine details, she would glance at Captain Sumpter's portrait. *They had so much in common.* And she knew that portrait was painted with integrity, far surpassing any of these present-day works. In a strange way, she needed its company.

Rachel had to pay a final visit to an estate in a southwest district of London. After crossing the London Bridge, her coachman inadvertently veered in the wrong direction, directing the horses left instead of right. She was soon aware they were entering an alien world; the regal monuments and classic architecture were quickly effaced. So, too, the stretches of parks and boulevards, men in top hats and women in Victorian dress. The coach funneled deeper into narrow, trash-strewn streets–endless rows of run-down houses, broken windows, and empty doorways. Expressionless people, boys in tattered caps, and girls like dirty rag dolls. She watched in silence as they passed by.

The coachman attempted to turn the horses, but the street was too narrow. On they went with no other recourse, deeper into the womb of this hidden city. Rachel felt uncomfortable and ashamed. Finally able to turn, the coachman awkwardly made his way out. Rachel looked back.

The imploring eyes of the children followed them. She made a mental note: *There will be another time...*

....

Chapter 53

The Parable of the Coin

The Victorian Era was ripe with parables. Was not the kingdom of Great Britain like a priceless coin? The head of this silver sovereign, embossed with the noble profile of Her Majesty, manifested everything glorious about the empire. The opposite side, however, was tarnished and worn, besmirched by slums, corruption, and countless calamities within the regime. Two sides of the same coin: lavish luxury, prosperity, and power to one and blatant flaws on the other. And, if society had its way, the underside would be effaced and embossed over with a more glorious note–heads and tails, black and white, deception and truth–all facades of life.

With all due respect, what could the Queen do about such insurmountable burdens? The vast migration from Ireland with impoverished families continued to grope their way into the city and flood the streets. Unfortunately, there was no gold to be found at the end of the rainbow, as the wheels of industry were far too large and merciless. Paradoxically, poverty became the sludge of industry.

And Rachel had, perchance, wandered into this foreboding land. The deplorable conditions were a bold-faced truth that lingered within her heart. Like a horse with blinders, she had been limited as to what she saw within her passages of pleasantries. Ensconced within the lap of luxury, she was as removed from the slums as if some far-off land in the Orient. And that one wrong turn by the coachman was about to give her a far more profound purpose than she had ever had.

One afternoon, while placing a beauty mark on a final commission, she cleaned her brushes and proceeded to the bank before the close of day.

....

"Who, being loved, is poor?" Oscar Wilde

···

Chapter 54

The year was drawing to a close; the days of December draped in gloom as the carriage trotted past the stone statues, legions of pigeons perched upon their noble heads. The horses clopped over the bridge and took the foreboding left turn, entering the city within the city – the opposite side of the coin.

Trash, the garden of poverty, was strewn everywhere; houses crammed together with dark pockets of narrow alleyways. Rachel noted that it should be painted with earth colors and black. Children began running out of the alleyways. Dressed in rags and faces covered with soot, they revealed a level of oppression that far surpassed her childhood.

Throngs of little ones followed, stretching out desperate hands. Rachel tapped her umbrella. The coachman pulled to the side and assisted her from the carriage. Children immediately pressed in. Though her previous venture has been a shameful mishap, this day would bear its silver lining. Opening a small bag, she began handing out six pennies. *What a gift!* It could have been Christmas. Rachel became flooded with emotions, little hands fluttering like hungry birds in the dead of winter with innocent eyes struggling to rise above the sea of heads. Older generations stood at a distance, observing with curiosity and caution. Slowly, they nodded their heads.

A haggard woman stood to the side, imploring with lifeless eyes, her frail hand extended. Retrieving several coins, Rachel reached over the little heads and placed them in her hand.

The bag was soon emptied, hands still frantically fluttering. *How could she tell them there were no more coins?* Considering this endless flow of starving souls, her gesture was nothing more than a bag of crumbs. Tentatively backing up, she repeated she would be returning. Then, awkwardly, she bumped into a child. Turning, it was a little girl, younger and smaller than the rest. *A precious face with large blue eyes. No more than four years of age?* Bewildered and clothed in tattered rags, her hand remained outstretched. Rachel thought of the little match girl. *A painting...* And it could prove to be far more valuable than her entire collection.

Leaning over, she inquired, "What is your name?"

"Wuff't." The little girl's voice was barely audible, her eyes downcast.

A woman nearby said, "Name be Muffet."

"Muffet?" Rachel smiled. "How peculiar. Who gave you such a name?" The little girl lifted her head and raised four fingers.

"Where are your parents?"

"Don't 'ave none," the woman added.

"What a shame." Rachel gently raised her into her arms. "I like your name, Miss Muffet." Something beyond words transpired. She found it difficult to release her. *Was it a want to fill the void over the loss of Captain Sumpter? The tender comfort after a demanding season? Or is it simply a natural maternal bonding?* Putting her down, she said, "Please be here when I return."

Assisting Rachel into the carriage, the coachman made his exit, multitudes of children following close behind, with more pouring out of the dark recesses. Looking back, she could see Muffet standing by the gutter, her hand still extended. There was far more to that than just a painting. Muffet became smaller and smaller, finally fading into the crowd.

....

Chapter 55

An Awkward Request

Rachel arrived at the Bradshaw estate early Sunday morning, planning on attending St. Paul's with Lady Bradshaw. Though the sun had dissipated in the winter sky, the ride was mercifully pleasant. They then returned to the estate for brunch. Rachel remained quiet throughout the morning, and the baroness perceived something was troubling her. *Possibly still lamenting over the loss of Captain Sumpter?* She did not press the matter.

After the repast, Rachel sighed, resigned to share what was weighing on her heart. Stumbling for words, the baroness waited patiently.

"Please forgive me, Lady Bradshaw... but I would like to ask a favor of you. I hope you won't find me presumptuous." The baroness raised a brow and gave a slight nod to continue.

"Not long ago, my coachman inadvertently made a wrong turn. We soon found ourselves in a bleak part of London, as if we had ventured into some strange and forbidden world. At first, I was intimidated, almost fearful. However, it didn't take long for me to grieve over the plight of all those impoverished children. The coachman eventually was able to turn around, and we quickly made our way out. For some odd reason, I had a deep sense of shame.

"It continued tugging at me. As you know, I have been quite busy of late. Finally having time, I returned yesterday morning. Quite an irony as the coachman knew the way." Rachel smiled. "I carried along a little bag of coins, desiring to give the children a gift. It was such a feeble gesture as I was overwhelmed, children streaming out of every door and alleyway. Upon leaving, I happened upon a little girl. She was standing behind the other children. Alone. Her small hand extended." Rachel looked down, her voice fading and broken. "It's difficult to put into words... I... I picked her up, held her in my arms..."

"That will be fine," Lady Bradshaw responded.

"Pardon me?"

"Yes, you may bring her home."

How did she know? Rachel whelmed with tears.

The following Saturday was but one of a long string of winter days. As the coachman headed south, Rachel thought the hour was not made for sunshine. To her dismay, the baroness had decided to come along.

The boulevards began funneling into narrow streets and endless rows of run-down houses. Old people, stooped and lifeless, watched the carriage pass by. Children began flooding the street, running after them with outstretched hands. *Please! Please!* The baroness studied Rachel, sensing the contained enthusiasm beneath her beauty.

Rachel tapped her umbrella, and the coachman pulled over. This time, she was better prepared with a more prodigious bag of six-pennies. Lady Bradshaw remained seated in the shadow and observed. The children pressed in as if the Pied Piper had arrived. She began handing out the coins, and, once again, the bag was soon empty. Wading through the never-ending flow of children, there was no sign of Muffet.

Then, there she was, standing alone, all but hidden in a dark passage. Extricating herself from the mass of children, Rachel finally reached her. Leaning down, she picked her up and asked a nearby woman, "Is everyone certain she has no mother?" The old woman's head swayed back and forth, "Nay. T'ain't no mum." Making her way to the carriage, Rachel embraced the child as if laying hold of a great treasure. The coachman assisted them into the carriage and slowly retreated into another world.

Muffet sat motionless and wide-eyed. Rachel pressed her hand, giving a reassuring smile. Looking out the window, the children were still following. *How could anyone in good conscience leave them behind?* The press of little faces faded. Lady Bradshaw was quietly taking it all in.

....

Chapter 56

A Broken Toy

Muffet did not come prancing into the estate as a little girl should but like a broken toy. A child was not meant to be so melancholy. Within a matter of days, she began raising her head and looking around as if awakened from the dead. In short order, she was properly dressed and spoon-fed the social graces. Tutors and a good education would eventually follow. So, too, the prancing. Though the dear little Muffet was now the beneficiary of an exceedingly abundant lifestyle, the tender process of healing would take time.

The baroness immediately took a liking to her, like a medicine for her aging soul, though she was far too discreet to admit how good it was to have her merrily making her way in and out of the rooms and playing with dolls. A special bonding occurred between the very young and old, which would invariably take its natural course.

Muffet also turned a page in Rachel's life, and it soon became her fervent ambition to help the multitudes of children left behind as much as humanly possible. One morning, there was a faint inspiration. *An orphanage*? She would soon find herself considering such a monumental task with more clarity.

After an extended season at the estate, Rachel returned to Westminster with Muffet in hand. It had been a special time as a little family had been knit together, three generations in one. She began structuring the days accordingly, teaching Muffet intangibles such as respect and honesty and nurturing a faith in God. The little girl was softening the edges over the loss of Captain Sumpter.

The winter days were short, but the season long. Spring finally made its way into the city. Pleasant smiles were evident beneath top hats and parasols, and the parks were lush with color. Rachel's brushes sang with the season, now finding immense pleasure in painting flowers: the prose, the delicate lines, and the variety of hues. Though she had grown fond of Nora's gardens, she was now seeing them in a new light, aesthetically speaking. She was especially fond of the frailty and beauty of the iris.

A series of floral paintings was completed throughout the summer. She thought it rather amusing how her studio was beginning to resemble Nora's gardens. She also started a painting of Muffet, though attired in Victorian dress and not as the little match girl. Posing her from time to time, Rachel had to work quickly as her youthful model could not keep still for more than a few brushstrokes. There were other works, with women holding parasols strolling through the parks and another painting of Cedric. Through it all, there would be those glances at the painting of Captain Sumpter, his eyes catching her unawares.

Though Muffet was of a tender age, with fingers lacking dexterity, Rachel could not help but give her art lessons. She especially loved to color. During the early evening hours, they would take walks in the park. Muffet always explored the world of nature as Rachel sat on a park bench doing a flurry of floral studies along with gesture drawings of pedestrians passing by.

The art world was running parallel with Rachel's newfound ambitions, evolving within its own rhyme and reason. Times were changing, and painting was finally coming out of its shell. The renowned art historian John Ruskin would be a forerunner in this awakening, promoting a rather radical group of English painters known as the Pre-Raphaelites. French plein air painters were also making their mark throughout Europe.

Miss Thomson continued to broaden her oeuvre, merging in more bold and dynamic paintings, some displayed in various galleries throughout the metropolitan area. And more and more patrons began patronizing her own transition.

Alas, the pure love of painting had taken hold of her. In retrospect, there had been far too many commissions. And she was adamant never to do another. There was a great relief in no longer having to concern herself with the fleck of a beauty mark, softening wrinkles, or toning flesh to warmer hues. It was so insincere and became evident after coming face to face with the destitute. However, contradictory to her firm line of resolve, she would acquiesce to do one more commission...

....

Chapter 57

𝕿𝖍𝖊 𝕮𝖔𝖒𝖕𝖗𝖔𝖒𝖎𝖘𝖊

Lord Byron was bred within the higher plain of British society, residing in one of the more prodigious estates throughout the area. A peculiar sort, though, abstaining from the pomp and ceremony of society, he desired little more than a portion of solitude, a good book, and the melodic notes of nature. Lord Byron was also a lover of art. Save for a few staid family portraits, the space upon his walls was for more personal preferences. There was even a Rembrandt in the collection. In recent years, he had expanded his gallery with more unaccepted styles, works that stirred his heart no matter what the critics might say.

He had recently taken note of an up-and-coming painter, Miss Rachel Thomson. Not only was he impressed with how she had severed herself from high society but also with the bold steps she was now taking in painting. Seeing some of her recent works in a gallery, the curator mentioned, "Miss Thomson is pursuing a purer purpose." *Quite extraordinary*, Lord Byron mused. *A rising star denouncing everything for a purer purpose? Could this not be a diamond in the rough?* He thus made it his aim to search her out. And it would not be long before he came knocking at her door.

After a cordial introduction, he politely requested a portrait. Rachel stalled as she was quite firm with her decision. She studied his impressive countenance for a few moments. *Possibly three score years? He held his age well*. He looked articulate and genteel, with softer edges than most of the aristocracy with whom she had become familiar. However, the wisdom in his eyes and the smile inspired her most. In a humble and gracious manner, he said she could paint the portrait as her heart dictated, with reckless abandon, for that matter. To him, a good painting was simply a good painting. It was the integrity of her brush, not a likeness, he desired.

Continuing to reflect, she smiled and consented. There would be stipulations, though. For one, she insisted on his coming to her studio for the sittings. Furthermore, it would be done when the time afforded. Nor would it be a full-length portrayal–simply a bust. He agreed wholeheartedly. The first session was then arranged for the following week.

It was a day in early autumn as Lord Byron made his way to Miss Thomson's studio. The valet escorted him up the stairs. After a few pleasantries, Rachel excused herself and prepared for the session. Her distinguished guest strolled around the room, taking in everything from her palette and brushes to the blank canvas waiting on an easel. Volumes of disheveled drawings were scattered on the floor. Making his way to a far corner, he paused in front of an unfinished painting of a young officer. *Rather bold and quite exceptional.*

Rachel interrupted his thoughts. Everything was ready. She directed him to a stool near the windows. Taking a few moments to situate him brought back memories of Captain Sumpter, the last one to take such a pose. Satisfied, she went behind the easel and commenced. There were no preliminary drawings as she began to lay in the composition with a large brush.

Having a deep respect for the art world, Lord Byron had always been intrigued by the creative process, considering it an extraordinary gift. And this lovely Miss Thomson, now absorbed in such an endeavor, made it all the more enlightening.

Within the hour, she gestured for him to take a break as she busied herself with adding more paint to her palette. Rising from the stool, he made his way around the easel. The portrait, though rough, had a flare of brilliance. He would gladly take it as is. Making no comment, he made his way around the room once again.

"You seem quite comfortable here," she said.

"The art of painting has always fascinated me." He stood before the portrait of the officer. "There seems to be an underlying message in this work–quite different and rather separated from the rest."

Rachel made no reply. Completing the palette, she politely requested him to return. Taking a moment, she positioned him in the same manner and then picked up a brush, the silence only interrupted by the faint sound of brushstrokes.

Another hour passed. She stood back and considered. Turning the easel around, he was amazed at how much had been accomplished. She had masterfully added various tones, accentuated the facial features, and captured his smile. Even, perchance, his soul?

Miss Thomson requested another session. However, it would be placed on hold until some indefinite time in the future. Unbeknownst to all, she had a more pressing commitment. Lord Byron would not return the following week nor, for that matter, the following season.

....

Chapter 58

Crimpus

L ord Byron was also making a transition. His vast estate had held little appeal in recent years, and having a house in Westminster, he resolved to relocate. And, within a season, he could be located in a charming part of the city. Though nestled in a lively metropolitan area, he maintained a life of relative solitude. One could observe him wearing his top hat and carrying a cane during the morning or evening hour, strolling through the parks. Quite often, he would pass a pleasant hour reading on a park bench. It was only by coincidence that his house was a short distance from Miss Thomson's.

All the while, Rachel returned into the depths of the inner city. During her long absence, she continually thought of those countless innocent faces. Yet, there was another reason for this venture, one more artistic in nature. She was inspired to put her portrait abilities to better use, this time bringing along a bag of six-pennies and her satchel of drawing materials.

The carriage made its way through the long, narrow streets, everything compacted and pressed together. Rachel thought *Only the affluent have the luxury of space.* Weathered faces began peering from broken windows, countless withered souls watching as the carriage trotted by. *A gallery of the poor. How do they survive these unbearable winters?*

An old man, cap askew, was seated on the front steps of a house. *A great face!* Rachel tapped the carriage, and the coachman pulled to a stop. The children quickly pressed in from all sides as she stepped into this estranged world once again. Handing out the coins, she gave each child a special moment, a slight pause and making eye contact. More cluttered around, and the bag was soon emptied. *There was never enough.*

She approached the old man. A closer look: wavy wrinkles above the brow, a gray, unshaven scruff, and a timeless smile. The weathered cap held a wisp of white hair in place; the face accentuated with gray-green eyes. She imagined a golden halo encompassing him, like some antiquated Irish saint. Never had she found such inspiration in all those regal countenances who had posed before her.

After a pleasant introduction, Rachel awkwardly inquired if she could draw his portrait. Having no comprehension of what she was saying, he nodded obligingly, "Aye. Aye." Whatever it was she wanted to do would be fine with him. Positioning herself at the base of the steps, she opened her sketchbook. Though standing in the midst of a crowd of children, it was a good vantage point, studying his face almost eye to eye.

Everyone became quiet. Never had they witnessed such a thing. Rachel was at first intimated, the scenario incredulous. What she was doing was almost absurd. It would have been easier to give him a few pounds and have the coachman bring him to her studio. Yet there was a raw energy here, and, like a gray-toned canvas, the air was heavy with oppression. She was soon immersed in her creative world, digging deeply with charcoal to capture his soul; several minutes passed before she broke the silence by asking his name.

"Crimp-ees." His voice was raspy, almost inaudible.

"Crimpus?" Rachel thought it a peculiar name but let it go, continuing to absorb herself in the drawing. Working quickly, she jotted a wealth of notes around the borders: *use earth colors... a dull green for the weathered door; soft light... gray day... not much contrast... raw umber, yellow ochre, a touch of burnt sienna in the flesh... no black accents, thicker paint in light areas... exaggerate the curve of the cap... eyes are the focal point...*

An older woman made her way out the door. Bent low, she carried a battered chair and placed it beside Rachel. The drawing had enough information to have the luxury of sitting while adding the final touches. The children huddled closer, many on tiptoe. *So intriguing how they love the process of creating, gravitating like ducklings to a pond.* All the while, the elders remained at a respectful distance, just as they had done in Sheppey. *Where was the dividing line? At what age do they drift away?* Adding a few more strokes, she considered the portrait complete.

Rachel was humorously amazed at how her model had remained motionless throughout the session, like an old stone statue. He did, however, give a slight nod upon seeing the finished drawing. Most assuredly, he would fade into oblivion, swept away and forgotten in that fathomless sinkhole of poverty. However, who knew the merit of the painting she was about to do? *Possibly the dear man's legacy.*

Making her way through the children, the coachman assisted her into the carriage and began to steer the horses out of the cluttered street. Her artistic eye was now insatiable as a gallery of faces passed by: scraggly, lifeless women, as barren as their wombs; beaten men, bowed down and defeated–all staring at her with those empty eyes. *Why not do a* series *of these weathered souls*?

Throughout the winter months, the carriage returned time and again. Quite often, Rachel had to bundle up to bear the cold. She was building upon her true oeuvre: priceless jewels of humanity, one after another. Though these people were naive about the world of art, they sensed she could be trusted. Little did they know their story was now to be told on canvas with paint and brush. Rachel continued to bring along a bag of coins.

....

Chapter 59

An Old Edifice

It would be with much hesitancy before Rachel proceeded with her ambition to establish an orphanage. Yet, she knew that such a monumental task would once again depend on the gracious assistance of Lady Bradshaw and finally told her of this aspiration. The baroness, always exceeding Rachel's expectations, consented. In a fortnight and through various connections, Rachel's prestigious friend found what she believed to be an ideal building on the south side of the city.

They set out early in the day, taking Muffet along. Passing through the wide boulevards, the coach crossed over the Thames and veered to the left. Knowing the path well, Rachel said a hushed prayer that the building was not near the slums as the orphanage would invariably remain closed to many. *Was it not a cruel selective process?* She diverted her thoughts to other concerns, imagining the size of the building, rooms, kitchen facilities, etc., continuing to place her trust in the good judgment of the baroness.

The coach traveled into a moribund industrial area in Peckham, close to Sir Wisham's workshops. The buildings were outdated amidst the rapid advancements with industry and lay to waste in the wake of progress. The horses were reined next to an old edifice with large brownstones on its façade. The surrounding area was relatively peaceful. Rachel was relieved that it was removed from the poorer districts.

A properly dressed middle-aged woman awaited them at the top of the steps. After an amiable greeting, she opened the door. She apologized for the disarray. The interior was musty but spacious. Rachel became enthusiastic, seeing it as Michelangelo might have envisioned that large block of abused marble in which he created his *David*. Cobwebbed, with heavy machinery and office furniture cluttering the space, the potential was unlimited. Looking around, Rachel calculated... *wonderful space, a decent neighborhood... high ceilings... large windows...* All the while, the baroness held Muffet's hand, following behind Rachel's trail of ideas.

They were then directed to the second floor. As if an answer to prayer, there was an abundance of smaller rooms essential for bedrooms and classrooms.

Her thoughts began to unravel after their departure, countless ideas merging one into another as she excitedly began sharing everything with Lady Bradshaw. Afterward, the baroness made a small request: "I would like the orphanage to be called 'Saved by Grace.' After all, will it not show God's compassion upon these children?"

....

Chapter 60

The Final Touches

It was a Saturday morning, the raw edge of winter still clinging to the initial days of spring, when Lord Byron finally found his appointed time. As the coach proceeded through the boulevards, he observed a few brave souls leaning into the wind. The cold air was invigorating, especially with the anticipation of returning to Miss Thomson's studio, not only for the completion of his portrait but also for the opportunity to become better acquainted with this young, brilliant artist.

It had been quite some time since their last meeting, and Rachel greeted him warmly before preparing for the session. The portrait was on the easel. He noticed thicker brushstrokes in the lighter areas and more clarity in the features. It seemed to breathe. Once again, he casually made his way through the studio and was soon confronted by the portrait of the officer unobtrusively placed in a corner. *Why was it so intriguing?* He then saw the incomplete painting of Crimpus and a trail of drawings scattered around the floor, all faces of poverty.

The painting consumed a good portion of the morning. In due time the easel was turned around. Lord Byron gave it a deep moment of reflection. The head was encompassed in a golden brown, with darker tones merging into the shaded areas. He sensed his very soul was being framed for posterity. "It far surpasses anything I had hoped for. Seeing such, I will pay you twice the amount we had agreed upon."

"Lord Byron, you are already being charged a handsome fee. And I cannot accept such benevolence."

"You most certainly will, my dear. It is worth every crown of it–a masterpiece that most assuredly will only appreciate with time. A good investment, I must say. Furthermore, the path you have now chosen may prove to be a difficult one. I noticed the series of impoverished faces strewn around your studio. Oh, how far removed they are from the social graces. Now, you are making a statement! And I would like to be a special patron, assisting in launching you into such untested waters." He looked at her tenderly, like a caring uncle. "It is also my desire to send you to Holland. Consider it a holiday. I find it essential that you study the works of the Dutch masters, especially Rembrandt. His works will speak volumes to you. He has rather fallen out of favor these days, that golden era of Dutch painting now centuries past. And the art world moves on. However, his works are as timeless as the pyramids of Egypt."

Rachel was grateful beyond words. "To be honest, that has been my heart's desire. I know so little about Rembrandt and do so admire his portraits, though I have only seen them in books." She immediately began making mental notes, allowing her mind to once again wander.

....

Chapter 61

One Last Request

Rachel's measure of time was now the anticipated day of her departure. In the meantime, she immersed in painting those dear faces, her empathy only increasing with every brushstroke.

On weekends, she would take a break from the studio and spend time with Muffet, strolling through the parks during the evening hour. There was an unexpected encounter with Lord Byron. Rachel was delighted to know he had moved to the city. They began meeting at a certain time of the day, taking their stroll together, always with talk of Holland.

Early one evening, while Rachel and Muffet were sitting on a park bench waiting for the arrival of Lord Byron, she inquired, "My dear Muffet, how did you ever receive such a name?"

Wiggling her feet, she shrugged, more focused on the daffodils in a nearby garden.

"Well, there's a tale about 'Little Miss Muffet.' I wonder if that is whom you were named after."

She gave another shrug.

Rachel began reciting; '*Little Miss Muffet sat on a tuffet.*' Do you know what a *'tuffet'* is?" Again, no response, her feet still wiggling, "It is something you sit on, like a small mound of grass or a stool, even a large mushroom." She continued: "*Eating her curds and whey.* I wonder what '*curds and whey*' are. Do you know?"

Lord Byron approached. Smiling, he took a seat, Muffet scampering away to explore the gardens. After a few pleasantries, he handed Rachel a package. "I have been meaning to give this to you for quite some time."

Carefully removing the wrapping, she uncovered a crucifix. It was rather heavy and slightly larger than her hand. The head of Christ was bowed, and a sublime curve to His body. She had always cherished crucifixes, large or small, considering each to be a masterpiece in its own right.

"It is sterling silver, given to me while in Rome. I could think of no better hands to place it in than yours."

A lamplighter was making his way through the park. A cadence of fireflies was blinking in the deep pockets of the gardens as Muffet gave chase.

"Would you kindly do me a favor?" He asked.

"Yes. You know I will."

"Could you find the time to do a little painting for me while in Holland? I have always been fond of those rustic fields and the old windmills."

....

"I am going into the fields to see what this hour yields."
Percy Shelley

....

Chapter 62

𝕿𝖍𝖊 𝕷𝖆𝖓𝖉 𝖔𝖋 𝖙𝖍𝖊 𝕸𝖆𝖘𝖙𝖊𝖗𝖘

With caring for Muffet on weekends and a new resolve in painting, Rachel's days remained full. The warmth of the sun permeated her studio, adding a sense of vitality to her brushes, the floor strewn with countless studies waiting for her attention. Canvases had been prepared, and each unheralded soul came to life one by one. She worked on several paintings at a time, spending an hour on one before moving to another. Dearest to her heart, though, was *Crimpus*, returning to it time and again. All the while, she thought of Holland. The day was drawing nigh.

She paid a final visit to Lady Bradshaw, placing Muffet in her care and making a mental note to do a landscape painting of tulips. *How else could she repay her*?

It was mid-April as Rachel boarded the vessel. The spring air breathed with life, the sun having its full liberty upon a slate of cerulean sky. Pulling up anchor and releasing its sails, the ship slowly made its way down the Thames, an abundance of gulls following in its wake. A new dimension of England opened before her with a wealth of inspiring subject matter passing along the shoreline. *Limitless paintings...* The wind picked up, the air cooled, and the sails tightened. Rachel was revitalized. It had been a long wait, far too long.

The vessel breached the estuary and broke free into the channel. In the distance, she could see Sheppey, picturesque and quaint. Several half-sunken ships clung to the sandbars. Squinting her eyes, she vaguely saw the pier jutting into the sea and only imagined Cedric being there. Facing the open channel, she pleasantly allowed her mind to drift into the foreign world that awaited her. It was her maiden voyage to the continent and would finally give her the opportunity to visit countless museums and study the masters. Foremost, though, was her ambition to see a Rembrandt. Nora's books introduced her to the Golden Age of Dutch painting, though the works were all black and white. She knew that the era of its days of glory had passed–the ebb and flow of various styles with many a great artist fading with time. However, the Dutch masters, especially the works of Rembrandt, Vermeer, and Hals, would never be outdated, no matter the whims of contemporary taste. Paintings done with integrity were timeless and never ceasing in their ability to touch the heart of man. And now the time had come to be afforded the luxury of standing before a Rembrandt and satiate its every brushstroke.

The vessel arrived at the docks in Hook van Holland late in the afternoon. Rachel, overwhelmed with emotions, took her first step upon the continent and beckoned for a carriage. Her first destination was Amsterdam, planning on remaining a week and absorbing the personality of the city along with visiting museums and galleries. Settling in a quaint hotel, she rested for the remainder of the day, sitting on a balcony enjoying a cup of Dutch coffee and watching a myriad of colorful cyclists pass by.

Early the next day, she walked along the thoroughfares of this new and bewildering city. The people were pleasant, many speaking English. Making her way to the canals and passing the long rows of tall houses, she occasionally took in the rare intricacies of the little shops. After lunch at an outdoor café, Rachel returned to the heart of the city. Finding her way to a museum (the stone edifice had to be older than the paintings it housed), she meandered from one spacious room to another, absorbing pictures by 17th and 18th-century masters: landscapes, still-lifes, seascapes, and cityscapes–all done with Dutch perfection. At last, several rooms dedicated to portraits, and she soon found herself standing before a Rembrandt, a self-portrait she knew well from one of Nora's books. It was one of his final works after losing his only son, Titus. His wife had also recently passed away. The tragedies were followed by bankruptcy. Rembrandt's eyes told it all. There he was, laying his heart bare for all the world to see. The painting breathed as if she were standing face to face with the great master, the most powerful portrait she had ever seen.

She spent the remaining days in Amsterdam taking in other galleries and museums, especially searching for Rembrandts while sketching and taking a wealth of notes. During the late afternoons, there would be long walks, soaking in the architecture and the warmth of the people.

....

"There are indeed few merrier spectacles than that of many windmills bickering together in a fresh breeze."
Robert Louis Stevenson

....

Chapter 63

𝕬 𝕯𝖎𝖕𝖙𝖞𝖈𝖍

T he week in Amsterdam drew to a close. Packing her belongings, Rachel took the short train ride to the village of Zaanse Schans. Her heart stirred, seeing the rustic windmills along the way, exclamation marks upon the land. She settled in a quaint inn. From here, she would venture out into the fields to find her paintings. After a delightful dinner in a small café, she retired for the remainder of the day.

The following morning, she walked the village, enjoying the shops and inquiring where she might find picturesque scenery. Late in the morning, satchel in hand, she journeyed into the countryside abounding in its countless aesthetic treasures. She reflected on her youthful years in Sheppey. There, too, she discovered a wealth of inspiring subject matter that the world seemed so impervious to.

Bursts of tulips began stretching out to either side of the road. *Color. That's what Lady Bradshaw would like.* Finding an ideal setting, she sat on a tree stump and began her first study. The air was cool, the sky gray. *Similar to that of England but different.* A breeze blew across the field as a solitary blackbird passed by, the caw of a distant crow piercing the silence. The long blades of the windmills slowly turned, creaking, only adding to the solace–peace and solitude unlike any she had ever known.

Using brown conte, she began with a high horizon line, revealing more land than sky. She then laid in the basic geometric shapes of her composition: narrowing rectangles suggesting the rows of tulips fading in the distance, more rectangular and square shapes for patches of fallow fields. And then the final touch, blocking in two windmills, one to the right and one closer to the left, everything done with a brevity of lines.

The clopping sound of horses. Looking over her shoulder, a farmer with horse and wagon was making his way toward her. He offered a congenial salutation, most likely amused to see an artist sitting in the countryside, especially one so fair. She thought it would be *another classic painting*. After ample notations, the sketch was complete–the first fruit of her glorious adventure. Packing up, she proceeded down the earthen road.

Stopping to rest upon a large stone, Rachel retrieved an apple and cheese from her satchel and breathed in the surroundings, her hair blowing slightly in the breeze. Looking around, this was her present-day studio: a broad, flat land abounding with the sky as a ceiling. Even on such an overcast day, the light was soft and pleasant on the landforms. Everything was alive. Though her studio in Westminster offered the luxury of convenience, materials easily at her disposal, and protection from the elements, there was something about being in the womb of nature. After a short reprieve, she rose and continued on her way, every-thing changing within a few steps, windmills stretching as far as the eye could see.

The sky became a slate of cool blue as the clouds were brushed aside and light spread across the land. She found an antiquated wind-mill and made ready, *possibly for Lord Byron*. Deciding to stand for a better vantage point, she worked rapidly, blocking in the shaded areas of the old structure with notations of earth tones and leaving patches of light. It was quick and abbreviated. Placing her supplies in the satchel, she headed through an open field–windmills and cottages lining the flat horizon.

By late afternoon, she began the journey back to the village. Another inspiring windmill was by the side of the road. She had passed it earlier but from a different perspective. *Masculine. Another study for Lord Byron?* She made notes of the tones: *burnt sienna, umbers, dull ochre, muted Venetian red... accents of black.*

Rachel returned to London with a wealth of sketches and immediately prepared a pair of blank canvases. The paintings were to be a practical size and a matching pair, more or less.

The year had been resurrected. At times, she reflected on those tedious commissions, all but draining the life out of her. *Perfected images, yet so flawed.* She remembered presenting a finished portrait to a patron and then the deadening silence followed by a forlorn expression; the duchess bemoaning, with hand on breast, *Is that really me? My gracious–why those colors? You made me look so old.*

It would take several weeks for the pair of Dutch paintings to come to fruition. Looking at them side by side, they reminded Rachel of a diptych–a two-fold depiction of Holland. The more colorful of the two, with its rows of tulips, was most assuredly for Lady Bradshaw.

It would take several days for the paint to dry and make a visit to the Bradshaw estate. Muffet had been amiably spending her weekdays at the orphanage and with the baroness on weekends. There was an overwhelming embrace within this special little family. It seemed as if she had been gone for ages.

The painting was a complete surprise, catching the baroness unawares. Absorbing every detail, Lady Bradshaw especially admired the way Rachel had masterfully painted peasants bending over rows of tulips. All the while, Rachel studied her emotions and was beginning to comprehend how priceless the gift of a painting could be.

Miss Thomson commenced with a vibrant industry as countless paintings were waiting to be birthed. Her palette was changing, the brushstrokes more pronounced. However, the tones were somber in her collection of those wretched souls, laying in humanity in its abject suffering: the humble, the meek, the contrite of spirit, the brokenhearted, all faces of Christ.

It was becoming a marriage; the paintings were her children (*that is, save for dear Muffet*). There were still vulnerable moments when catching a glimpse of Captain Sumpter. *Life could have been so different–marriage... children... even painting together.* She would blink and return to her reality.

Lord Byron was invited to her studio and presented with the painting. Upon entering, he noticed many of the drawings that had been scattered around the floor had come to fruition on canvas. They were peculiarly similar to Rembrandt's portrayals yet different from Miss Thomson's touch. *They would hold their own in any museum.*

Then, upon the easel, he saw a painting of two windmills. It was his Holland and surpassed anything he had hoped for. It would be prized in his collection, juxtaposed next to a painting by Millet he had recently purchased. Rachel thought of her gifts again–the only thing she could give to those who meant so much.

....

"And I looked, and, behold, a whirlwind came out of the north..."
Ezekiel 1:4 KJV

....

Chapter 64

A Condensed Notch

The bosun approached Captain Hawkins, yelling, "To the stern, sir! It's com'n!" The captain, already aware of what was impending, had been observing the distant sea and sky merged into a swirl of ominous umbers. The wind picked up, and the sails pressed tight. Though the coast was but a hare's breath away, he knew full well he could not outrun it as if the hounds of hell were in pursuit.

The *Fontainebleau* soon became embroiled within the whirlwind, the ship all but defeated, as insurmountable waves crashed against its bulwarks with all their fury. The main sail ripped from its halyards, flapping recklessly as if half-crazed. Rudderless, the vessel was aimlessly tossed about. Though a classic vessel from topsail to haul, proud and invincible through many a storm, the *Fontainebleau* was now a paper sailboat; its pride had turned to prayer. A hopeless dread fell upon one and all.

One could say it was good fortune, the first tempest to hit Sheppey in quite some time, like a long peace between wars. Then, throughout the night, it came, relentlessly pounding the village and wreaking its havoc before departing. As the pale light of day made its note upon gray, the villagers began peeking through the slabs and opening their doors, seeing what damage had been done. The sea was calm.

Sammy made his way to the beach. The pier was still standing. Though he had seen a ship in distress the previous evening, there was no sign of another wreck stranded upon the shoals. Strange, there was a legion of footprints along the beach, as if a small army had moved down the coast throughout the night. Following the trail, it terminated at the door of the Inn. In the mix were prints as large as a bear's paws. *Cedric's...?*

Pinky had kept a diligent eye on Cedric as the storm rolled in. Wiping the window and squinting, he vaguely saw him take the leap and then vanish. Everything became lost and entangled in the storm. And it would take some time before he could comprehend the magnitude of what had literally gone down.

Indeed, a ship was most assuredly struggling to make its way to the coast, and there would likely be another notch upon the beam. However, when all was settled and tallied, Pinky would have to merit this mark as *the condensed notch*. Certainly, each one attested to a miracle in its own right, but this notch would go far beyond the measure of man's comprehension. A single mark could not do it justice. For, with the sinking of the *Fontainebleau*, Cedric would rescue more souls than all the other notches combined. In the years that followed, with all the tales to tell, Pinky would point to this one the most as Cedric not only saved a lad from the depths of the sea but also a flotilla of lifeboats, directing a legion of bedraggled survivors to the beach and then to the doorstep of the Inn. *Aye, 'tis compact 'ndeed.*

Chapter 65

"Follow That Dog!"

P ounded into submission, the *Fontainebleau* rammed against a reef. A mast had shattered and fallen into the sea as the remaining masts precariously creaked and wavered, the ship listing heavily to the lee side. Captain Hawkins commanded everyone to take hold of the bulwarks: "Hold firm!" The raging storm all but muffled the hysterical screams and pleas to God.

A large wave crashed over the vessel and released it from its snare. The ship groaned as it drifted. Flooding with water, the captain ordered his crew to man the lifeboats. The passengers frantically scurried over the side, many falling into the sea.

There were three lifeboats in all, filled to capacity. Drifting away from the sinking *Fontainebleau*, everyone solemnly watching it capsize. Shattered remains surfaced, encompassing the swirling void like a wreath.

The boats bobbed like corks, oars motionless as the crew waited for the captain to set their course. Passengers huddled together–cold, wet, and frightened, the froth of the waves soaking them to the bone. A heavy gray consumed the sea and sky. With no land or stars to set the course nor a compass in hand, Captain Hawkins stalled. *How, in God's name, was he to direct them to safety?*

An apparition then appeared, illusory, like a mirage within the tumultuous waves and furiously paddling toward them. It had a large bear-like head and was clenching something in its jaws. *A boy?* A woman exclaimed, "It's Johnny! Oh, thank God!"

The creature pulled alongside one of the lifeboats as the hysterical mother and several crew members hoisted the boy into her arms. One of the men then blurted out, "'At 'ere's ah dog!" Perplexed, the captain studied the creature. What! *Where did it come from?* However, there were more pressing concerns. The crew continued waiting, the wind blowing relentlessly as Captain Hawkins remained in a quandary.

The dog paddled in front of the lead boat, suggesting they follow his lead. Cast in heavy doubt, the captain sighed and gave the command, "Follow that dog, men!" Immediately the oars were put to sea, and they rowed with all their might, the captain keeping a vigilant eye on their guide as he chugged into the dark, his head drifting out of sight into the edge of night. *At least there was hope, as ludicrous as it may seem.*

Soon the surf could be heard, and waves began pushing the lifeboats to shore. The dog was the first to arrive, remaining steadfast on the beach as a landmark. He presented himself full-bodied and four-pawed in the waning light. The captain approached and bent over, giving him a hearty pat on the head and saying, "Good job, ol' boy!"

A motley assortment of crew and passengers awaited the next command, their silhouettes barely outlined against the darkening sky. Taking a few steps down the beach, the dog once again implored them to follow. Shrugging and resigning himself to the simple fact that there was no other recourse, the captain muttered, "Why not?" And like a haggard band of nomads, they fumbled their way southward. A faint light could be seen in the distance.

Pinky faced the north wind. Holding a lantern high, he scanned the shoreline for any sign of Cedric. A vessel must have gone down. *Why else would 'ol Cedie boy 'ave leapt from the pier?* And now he waited, not only for his return but hoping he would be bringing along a survivor.

'An wat ta me wonder'n eye should 'pear, Pinky exclaimed under his breath as he saw Cedric emerge from the dark followed by a mass of figures. They drew closer. More and more. It seemed as if Cedric had brought an entire shipload to shore! Pinky jostled about and hollered for Jarvis to come quickly. "An' bring plenty ov blankets!" He then hobbled his way out to meet them. Jarvis, panting and catching his breath, was soon by his side, a bundle of blankets in hand. Countless faces appeared in the light of the lantern. "Amazing!" Jarvis whispered. Taking a quick tally, he handed the blankets to Pinky and hurried back to the Inn, yelling to Bertie, "Make ready with all the bedding in the house!"

Disheveled and freezing, they staggered into the door by twos and threes as if filling the ark. Every chair in the house was soon occupied, the overflow taking a place on the floor or sitting on the stairs leading to the second floor. Many children gathered around the hearth with Cedric. Bertie began rubbing the little ones down and wrapping them in blankets. All the while, Jarvis stoked the fire and hung wet clothes to dry. Pinky went to the kitchen and began preparing several cauldrons of stew for the morning. The roaring blaze from the hearth was comforting. Wrapped in blankets, benumbed, and thanking God with hushed utterings, the survivors silently stared at their gracious hosts.

The Merriweathers did their best to prepare the rooms, though it was not a time for tidying up but to offer rest for their weary survivors. The adults were directed to rooms up the stairs, and most of the children were bedded on the floor, the younger ones snuggling next to Cedric. Like a bee going from flower to flower, Bertie made her way around the children, tucking them in with prayerful words and motherly care. Faint smiles appeared as they faded off to sleep. The fire was stoked and given a final stuffing. All fell peacefully silent. Pinky snuffed the lanterns and bid everyone a coarse but gentle good night. Jarvis and Bertie were in awe as they headed up the stairs. It was the first time the Inn had ever been filled.

Early the following day, while everyone was still asleep, Jarvis tiptoed over and around the children and quietly made his way outside, where he merrily posted his *No Vacancy* sign, something that had been tucked away since the Inn's beginning. It was one of those distant stars he had held so dear to his heart for many years.

As the sun rose, one yawn stretched into another. The adults began descending the stairs, and the tavern was soon full of life. Everyone had regained their well-being, and a flow of tales commenced from table to table. In the midst of the incessant chatter, the women and older girls assisted Bertie in serving breakfast. Each and every soul had their own extraordinary story to tell. Naturally, Cedric was the main topic of conversation.

The cauldrons of mutton stew simmered throughout the night. The pantry was ill-prepared for such a time as this, and each pot had its own unique taste. The shelves were laid bare as Pinky added herbs and spices along with an assortment of chopped vegetables into the pots of lamb bones. No matter the variance, everyone voraciously devoured the meal, exclaiming it to be the most delicious stew they had ever tasted. A large bone was given to Cedric, who found his way to the hearth with an entourage of children following him like little birds on a whale's back. Thawed out, rid of fear, soothed and comforted, everyone feasted on a king's meal and was thankful indeed. The motto for the day could easily have been, *Eat, drink, and be merry–for today you live!*

After the meal, the children scampered outside chasing seagulls, playing on the beach, or exploring every nook and cranny in the village. Being claimed by all, Cedric amiably lumbered along. The villagers stood outside their cottages in disbelief at such a flood of youthful souls prancing around the muddied path. *And there was ol' Cedie boy!*

The adults remained in the tavern as the stories continued to flow, one table jabbering as much as the next. However, there was one tale of special interest, which Captain Hawkins had discreetly kept close to the hilt. Now, in the good company of the Merriweathers and Pinky, he found it to be an opportune time for its disclosure. Knowing that the captain was a respectable man and not one to stretch the truth or banter about, the threesome leaned in. Lowering his voice, he began...

It was during the most climactic moment of the storm, as the lifeboats were being lowered. The *Fontainebleau* was sighing its last. In the midst of the consternation, with passengers weeping and wailing while boarding the boats, he noticed a boy being swept overboard. Crying and splashing about frantically, the lad then faded into the dark sea. The captain knew any effort to retrieve him was futile and returned to other pressing concerns. Shortly thereafter, he caught sight of a vague creature paddling near the ship, the little boy clutched in its jowls. In the blink of an eye, waves began crashing over the deck, and the captain was again diverted.

At this time, Cedric, exhausted from playing outside with the children, returned and rested by the captain's side. Looking down and giving him a pat, Captain Hawkins said, "There's no way of knowing how long this-here creature held on to that boy or how he had the strength to prevail during that storm. For that matter, from whence he came?"

A little boy was seated next to his mother at a nearby table. Captain Hawkins called for him. The boy arose and proceeded to stand before him, a small, timid lad of seven or eight. When addressed, he meekly replied that his name was Johnny. The captain smiled and leaned over, looking him in the eyes. "Did this here dog save your life?"

The boy looked at Cedric and lit up with large eyes and a big smile. "Indeed, 'ee did, sir! 'Ee's the best dog in the 'ole world! An' the biggest too!" The boy was then released to the care of his mother.

....

Chapter 66

"Pass'n the cap 'round."

Shortly after posting the *No Vacancy* sign, Jarvis tapped on the grocer's door. Mrs. Filmore groggily greeted him. They were in dire need of more staples to feed their unexpected guests. Stocking up with armloads of ware, he excitedly divulged everything that had happened. The grocer's wife, now wide awake, quickly broadcast the incredible news after his departure to everyone who entered the shop, even proclaiming it at her doorpost to passersby. If there were a bullhorn, she would have heralded it from the rooftop. Cedric's unbelievable feat was trumpeted throughout Sheppey with as much enthusiasm as the day Wellington defeated Napoleon. Like carrier pigeons, the villagers would flit throughout the rest of the village, sharing the news with late sleepers or enfeebled souls. Those who were hard of hearing cupped their ears and leaned in, giving an astonishing nod and dropping their jaws. Not a word fell to the ground void.

By mid-afternoon, the Sheppians had come out of their shells, watching the children skip around the muddied path or splash in the puddles. Even the gulls joined in, weaving their joyful patterns in the sky. Many a withered soul rubbed their chins, wondering how such a festive time could have been birthed from that horrific storm.

Within a few days, a vessel arrived to retrieve the survivors. Unfortunately, no rooms were available in the Inn, and the authorities remained on board. Staying longer than anticipated, they ironed out many of the wrinkles in the sinking of the *Fontainebleau* with volumes of paperwork, along with taking a tally of the wreckage along the shoreline and the tedious process of finding relatives of the deceased. During the evening hours, they joined in with the festivities in the tavern, dining on Pinky's mutton stew and a pint or two, enthralled with the countless stories being told.

Foregoing the sign in the lobby, *Pay on Your Way Out*, there was no bill for the shipwrecked souls that had lodged at the Inn, nor for the cauldrons of mutton stew, not even for the generous flow of libations– for Christian hospitality outweighed the filling of the Inn's till. How could the Merriweathers, in good conscience, put a price tag on such a tragedy? Nor was it in their fiber to extend one hand with compassion and collect a fair share of coins in the other.

Before departing, Captain Hawkins took Jarvis aside. He mentioned that the shipping company would be donating something to the Inn for the care of the survivors. Then, added, though empty of pocket when the ship went down, he also desired to show a token of his appreciation. A pocket watch was the only thing on his person when the Fontainebleau went down. It was sterling silver and made in Switzerland, bequeathed to him from his grandfather. Clasping it in Jarvis's hand, he insisted on his taking it.

The other guests also donated. Early on the morning of their departure, they gathered 'round. Retrieving every shilling, farthing, or sixpenny that had clung to their pockets when abandoning ship, they emptied every last coin into a cap that was passed around. One of the younger boys even donated his prized marbles. A crew member jovially commented, "Naked 'ah came into 'is world, and naked 'ah'll d'part." Though the donations amounted to a meager sum, it was as heartfelt a gesture as the widow's mite. A woman had even discreetly placed a rosary in the mix. Upon taking tally later in the day, Bertie tenderly took hold of it and would carry it with her throughout the remainder of her days.

Before the vessel set sail, two distinguished officials personally thanked Jarvis and Bertie for their gracious hospitality and, after handshakes and approbations, handed them a small purse in the Queen's name containing one hundred crowns.

Though the day was heavy with clouds and windswept, there was a warm farewell as the guests gave their tearful goodbyes and proceeded to the cove, Cedric following along by the captain's side. As the vessel made its way up the Thames, Captain Hawkins kept his eye on Cedric until he faded in the distance. *Amazing. Who would ever believe it?* The *Wayfarer Inn* returned to peace and solitude; the animated spirit of that houseful of guests continued to linger throughout the day.

The following morning, Pinky made his way to the beam. It was so incomprehensible, like a far-fetched dream. Rubbing his chin and considering, he concluded it would be recorded as one notch and could be regarded as Cedric's rescue of the boy. Though Pinky knew full well that far more lives were saved than one. Yes, it was a condensed notch indeed, with as many tales to tell as the stars in the sky. He notched it to the side of the others, next to that of Miss Gertrude's. Returning to the table by the window, he could see Cedric, looking out upon the sea, the stalwart sentry of Sheppey, and wondered, once again, how many more shipwrecked souls would be brought to the Inn and tallied upon the beam and how many more tales were to be told?

....

Chapter 67

A Final Visit

It was mid-August, and the time was drawing nigh for Adaline's departure. It had been many years since being stranded on the shores of Sheppey. News from Ireland was becoming bleaker (if that were possible), and there was a sense of urgency. Though the wedding was drawing nigh, she would not be attending. The decision to leave immediately all but broke Faith's heart. Yet she knew she could not deter her dear friend.

The evening air was crisp. The pair sat around the campfire, poking embers with glowing ash sailing into the night. A note of melancholia hung over the silence. Faith rose and went into the cottage. Returning with a small purse, she placed three gold doubloons in Adaline's hand. "Rachel gave these to me before you arrived. They were a gift from Lady Bradshaw. Her only request was that I put them to good use. I don't know how much they are worth, but I can't think of a better cause than to give them to you."

"You are so kind." Tears glistened in the light of the fire as they embraced. Adaline then retired, leaving Faith to stoke the fire and reflect.

Faith wrote to Rachel the following day, telling her that Adaline was departing for Ireland. They had become as close as sisters, and she had been a great help to Nora and had filled many an hour with joy. Not to mention all the good she had done for Miss Agnes and Miss Gertrude and then said she had given Adaline the gold coins to help with her cause. *Seeing that time was short, I could not wait for your approval, knowing you would understand.*

The next day, Adaline took her final trip to the village. The hike did her good, as there was much to consider. A brisk wind greeted her on the coast. Save for the flight of a wandering gull, the beach was desolate. Proceeding north, she paused at Roger's cottage. The shades were drawn. *Hopefully, they will be opened later in the day.* In the distance, she could see the old pier. And there was Cedric–as fixed in his resolve as she was.

Reaching the pier, she called out to him. He immediately rose to his feet and lumbered over the planks. She always marveled at how he navigated the precarious planks like a dancing bear. Bending down and coaxing him, she took hold of the scruff of his head, stared into his eyes, and spoke a few tender words, his tail wagging fervently. It was a universal dialogue. Wiping away tears, she whispered a farewell and headed to the Inn. Cedric looked on.

Mrs. Filmore had told Pinky of Adaline's impending departure, and he had anticipated a visit. Adaline took her favorite seat next to the window and watched Cedric return to the end of the pier. Pinky shuffled over with a pot of tea, smiling with that all-knowing glint in his eye. *A memory she would always hold dear.* She thought of that first day, wet to the bone, when he covered her with blankets.

Pinky had always admired Adaline. She was of a different cut, bright, and gifted with a precious Irish soul. She could hold her own in any conversation and, at times, even keep him at bay with her never-ending enthusiasm. There was also a deep empathy for what she had endured as a child, emotional wounds so well concealed. He knew it was the stuff that had tempered her soul, just as battle had for him; her Irish grit entwined within an indomitable spirit. She would rise to the occasion wherever she may wander, just as he had done. And success, whatever it may be, would not come from the direction of the stars or hap and circumstance, but through her own will and industry.

It was a short hour when their conversation came to its conclusion. As Adaline rose, she said, "Mr. Pinky, may I pry a bit?"

He grinned and nodded, never knowing what to expect.

"Though I find your name quite apropos, I have often wondered what may your birth name be."

"Aye…" Looking at her with that one good eye and a broadening smile, he replied, "Long-kept secret, me lassie. But fer you…" He turned, making sure no one was pressing in. "'Tis Cee-sool. Cee-sool Chizzl'wick, eet ess. At yur service." Adaline laughed. *It was good to see her face light up.* That was his memory.

"Oh, Mr. Chizzlewik! If only the world knew. 'Chizzie and ol' Cedie boy'–has a ring to it. But I'll leave it be for now." There were a few more humorous tidbits and then a tear or two as they embraced. Jarvis and Bertie made their way over and added to the emotional farewell.

The wind picked up, the day carrying its all-too-familiar note of somberness. She looked out at the pier. Cedric's eyes were set upon the sea. Proceeding past the grocer's, she came to the cottage of Agnes and Gertrude. Gently tapping on the door, Adaline was greeted by the sisters. She marveled at how much they had changed since that first encounter, everything softer. She said she would not stay long as she was leaving for Ireland in the morning but wanted to see them before departing. Gertrude began praising her, stammering as she attempted to put her heartfelt words together. She gave them a hug and bid farewell.

Roger was the final stop. *Alas, the shades were pulled aside.* Throughout the seasons, she had passed by countless times but remained hesitant. *How many years had it been since that evening in the tavern?* She stalled. Unexpected visits were likely an intrusion. Knocking…

Otto barked, and the door opened. Roger greeted her with a pleasant smile. Much relieved, she extended her hand, which he tenderly shook. She discerned *That was as far as he would go with any form of physical display.*

He paused and studied her. Though it was the same young girl he had met in the tavern years ago, she had matured. Her smile was tempered, and there was now a serene quality about her. He invited her in, Otto scurrying around her feet and manifesting all the emotions Roger lacked.

Adaline was finally within the womb of his industry. She looked around. Spartan and pure in its simplicity, reminiscent of a monastic cell. There was a small library with several shelves of books on a far wall. The only contradiction was his desk. Situated in a corner by the window, it was cluttered with pens and reams of paper.

He invited her to have a seat.

"I shan't be staying long as the day is short. I leave for Ireland tomorrow and wanted to pay you a visit before departing." Otto jumped on her lap. She gave him a few moments of undivided attention. "What a rarity," she commented. "How is it that Otto and Cedric are the only dogs in the village? You should take him out on occasion to meet the villagers. They would enjoy his energy. One cannot help but adore your little friend."

"I have been anticipating your visit for quite some time." He said. "Our conversation that evening... How many seasons ago was it? Though never quite sure you would come tapping at my door, I sensed you would not be tethered to Sheppey for long."

"I so much wanted to pay you a visit. Time and again, I passed by but was always hesitant, respectful of your desire to be left alone. You have been a great inspiration to me, though our time together was but a fleeting moment. My desire to write is quite alien to those around me. I often feel like one of those solitary gulls far out at sea." Looking around the cottage, "I must say, you seem to be quite stoic and cluttered at the same time." She retrieved an envelope from her pocket and handed it to him, "I wanted to leave this with you. 'Tis a poem. And certainly not worthy of your consideration. However, I feel led to place it in your hands. I often wonder how much you could have assisted me in my ongoing struggle to put thoughts to verse, words that truly ring within my heart. Hopefully, you will find a measure of good intent in my feeble effort."

He placed the envelope on his desk. "Thank you. I'll reflect on it later." They continued talking idly for a brief time. Daylight was fading. "I must be going."

Roger walked her to the door and offered an extended hand with a dried-eye farewell. Adaline mused *If only there was some Irish blood in those veins*. Otto did much better, frolicking around her with uncontained ebullience and following her out the door, his little barks fading as she made her way past the church and through the woods.

As the day drew to its conclusion, she thought of all those tender souls now being left behind. Nora had grafted her in with tender motherly care; Faith, the dearest friend she had ever had; Pinky was nothing short of an exclamation mark upon mankind; Cedric, a remarkable story if ever there was one; Miss Agnes and Miss Gertrude, an unbelievably happy note upon the face of humanity; and the professor, with that mind filled with its unlimited depth of knowledge and prose.

Roger put on his spectacles and opened the envelope. The penmanship was good.

We speak in silence,
As soft as the stars.
Alone, we hear the lark ascending;
'Tis the path we chose.
Not to quail in life's sad offerings,
But to hear that songbird and endure,
And so aspiring, we lay hold of the beauty of God.

He looked out on the horizon. Daylight was spent. Lighting a candle, he picked up his pen and began writing.

Chapter 68

Sealed With a Kiss

⸺

T he day of the wedding finally drew nigh. An attentive eye would observe a new bounce in the old pastor's step. To Theo, Thomas was like the young Timothy by the side of Paul. And he cherished this honor now bestowed upon him to wed this precious couple. After all his years of spiritual travail, a revival seemed to be stirring in this barren land. *Was it not evident in the transformation of Agnes and Gertrude? And to think, there could even be a newborn child?* Pastor Theo let his mind pleasantly continue to wander, imagining lifting an infant up to God just as Simeon had done in days of old.

It was mid-autumn, the air fresh and the day pleasant enough. Though the bell in the old belfry rang out a merry tune, only a few intimate souls attended. Nora was seated in the front row next to Mildred. Gertrude and Agnes were to her other side, not to miss it for the world, the first such ceremony they had ever attended. With shillings overflowing in their jar, they had even purchased new dresses for the occasion. Jarvis and Bertie and a handful of faithful church members were also present. So, too, were Thomas's parents, as teary-eyed as any. Nor would Pinky pass it by, more spit-and-polished than anyone had ever seen him. There was one other guest. At the appointed time, Cedric came sauntering down the aisle, wagging his tail fervently. Bathed and groomed by Mildred, he handsomely presented himself, delivering the wedding rings attached to a red ribbon around his neck to the altar.

When Pastor Theo pronounced Thomas and Faith husband and wife, there was no sweeping of the young bride off her feet or any other display of passion. A tender kiss sufficed to tell it all with ne'er a dry eye in the house. That is, save for Cedric.

....

Chapter 69

Enter Mr. Percival

At long last, Thomas's cottage was brought to life just in time for the anticipated honeymoon. After he departed from the Inn, the rooms were vacant once again. Like the ever-present gray sky, nothing seemed to change in the Wayfarer Inn. However, a Mr. Claude Percival would make his way to Sheppey at such a time as this. Traveling by coach, he was greeted in the lobby of the Inn by Jarvis, attended to promptly, and, seeing he was a man of prominence, lodged on the second floor in what was considered the Inn's suite. The coachman took his lodging on the third floor, the same room recently vacated by Thomas.

Mr. Percival was the editor-in-chief of the *London Illustrated News*. A weekly journal that hit the stands several years past, quickly becoming the most prominent paper throughout London. The immense success was due to the fact that it was the first publication to have illustrations complementing the articles. However, sales were brisk; the long and bloody wars of the British Empire and a myriad other ongoing travails made for dismal news. And, like the Queen, Mr. Percival realized the people needed a good report, something to read about that was uplifting, something to mend their hearts. A decade had passed since Captain Sumpter's luncheon, with the Queen being honored as the sole survivor of the battle of Kabul. That in itself, along with the shipwreck, would have been an excellent story if not for the simple fact that it had all taken place far before his paper went into print.

It was the hearsay about some dog that had rescued him from the shipwreck that truly piqued his interest. Certainly, if true, it would make for an amazing story, especially in this present day. And so, Mr. Percival was patient but always attentive to this extraordinary tale. He had recently heard through the grapevine that abounded around the Monarchy that the Queen was considering knighting this remarkable creature. That would be the climax to it all, the exclamation mark upon an outstanding article! In the meantime, the editor-in-chief began formulating the story and, rolling up his sleeves, he set to the task of investigating the heroics of this dog by venturing to the village from whence he came.

The first evening at the Inn, Mr. Percival invariably took the jaunt down the stairs to the tavern to indulge in a glass of port fireside. Naturally, he made the acquaintance of Pinky. By all appearance and surmising, they were most assuredly opposing bookends; the guest of the Inn was refined, articulate in dress, educated, and soft of hand, while the latter could best be described as Black Beard the pirate himself. Needless to say, the distinguished Mr. Percival was perceptive and well-versed in the variances of man and not intimidated by such crudity. For, being patient, he had oft discovered a jewel in the rough. Was that not his profession? And the experienced editor-in-chief sensed this bedraggled, patch-eyed man, who blatantly shredded the English language, could possibly be a page-turner.

Naturally, Pinky recommended the mutton stew, to which Mr. Percival nodded favorably. While waiting, he noticed the drawings hanging on a wall. When Pinky returned, he inquired as to the picture of the dog. "'At's ol' Cedie boy. 'Tis done by the lovely Mus Rachel. Spent 'er youthful years in Sheppey an' now liv'n in London. A painter she 'ees. Mak'n quite ah name fer 'erself." Pinky puffed out his chest and let it be known that the other picture, done by the same lovely hand, was of *meself.* Mr. Percival made a mental note to search her out. *Could she not prove to be the perfect illustrator for the article?* Upon tasting the stew, he praised Pinky for its culinary merit and then settled back to listen to several of his tales about Cedric and the shipwrecks.

The next morning, Claude Percival returned to the table by the hearth. Having a pot of hot tea, he coddled his body after a bone-chilling night and spent the early hour enjoying the warmth and reviewing his notes. Astute in his research, he began probing into all the facts pertaining to this dog.

Pinky hobbled over. Cedric was by his side. Mr. Percival put his pencil down and sat back. His first impression was that it was a remarkable creature. *And quite large at that.* After several more tales, Pinky persuaded him to take a brief tour, "Ta see fer yerself." Taking a moment to organize his paperwork, the distinguished guest set out with his guide along with the hero of Sheppey.

Venturing into the brisk morning air, Pinky pointed to the pier. They then watched Cedric saunter to the end of the dilapidated structure and come to rest. *How could he possibly reside there throughout these brutal winters?* Pinky pointed his cane to the skeletal remains of several vessels still clinging to the bars and told the tale of each. Mr. Percival was quite impressed at how Pinky knew the vessels' names and their fatal stories. He then guided him along the shoreline. Fortunately, with his limp, it was at a pace Mr. Percival found almost accommodating. Rusted remnants of bygone wrecks, like half-buried seashells, were strewn across the beach. *Marvelous.* Pausing and taking mental notes, he considered the distance Cedric had to swim from the pier to a ship and then bring a survivor to shore. *Remarkable. Especially in a storm...* Farther north, Pinky pointed to where the Thames clashed with the North Atlantic.

Cold and windblown, they returned to the Inn, where the editor-in-chief would spend the afternoon indulging in another bowl of the house specialty and taking down a wealth of notations while everything was still fresh in his mind. During the early evening hour, the

Merriweathers joined in. He invited them to have a seat. Over the next hour, they shared their perspective on Cedric's heroics, telling how he had arrived on that rainy day in '39 and anecdotes about many of the survivors of various shipwrecks, spending an inordinate amount of time speaking of the epic rescue of Captain Hawkins and the three lifeboats. Mr. Percival was in awe. *How in the world would he be able to compact it all in one article, let alone the knighting?*

The light of day faded, the lanterns were lit, and the fire stoked. Mr. Percival lingered over a glass of port, trying to consume it all before packing his materials and returning to his room. He removed his damp and gritty socks and painstakingly cleaned the once-polished two-toned wingtip boots. In hindsight, he regretted not bringing along his button spats.

The following morning, after tea, the honorable guest ventured down the muddied path, his intention being to go from cottage to cottage and obtain more firsthand accounts. Pad and pencil in hand, he approached the first cottage and tapped on the door. An elderly woman greeted him in a stoic and uninviting manner, though rather dismayed at such a visitor. After a pleasant introduction, he commenced with his inquiry. Upon hearing Cedric's name, she immediately became animated, responding with a raspy voice, "'Ee's me 'ero!" That much said, and little more, he bid her a fond farewell and ventured to the next dwelling, soon to be greeted by another withered soul and a similar abbreviated statement. With fresh mud caked upon his wingtips, Mr. Percival put his pad and paper aside and retreated to the Inn.

Late in the afternoon, Pinky again approached with Cedric, to which the editor took off his glasses, ordered a glass of port, and once again leaned back to have the pleasure of a more thorough introduction. Never investing time in a dog, he found this Cedric delightful and rather good company. *Possibly something to consider some time in the future.*

Mr. Percival departed early on the third day. He felt it best to leave first thing with his reams of notes. The Merriweathers were given a generous sum for his stay, and after the coach was packed and ready, he bid them all a fond adieu. Turning aside in the brisk wind, he saw Cedric on the pier. That regal pose, facing the North Sea, reminded him of one of the bronze lions encompassing the monument of Lord Nelson on Trafalgar Square. *Fascinating indeed.*

....

Chapter 70

𝕷amentations

Nor would Rachel attend the wedding. Most assuredly, it would have been a family reunion she had yearned for all these years. There was also a recent desire to return home to her roots, dearly missing Nora and giving Muffet a home in the country. And with her perspective on painting changing, she longed to paint the various nuances of Sheppey and its people before it was gone. However, outweighing her heartfelt sentiments was a deep concern for Lady Bradshaw. Her health was deteriorating, and she realized she would have to remain by her side. After sending a letter to Faith with the deepest regrets, the book was closed on such aspirations.

The baroness's complexion began losing its color, and her once-engaging eyes dulled. She slept throughout most of the days. During the quiet hours, Rachel continued to give Muffet art lessons, reflecting on how she had the same joy with color and creating as a child. Muffet accompanied her to Lady Bradshaw's bedside, showing her artwork and prancing around the room. In time, Rachel perceived the animation was too draining and made the visits alone.

It was late autumn. A touch of warmth lingered in the bedroom; the window was opened with a gentle breeze passing through the curtains. There was an immense peace. The baroness stared at the ceiling.

Her eyes then gently closed, and she breathed her last. Death, the sorrowful moment that awaits us all, held no fear or dread within her soul. For within all God's paradoxes, Lady Bradshaw faded into the sublime beauty of another world. The pale light from the window cast a veil of rest upon her.

The protocol for family members was black: dress, hat, gloves, and shoes. Lady Bradshaw's extended family attended the funeral, along with Rachel and Muffet. Though the latter had no family ties, Rachel wore the appropriate dress for mourning. It was a simple service. A priest from St. Paul's gave the eulogy. He focused on the baroness's years after the tragic shipwreck and her resurrected life. Lady Bradshaw bequeathed to all; a large sum was also set aside for the orphanage. The house in Westminster, the carriage, and a stipend for the coachman would go to Miss Thomson. And, quite discreetly, a substantial amount was put into an account for the care of Muffet. Rachel remained in a state of mourning throughout the season, Faith's wedding all but a faded hope.

Rachel and Muffet returned to Westminster before winter had set in. The studio lay dormant, the brushes silent. Putting painting aside, she invested her time and energy in the orphanage: refurbishing the building and purchasing beds, tables, chairs, and kitchen necessities. A staff was selected with countless meetings throughout the days as every detail took painstaking time. Several staff members were then sent into the slums to gather orphans, a flow of children funneling into the caring hands of the staff, and every bed quickly taken. Sadly, an infinite number of children still waited in that illusory queue.

Though Mr. Percival was consumed with various deadlines, he made it a priority to inquire as to the whereabouts of Miss Rachel Thomson. In due time, he came knocking at her door and was immediately taken aback by both her beauty and congeniality. *To think, the possibility of having her do the illustrations!* He proceeded to tell her that he was the editor-in-chief of the *London Illustrated News* and the ensuing article and the impending knighting of Cedric–and that he would be honored if she would do a series of pen-and-ink drawings to go along with the storyline. (For which she would be paid handsomely.) He concluded that from what he knew, the appointed date for the ceremony would be sometime this summer, and she could work on the illustrations whenever time afforded.

Rachel was delighted. It was the first she had heard any mention of Cedric being knighted! And she relished the opportunity to let her abilities run their creative course with the illustrations. Throughout the ensuing season, she began recollecting the memories, many of which were soon to come to life with a pen and ink.

....

Part III
(1852–1867)

Chapter 71

"Let us proceed."

A handful of years passed since the seed had been planted in the Queen's heart pertaining to knighting Cedric. In the meantime, there would be many more storms upon the coast of Sheppey, more shipwrecks, and more notches upon the wooden scroll. The *Princess Lily* went asunder. So, too, the *Billie-Boy,* the *HMS Unicorn,* and the *Lizzie May,* all of which the Queen had taken note. However, entangled within the overwhelming demands of endless wars, reams of documents, and the ongoing concern of poverty throughout London, her ambition for knighting Cedric would all but be swept aside and lost in the shuffle. However, one should be mindful that Her Majesty was of steadfast resolve and had not forgotten. *There will be a time.* Mr. Percival also waited patiently.

By mid-century, Queen Victoria had reached the zenith of her reign, the Union Jack flying majestically throughout the world, for it was a truism that *the sun never sets on the British Empire.* A righteous monarch with a sincere desire to instill the virtues of Christianity in her people, she also had a handful of other ambitions. For one, she appreciated good art and desired to bring her people to a higher level in its appreciation, to embrace art that was of a good report, sublime, enlightening, noble, even chivalrous. Art, too, should have its standard of ethics.

It was well known throughout the kingdom how much Her Majesty adored her beloved dogs and Shetland ponies. During more vulnerable moments, she was known to have muttered that she cherished them more than people. Throughout her reign, she commissioned the very best animal artists to portray her pets.

Which eventually leads to Cedric. Could we not say that seeing her love for God's creatures and his heroics, this unlikely pair would invariably become entwined within the grand scheme of things? Most assuredly, the commonwealth was long overdue for something to celebrate, especially a great dog story.

Though knighting Cedric was quite irregular, especially within the prim-and-proper protocol of the Queen's court with its antiquated mindset, she knew the consensus of the commoners would be one of overwhelming support. More often than not, her court and so-called advisors smothered her with their staid sentiments, leaving her to muse they were not far distanced from the supercilious airs of King Louis XIV's court. Born and bred with an independent temperament, Her Majesty remained dauntless in this pursuit, all but assured that her people would rise to the occasion.

And so, one morning after the business of the day was pushed aside, she nonchalantly mentioned her intention to an assortment of counselors and parliamentarians. Immediately, ears perked, and dubious looks arose, finding such an ambition absurd. With every feather ruffled and all but stomping their feet, they mentally blurted, *Knighting a dog is an indignity to the crown! Tradition is the lion that guards our heritage!*

The Queen nonchalantly placed her request aside, and, keeping her head high and fanning the air, she brushed past the assembled advisers, knowing she would simply bypass such indignation–n*o need to raise a fuss. For now, more pressing matters must be attended to.* When the hour was right, she would also put her foot down and proclaim, *Cedric will be knighted! Mark it well on the calendar! What could be a greater exclamation mark upon these harrowed times than knighting such a fine creature? Is he not just as valiant as Lord Nelson? Yes, the time is drawing nigh.*

Most assuredly, the Queen had her concerns about such a ceremony. *Could she truly knight a dog? For that matter, how does one go about it?* Her Majesty knew full well it would not be feasible to use the standard protocol of tapping Cedric on the shoulders with a sword. Such finer nuances would have to be researched. She called upon her loyal and trusted advisor, Sir Elliot Barton. An elderly gentleman who had been by her side since the coronation, she continually gleaned from his insight, trusting him as much as her pets. Alas, her venerable counselor would be put to the test once again.

Standing stalwart before the Queen, she let her concerns be known. There was a long pause. Raising his head, he smiled, gave an assuring nod, bowed, and departed. The Queen also smiled, knowing he would thoroughly delve within the archives and find a buried clause confirming that her ambition could be accomplished.

Several days passed before Lord Barton returned, an all-knowing smile upon his countenance. He commenced by saying the bylaws clearly stated that knighthood could be bestowed for any special achievement *or any major, long-term contribution to any activity of national interest.* "Most assuredly, Your Highness, seeing how Cedric has rescued countless souls from the sea, he fits quite well into this category. Furthermore, his knighting may be logged as a *special achievement* and a *contribution to our nation's best interest.*"

With that settled, the Queen inquired, "And how, may I ask, shall I go about bestowing knighthood without a sword?" Her courtier, reflective with the years, reflected for another moment and mentioned an alternative. Placing his hands to his side, he stated, "If you so desire, Your Majesty may bequeath this noble act simply with a hug."

"A hug?"

"Indeed. My research ascertains that if Your Highness deems it so, an embrace will more than suffice."

The Queen arose like a lark ascending. Raising her arms in the air, she proclaimed, "Then, by God, that is what I will do!" With that, the diminutive figure departed, followed by an entourage of ladies-in-waiting and her three small furry companions.

Later that day, after an assortment of government issues were taken care of, the Queen found her opening. Pushing aside the red box with its reams of paperwork, she let it be known, "This marvelous dog from Sheppey, Cedric that is, is to be knighted." A dead silence followed. One could almost hear a groan. *Oh, no–she is actually going to do it.* There were no smiles, or affirming heads bobbing, or mutterings of "Hear. Hear". Rising slowly, they bowed in deference and staggered backward as they departed. Once the door was closed, some were heard to mumble she had lost touch with her faculties.

The Queen was fully aware of the outdated traditionalists who abounded around her, their mindsets as thick as the stone statues throughout the palace. However, she knew, with time, they would see her reasoning. Meanwhile, Queen Victoria would stand alone in her conviction. For is it not the sign of a truly great leader to sometimes go against the whims of one's counsel? And it would not be the Victorian Era without Victoria. Casting their sentiments aside, she requested the glorious ceremony to be held at St. Paul's Cathedral. *If it could hold funeral services for Nelson and Wellington, we most assuredly could knight Cedric there!* She made a note that palace guards would not be sufficient to keep the commoners at bay as all Great Britain would want to be present, and fences would also have to be put in place. So the stage was set, the announcement released to the tabloids, the headlines reading: *Sir Cedric!* As quickly as it hit the stands, the Queen received her confirmation with an overwhelming "Hoorah!" from the masses.

There were still other minor details that had to be tended to. Though it would be a regal ceremony, prim and proper and manifesting the monarchy at its best, the Queen had no desire for it to be as rigid as the polished armor abounding throughout the palace, delightfully bringing her own dogs along for the occasion. *They would not miss it for all the world!* There was one other finer nuance: *Who would walk the dog down the aisle? Being led down the red carpet by a dignitary, or even a valet, would miss the essence of it all. Let's see... possibly someone whom the dog had rescued? That young officer would have been ideal, a glorious accent. But that is a foregone conclusion. Was there not another? The seaman rescued from the HMS Prince Edward... Was he not a member of our Royal Navy? Put him in his military best and give him the honor of escorting Cedric down the aisle. Most assuredly, it fits like a royal glove.*

Bosun Oscar Bluthers resided in a ramshackle to the east side of London, a neighborhood scraping the very edge of the slums. His many years in Her Majesty's Royal Navy were behind him, and his life of ser-vitude all but fading.

One morning, there came a knocking at the door. In due time it was opened. Garbed in a stained undershirt and pajama bottoms, unshaven and scruffy, he looked as if awakened from a heavy slumber. Coming to his senses, he was perplexed to find two well-attired men standing before him. After introducing themselves as emissaries of the Queen, one of the officials stated, "Her Majesty requests your services one more time. Being the sole survivor of the *HMS Prince Edward*, you are to be present for the knighting of Cedric and given the honor of escorting him down the aisle for the ceremony."

"Oh, mercy me! Ah can't b'lieve me ears! Ethel, com' 'ere! Quick!" A small, rotund woman came scurrying to the door, wiping her hands on an apron.

"'Ees 'ere gentl'm'n seys our belov'd Queen wants me ta 'scort 'at dog 'at saved me life 'down the roy'l carpet. 'Ees ta be knighted!'"

Ethel gasped, placed her hands aside her cheeks, and blurted, "Oh, mercy me!"

The ceremony would be sometime in mid-summer, and the palace would send a carriage for him a day in advance. He would be provided lodging and *polished up a bit* with a new uniform. Taking note that the sailor had only a few teeth (and those being stained and contorted), they went on to state, *Not a word is to escape your mouth throughout the entire ceremony, not even a smile. You are a representative of the Crown and will stand stalwart before the Queen, remaining buttoned up from top to bottom–from beginning to end.*

Chapter 72

𝕶nighted

As the day approached, a carriage was sent to Sheppey to deliver Cedric to London. The palace had requested someone from the village to accompany him, to which Thomas and Faith gladly responded. It would not take long for Rachel to receive word they were coming, overjoyed to know she would soon embrace them and hear about the wedding. She would also have the opportunity to introduce them to Muffet–and Muffet to Cedric.

The two coaches arrived in London on the same day: one escorting the bosun to the palace and the other going to Rachel's home in Westminster. Muffet immediately gravitated to Cedric and led him around the house to play. Rachel was more than pleased with Thomas, everything and more she had hoped for, and the next several days proved to be an extended family reunion.

The palace had requested Miss Thomson to escort Cedric to the ceremony. Invitations were selective and kept to a minimum. Though Thomas and Faith were not invited, their time in Westminster would be just as enjoyable. There was another purpose for their visit, though, as they desired to visit the orphanage.

The day of the ceremony arrived, a glorious summer morning casting its warmth upon the land. The entire nation was as exhilarated as if it were the Queen's coronation. As intended, Her Majesty added her personal touch by bringing along her three little companions. Tamed but excited, they took their place next to the throne. The Queen, too, was excited beyond measure, knowing how monumental the day was, *A time to mend wounds, rejoice, and exalt Great Britain's newfound hero.* As Victoria's beloved Tennyson proclaimed, *Ring out wild bells across the land!*

Dignitaries, officials, generals, and ambassadors were neatly compacted in rows to both sides of the aisle, a long, red carpet separating the two, all attending at the request of the Queen. Remaining supercilious, they were discreetly appalled with such a ceremony. Whereas the commoners, literally on the other side of the fence, pressed against the black-speared gates, elated beyond measure.

Rachel was seated near the front. Her season for mourning was over, and she was now dressed for the occasion. Barely able to contain her joy, she knew Lady Bradshaw would have cherished this moment. Casting a glance throughout the gathering, there was a somber mood. *Why were they not embracing such a joyous occasion?* She then caught sight of Lord Byron seated across the aisle. Their eyes met. He gave a soft smile and a reassuring nod. Looking to the rear of the cathedral, she could see Cedric patiently waiting. More majestic than ever.

Bosun Oscar Bluthers stood tall. Donned in the Royal Navy's best (a uniform most assuredly above his rank), he was as stalwart as a tin soldier. Proud as a peacock, eyes remaining front and center, everything was *buttoned up* from top to bottom. *To think he would soon be standing before the Queen herself!* Bursting with pride, he could barely keep from pinning a smile from ear to ear, let alone gushing forth with his incessant blather. But *button-up* was the order of the day, and button-up it would be. Cedric, too, remained stoically poised, a royal leash connecting the pair.

All stood as the procession moved down the aisle, a young officer to either side, fading two steps behind. Stopping just short of the throne, they remained at attention. All was silent, the Queen's dogs watching their every move.

The Queen rose and commenced: "Knighthood is the greatest honor our nation can bestow upon an individual. It is granted to someone who has far surpassed his call of duty to God, Queen, and country." The acoustics within the cathedral carried her every word. Looking at Cedric, she added, "And, in this case, even the chivalrous deeds of a dog."

Cedric drew closer to the throne as if comprehending her words, wagging his tail with his head bowed in deference. At which time, the Queen's small companions did away with protocol, leaping down and doing a merry dance around the large and gentle creature. Queen Victoria smiled and called them to her side.

"Bestowing knighthood upon those who have shown exceptional merit has been part of our centuries-old tradition. Sacrifice and an undaunted heroism are what we Britons esteem." The morning sun crowned her in a golden aura; though stout and diminutive of stature, she was as grand as the cathedral itself. "Much thought has gone into my decision to knight this noble creature to which so many are indebted, one being Bosun Oscar Bluthers. The sole survivor of the *HMS Prince Edward*, he now stands by the side of our beloved Cedric." The Queen paused, mastering the silence. "Most assuredly, we want to maintain our fine traditions. However, today, more from the law of heart than the rule of stone, we will make a slight amendment with our dear Cedric for his remarkable acts of valor." Taking a step forward, "Therefore, I now bestow our highest honor upon him." She let the words sink in as she faced the sea of dignitaries. "There is a clause within our archives stating that, without the ritual of a sword, I may deem it appropriate to bequeath this knighting with nothing more than a warm embrace."

Queen Victoria then proceeded down the several steps, her three dogs bounding around her. Sensing the honor, Cedric instinctively stepped closer. Leaning over, she tenderly wrapped her arms around his broad shoulders with a warm embrace. It was done to perfection, partially due to the Queen's small stature and Cedric's large proportions. Rising, she proclaimed, "On behalf of all Great Britain, I invest upon Cedric the Order of St. Michael and St. George for his undaunting valor. All for the good of our Commonwealth." One of the officers stepped forward and handed her the medallion with its gilded chain, which she tenderly draped around Cedric's shoulders. At this silent and tender moment, the assembly of skeptics and antiquated mindsets began to soften, the stone walls crumbling down as one and all gave a heartfelt, "Hear. Hear".

Boson Bluthers and Cedric took an about-face and proceeded back down the aisle, the two officers several steps behind. With a constrained smile, the proud sailor could not help but let his eyes wander from left to right and back again, believing the honor was as much for him. Finally, near the last row, he broke rank and, turning from side to side, began thanking everyone for coming. Fortunately, the ceremony had ended, and the unauthorized antics were lost in the shuffle. Cedric waited stoically, receiving a flurry of pats and adulations from the dignitaries as they passed by. All the while, Bosun Bluthers blathered on.

It had been arranged for Rachel to escort Cedric to her place when the ceremony ended. Waiting patiently for the flood of praise to pass and the last of the dignitaries had left, she led Cedric outside, the medallion still draped around his shoulders. The commoners, pressed against the gates, finally had the opportunity to see their hero and were thrilled beyond measure. Two orderlies then assisted in prodding Sir Cedric into the carriage. The moment proved entertaining as they witnessed the monumental task of hoisting the noble creature into the door. The orderlies stooped low, raised his hindquarters on their shoulders, and heaved with all their might. Cedric assisted as best he could, furiously paddling with his front paws. Fortunately, the dignitaries had all departed, for it was an undignified procedure indeed. All the while, the crowd laughed uproariously.

Rachel entered from the other side, and the carriage departed. Consuming an entire seat, Cedric's head protruded from the window, responding to the crowd's exaltations with a splash of his rosy tongue and flapping his tail vigorously from side to side. Passing by the masses, he looked at them with his innocent, loving expression; many hands reached out to touch him as if royalty was passing by.

Rachel glowed. The ride afforded her the time to study this newly acclaimed hero of all Great Britain. Coming to rest in the seat, Cedric returned her stare, the medallion still draped around his shoulders. She sensed he knew far more than she perceived. He also made for good company.

Thomas and Faith awaited them, Muffet running forward to embrace Cedric. Rachel removed the gilded chain as Muffet took hold of him and scampered away. Rachel then shared all the events of the glorious ceremony. Thomas and Faith eventually mentioned their desire to visit the orphanage.

The next day an appointment had been arranged. Rachel provided her carriage but remained behind. However, Muffet would go along, as she had come to know her way around the facility quite well.

"For the oppression of the poor... now will I arise, saith the Lord." Psalm 12:5 KJV

....

Chapter 73

"Take me! Take me!"

At noon the following day, the coach arrived at the orphanage. Greeted by several staff members, Thomas and Faith were directed to the dining hall as the children were having their noonday meal. The hall was large, compressed with orphans seated at long tables. Muffet was released and quickly merged in with the other children. Thomas and Faith stood in awe at the overflow of boys and girls. Everything was orderly. Looking over the sea of faces, they realized selecting just one would be most difficult. If it were humanly possible, they would take them all. Passing by each row, innocent eyes silently watched their every move as if imploring, *Take me! Take me!* It seemed so unfair. Almost cruel.

The couple remained for several hours. Stalled, indecisive, and overwhelmed, they returned to Westminster with the decision still weighing heavily on their hearts. That evening, they walked through the park with Rachel and Muffet, Cedric tethered to the side of Thomas, who continued to draw the attention and praise of passersby.

The couple aired out their deep concern with Rachel. After much consideration, they agreed to adopt three children; Faith would select two, preferably a brother and sister, Thomas the other. That was the best they could do for now.

Thomas and Faith met with the director in his office the following day. A pleasant elderly man, bespectacled and balding, he was neatly attired in a tweed suit. After jotting down a few notes, he handed the paper to an assistant and waited patiently. Half past the hour, the assistant returned with two siblings: a boy and his little sister, ages five and three, respectively. Bewildered, the children remained silent with downcast eyes. Faith remembered how shame and brokenness had been an integral part of her own poverty after their father died. Looking into those innocent faces, she knew the hurt with that feeling of rejection, the ill-conceived notion she had been abandoned. If not for Nora, she and her sister would most likely have found themselves in a similar situation as these two little ones. She saw beauty, even a sense of purity, in the siblings. Giving them a reassuring smile, she said to the director, "They will be fine. Thank you. We will take them." Bending down, she introduced herself.

"I think you have made a good decision. We'll draw up the papers and have them ready within the hour." He said.

The woman soon returned with another boy, several years older. Frowning, with freckled face and amber hair, his head was downcast as he shuffled his feet. Thomas immediately liked him. He was tough-looking, the type of boy he would love to work with. Like Faith, he gave a quick nod of approval. The names of the younger pair were John and Mary. The older boy was Patrick. All three were Irish. With an instant family and a full carriage, they returned to Westminster, Muffet squeezing into the mix.

Cedric greeted them with licks and wags of his tail upon their arrival. The children immediately began hugging and petting him. Muffet then led them throughout the rooms to play.

The next several days passed by amiably. At the appointed time, the palace sent a coach to return Thomas and Faith to Sheppey. Being quite cramped, Rachel decided to keep Cedric. He would be a good companion for Muffet and allow her to become better acquainted with him. Giving them a warm farewell, Rachel said she would soon return home.

Muffet remained in the hands of the orphanage throughout the weeks. At last, Rachel found time behind her easel. She decided to do another painting of Crimpus. *So much to say in that simple face.* Cedric proved to be the best of company. The only intrusion within these pristine hours was the ongoing flow of visitors–dignitaries and reporters desiring to meet Sir Cedric. Rachel's coachman was put to the task, frequently bathing and brushing him to make him presentable. She humorously mused that he was beginning to look more like a show dog than that rugged dog she remembered on the pier.

During the morning and evening hours, they would take long walks throughout the parks, always greeted with an abundance of pats, praise, and animated conversation. Throughout the quiet afternoons, Cedric would saunter up the stairs and rest near the easel, patiently watching her every brushstroke. Not intrusive; he never placed demands on her. He would give a soft whimper if hungry or desiring to go out. This intimate time revealed far more than Rachel ever expected. She felt he was looking at her with a deep love, and the bonding continued without words. What concerned her, though, was that he was aging. There were now white flecks within the black fur, and he was sleeping more throughout the days. His steps had also slowed. There was often a sadness in his eyes. *Be patient... in time, we will all be going home.*

One afternoon, while studying Cedric's melancholy look, she had an epiphany: "Why don't I take you for a visit to the inner city? Would you like that? The children will love you!" He flopped his tail.

After Muffet was taken to the orphanage on Monday morning, Rachel prepared for the venture by going to the bank and filling her purse with coins. She had completed the second painting of Crimpus, which the coachman had secured to the back of the coach. Then, after much tribulation, Rachel and her elderly assistant managed to hoist Cedric into the carriage.

The team of horses made its way south and over the London Bridge, Cedric's head protruding from the window and making quite a stir as everyone recognized him. The coachman took the familiar turn, proceeding into the dismal depths of the city with the long rows of congested houses, broken windows, and empty doors.

Heads began rising, people vaguely remembering the sound of those clopping hooves. Older generations peered from windows. Smiles surfaced, and some heads nodded as a flood of children scurried out of every crevice. Cedric began wagging his tail fervently.

Crimpus was standing in his doorway. Rachel tapped for the driver to pull over. The old Irishman's smile broadened. The coachman opened the door, and Cedric leaped to the ground, immediately immersed in children pressing in and trying to lay claim to him. He was not only big and strong but loveable. Never had they seen such a fine creature. Ironically, not a soul knew of his acclaim, for news rarely found its way into such a place. The children kept reaching out, trying to pet him and give him hugs. Cedric obliged, licking little hands and faces. Rachel noticed his youthful energy had returned.

She opened her purse and began distributing the coins. Within the animated flurry, the bag was soon empty. She requested the coachman to retrieve the painting and presented it to Crimpus. Looking at it with the same ongoing smile, he gave a slight nod. Others came out of the house, arms folded and nodding. "At's 'im all right." Rachel requested the coachman to hand it to them, knowing full well it would be nailed on some paint-chipped wall or placed in a corner.

Wading through the masses, the coachman held the door open. Cedric extended his body and fumbled with his front paws, struggling to enter. The coachman obligingly bent low and did his best to prod him along. Older boys quickly came to his aid and shoved Cedric into the cabin with a burst of energy and a hearty heave-ho. Everyone laughed a peal of laughter that had been vacant for countless years.

Cedric's head protruded from the window as the horses slowly galloped away. He then gave out several loud barks, echoing in the streets. *What an irony!* Rachel thought. *The first time I have ever heard him do that.*

....

Chapter 74

An Eager Queue

Claude Percival's article was finally put to press. The headlines of the *London Illustrated News* read, "'Ol' Cedie Boy'–Hero of Great Britain." It was all the more enhanced with illustrations by the noted Miss Rachel Thomson. To date, the edition was Mr. Percival's proudest accomplishment, and the sales were record-breaking.

A courier eventually made his way south by southwest to Sheppey, delivering a stack of the weekly tribune to the doorstep of the Wayfarer Inn. The papers were then proudly displayed on the counter in the lobby with a sign, *One Sixpence*. By late morning, villagers and fishermen were pressed in a queue that meandered out the door and down the muddied path. Even Mrs. Filmore and Roger had merged within the bedraggled line, everyone with a sixpence in hand.

During the pleasant midday hours, many of the villagers could be seen outside their cottages seated on crates or rickety chairs with the weekly spread wide. Even the eyes of the illiterate were pressed to the pages, relishing the familiar images illustrated by the young Rachel. Mrs. Filmore took it upon herself to have reading sessions for those who stopped by the shop. The scene throughout the village on that sunny day was the closest thing to a library that Sheppey had ever known.

The editor-in-chief concluded his article by stating that Sheppey was a quaint little village nestled on the channel, a stone's throw from the estuary of the mighty Thames and a delightful getaway from the fast pace of London. Furthermore, the stay at the Wayfarer Inn was *most pleasant indeed.* Mr. Percival concluded with an epicurean touch: *And Pinky's mutton stew was the best I have ever tasted!*

....

Chapter 75

Disfavor

Rachel continued to fill her hours behind the easel, working on countless portraits of those precious souls within the city. In late summer of 1852, she submitted *Crimpus* in the prestigious annual exhibit at the London Royal Academy. Ironically, it was accepted not on the merit of style or subject matter but its profound statement. Most assuredly, *Crimpus* was not a thing of beauty nor sublime in lifting one's soul to a higher plane, for that face, in all its crudity, bared itself to the world. Then, again, who would dare hang such a thing upon their walls?

Though *Crimpus* was an affront to the art world, it was juxtaposed next to the best of contemporary masterpieces. And it had its uncanny way of making patrons pause. Redolent in earth colors and bold strokes, the portrait captured him in stark simplicity, and as base as it was, one could not deny its integrity. Lord Byron made his way through the throngs of patrons on the first day of the exhibit and eventually stood before it. Rather unobtrusively, he remained there longer than anyone.

Though it may be true that many people stalled and studied *Crimpus* more than any other work in the exhibit, the judges, born and bred in tradition, bestowed their colorful ribbons and approbations upon more *worthy* paintings–ones that were *truly art*.

Rachel was well acquainted with the mindset of the art world. In a peculiar sort of way, finding it similar to the stubborn mindsets of the villagers in Sheppey. In recent years, she had been tempered by the whims and fancy of critics and held to her convictions. However, she would, at times, be vulnerable, proving to be quite fragile indeed. Yet, she knew full well that fiend of narcissism and being enamored with her works. And who knew the actual value of *Crimpus*? Or, for that matter, her true merit? Despite the whirlwind of opinions and her sway of emotions, *Crimpus* prevailed, standing unashamed amid all the pomp and ceremony.

Several weeks passed. One pleasant Saturday evening, as Lord Byron was taking his stroll, he noticed Rachel and Muffet sitting on a park bench. Rachel smiled and invited him to sit, releasing Muffet to explore the flowers and butterflies.

"It is always good to see you, Lord Byron. A pleasant evening, is it not?"

"Yes, indeed." There was a pause. "I would like to say, Rachel, that your *Crimpus* painting is exceptional. Actually, I consider it to be one of the most profound paintings I have ever seen. Going to Holland proved to be a good investment."

"Thank you."

"Don't take it personally that it was not awarded a medal. You know how these things go. I've known the nature of the beast for quite some time." He gently touched her hand, "You are far better than they perceive. Remember–you are no longer painting for the pleasure of others. Your heart and brilliance now direct the hand that holds your brushes. Be patient. Times are changing."

Rachel's eyes were downcast.

"The last time I visited your studio, I noticed quite a collection of *Crimpuses*. How many have you completed?"

"Twenty-one." Muffet was immersed in a garden with fireflies blinking in the darker pockets of the hedges.

"I see..." He thought for a moment. "I have a splendid idea. Why don't we put together a show? Here in Westminster? It may prove to be quite remarkable."

Immediately, there was a myriad of unsettling thoughts. *It would be another lesson in futility. Why go through the effort if I already know the outcome? Too much time and labor, let alone the unnecessary pain and frustration.* She then began to settle in a more positive direction. *Why not? Did she or did she not believe in herself? And this remarkable man is such an encouragement.* Rachel softly replied, "That will be fine."

"Splendid." He raised himself on his cane. "I will be in touch. In the meantime, keep doing what you are doing."

Watching him make his way through the park, she realized how rare he was, the likes of whom would only pass her way once in a lifetime. There was always a sense of comfort in his company.

Lord Byron's exhibit was set for early autumn. Although Rachel was well aware of his prestige and great influence, the exhibit proved exceptional. The hall was spacious, with hanging candelabras and excellent lighting to showcase her paintings.

Opening night overflowed with London's best, donned in black ties and eloquent gowns, servants with hors d'oeuvres and champagne trays, weaving in and out of animated clusters. A wind ensemble played in the background. Rachel was an accent on the evening, as splendid as a neo-classical painting. There were familiar faces–acquaintances of Lady Bradshaw's and others she had become acquainted with from portrait sessions. Miss Thomson remained pleasant but subtly detached.

Twenty-four paintings were exhibited in all. Lord Byron had requested the painting of Cedric to be hung along with his Dutch landscape. Neither was for sale. By now, all of London was aware of Cedric's heroics, which was the highlighted centerpiece. There was another work, more a side note that was discreetly exhibited – for Lord Byron also requested the portrait of the young officer to be on display.

The paintings remained on exhibit for a week. However, it was the opening soiree that would reveal its measure of success, and, unfortunately, the bare face of poverty proved, once again, to be too coarse a statement, and none were sold. That is, save for *Crimpus*. As fate would have it, an emissary of the Queen arrived. Was it the Queen's statement of her empathy for the impoverished souls within the slums or her aesthetic taste that stirred the sale? It should be noted that she had visited the exhibit at the Academy one evening after its doors were closed and studied *Crimpus* undeterred. Most likely, she knew it had indeed captured the heart of the destitute.

The Dutch landscape generated some interest, with several guests inquiring about Miss Thomson's availability to do a landscape of their estates. Naturally, the painting of Cedric received the most significant response, with more than a handful of requests for animal portraits. The portrait of Captain Sumpter drew little attention.

Rachel thanked Lord Byron the final evening and bid him a good night. The carriage ride was one of solitude and reflection, her heart heavy again. It was far too personal. A soft rain was falling, and the city lay quiet; the warm glow of lamps within the homes added to her sense of isolation.

She was thankful for the honor of having the Queen purchase *Crimpus*. The requests for landscape paintings, along with the praise of *Cedric,* were encouraging. Yet the pain of rejection was like a dead weight. She felt empty and alone. Thank God for Nora and Muffet. The rain fell late into the night.

....

"Plus ca change, plus c'est la meme change."
French Proverb

....

Chapter 76

A New Season

Rachel's heart was set on returning home. However, the transition from one world to another would take longer than anticipated with planning, packing, and placing the house in order. Transporting her studio alone was overwhelming. There was a sense of apathy in her steps, so many emotions compacted within the years in London. However, it was a definitive farewell as the house was put up for sale.

The day drew nigh, her faithful coachman having packed and strapped crates upon the carriage. The painting of Cedric was also brought along and secured to the rear. It was the only thing she had taken from the Bradshaw estate.

With everything ready, it was time to perform the monumental task of hoisting Cedric into the coach. Though he had braved countless storms with many an undaunted leap into the sea, he could not jump. It was an inability that always had its touch of humor, save for with the coachman, that is. Not getting any younger, he dreaded the thought of heave-hoeing the heavy-coated leviathan into the carriage. Muffet was more than willing to assist. Resigning himself to the task proved to be an extraordinary accomplishment as the unlikely pair managed to pry him in, Cedric doing his part by paddling fervently with his front paws.

With a great sigh of relief, the venerable coachman knew it would be the last time he would have to perform such a duty.

Cedric situated himself on the entire seat, consuming the space from side to side. Muffet joyfully squirmed in. Rachel was amused seeing them pressed together, Cedric's large head jutting out the window and his tail sweeping across his small companion, adding another note of humor to the departure.

The ride across the country road was long and arduous, but no one seemed to mind. Cedric looked out upon the farmlands and lapped the air, Muffet being just as preoccupied looking out the other window. Rachel observed Cedric, from time to time, giving a low whimper. *Did he know they were going home?*

By late afternoon, the cottage was in sight, perched upon the same hill and dappled with sheep. As the French would say, *Plus ca change, plus c'est la meme chose.* Though so much had changed within her life, the scene was just as it had always been: every rock and tree, every rolling hill–even the sheep seemed the same. *How long had it been?* Pleasant memories continued... She now knew she had made the right decision.

Cedric was the first to leap from the carriage. Exiting quite effortlessly, he was greeted by Nora. After tender strokes and praise, she turned her attention to the little girl, coaxing her in the same manner and admiring her ladylike demeanor. Though Muffet was much younger than Rachel when she had first arrived, there was something similar in their nature.

Nora rose and gave Rachel a long-overdue embrace, silently expressing how good it was to have her home. Rachel was pleased to see she still had that sparkle in her eyes with that insightful wisdom and had maintained that natural beauty. However, she seemed frailer, and her movements, like Cedric's, had slowed. Rachel's assistance and having Muffet around would do her good. Nora was also studying Rachel. No longer the blossom of youth, she had been tempered by the years and evolved into a matured beauty.

Thomas and Faith stood by the door. The children hurried out and surrounded Cedric, who followed with an overflowing abundance of persuasion as they scampered out on the hillside.

Thomas assisted the coachman in tending to the horses and bringing in the luggage as Faith prepared dinner. The painting of Cedric was placed over the mantel. Nora paused. It was the first painting she had ever seen by Rachel. There he was, majestically poised upon the pier, the suggestion of a ship and seagulls in the distance. She admired the brushstrokes and the mastery of tones. The colors, though limited, were rich. Nora had appreciated countless masterpieces while visiting museums in years past, and Rachel's painting held its own. To think– she would now have the opportunity to watch the entire process. "My dear, you have come so far."

"It's good to be home. And I know you will come to love our dear little Muffet."

"I do believe we will have to give her a more suitable name, though. *Muffet* seems rather inappropriate for such a sweet child." Rachel agreed. But that would be for another time.

Throughout the evening, Rachel unpacked, organized, and planned. There was much to take in. The cottage was tidy, the gardens well-kept, and the view of Sheppey in the distance held the fondest of memories.

The children returned, exhilarated, laughing, and exhausted. Cedric helped himself to a large bowl of water and rested by the potbelly stove. Nora invited the coachman to join them for dinner, the children being served around the campfire. Thomas said grace with a few heartfelt words. Everyone then dined on roast mutton.

Late in the evening, Thomas hitched up Mr. Wilson and headed home with his family. The coachman spent the night at the cottage. He would be returning to Westminster in the morning. There would be many trips to follow.

Rachel's lines had fallen on pleasant places. Ensconced in the peace of nature and comforted by being home, she set to the task at hand. In a matter of days, she hired several men to construct her studio. It was to be adjacent to the cottage and, weather permitting, would be completed before winter. A wood-burning stove was to be on one side, with a large window facing the panoramic view of Sheppey and the sea.

The days began fading into winter; the air was brisk, and the sky laden with those all-too-familiar heavy clouds. The coachman made his final trip, delivering the last of Rachel's paintings and supplies along with the unfinished portrait of Captain Sumpter. Seeing it for the first time in many months was like being reacquainted with an old friend. *But if the while I think on thee...*

The studio was completed before winter set in. Paints and brushes were ready, and a new excitement stirred within her. It had been a long time since she had been behind the easel, and countless paintings were now envisioned, the first of which was the landscape outside the window. A light snow began falling as she began brushing in the scene.

While sharing a pot of tea with Nora and watching Cedric outside with Muffet, Nora commented on how his movements had slowed one afternoon. She mentioned he was also sleeping more throughout the day.

Rachel had hesitated to take him to the village, believing he had served his purpose well and it would be cruel to allow him to return to the pier. Though her thinking was rational and for the best, there was no denying he was an integral part of the village, within the heart and soul of everyone.

Cedric could often be seen lying by the door, his head resting on his paws with that imploring look, often giving a low whimper. Rachel played over such sentiments but knew he had to be taken to town. *How can I deny you? Especially with that look. We'll go. But only for a visit. And no going onto the pier!*

The day was bleak and windy as Rachel hitched up Mr. Wilson. Then came the arduous task of hoisting Cedric into the wagon. With a little ingenuity, she placed several crates on the ground, and with a little persuasion and assistance from Muffet, he lumbered up and aboard.

Rachel placed Cedric's medallion around his shoulders and told Muffet to remain at home.

Mr. Wilson was also slowing with age, and the journey to Sheppey was at his own pace. At times, Rachel missed her coach. In all fairness, though, she had released her faithful coachman, bequeathing him a healthy stipend along with the carriage and horses. *All for the best.* The hour was tentative. A storm seemed to be brooding upon the sky.

....

Chapter 77

With Deep Remorse

⎯⎯⎯⎯

The broad stretch of sea and sky greeted her. The little church had remained stalwart; its cross, though bowed and worn, still proclaimed the presence of God. Dark clouds loomed on the horizon. Seagulls tossed about in the wind. Rachel would have to make it a brief visit.

Heading up the muddied path, she noticed everything had remained the same, bereft of color–a painting in its own right. In recent years, she had been saturated with fashions, lavish dresses, a palette of vibrant colors, and the burst of blossoms within the parks. Yet, Sheppey continued to hold its own inspiration.

Cedric immediately came to life, chomping at the wind, his tail wagging with renewed enthusiasm. The villagers were battening down and overjoyed when they saw him. More surfaced from their cottages. There were no wreaths to cast upon their returning hero, just smiles and lowly nods.

Rachel pulled in the reins, allowing them to admire his medallion and bestow their praise. *There was change... so evident... these once hard-hearted people had softened.* Unbiased, Cedric responded with tender licks upon every hand that touched him. *Who has ever loved them like this?*

As soon as they reached the Inn, Cedric leaped from the wagon. Its battered sign flapping in the wind. Rachel looked through the window. A blazing fire was in the hearth, and several tables were occupied, people she had never seen before. Having a seat by the window, she took off Cedric's medallion, and he made his way to the hearth. The guests became animated, cupping a hand and disclosing in half-whispers, *It's him!* A distinguished lady approached him and spoke a few kind words.

Rachel studied the sea. The surging surf was coming hard against the pier, and she knew the hour was tentative. She turned her attention to her drawings still hanging on the wall. *They held their own over time.* She heard the familiar thump and shuffle. Turning, Pinky was hobbling her way, a glass of port in one hand, his white hair still held in place by the same old tattered cap, that smile always accenting the patch.

"Fer me most fav'rite lady." He placed the glass in front of her. Like Crimpus, countless stories were etched within the creases and wrinkles, and that good eye still held its sparkle. His smile broadened. "Oh, ter see the sun smil'n on such ah dreary day." Pulling up a chair, he awkwardly took a seat. Cedric rose and came to his side. She showed him the medallion and began sharing all the details of his knighthood. Pride overwhelmed Pinky.

The conversation took its familiar course as he began filling in many of the blanks throughout her absence–the shipwrecks and all the rescues. He told of Captain Hawkins and the three lifeboats, along with the amazing story of Miss Gertrude's religious transformation and that of Agnes as well. "Ev'n attend'n church." Leaning in, he commented, "Mus' say—ol' tarts certn'ly changed." He added, "Mus Agnes pass'd 'way two years 'go." Continuing... Business was on the up. Ever since the story in that London paper, curiosity-seekers *'av been com'n down fer a look'n see.* Shortly after Cedric was knighted, a young couple from London, *entreepreenoors 'ey was,* had taken a liking to the place and purchased the Inn, *fix'n it up a mite.* The rooms filled during summer, and everyone enjoyed his mutton stew. Young families were even coming down from the city to work. On a sadder note, Bertie had not been up to snuff. *T'was tak'n 'eets toll on ol' Jarvis.*

Rachel stared out the window. The sky was foreboding, whitecaps agitating the sea and whipping spray into the air. She knew bringing him to the village was a bad choice, even for a brief visit.

Cedric went to the door and gave a soft whimper. There was a dreaded moment of silence. She knew his imploration. A tear surfaced in her eye. *How could she deny him his purpose?* Giving a slight nod, Pinky rose, made his way to the door, and released Cedric. The wind was blowing furiously, waves relentlessly hammering the pilings as he slowly made his way to the end of the pier. Cedric came to rest and set his face like an old lion toward the sea. The structure teetered precariously. Rachel felt a deep dread. *It would have been best to have left him at home. Then again, she realized he had been created for such a time as this. Sheppey was his home, and this was his legacy.*

Pinky urged her to stay and wait out the storm. However, she thought it best to go while there was still time. Folding Cedric's medallion and placing it into her satchel, she pulled out the silver crucifix given to her by Lord Byron, laid it on the table, smiled, and departed. He studied it for a moment. Perplexed, he had never considered such a thing except when he saw that rosary in Bertie's hand. Placing it aside, he watched Rachel board the wagon and make her way southward. Fortunately, the wind was behind her.

The rain came down hard, and the storm beat against the coast. The wind eerily made its way through the seams of the window, and soon everything became a blur. As best as Pinky could tell, Cedric was within the vertigo of the swirling sea and sky. Buttoning up, he headed outside.

Bent low, hands pressed against the cane, he pushed on against the fury of the wind. The sea was at full strength, waves crashing over the pier. A plank loosened, flying recklessly in the air. He stopped. Cedric was poised like an old sentry. Pinky wanted to go farther, but wisdom prevailed, knowing full well that his days of bravado were behind him.

Cedric rose to his feet, his eyes intently focused somewhere to the northeast. Pinky had a suspicion that a vessel was in distress. Raising his cane, the wind howling around him, he yelled out a final salutation, one old soldier to another, "Cedie boy!" Cedric did not hear him. Pinky remained motionless, shoulders bent into the gale. Bleary-eyed, he vaguely saw Cedric leap. He then turned and made his way back to the tavern.

....

"But thou who rulest the raging of the sea and stills the waves thereof when they arise, rise up and help me."

Thomas à Kempis

....

Chapter 78

"Women and children first!"

History recorded the events of the sinking of the *HMS Birkenhead*. It's tragic demise happened while transporting British soldiers and family members homeward. A squall had caught the vessel unawares off the coast of Africa. With tattered sails whipping in the wind and the ship taking on water, the captain bellowed, "Abandon ship!" To his dismay, he quickly realized there were not enough lifeboats. Considering all the grief-stricken women and children on board, he gave another order, though now directed at his troops. Raising his voice above the wind, he commanded, "Stand fast!" followed by a resounding, "Women and children first!"

The men formed their ranks, line upon line, and remained steadfast as the storm beat against them. Stalwart for God, Queen, and country, no one broke formation as they watched their families being placed into the lifeboats. Weeping and in deep anguish, women and children reached out to husbands and fathers left behind. The soldiers continued to look on, front and center, as the boats were lowered upon the sea. Brave beyond measure, they all went down with the *HMS Birkenhead*. Records state that not a woman or child was lost.

The message of the valor on the *HMS Birkenhead* swept across the sea and settled within the heart of Great Britain. It would not be long before the Royal Navy made an ethical proclamation that whenever a naval vessel was going down, the command would be given, "Women and children first!"

The *HMS Wellington* was a forty-eight-gun frigate. It, too, was transporting British troops and family members to the port in London. The voyage from India had been long and pleasant enough. Then, just as the vessel neared the coast of England, it succumbed to the wrath of nature. Pounded mercilessly by an unforgiving storm, its sails blowing hopelessly in the wind as waves crashed over the bulwarks. The lifeboats were made ready. The captain hesitated. Looking around at all his good men, he knew full well of the recent proclamation and, with a heavy heart, bellowed out, "Women and children first!" (Was it the wind that put a tear upon his cheek?) He then commanded, "Men, form your ranks and hold firm!" The troops assembled rank and file, obliquely watching their wives and children being lowered into the sea, grieving members of their families weeping uncontrollably. The lifeboats drifted away as the *HMS Wellington* took its final journey to the bottom of the sea.

Sadly, this ineffable act of bravery would be all for naught as the lifeboats, tossed about in the rough seas, also went asunder, children and wives meeting with the same sorrowful fate as husbands and fathers. That is, save for one...

A little girl, a dangling remnant of this travesty, was holding fast to the sides of a half-submerged lifeboat, its aft laden with water, crying and terrified as it began to sink; her head barely breaching the waves as the little one flapped her arms frantically. Then, a large, furry creature appeared alongside the frantic child. Coughing, splashing, and weeping, she took hold of its collar.

As fate would have it, a wave passed over them, miraculously placing her onto the creature's large back, and, like some little princess in a fairy tale, she held tightly, weeping all the way. In the years to come, some would say it was a guardian angel that had saved her life.

....

Chapter 79

𝔉𝔯𝔞𝔪𝔢𝔡 𝔦𝔫 𝔖𝔢𝔞𝔰𝔥𝔢𝔩𝔩𝔰

T he storm did its damage and moved inland. The sea returned to calm, though the sky remained a steel gray, and all became peacefully still. Pinky was the first to notice that the pier was gone. Like broken teeth, a few pilings remained as a solemn reminder. There had been no sign of Cedric.

Pinky made his way north along the coast. It was low tide, and the beach was strewn with telltale flotsam. Limping over the carnage of halyards and shattered planks, lifeless bodies washed in and out of the waves, many bearing the red uniform of the British army.

He stopped, all but stumbling over a body–a little girl. Petite, like some ceramic doll framed within a wreath of seaweed and shells, her flesh was the tone of marble. Three gulls circled overhead, white against the pale sky as if crying out a lamentation. Pinky thought how cruel death was. It was not meant for such a little one but for men in battle or those who had had their fair share of years. Large dog prints were circumventing the body that faded into the surf. Looking out upon the sea, he knew it was the final vestige of Cedric.

Bending over, he struggled to lift the little one. The body was still soft and warm, and she was breathing! Pinky dropped his cane. Staggering, the load was too arduous for his aging bones, and he awkwardly laid her back on the sand. Lifting her again, he stumbled toward the Inn, almost falling. Jarvis was in the distance, excitedly coming toward him.

Lurching forward, Pinky all but cast the child into his arms. Like a pair of old bookends, stalwart in battle and friendship, they made their way south, carrying the only survivor of the *HMS Wellington.*

....

Chapter 80

"'Aven't seen 'im."

Mildred arose early the next morning and peeked outside. A few drops of rain were still dripping from the roof. She had seen Cedric pass by the previous day in the back of the wagon, but Rachel was gone before she had time to scurry out. And she knew full well, with a storm coming, Cedric would be traipsing out to the end of the pier. There was an unsettled grief as she prepared to make her way north.

The morning was inviting, with little wind and a soft gray sky upon the sky. Roger was smoking his pipe, taking in the aftermath. She gave a pleasant nod and continued on her way. The path was dappled with large puddles and windblown objects. Prevailing with a merry heart and not a day younger, she was thankful she could still make the journey north. The sun made its way through the veil of clouds and cast its warmth upon the village. Pausing and squinting, she looked up the beach. The pier seemed to have vanished. *Must be seeing things.* Trudging onward, Cedric continued to weigh heavy upon her heart.

Traversing the puddles as best she could, Mildred finally arrived at the Inn. The sign over the door hung from one hinge, and debris was scattered everywhere. Weary, she sat on a wooden crate to catch her breath. And then a grievous moan, *Oh, dear...* The pier was indeed gone.

"'Aven't seen 'im, Millie." Sammy was standing by her side. "Not hide nor hair. A frig'te went down to the nor' east. British naval vessel it was.

Pinky an' Jarvis retrieved a young'un. Litt'l girl... still 'live. Sure took its toll on the ol' pier." Mildred remained silent. Grief-stricken, she knew her dearly beloved Mats was gone. Tears made everything blur.

Slowly rising, she said, "Tell Miss Bertie we will be praying for her and that dear child. If Cedric returns, please let me know." Bidding him farewell, she headed in the direction from whence she came.

Sammy watched her go homeward, the sun casting its light upon the diminutive figure. Turning and looking north across the sea, he imagined where the vessel had gone down. The coast was windswept. Sandpipers danced in and out of the lapping waves, the sea sparkling in the sunlight.

···

"And now, the hand that traces these words falters, as it approaches the conclusion of its task and would weave, for a little longer space, the thread of these adventures."

Charles Dickens

···

Chapter 81

Fading Footprints

W hat is a miracle? Is it not some intangible that stirs one's imagination to greater heights and blurs the edges of reality? Then again, is it not something mysteriously tangible that man can put his finger to? Miracles come in disproportionate sizes, as great as the parting of the Red Sea or as small as the little girl who survived the sinking of the *HMS Wellington*. Lo and behold, the child was not only the lone survivor of the shipwreck and safely delivered to shore by a dog, but there was ne'er a touch of frostbite on her frail little body.

And so, another soul was stranded on the shores of Sheppey and delivered to the Inn. Though ailing, Bertie rose to the occasion, doing her best to care for the child. Drying her off and wrapping blankets around her tender body, she cradled her in her arms and prayed. Though racked with trauma, the child rested peacefully. In time her eyes would open. A nervous blink. Bertie stroked her hair and whispered, "You are blessed by the Lord."

Pinky drew near. He reasoned her to be no more than three or four years of age. "What be yer name, lassie?"

Her eyes twitched and wandered around the room. Then a low murmur: "Momma."

He tried again. "Momma... Momma." Too young for words, they would possibly never know her name–or, for that matter, the tale of the sinking of the *HMS Wellington*. Her eyes continued blinking as she looked at him innocently.

He then surmised, "We'll call yer Mus Winkie."

Though the child now had a name, it was far removed from a true identity, and throughout the ensuing days, she would remain disconnected from the world and any next of kin. For *Mus Winkie* was nothing more than another castaway in the inextricable web of industry, wars, and shipwrecks and invariably would be lost in the shuffle.

The port authorities had made a feeble attempt to sort things out. Complicating matters, however, were the immigrant families that had boarded the vessel in Lisbon, making a search for the child's identity through the civil registrations and customs registers all but impossible. If truth be told, who really cared? Most likely, a clerk within the lower tier of things was assigned the task. Quite possibly, late one afternoon, with countless reams of records piled before him and no one looking over his shoulder, he nonchalantly placed the child's paperwork into a heap with other unresolved papers and muttered, *Whatever.*

Several days after the storm passed, a vessel arrived and anchored in the cove. Serious-minded authorities set to the task once again of logging the various details and tending to the deceased who had washed ashore. There was little concern for the proper whereabouts of Miss Winkie, the streets of London being glutted with such. Stamped *Unknown,* the issue was resolved, conveniently letting her remain in the care of the innkeepers. As the vessel departed, Pinky held the little girl's hand as they followed the dignitaries to the cove and watched the ship sail up the Thames.

Late in the day, Pinky made his way to the beam. It was a painful moment of reflection. He then took out his knife and carved a final notch. There would be a mental asterisk, though, marking the end of an era, the beam now holding all the tales from beginning to end. Like an ancient scribe scripting upon a scroll, he had documented them well, every jot and tittle of each also logged within his mind. In time, the marks upon the beam would seem like fables. There was not another soul on the face of the earth who knew these actual events–that is, save for Jarvis and Bertie.

Putting away his knife, he opened the door and looked out at the remnants of the pier–*Cedric's memorial*. With the waning years, the sea would take that too, immersing the remaining pilings in its vast caldron, laying it to rest with all the other broken planks and masts in that bottomless graveyard. All fading memories–just like Cedric's footprints in the sand.

....

Chapter 82

The Solace of Silence

W ith the ebb and flow of the tides, flotsam continued to make its way to shore. Still no sign of Cedric. Several days passed before Nora and Rachel hitched up Mr. Wilson and took Muffet to the village. Mrs. Filmore immediately commenced in telling of the shipwreck and the rescue of that dear child: *She is now in the care of Jarvis and Bertie. No one has claimed poor thing! Yes, as you can see, the pier is gone. And so it seems is our dear Cedric. Many of the villagers have been weeping these past few days. Bertie's health is fading, and Jarvis is wrought with grief. Pinky has been given more responsibilities and is also caring for the child. Never one to complain, it is quite apparent he no longer has the energy for such a task, nor is he gifted with the tender ways of mother-hood. Dear man is taking care of her as best he can, attempting to dress her in the morning, brushing her hair, and preparing meals. Her name is Lee-sha, or something like that. He nicknamed her Miss Winkie. Said she is beginning to speak a few more words like Pa-Pa. The new proprietors are in London and in the process of hiring a staff. But for now, everything is in his hands.*

Mrs. Filmore was a run-on sentence, "Pinky was the first to find her, strewn on the beach like a fallen angel. All but given up for dead. Cedric's footprints were all around her and faded into the sea. No one has seen him since."

Muffet listened attentively. It was the saddest expression Rachel had seen on her face since those initial days in the slums. Rachel also had a deeper, more empty feeling, grieving all the more over her fateful decision to take him to town and let him return to the pier. There had been a unique bond since his stay in Westminster. And how proud she was when he was knighted, not to mention his special bond with Muffet.

Late in the day, Rachel returned to her easel, working on another landscape outside her window, her escape whenever deeply troubled. It was a cold day, and the studio fended well against the cold with the wood-burning stove. She had come to cherish the stark beauty of winter and the vista of undulating hills and sea before her. *A world apart from Westminster.* She glanced over at the painting of Captain Sumpter, the gray light of day making the colors all the more somber.

Her thoughts turned to the little girl. She thought of bringing her home and grafting her into their little family. *It would be good for Muffet.* Upon further consideration, *It would not be fair to Nora. Though all-loving and tenderhearted, she no longer had the energy to tend to another child. Conceivably, it would even be too much for her; raising Muffet, assisting with chores, and painting were consuming. Was there the possibility of placing her in the orphanage? That would be far too impersonal, almost cruel. What else could be done?* She dreaded making another poor decision.

....

Chapter 83

In Full Bloom

⎯⎯⎯⎯

I n time, Mildred visited the grocer's. It was evident to Mrs. Filmore that she was still grieving, and only made matters worse when she told her how much everyone missed Cedric and appreciated Theo ringing the church bell. Packing her goods, Mildred remained silent. Mrs. Filmore went on to mention the poor orphaned girl. "What is to become of her? Bertie is all but bedridden, and the child is totally in Pinky's care."

As fate would have it, Pinky hobbled in with the little girl in hand holding a basket. It was the first time Mildred had laid eyes on her. *Adorable... though quite shoddy. Poor thing–her hair is as matted as Cedric's after a storm. And she is in dire need of new clothing!*

She inquired as to how things were going at the Inn. Keeping a good face, Pinky suggested things could be a wee bit better. She then affronted him, stating she would find a good home for that precious little girl. Would he mind? Pinky's expression told it all, obviously, he had grown fond of her. He then said, "'Tis best."

That evening, Mildred made her way to Thomas's cottage and shared the plight of the child, mentioning she was in a dreadful state, Bertie's health was failing, and Jarvis was too distraught to do much of anything as he remained by her side day and night.

It did not take long for Faith to respond, "Why not bring her here? After all, we still have a vacant bed, and another girl would balance out our family." It was the missing puzzle piece they had been hoping for–a pair of boys and a pair of girls. Thomas smiled and nodded, confirming the decision.

The next day, Thomas rode to Nora's cottage to tell of their decision and requested that Rachel bring the horse and wagon and go with Faith to fetch the little girl. Rachel was much relieved; her concern solved most perfectly.

The following morning, she made her way to Thomas and Faith's cottage, Muffet accompanying her to be part of the welcoming committee. Throughout breakfast, Rachel observed how Faith had matured and how much more she was beginning to resemble their father. It was easy to discern the endearing intimacy within the marriage.

They arrived at the Inn by midday. Pinky was seated by the window, the little girl by his side. She was at peace and seemed to be enjoying his company. Rachel saw how much she resembled Muffet the first time she had seen her on the streets. There was a moment of remorse, considering how good it might have been if she had taken her home. The thought was quickly dismissed as she realized the child would now be in the best of hands. Pinky rose and introduced them.

Sitting around the table, he cheerfully said the child had told him her name was *Leesha*. "Been call'n 'er Mus Winkie."

"That name will never do, Mr. Pinky.", Rachel amiably replied. "A little girl deserves to be called something more ladylike. Though you have good intentions with your notable pet names, there are exceptions to the rule. Possibly, she has been trying to tell you her name is Felicia. Certainly an improvement over 'Mus Winkie.'"

He smiled and nodded. Looking at her with that astute eye, he jested, "Well, yer gots a litt'l 'un yer calls Mus Muffet, do yer?"

"A point well taken. I will certainly address that in the near future."

There was nothing to pack. Pinky said it was the same dress she wore when he carried her from the beach. Though he had washed her clothing, it was to little avail.

As they departed, the child nestled with Muffet between Faith and Rachel. Glancing in the tavern window, Rachel saw a sad expression on Pinky's face, one she had never seen before. For the first time, she realized how alone he was. During the ride, Faith shared with her that she was with child.

Upon arriving, *Mus Winkie* quickly blended in with the other children, following them outside to play in the brisk air, Faith placing a warm coat on her before they scampered out. Late in the day, Rachel headed home, relieved that the child's future was secure. She then considered what Faith had mentioned. A pleasant smile surfaced. Youth was arriving in Sheppey in full bloom.

....

"For Thou hast even ordained angels for the service of man."
Thomas à Kempis

....

Chapter 84

The Eulogy

He rain began falling in early morn as the bell in the belfry gave
out its rusted lamentation. The somber day marked the first time
the church had filled; everyone pressed together in the pews and soaked
to the brim. Pastor Theo mused… N*ot even during the worst of storms
was there such a gathering.*

Mildred was seated in the front row. Nora, Thomas, Faith, Rachel,
the children, and Gertrude filled the remainder of the pew. The fishermen stood to the rear, hats off and heads bowed. There was also Mr.
and Mrs. Filmore (the only ones to arrive with an umbrella). As was
Roger Osborne. The door opened once more as the wind and rain
prodded Pinky inward, nudging into the far pew. *Another irony. How
many times had Mildred invited him to church? To which he always
replied, 'When the storm blows in.'*

As old as the belfry, Theo would make his way to the altar one
more time, Thomas being more than obliging to step aside, knowing his
uncle's eulogy would especially console Mildred, who was still wrought
with grief.

Throughout the years, Theo had observed how much his dear wife
had adored Cedric, loving him like the son they never had. He thought

it rather odd, though, how she called him *Mats*. As time passed, he resigned himself to the simple fact that Cedric was nothing less than an instrument of God—using this amazing creature to save countless souls from the sea and soften the hearts of the entire village. Looking out upon the forlorn gathering, he sensed a peculiar unity.

The Sheppians had always been at arm's length to the church and rarely acquainted themselves with the pastor. On occasions, he made his way to the fish house to purchase a piece of cod, amiably greeting everyone along the way, and once in a harvest moon, he could be found at the grocer's. He now presented himself on the podium, slightly bent, with his hoary head more a thinning gray, revealing how much he had aged.

"Good morning." The wind and rain beat against the windows, the wood-burning stove glowing warmly. "It is good to see all of you. I know how difficult it must be to come to church on such a dreary day. Yet we gather today for a very special reason: to pay homage to our dearly beloved Cedric."

Looking throughout the downcast faces, he continued: "You're a good people. God knows that. And you should all know by now how compassionate and forgiving He is. For, did He not send Cedric our way?" All was silent. "If nothing else, please know God's mercy endures forever. For each and every one of you. Let us pray." Pastor Theo bowed his head and began by praying for all those who had lost loved ones on the *HMS Wellington*. He then thanked God for the little stranded girl who had found a good home. He closed by praying for all those now before him that they would truly find the peace and joy that only God can provide. After a soft *Amen*, he raised his head and began the eulogy.

"In 1839, Cedric placed his first imprints upon our shores. His arrival has always been a mystery. Where did he come from? How old was he when he arrived? Why did he make Sheppey his home? And what was his real name? Now that he is gone, the questions remain. Some of you may have heard my dear Mildred call him *Mats*. She often told me it means 'a gift from God'. Possibly, she realized it long before the rest of us.

"I became acquainted with Cedric through her. Mildred always found time for him, making those laborsome journeys to the pier time and again and persuading him to follow her home. She would bathe and brush him, give him a hearty meal, and settle him down for the evening outside under the stars. By morning, Cedric would always be gone. For we know what his purpose was—to be our beacon of light and, like God, to save souls.

"Not long after his arrival, as you all remember, there was another shipwreck. That seems to be the way it is here. Saving a drowning seaman would mark his first extraordinary rescue. When all was said and done, Cedric would rescue twenty-three souls.

"And how could we ever forget that tale, which is almost too miraculous to believe when he led those three lifeboats to safety the night the *Fontainebleau* went down? As you know, it made for one of the most joyous occasions in memory. Nor shall we forget how he saved Miss Gertrude during that blizzard, a deed that changed her life in the most wonderful of ways. And, certainly, we all know how our hero went to London to visit the Queen and received our nation's greatest honor with knighthood. Our beloved Sir Cedric then made headlines throughout all of Great Britain, and after countless centuries, our little village was finally placed on the map.

"As with all of life, the years eventually took their toll on him. Mildred and I noticed he was slowing down and dozing throughout the afternoons. For some odd reason, I thought he would never age. Ol' Cedie's heart remained that of a lion, and the years would not deter him from doing what he was called to do. I have recently considered he had simply fulfilled his mission." A long pause. Only the sound of the rain and wind as tears began to glisten in the pews.

"Now then, can we not believe God used this dog like an angel? Strange... under my breath, I began calling him *Gabriel*. We may adore Cedric simply for being a faithful friend; however, it is all but impossible not to sense that God had His hand upon him. And can we not believe that each and every soul he rescued was divinely touched?" Another pause. "I believe that God, in His own gentle way, is doing the same within all of you."

Pastor Theo placed a forefinger to his chin and reflected... "Which leads to another of my many unanswerable questions. Gazing up to heaven, I have often wondered if there will be animals within the pearly gates. Sometimes, I allow my imagination to wander, seeing Cedric next to the throne of God.

"Now then, we may also inquire, *Why did God bestow His mercy on some shipwrecked souls and not others*? I envision Cedric paddling within a whirlwind of roaring waves, weeping, and death all around. How was he able to choose whom to save? So many questions... so much going beyond the comprehension of man.

"At times, I have even compared him to Samson. Was he not an excellent swimmer? And did he not have supernatural abilities to accomplish those remarkable feats? Even during that final storm, without the strength of his younger years, he rose to the occasion one more time, just as God had given Samson the strength to pull down the pillars of that temple. And do you not find it an extraordinary miracle that ne'er a survivor suffered from the freezing cold? Not even Miss Gertrude, raised from a mound of ice and snow, had a single touch of frostbite on her body.

"It is common for mankind to become attached to a dog, though we have had a lack of such throughout our years. In many ways, a dog can become closer than a brother. They are trusting and bring comfort and joy. I find it rather peculiar that there is nothing worth mentioning about dogs in the Bible. Undeniably, God has created them for our good. And, when it comes to compassion, a dog can teach us a thing or two. You know that Cedric had an unwavering love for all of you. How many times did he look at you with those innocent eyes, wag his tail, and lick your hand? The affection was unbiased, even to those most hostile toward him." Gertrude's head was bowed. St. Paul said, *Follow my example as I follow Christ Jesus.* Can we not say the same of Cedric?

"As I stand before you this morning, I find it awkward to pray for a dog's eternal life. However, I have to smile, realizing God's ways are not our ways, and He can do whatever He pleases. So, I simply shrug and believe Cedric is in heaven.

"The words of Jesus Christ ring true: *Greater love hath no man than this, to lay down one's life for a friend.*" All was still, every eye fixed on the old pastor. "Though the pier is gone, we still see him out there, do we not? And we will forevermore be telling his story."

The venerable pastor did not fumble his words throughout the eulogy; though his voice was raspy, it carried throughout the entire church. He concluded by saying that Sheppians were a hearty people and that the sea and countless storms had always been a part of their lives. "We are now on another voyage, soon to reach its final destination. Eternity is but a breath away, and we will all come to know there truly is a God. This altar symbolizes trust, a stepping-stone to meet God, a place to bare one's soul. The first step may be awkward: coming forward and placing one's faith in Christ. Strange, is it not that in the end, we all have to take that walk alone? As you can see, the carpet is the only thing in our church that has not worn thin. I implore you to reflect on the limited days you have remaining. And I assure you that, in giving your life to Him, you will be making the most wonderful decision in your life." Heads bowed. No one stirred.

In the last pew, an old man rose, his white hair disheveled, his body bent. With a cane in hand, he hobbled past the pews and made his way to the altar. Still soaked from the rain, he bowed low as best he could with his one good leg.

Pinky had defied the wind and whatever else might come against him throughout his life. However, during this recent season, despair had begun to weigh heavily upon his soul. Nothing could soothe his grief over the loss of Cedric, let alone the departure of little *Mus Winkie.*

Then, too, Bertie's health was failing. And on this hollow morning, the pastor's words rang out as clearly to him as the old bell in the belfry.

Everyone donned their coats and hats and shuffled out into the heavy morn as Pinky remained bent and bowed. Pastor Theo and Mildred let him be, knowing it was a time for him to be alone and bear his heart to God. Awkwardly standing to his feet, he finally made his way down the aisle and quietly exited, hobbling north in the rain.

....

"He made the Bear, Orion, and the Pleiades..." Job 9:9 NKJV

....

Chapter 85

"Lo! Look upon the stars!"

E arly one morning, before the break of dawn, the clouds dispersed, and a clearing of deep blue spanned the heavens with a vast candelabra of stars. An old fisherman studied the sky, pleased to see a good omen for the coming day. To his dismay, he noticed a peculiar cluster. Seasoned by his many years at sea and as versed in the constellations as the ancient mariners, he had never seen such a formation. It was bright and polished as if making its grand debut. And lo, an epiphany! It was Cedric outlined in silverpoint. In all his years of coming and going, passing him on the pier, or greeting him at the fish house, he knew him well. And now there he was, emblazoned upon the universe for the world to see. Less knowledgeable souls might have assumed he had seen Leo the lion. Others might consider the constellation was Taurus the bull. "Nay, nay," said the wise old fisherman. "'Tis ol' Cedie boy, eet is."

In the days to follow, the revelation was passed along to the other fishermen. One matter-of-factly mentioned it to his wife. Being of the more curious sort, she stood outside that evening to see for herself. And, as the clouds cleared, there he was! The following day she hurriedly approached Mrs. Filmore, "I sees 'im meself! Lo! Look upon the stars!"

Most assuredly, Mrs. Filmore would have to ascertain such a bizarre sighting before it would make headlines. The following evening, the sky was once again clear. Gazing heavenward... and there he was, Cedric in all his glory!

The news carried more quickly than a weaver's shuttle. And, as the days passed, during those more pleasant evenings, villagers could be seen outside their cottages, lifting their heads heavenward and gazing upon the stars, nodding pensively and confirming, "Tis 'im aw right. 'Tis ol' Cedie boy."

....

Chapter 86

The Rosary

A fortnight after the eulogy, Thomas made his way to the Inn. He had become acquainted with Bertie during his stay at the Inn. However, their time together was minimal. Though the Merriweathers had not attended church for years, they were as Christ-bearing as anyone in the village. Knowing her faith and compassion for others, Thomas held her in the highest regard. Sensing her days were numbered, he knew it was time to pay his respects. Mounting his horse at an early hour, he headed north into the wind; puddles, caked in ice, cracking under the horse's hooves. The cottages were shut tight, more from the weather than his appearance. He thought how futile his attempt had been in swaying the villagers. A stranger in a strange land – and that is what he would always be. They were dying off, and he fervently desired to reach as many as possible while there was time. The eulogy of Cedric had touched their hearts, yet their doors remained closed. Pastor Theo often mentioned they were a hard-hearted sort and that his prayers seemed so futile. Even with unwavering faith and enthusiasm, Thomas was finding the same. There was never an invitation to visit nor prayer requests, yet the church was always obliging for their burials. Giving a brief sermon over a grave, a handful of villagers gathered round, he would end, "Ashes to ashes, dust to dust." Pastor Thomas was never one for flowery endings and could only hope that the few times they had made their way to church, the message had been taken to heart. *Who knows the heart of man during that final hour?*

The tavern lay still. Jarvis sat in the shadows at an isolated table. Thomas approached. Mr. Merriweather was wrought with grief; his hair disheveled, eyes bloodshot, with deep creases etched within his face. There was the impression he had slept in his clothes.

Pulling up a chair, Thomas did his best to console him. However, he knew that during times of heavy grief, words never sufficed a, silence proving to be the best medicine. He finally mentioned he had come to visit Bertie. Jarvis looked up, slowly rose, and guided him to her room.

It was on the first floor, down the hall on the south side. Jarvis quietly opened the door and sat to the side of her bed. Thomas stood to the other side. She was resting peacefully, her eyes closed. A rosary was in her hand. Thomas bowed his head and remained silent. No prayer was necessary, save that she go peacefully into the hands of God. He then made his way out and returned home.

Bertie had always been an anomaly in the village. Born and bred in Sheppey, she had a spiritual awakening as a young girl and dedicating her life to God, she subtly came out from among them. Though spiritually estranged, she loved every villager, caring for them whenever the need arose. Upon her return to Sheppey and her marriage to Jarvis, her time was consumed with tending to her mother and then the construction of the Inn; ongoing commitments that, naturally, had distanced herself from them. There were occasions, though, when she made her way to the bedside of an ailing neighbor, oft times praying before they breathed their last. They say some gave a slight nod before dying. Who knows how many entered the pearly gates because of Bertie?

There would be little mention of Bertie Merriweather's life upon the battered scrolls of Sheppey. Nor would a wreath of laurel be hung upon the door of the Inn, or a team of white horses to draw the caisson, nor fife and drums to lead a mournful procession to the cemetery. It may seem that all her little acts of kindness went for naught, like dandelion seeds blown across the barren beach. However, in another world, the angels were rejoicing.

Every soul who could manage down the muddied path attended the service. Those too feeble sat in silence within their cottages, recollecting all the good she had done. Pastor Thomas spoke over her grave; his words were sincere and heartfelt. Jarvis also spoke his tearful words, all but lost in the wind. When the service concluded, Thomas led the humble gathering in a hymn, their singing as broken as Jarvis's eulogy. And then the earth was shoveled upon her coffin.

....

Chapter 87

Roger

Roger groggily opened the door. It was late afternoon. The noonday nap had done him good, though the heavy slumber had overlapped a good portion of the daylight hours. The demanding nights were taking their toll. Though his inkwell had not gone dry, he had not reached a satisfactory conclusion; his mind as crumpled as the scribbled pages. Entangled in words and thought, his candle had burned too long. The fresh air was stimulating, the sea spreading out calmly before him as the sun cast flecks of light upon the gulls. He took out his pipe and lit it, puffing and pulling; wisps of smoke quickly swept away. The village was changing. Far before the knighting of Cedric, Londoners had begun making their way to Sheppey to see him for themselves. The clopping of horses' hooves and the merry sounds of tourists became a familiar sound passing by his cottage. A young family had purchased a vacant cottage near him, bringing it to life. Sheppey was losing its charm. Otto had recently passed away, and he missed him dearly. *Alas, death waits for no one.* Roger was well-versed in solitude.

It had been some time since the *HMS Wellington* went down. He remembered seeing Mildred in her coming and going. *Poor soul, grief stricken.* And that dog continued to remain a mystery. His encounters with Cedric had been few and far between. Naturally, there were updates from Mrs. Filmore and brief chit-chats with villagers. The article in the *Illustrated London Times* also provided insight. The only other information he had gathered throughout the years was that evening with the loquacious Bosun Bluthers and the eulogy by the venerable pastor. *So much was still missing...*

The day was inviting enough to consider a venture north. The last time he had been with Otto. The sea air and a long walk would allow his thoughts to untangle. He was also drawn to the allure of that pier, its remnant vaguely etched against the sea. For some peculiar reason, the spirit of that dog remained. Tapping his pipe, he returned inside and bundled up.

Roger made his way to the shoreline, distancing himself from the cottages. The village looked quaint, the beach desolate and peaceful. Following the sandpipers with the ebb and flow of the foam, he remembered how Otto had pranced in and out of his legs. His mind became crisp, and he gave it the luxury to wander. *How many years had it been since he settled in Sheppey? Shortly after the Napoleonic Wars. Though never following the call of duty... Would it have made a difference? War is brutally cruel. And who was to say how many dark crevices would have settled upon the pages?*

The sun bedded down in quilted clouds, and the late afternoon hour cooled; the wind increased, whipping up the waves, whitecaps agitating the sea. Lanterns glowed in the far-off cottages. Keeping his head low, he picked up his stride.

The skeleton of the pier was clearly seen, the few remaining pilings making a futile attempt to fend against the sea. Silhouettes of shipwrecks were etched against the fading sky.

The light in the tavern window became closer and more inviting. He took a moment to marvel at the Inn, the weathered fish house to one side... all the tales it told. Throughout the years, he had only ventured this far north on several occasions. *How many moons ago had he heard the bosun's tale? And that engaging evening with the ebullient Irish girl?*

Though not one for imbibing, the hour presented a rare opportunity to hang his hat and have a hot toddy. *Yes, a hot toddy would do just fine. Only one, though–not to overindulge.* Common sense ruled the hour, knowing he would have to make the same journey homeward. Looking in the window, the tavern was peacefully still, a fire blazing in the hearth as if awaiting his arrival.

....

"I had endured through watches of the dark the abashless inquisition of each star." William Shakespeare

....

Chapter 88

𝔖𝔱𝔞𝔯𝔰 𝔣𝔬𝔯 𝔗𝔥𝔬𝔲𝔤𝔥𝔱

U nraveling his scarf, Roger took a seat near the hearth. *There were changes...* Mrs. Filmore had mentioned the Inn had passed hands and was going through renovations. *Whoever it was has impeccable taste... a little on the feminine side with the frills and nic- nacks, but all for the better.*

He heard a shuffle and a thud between each step. Turning, Pinky was making his way to the table. Roger humorously mused he could have been a typecast for Quasimodo. Though having never made his acquaintance, he remembered his dramatic oratory that evening with Bosun Bluthers. *Hopefully, a hot toddy would soften the edges.*

"Gd-day, sur. Someth'n ta warm yer bones?" *Was that a smile or a grin?* Upon closer scrutiny, Roger noticed a sooted apron draped over a battered military jacket. He wore the same tattered cap. *When was the last time he shaved?*

"I'll take a hot rum toddy."

"Aye, 'tis ah good 'un." *Not exactly the King's English.* Roger settled back and studied the pair of drawings above the mantel. *That young girl–Rachel, was it? She captured a good likeness of this Pinky character.*

Pinky returned, adroitly carrying the hot toddy in one hand, "Cheers to yer." He lingered. "Yer live 'at the far end, don't yer?"

"I do."

"Seys yer ah pecul'r sort. 'A gentlm'n 'ee ees.' Calls 'yer 'profess'r'?"

"That's very gracious of them."

"Seys yer be a writer?"

"This is true."

"'T'ain't much ta quibble 'bout 'ere." His smile (or grin) broadened.

"Well, you could say what I write is somewhere between the realm of reality and one's imagination–simply snatching thoughts before they flit away and trying to make sense of it all."

"Yer knows ol' Cedie boy?"

"Is that Cedric? I had the honor of making his acquaintance on several occasions. Otto, my little companion, was especially fond of him. Quite an exceptional breed, that Cedric. A Newfoundland, I believe. Strong swimmer, as you know. Did you ever notice the webs between his toes? That's what helped him paddle through the storms."

"T'were yer at 'ees serm'n?"

"Don't make a habit of attending church. Not my social hour. But, yes, I attended."

Pinky would have liked to tell him of his experience that morning what he felt when he went to the altar. But it was one of those rare occasions he found too awkward for words.

The drink was warm and soothing, taking the edge off the raw evening and making Roger more amiable. "You seem to be wearing an old military jacket. Did you serve in the Queen's service?"

"Nay, King George 'ah served. 'Gainst Napol'yeon. 4th Dragoons. Best in the King's army. 'Napol'yeon, a great man, ee was. Saw 'im once b'hind lines."

Roger added, "Story has it that one night while Napoleon was upon a ship, he fell overboard, and a Newfoundland dove into the sea and rescued him." He continued on a different note, "Few generals in history could measure up to his brilliance. Ironically, some say the exiled emperor found religion late in life. However, I find it rather unlikely. During his confinement on the Isle of Saint Helena, he began reading the Bible. Hearsay has it he eventually came to the conclusion that no greater man ever walked the face of the earth than Christ and that countless thousands would gladly lay down their lives for Jesus Christ– far more than for any other emperor."

Pinky was intrigued by Roger's ongoing knowledge. He then began telling of his military engagements and that final battle at Salamanca in the spring of 1812, how he had been wounded, and that his beautiful steed, Ketch, had gone down in the heat of battle. "Me best friend.", adding that Cedric was just as endearing. One of the most remarkable creatures he had ever known.

"And all those tales about Cedric...?"

"'Tis true. True 'ndeed." Several guests descended the stairs and seated themselves at a nearby table. Pinky gave a slight nod and made his way to them.

Roger put on his hat and coat and placed a pound on the table, the toddy proving more than ample to send him on his way.

Before making it to the door, Pinky approached. "If yer got a minute, 'ave somethin' may int'rest yer."

"Most assuredly."

He directed Roger to the beam and pointed out the notches, abbreviating each tale therein. Roger followed along, impressed with the chronology and various details. He then thanked him and departed, for the hour was late. Pinky followed him out the door. "One more moment, if yer would?"

Pinky had noticed that the sky was opened by the moon's reflection upon the sea. Stepping away from the Inn, he looked up into its depths with its showcase of stars and a lazy half-moon. Raising his cane, he directed Roger's attention to a unique cluster, "'Ere's ol' Cedie boy." Roger followed along. To his amazement, he saw the silhouette of Cedric. Gazing as if staring at the ceiling of the Sistine Chapel, he whispered, "Remarkable." Pausing for another moment, he again thanked

Pinky and headed south. The wind had picked up. Fortunately, it was behind him as he prodded him along. The cottage lanterns had all been snuffed out, and all was silent.

He decided to take the beach instead of the muddied path. Heavy clouds had tightened the sky, leaving only a faint silver glow where the moon was tucked. The shoreline held its appeal, the sound of the surf soothing, and the pale edges of the foam, lapping near his feet, assisted in guiding him southward.

His mind drifted to the notches upon that beam. *A story to be told in each? And that bizarre Pinky, Sheppey's sage, knows the story within every mark. Archives of those past years, the ships, and rescued souls all accounted for. It was already turning into lore. Truth has a way of compromising with time. Where would the line be drawn between fiction and fact as the years pass?* Roger amused himself with the thought that Cedric's long trail of stories was somewhat similar to the tales of the Battle of Hastings woven within the Bayeux Tapestry.

A patch of blue opened up. Looking up at the sampling of stars, his mind began to travel within its depths. *Infinity...?* Something he could never comprehend. The clouds continued to disperse, and Cedric's constellation appeared again. He saw it with more clarity. *Yes, he had been immortalized.*

Entering his cottage, Roger lit a candle. Tired but enervated, he sat at his desk. The moonlight danced upon the sea. His thoughts remained on Cedric. *There seemed to be a profound purpose in it all. Mrs. Filmore mentioned that every one of those survivors had been awakened religiously–that is, save for Bosun Bluthers. And who knew about him?* He considered the unlikely pair of Lady Bradshaw and Gertrude as diametrically opposed as heaven was to hell. *How was it conceivable that they had come to bear the same cross? Gertrude and her sister, unsheathed from that hellish attire, were like Lazarus coming out of the tomb. They even began looking quite normal as he watched them pass by on their way to church, even offering a warm smile. Most peculiar...*

As far as having any sentiments toward a supreme being, Roger had remained evasive, almost adamant. Throughout the years, such a consideration was always swept aside. *Why was it that he struggled to even utter the name of God?* For a moment, he felt vulnerable. Seeing his dim reflection in the window, he felt a flicker of faith, a flicker of a possibility...? He shrugged and resigned himself to the simple fact that there had to be a supernatural force somewhere out there. *Did not the stars attest to as much?* Possibly, it was the lingering effect of the hot toddy, but Roger began pondering the likelihood of Otto being within those pearly gates. If so, most assuredly, Cedric was also there.

His mind was lucid, the candlelight echoing the light of the moon. Placing a clean sheet of paper on his desk, he dipped his pen in the ink-well and began writing.

....

Chapter 89

A Special Event

Alas, Rachel was finally home and nestled within the cottage of her youth. There was now a new perspective on both life and painting. Though the path had been awkward and sometimes painful throughout her years in London, she was evolving into what she had always intended to be. She quickly began to delve into the creative wellspring of Sheppey as an abundance of new subject matter filled her studio, capturing its antiquated charm. Painting after painting came to life: old cottages, the fish house, remnants of the pier with the suggestion of shattered vessels in the distance, and a growing collection of portraits of the villagers. There was also a series of floral paintings capturing portions of Nora's gardens. It was to replace the painting of Cedric, as the latter was soon to serve a broader purpose.

It was a vibrant day in early spring. A large painting of purple irises was on Rachel's easel for Nora's birthday. A letter arrived from Lord Byron the previous day, and she was considering his words between brushstrokes. He was following her progress, seeing her paintings in several galleries, and was especially fond of her most recent works. How wonderful. Though she had vanished from the spotlight, the art world was enthusiastic about what she was now doing. Several patrons had even purchased paintings from her *Crimpus* collection. For no one could deny the masterful touch of Miss Rachel Thomson. A curator mentioned he would like to venture down to Sheppey to see more of her recent paintings. Lord Byron concluded by saying he would like to visit her studio and the village from which she came. To be honest, though, he missed the comradery, for she was part of that rare breed who left a void when gone.

Rachel's sentiments were likewise. She had been leaning more on their friendship since the departure of Lady Bradshaw. Though the baroness was irreplaceable, he carried the same qualities of wisdom, trust, and integrity. She also found him enlightening and encouraging.

Putting her brushes aside, she responded with an enthusiastic note: *Yes, I would very much like to show you my recent works and relish the thought of introducing you to Pinky and the village.* However, *since our cottage would not be accommodating, it may be more appropriate for you to stay at the Wayfarer Inn. You might find it quaint being cut from a different cloth than our great society.* She added in jest, *You will be one of its most distinguished guests.* (That is, save for the baroness.) However, Lord Byron would be arriving by coach and not by shipwreck, unlike Lady Bradshaw. There was something else, quite undisclosed, as a visit would present an opportunity for him to finally meet Nora.

....

Chapter 90

A Warm Embrace

Lord Byron's carriage trotted through Sheppey in early June. It was a rather unpretentious entry with an informal coachman and carriage. He pleasantly smiled, observing the line of cottages passing by and the vast shoreline with its wandering gulls, everything just as he envisioned it through Rachel's many stories.

The suite at the Wayfarer Inn awaited him. Rachel had left a message suggesting he should rest and she would meet with him in the morning. After settling in, he proceeded to the tavern. It was early evening, and there were several well-attired diners. *Most likely Londoners.* He noticed a pair of drawings over the mantel, one of which was Cedric, the other looking like a weathered seaman. *Undoubtedly Pinky.* He knew they were done by Rachel during her youthful years.

A young server approached, neatly attired and courteous. She recommended Pinky's mutton stew, to which Lord Byron consented, along with a glass of sherry. During the meal, Pinky made his way to the table. The patch and hobble were his apparent trademarks. *Most assuredly a true rarity.*

Knowing the guest was Rachel's honorable friend, he gave a coarse though warm greeting. Lord Byron gestured for him to take a seat. *A friend of Rachel's was a friend of his.* After a few pleasantries and sharing some idiosyncrasies of his recipe, Pinky commenced with tales of Cedric. Lord Byron found him rather pleasant and quite entertaining, and it did not take long to comprehend why Rachel was so fond of him. After a second glass of sherry, Lord Byron excused himself and retired, ascending the stairs to his room to read as the sea faded in the waning light.

During his latter years, Mr. Wilson could be found grazing on the hillside with the sheep. Rachel had recently purchased Ben, a larger horse, and found it a pleasure, with his livelier gait, to hitch him up and take him to the village. Quite often, she realized how little she missed her carriage and the days in Westminster.

Arriving in mid-morning, Rachel found Lord Byron seated by the window. He rose and greeted her with his warm congeniality. The sun had settled in a mist, casting a soft light upon them from the window. She noticed he was dressed comfortably in a flannel shirt and tweed jacket; the years had been gracious to him.

He, too, was reflecting... denuded of her Victorian lifestyle, Miss Thomson was more relaxed and quite authentic in her country dress, and her beauty continued to blossom. A waitress approached, and he ordered tea and crumpets.

"What a charming place. My room provided a most pleasant rest, and the view is delightful. Your friend, Mr. Pinky, made his introduction last evening. Out of the ordinary, I must say." Looking around at the guests, "I see the Londoners have taken to Sheppey. Several of the cottages have had a nice refurbishment, though the village still has that vintaged touch. Quite idyllic."

"Yes, things are changing. And all because of our beloved Cedric."

"I read the article several years ago. Your illustrations were excellent, truly enriching the story. Bravo." Looking out to sea, "Are those the remnants of the pier?"

"Yes. It still holds its memories."

The light fare was served.

"I find the staff here most congenial–young and vibrant."

"It has been long awaited. Young families are arriving and pur-chasing the old cottages, fixing them up quite nicely." Rachel went on to say how much she cherished being home. He praised her for the move and said that the direction she was now taking as an artist was far more authentic. She told him about her recent works and her new studio.

The sun rose past the mist and was resplendent upon the coast. She persuaded him to take a short walk. Before departing, he casually placed a crumpet in his jacket pocket.

Rachel began sharing her adventures as a girl and fond memories on the old pier. *That was where she had drawn Cedric, the picture over the mantel in the Inn.* She thought it a sad irony that Cedric and the pier had reached their fatal end on the same day. The remaining stumps still held their lore. In a melancholic way, they complemented the remnants of shipwrecks upon the shoals.

Several seagulls passed overhead. Lord Byron pulled out the crumpet and began tossing pieces into the air. The gulls became enliv-ened, circling above and waiting. Soon, others could be seen coming from far off. Hovering overhead and clamoring with their cries, they waited for a morsel to be tossed in the air and swooped down upon it.

"The last time I did this, I was a boy.", he said, heaving the final crumbs into the air. Rachel was pleased to see him enjoying himself. As they strolled along the shore, the rolling surf and sandpipers added a soothing note to the conversation.

Returning to the Inn, she invited him to their cottage for dinner the next day–*Possibly late afternoon?* Giving directions and a warm farewell, she then headed home. He continued to take great amusement as he watched her ride away in a horse-drawn wagon.

Chapter 91

A Natural Harmony

L ord Byron arrived at an appropriate hour. Gently knocking on the door, a young girl soon greeted him.

"Could this be little Miss Muffet? My, my–how you have grown! You have become quite the young lady."

"Yes, sir."

"Let's see–you must be ten years of age by now. Is that correct?"

"Yes, sir. My birthday is next week."

Rachel and Nora joined in. "Lord Byron, this is my Aunt Nora."

He politely shook her hand, "I'm so glad to meet you. Rachel has spoken of you so often that I feel we have already met." She had a subtle beauty and the glow of health. Nor was there any fine dress or jewelry as simple as nature itself. He sensed wisdom in her eyes.

"Rachel has spoken quite highly of you also." Nora's voice was soft and gentle.

"Muffet has grown into quite the lady, hasn't she?" Rachel interjected. "We have decided to name her Esther. In due time, though, as she persists in being called Muffet."

"Well, I will have to remember that. Esther is such a fine name. However, 'Miss Muffet,' it will be until further notice." Lord Byron told his coachman to go to the Inn and return by mid-evening.

His introduction to Nora flowed naturally. Almost immediately, Rachel noted a tone of affection. She had always thought they were like complementary colors–of good character and tenderheartedness. However, she put the thought aside, knowing that something being kindled between them was out of the realm of reasoning. Besides the perfect gentleman that he was, he most likely bestowed such warmth on everyone. Yet, purist that she was, she held a faint glimmer of hope for a happy ending.

The meal was served. Naturally roasted lamb. Rachel mentioned Nora had butchered it. Lord Byron was most impressed, and the feast surpassed his epicurean expectations. He began discussing Rachel's recent paintings and how the art world was changing with new styles on the horizon and was pleased to find Nora knowledgeable on the topic, and the conversation had no end. Muffet remained quiet and attentive. Lord Byron discreetly observed her demeanor.

Rachel could not help herself as she entertained her creative mind with that far-fetched romantic notion, having the ludicrous thought that it was love at first sight. Studying them, she drifted; *Age has its reasoning that youth knows not. Seasoned with wisdom and tempered by the years, they no longer see love in its blinding beauty but appreciate more redeeming qualities.* She rose to clear the table and persuaded him to tour her studio while there was still light.

Dusk was settling in, and she lit several lanterns. It was a medium-sized barn. The interior was spacious and rather masculine, with beams and wooden siding. He was especially fond of the large window facing the vista. There was enough light to see the distant village and sea. Though a world apart from the studio in Westminster, it had its touch of ambiance. Then again, her precious spirit would follow her anywhere.

Taking his time… there were a handful of unfinished works. *Portraits of villagers? Quite good. A new style… generated by the trip to Holland?* There was an incomplete landscape on the easel. *Brilliant. A touch of Corot?* He then caught sight of the portrait of the officer tucked in a corner. *Strange… that it had never been completed.*

The evening was brisk, and Nora and Muffet had started a campfire. The first stars of evening were making themselves known in a deepening blue. Rachel invited him to join them and returned to the cottage, continuing to discreetly observe from the window. "Let intimacy take its course." There had been a time when she considered Lady Bradshaw his perfect match. To which he responded that he had always held the baroness in high regard, though they were too much alike. *Could this not also be said of Nora*? Something within her entangled thoughts unraveled as she studied them, seeing Lord Byron and Nora like a pair of finely tuned violins.

The coachman arrived. Lord Byron rose and bid them a cordial farewell, mentioning he would return to London the next day. Rachel agreed to meet him for tea before his departure.

She joined Lord Byron at a table near the hearth the following morning. The tavern was alive with patrons. Pouring tea, he said, "I have been giving much thought to this visit." His smile revealed more than the words. "Certainly, there is much to consider, and I would like to return from time to time. I am impressed with your progress and have grown quite fond of this little village." He folded his hands. There was something in that smile. "I believe this would be an excellent place for an extension of your orphanage, a place for older youth to learn a trade. It seems Sheppey could use some more vim and vigor." Pausing... "Wealth is such a strange companion, and as I age, it holds less appeal. And where could I find a better place to invest my earthly treasures? For when the final nail is pounded, and the doors opened, could it not prove to be a true legacy? Though I don't aspire for such." He was rather excited. "I envision it on the other side of the woodlands... teaching young men and women trades that will benefit them and the community." Leaning closer, "It could prove to be a grand venture."

It was another one of Lord Byron's well-tempered aspirations. Rachel was well-versed in his integrity and resolve and became enthusiastic, for he was not a man of whims or fancies.

Before departing, he handed her a letter. It was addressed to Nora. Thoughts lingered as she watched the coach depart, once again thinking of Lady Bradshaw. She and Lord Byron were two of the most remarkable people she had ever known, and both had embraced her as a dear friend.

Returning to the cottage, she gave the envelope to Nora. Late in the day, Nora went outside, sat under the elm, and opened it.

Dearest Nora:

Spending time with you has been a priceless treasure, and I would very much like to return. Hopefully, you will share more of your world with me in the near future. You have left a lasting impression.

Sincerely,

Lord Byron

....

"Pray, look better, sir...those things yonder are no giants but windmills." Cervantes

....

Chapter 92

𝔑𝔬𝔱 𝔞 𝔚𝔦𝔫𝔡𝔪𝔦𝔩𝔩

L ike Jarvis, Lord Byron set his aspirations high upon the sky. However, more than chasing windmills, his imaginings were lodged within a tempered soul, a prudent compass directing such intangibles. And so, a seed had been planted in his visit to Sheppey. As the days passed, it began taking root, the trade center firmly embedded within a concrete ideal. No, it was not some illusory far-off star, but something one could put their finger to.

Upon further consideration, the project began to have its corollaries. *For could not these youthful souls find a mate as well? New little families birthing upon the coast...? And could we not believe it is but a part of Queen Victoria's vision–to raise up a people with good work ethics and righteous values?*

The foundation was laid in the early spring of 1862. Thomas made several trips to London, selecting a dozen older boys from the orphanage to assist in laying the groundwork. They were Irish to the bone, loved the freedom and the fresh air, and proved to be industrious. Lord Byron also imported carpenters, the best in the trade. It went without saying that a mark of excellence was placed on everything he set his mind to.

After the framing was erected, sleeping quarters were nailed into place, and a room was hammered together for the kitchen. Nora assisted and, in time, became a mainstay, tending to many of the secondary aspects, such as overseeing the needs of the workers and preparing meals. She especially made sure the boys walked the line, watching over them like a mother hen. Faith also gave a helping hand. Her children, coming of age, tended to many menial chores and enjoyed interacting with the workers.

Lord Byron became a prolonged guest at the Inn. Always perceptive to details, he made his way to the site each morning. It would not be long before he invested in another property. He found the ideal place to build a future home on an adjacent hill that breached the woodlands and faced an expanse of sea.

The trade school opened in late autumn. The finishing touch was the large sign above the front doors. Having no desire to label it as an extension of the orphanage, Lord Byron gave it the title *Tools of the Trade*.

His house was completed the following year, and he made a point of inviting Nora as his first guest. Arriving early in the morning, she pulled in Ben's reins, and a valet assisted her. Lord Byron was reading on the porch. He stood to greet her, waiting patiently and presenting himself as a perfect gentleman. Nora took a seat and was served tea. Dawn passed into a brighter stage, the sun's golden light cast upon the sea with distant gulls giving their piercing cries.

"Nothing as serene as the morning hour." She said. "If I had arrived a little earlier, we could have enjoyed the colors of dawn. However, I believe my gardens can contend with any of the glorious touches of nature. Flowers bring me joy. They symbolize all that is good. And are we not given a new beginning each spring?" She trailed away... "God brings such hope in this life, and the earth will always hold His beauty."

"Well, hopefully, I shall give gardening a try–put my hands into the good earth and see what I have been missing." Giving a quick survey of the grounds, "Possibly a splash of color over there."

"May I ask what you are reading?"

"Why, yes. A collection of Tennyson's poems. I find it consoling to have such a contemporary by my side and have recently acquired a deep appreciation for his verse. Have been reflecting on Ulysses, the mythological King of Ithaca. He is returning home after conquering Troy, aged and weary of the world around him. However, he faces the day with a new resolve, believing, like you, that life still holds its value." Lord Byron opened to a page. "I especially like this verse: *Come, my friends. 'Tis not too late to seek a newer world. Push off, and sitting well in order, smite the sounding furrows, for my purpose holds to sail beyond the sunset and the baths of all the western stars until I die.*"

Nora listened quietly, appreciating the eloquent manner in which he read. She considered that more could be added to the king's thoughts as the Bible holds truths far surpassing mythology. Solomon, like Ulysses, was a rich and powerful king who despaired late in life, though his thoughts reflected hope with a godly perspective. Possibly, she would have the opportunity to discuss this with him at another time. "Thank you for sharing that with me, Lord Byron."

"Please call me David." He pulled out a folded sheet of paper from the book. "Something else I would like to read. It's from the pen of Lord Byron. Not that I am impressed with his writings because we share the same name. I find him more a namesake in thought." Staring out upon the sea, "I cannot say that I have any regrets about never marrying. Life has been very good to me. However, I find myself vulnerable in these latter years. And it is rather peculiar, never having an intimate relationship. That is, until recently." He began reading: "*What is the worst of woes that wait on age? What stamps the wrinkle deeper on the brow? To view each loved one blotted from life's page and be alone on earth, as I am now.*"

Who knows the final page in this intimate rapport? Though one may sense, during this golden hour with its new dawn, that this unlikely pair was about to give each other a priceless gift. As far as they were concerned, it was *not too late to seek a newer world.*

....

Chapter 93

All for the Good

More than a decade had passed since Cedric's final footprints had faded into the sea; his fame now settled in the hearts of all Great Britain and even emblazoned upon the celestials. Some speculated it was more than coincidental that the Queen and this fine creature had joined together. And could it not be conceived as a spiritual blessing as well? Everything had changed, even the hearts of the Sheppians.

The Wayfarer Inn manifested some of the first signs of this change. Renovations commenced soon after the ink had dried on its sale. Within the ensuing years, the establishment would prosper more than Jarvis and Bertie had ever imagined. By the summer of 1863, the rooms were full, and a new large hand-painted sign of a three-masted vessel swayed from the hinges. The young proprietors continued with renovations, the wife adding tasteful touches to the décor. Barring no expense, lamps, bedding, and curtains were replaced in every room. However, the tavern truly manifested her touch. It was transformed into a teahouse, which came naturally, for Bertie had long ago laid its foundation.

Bottles of spirits were replaced with teas from India, China, and Russia, along with an assortment of teacakes served on the finest porcelain. Though most of the libations were taken off the shelves, a selection of French wines and good ales was added to the menu, along with a bottle of the finest rum for hot toddies to comfort lodgers during the brisk evenings. Brunch was served throughout the noonday hours, and fine dining in the evenings, having its flare for French cuisine and the fresh catch of the day. Though not contending with such culinary entrees, Pinky's mutton stew received its own acclaim, for it went without saying that an Englishman invariably preferred a good mutton stew over a beef bourguignon.

Jarvis made his presence known, all but leaping for joy as he merrily made his way around the tables. For Bertie's teahouse had become a dream come true. Whelming with tears, he would clasp his hands and look up, thanking God and believing Bertie was looking down upon it all.

New families continued to flow into the village. Contrary to the mass exodus from Ireland to London, it was a subtle and simple migration. Foregoing the oppressive wheels of industry, adventurous young couples were resettling on the coast. For word had spread, there was work to be had, and cottages could be purchased at a very reasonable price. The sound of hammering nails soon intermingled with the roll of the surf as one disparaging cottage after another was revived, each having its unique personality. Wives framed the windows with latticed curtains and potted plants. What naturally followed was the laughter of children and the sounds of barking dogs. It would not be long before more cottages were constructed north of the fish house. Like the human soul, Sheppey was resurrected.

A handful of the old villagers lingered on. Shuttered and passed aside, they remained in solitude. There was also a remnant of weathered fishermen, aged in sinew and bone, who merged with the young men now tending to the boats. One wise mariner commented how much the weather had changed–those never-ending storms had all but gone out with the tide.

Gertrude's cottage prevailed. Some would say it was like an old tooth with a bright smile. Yet, like the remaining pilings, it proved to be a treasure, a landmark of times past.

The new proprietors continued seizing upon the window of opportunity, placing umbrellas on the beach and lounge chairs. During the lazy summer evenings, kites intermingled with the gulls within the tones of a setting sun. There would be a pleasant calm upon the seashore. As the hour waned, a full moon would make its way heavenward, its silver light shimmering upon the sea. Lanterns would be lit within the cozy cottages, complementing the lighting of the stars. At such a time, some would gaze heavenward and see the constellation of Cedric.

....

Chapter 94

Jack the Lumberjack

———

Quite often, an adage will teeter as much as the old pier. And the saying, *Plus ça change, plus c'est la même change*, swayed and bent within this new era. For, behold, a town hall was constructed in Sheppey. One of its first ambitions was to fund a memorial for Cedric. The officials commissioned a sculptor from London and requested it be completed in time for the ribbon-cutting ceremony in early autumn. At that time, Miss Rachel Thomson would also be presenting a painting of Cedric to be hung within the interior of the building.

It was a pleasant day as Rachel hooked up Ben and rode to town. Being absorbed behind her easel, caring for Muffet, and assisting Nora had consumed the season.

The ceremony commenced in mid-morning. The sky was a broad slate of blue, the sand and sea basking in the sun's warmth. Dignitaries and reporters had arrived, and a younger generation of villagers was present. Several officials took the podium to speak of days past. They told of the shipwrecks and the countless heroics of Cedric. Though their speeches were impressive, they read from scripts, and Rachel knew they were not speaking from the heart. Looking around, most everyone in attendance had never known Cedric. The pier was gone, the cottages renovated, and the old villagers fading away.

Finally came the unveiling of the sculpture. Two young men gently pulled away the cover. There he was, raised high upon a foundation for all the world to see. Poised like a lion, Cedric gazed out upon the sea. The piece was larger than life and chiseled with conviction, even capturing the texture of his heavy coat blowing in the wind. Rachel had given the committee Cedric's medallion, which was draped around his shoulders. A plaque underneath read, *For what greater love is there than to lay down your life for another?*

An official praised the artist, telling of his many credentials and pointing him out to the crowd, to which he paid little heed. Rachel noted his rather impervious air, indifferent to the applause and praise.

There was a second unveiling as the clerks brought forth Rachel's painting and uncovered it. It was handsomely framed, and even in the bright sun, the tones held up remarkably well. An official then directed everyone's attention to Miss Thomson, praising her for the wonderful contribution. The sculptor became attentive.

In an indirect way, Rachel had been introduced to him. There had been a trip to town early in the spring to purchase groceries and spend time with Pinky. He told her of an encounter he had with a strapping young man named Jack Crenshaw. He was a good man who had done his service for God, Queen, and country. And, like her, he was a successful artist, having established a reputation for himself in London. One afternoon, he had ventured into the Inn. By his dress and a ponytail strapped behind his head, Pinky knew he was not one of the fancier sorts who were making their way down from the city. Sitting at a far table and having a pint of ale, he kept to himself. At which time, Pinky made his way over.

Quite unabashed, he took a liking to Pinky, only taking a moment for him to pull out a chair and invite him to have a seat. An enlivened conversation ensued, and after a few hearty laughs this Jack Crenshaw mentioned he was a sculptor. He had arrived late in the winter to begin a commission work on a dog named Cedric. Though not considering himself an animal artist, he was inspired to do the work after reading the article in the *London Illustrated Times*. He had recently settled in a cottage on a hillside a few miles west of town.

With a twinkle in his eye, Pinky gave Rachel a nod of approval. She remained placid, knowing his propensity for matchmaking and his romantic wanderings.

Now, amidst the crowd, Rachel had the opportunity to see this Jack Crenshaw for herself. *Very peculiar. Not fawning over anyone. His dress and that ponytail... most assuredly on the periphery of English society.* Possibly a few years Rachel's senior, he was quite contrary to military stalwartness. Yet she found him rather dashing and entertained the thought that he could easily be construed as a woodsman. *After all, was he not chipping away at large blocks of wood*? She had recently read an article about lumberjacks in America... *Jack, Jack, the lumberjack.*

Continuing to entertain herself, Rachel discreetly followed him as he casually weaved in and around the mass of people. Their eyes met. Only a glance, but penetrating. He made his way closer. Something came over her that she had not felt for years. Turning aside, she merged within a flurry of admirers. The ceremony ended, and she prepared to leave.

"Pardon me."

Rachel turned. It was him. His eyes were full of life. "I wanted to commend you on your painting. You made a heartfelt statement. Never met Cedric, but you seem to have done him justice."

"Thank you. I was thinking the same of your work, putting our noble Cedric in a light he so well deserves."

"I made the acquaintance of an old friend of yours. Mr. Pinky, I believe? Quite a character. Odd sort, I must say. He did quite a bit of bragging on you. In all fairness, it suits you well. He pointed out your drawings hanging on the wall."

Rachel then inquired, "If I may ask, what inspired you to give Cedric such a regal pose? Though every stroke of your chisel was done with conviction, it's the pose that truly captures him. Considering you never met our dear Cedric, you did him justice."

"In actuality, you could give your Mr. Pinky credit for that too. We became good sorts, and I began frequenting the Inn on Friday afternoons. The more time I spent with him, the more insight he gave me on 'ol' Cedie boy.' Late one evening, he told me Cedric's image was actually upon the stars. He grabbed his cane and proceeded to take me outside. It was quite calm, and the sky was clear as he guided me through the stars and directed my attention to a peculiar constellation. And there he was, Sir Cedric, as vivid as day. It was then and there I found my inspiration."

"A constellation?" Rachel was amused and puzzled. Ironically, she had never heard mention of it.

"Yes, found my subject matter upon the stars, so to say. Story has it Michelangelo found his inspiration upon a hillside in Tuscany, seeing the image of God touching Adam in a cloud formation." He smiled. "My name is Jack–Jack Crenshaw."

"Jack, Jack, the lumberjack?"

His laugh was as full of life as his personality. "Not quite. Actually, if you desire to give me a title, call me *Jack the Woodsman*. And don't let my image ruffle you. It's proper attire for my livelihood. Michelangelo was often seen walking the streets of Florence covered in marble dust. Hopefully, there's a little more to me than this rough hew." He looked into her eyes with a penetrating depth. "Appearance aside, a creative nature connects you and me, artist-to-artist. I like that." Silence stirred within the breeze. She found no flaws in this Jack Crenshaw.

"Possibly we could have dinner at the Inn one evening?", he asked. "As you know, your Mr. Pinky makes an excellent mutton stew. I received a handsome commission for my work, so it will be on me. I will also make a concerted effort to be more presentable. If a clear night presents itself, I could even take you out under the stars and point out your dearly beloved Cedric."

"I would like that."

Late in the afternoon the following Saturday, Jack Crenshaw rode up to the cottage upon a horse. Nora was immediately pleased with him, and Muffet instinctively liked him. Rachel suggested they take Ben, and he proceeded to hitch the wagon and take the reins as they headed into Sheppey.

Ben took his time as he passed through the countryside, giving this newfound pair time to become better acquainted. As always, Rachel had much to consider and did not want to wander too far with her emotions. Her heart still needed time to mend. However, she could not deny that this Jack Crenshaw had entered her life. Simply put, she felt good. As they reached the shoreline, a span of clouds was on the horizon reflecting the warm colors of the setting sun, the gulls sailing open-winged. She had never seen it so beautiful.

....

"Then Naomi took the child and laid him on her bosom..."

Ruth 4:16 NKJV

....

Chapter 95

In the Twinkling of an Eye

L ord Byron also had lesser aspirations. One of which would come to fruition soon after the *Tools of the Trade* opened its doors when a young apprentice named Peetie joined hands with a lovely young lady named Becky. Peetie was one of the first boys to arrive with Thomas, and Lord Byron had grown particularly fond of him, a respectful lad whom he sensed was earmarked for success. Peetie became a master carpenter, even handcrafting many of the artifacts within the home of Lord Byron.

The wedding was set for mid-autumn. It was quite an event with all the students attending. (A discerning eye perceived some of the youth discreetly holding hands within the pews.) Pastor Thomas presided over the ceremony. They say he was more enthusiastic than anyone had ever seen him.

Upon hearing of the engagement, Lord Byron presented Peetie with a handsome dowry, a gift received well in advance of the appointed day. The young man went right to work building a cottage north of the fish house that was completed in time for the celebrated honeymoon. They say it was nine months to the day that an infant's cry could be heard emanating from the cottage window. Named Mackie Byron McIntosh, the child became known as *Mackie.*

On a fine summer's day, the young couple was taking a stroll, Peetie cradling the young Mackie in his arms. Passing by one of the few remaining cottages of days past, a woman beyond the years of measure was sitting outside on a rickety chair. She addressed them with a wane smile and a slight nod. Peetie paused. Approaching her, he asked if she would like to hold the infant. Tears whelmed in the old woman's eyes as he gently placed the child into her arms.

The town continued to prosper. A new bank was constructed to the north side of Mr. Filmore's grocery–a bookend to the town hall. Never before had there been a bank in Sheppey. To think, a place to deposit one's sixpence, which, in time, would grow into pounds and crowns! Gone was the ancient path with its soppy mud and myriad puddles. Londoners donned in their Victorian best strolled along the boarded walkway, taking in the sea air and the gallery of charming cottages as carriages trotted by in their coming and going.

Mr. Filmore, shrewd businessman that he was, knew when the iron was hot and rose to the occasion. Though his ledger had always been lined in black, old man Herman was not one to miss a beat. Keenly aware that times and tastes were changing, he was quick to make adjustments. Purchasing items of luxury delicacies from every port, his new patrons found such dainties most appealing. An extension was added to the rear of the store, stockpiling his inventory and putting more young men and women on the payroll to tend to the ongoing sales.

Being crafty of mind, Mr. Filmore innovated a handsomely wrapped basket filled with an assortment of cheeses, fruit, tea cakes, bonbons, a bottle of good wine, and a French baguette extending from its side. The baskets were stacked and showcased near the front door, the first things the flow of tourists would notice as they entered. Gravitating to the display, they merrily dispensed with a few pounds for such a treat. Later in the day, sitting seaside, they could be seen tossing morsels to the gulls and enjoying their picnic cuisine.

Jarvis was rejuvenated beyond measure. Overflowing with enthusiasm, there was a youthful bounce in his step as the rooms in the Inn were overflowing and prosperity abounded. Unfortunately, it was but a fleeting moment, for Jarvis's pail could never be filled without Bertie. And, within a brief season, he, too, was bedridden. However, one would find the final days of Mr. Merriweather filled with a rare joy. For there was hope beyond measure, his mind wandering upward with the thought of being reunited with his beloved Bertie.

It was a pleasant Sunday afternoon in early autumn when old Jarvis, with folded hands upon his chest, expired his last breath, making that inexplicable transition from one world to another–all in the twinkling of an eye.

Naturally, the Wayfarer Inn became dormant when the cold, bleak days settled upon the coast. Pinky became as whittled as the barren days. More like a rusted anchor on the bottom of the sea, he no longer found solace in his solitude. Bidding his farewell, one old soldier to another, his comrade-in-arms had been shoveled asunder. *What was left in this dreary world?* The long, hollow hours were now filled with lamentations and reflections.

Late one evening, a candle flickering on the table, he looked at the Bible that Bertie had given him. He knew the heart behind the gift. For this alone, it was kept in high regard, and there had been a silent pledge to one day give it a try. Upon further consideration, he placed it aside.

Through it all, there was a silver lining within the clouds as Pinky had risen to celebratory status and was bestowed with the title of concierge in the Wayfarer Inn. The proprietors had even commissioned Miss Thomson to do a full standing portrait of him which was proudly hung in the lobby. And during the last week in October, he was scheduled to give his first tour on the life and times of Cedric.

"It seems to me we can never give up longing and wishing while we are thoroughly alive. There are certain things we feel to be beautiful and good, and we must hunger after them."
George Elliot

....

Chapter 96

To Everything a Season

Adaline, too, returned to Sheppey. It was in the autumn of 1864. The freckles and pigtails were gone, her hair was cropped, and her body lean, and there was a subtle beauty that bore the years of the travesty now behind her. Her eyes revealed it all. During more whimsical moments, one would still see that flare of youthful ebullience.

After countless years in Ireland, expending both her heart and soul, she was emotionally and physically drained. Like an impassioned sponge, she had absorbed too much death and sorrow. However, immersed in such travails, she had fallen in love and married. John Clancey was the dearest man she had ever known. Unfortunately, as with everything else birthed upon that dismal land, love quickly slipped away, like sand sifting through her fingers. He died for the same cause as her father in the fight against English rule. And like Rachel's all-too-brief romance, Adaline was left with only a lingering memory of a love that flickered out far before its time. Wrought with fatigue and sorrow, she turned her eyes toward the only place where there was a semblance of home, a place to withdraw and heal.

There were other reasons for returning. Faith had written and mentioned a trade center had been constructed west of the village with many orphans from Ireland learning trades. Then, there was Roger and her rather abstract attraction toward him. He revealed so much insight in their brief encounters, and poetry was still within her bone and marrow. And there was an intuitive sense that, past his rigid formalities, there could be a special rapport. Faith mentioned that Nora had married. *What a surprise!* A delightful man and quite wealthy. They were living in a beautiful home on a hillside overlooking the sea. But there was more. Rachel had also wed! A strikingly handsome artist from London and quite successful. Thomas presided over Rachel's wedding in the little church. Muffet had turned into quite the young lady and had also wed, a dashing young officer and was now living in London. Rachel and Mr. Crenshaw were residing in Nora's cottage.

Faith closed by mentioning Roger's health. It had been failing, and his cottage remained shuttered. Mrs. Filmore was sending a clerk down to deliver groceries. Rarely did anyone see him. More than anything, this was the catalyst that started Adaline packing–a desire to sit at his feet and glean from whatever days he had remaining.

Upon arriving, Adaline knocked at the door of Thomas and Faith. There was an inviting glow from within. Remembering the dilapidated cottage, it was difficult to perceive it was the same place. Faith came to the door. After a long-overdue embrace, she introduced her family. Seeing the man upon the horse was now her husband was good. Most of the children were in their teen years, mature and polite. She said they all had been adopted from the orphanage save for the two younger ones. Elisha was eleven, the last to be rescued by Cedric. Hannah, the youngest, was born out of undue season.

During the evening, Thomas mentioned Theo passed away several years ago and Aunt Mildred the following year. When Faith mentioned to him Adaline's desire to return, they agreed the cottage would be ideal for her. After all, she was an extended member of the family. Adaline enthusiastically accepted the offer and spent the night in the warmth and comfort of their home, something long absent in her own life.

The next morning, she made her way to Pastor Theo and Mildred's cottage. The air was brisk, the sun dormant behind the clouds. A strong wind greeted her as she passed the old church. She stopped and breathed in the memories. Looking north, the muddied path was gone, a boarded walkway stretching north as far as the eye could see. Some of the cottages had been renovated and were quite colorful. In the far distance, she vaguely saw the remnants of the pier, snaggled pilings, like headstones standing in some forgotten cemetery. Her heart sank. The stark realization that Cedric was truly gone.

She turned her attention to the cottage. It seemed to be peacefully awaiting her. The door creaked. The interior was musty. *A little fresh air and touching up, and it would be fine. Far more than hoped for.* Everything was coming together effortlessly. Throughout the ensuing days, she would focus on bringing it to life and then make her way to Roger's.

Several days passed, the cottage was in order, and Adaline prepared herself for the impending visit with Roger. It was early morning as she approached his cottage. *Was it but the blink of an eye when last she stood there?* The shades were drawn. Hesitant, she thought it best to return later.

By mid-morning, the shades were still drawn. She approached and gently tapped on the door. There was a rustle inside, and the door opened. There he stood, disheveled and groggy, furrows upon his brow. His hair had thinned, and his body was frail, whittled with the years. However, she sensed the same pensive soul still resided within the shell.

Roger thought she looked familiar. Then, a faint recognition and a wane smile, as if awakening from his slumber. "My dear Adaline. Come in. Come in." Reaching out, she embraced him with open arms. He remained stiff and irresponsive. She knew such a physical display was not in his nature.

He made his way to his desk and took a seat, suggesting she sit on a wooden chair across from him. The gray light of day made everything soft. She inquired as to where his little friend was. He replied that Otto had passed away several years ago, the same year as Mildred.

They chatted for several minutes before she mentioned she had returned for good and was presently residing in Theo and Mildred's cottage. Since they were neighbors, and with his permission, she would like to visit, possibly even assist with the chores. Independent soul that he was, Roger surprisingly consented. An hour passed with more pleasantries, and she departed, believing the visit was an immense success.

Adaline soon set to the task in tidying up odds and ends up in Roger's cottage along with preparing meals. The spartan dwelling took little effort in dusting and cleaning. As the days passed, she took on more responsibilities. Arriving by mid-morning, she pulled up the shades and opened the window, laid out his clothes, and prepared tea. In a discreet way, he expressed his appreciation.

Roger was still writing, though piecemeal. Sleeping away his once-industrious hours and taking deeper naps throughout the afternoons, the sessions were brief, if at all. After morning tea, he would sometimes go to his desk and scribble a page of obscure lines. Adaline wondered if it had been a gradual digression. There were intervals when they ambled away an hour or two, and she gleaned from his insight. While he napped in the afternoons, she would make her way to the desk and quietly peruse the manuscripts haphazardly stacked on the floor.

Whenever the weather permitted, she would take him outdoors, holding his arm, and saunter along the shoreline. His words flowed more easily in the fresh air. Thomas had provided lounge chairs; on calmer days, they would sit in front of the cottage and watch the seagulls passing by. One clear evening, she wrapped him in a blanket and sat in the crisp air. Quite unexpectedly, he looked up into the sky and pointed a finger. "Look–there's Cedric... You see? To the bottom of that bright star... that's his head, and there's his paws." She whispered, "Yes. Yes, I see him."

One day, while sitting outside in the late autumn air, Roger shared the craft of making quills with her. To him, it was a dying art. He requested her to go to his desk and retrieve several quills along with a penknife from a drawer and proceeded to give his protégé a lesson in making pens, just as the ancient scribes had done. Years ago, he requested Mr. Filmore to visit a turkey farm in his coming and going and ask the farmer to save the feathers, eventually delivering a fine selection to Roger. The larger the feather, the better the quill. *Seagull feathers will do in a pinch. However, the turkey feather is supreme.* He then commenced with the process. Heating and flattening the point, he cut a slit at the tip while it was still hot. Adaline proved to be a good student, collecting seagull feathers and becoming an artisan of the craft. While sitting at Roger's desk during the quiet hours, she would often dip one of her newly made quills in an inkwell and practice lines. In time, more and more lines filled the paper.

....

Chapter 97

If Truth Be Told

The days invariably became colder as winter set in, shorter and more confining. Though tending to Roger and working at the trade center had consumed Adaline's hours, she finally found the opportunity to journey to the Inn and visit Pinky.

The boardwalk proved more delightful than she had imagined. Many of the cottages had colorfully painted doors with curtains draping the windows and picket fences bordering the yards. Friendly dogs barked as she passed by. She encountered new faces, amiable in their greetings. *Is it the same village I left behind so many years ago*? She knew she was now a stranger.

She paused in front of the cottage of Agnes and Gertrude–a *relic of the past*. Faith had mentioned Miss Agnes had passed away. And that, in recent years, Miss Gertrude had become the village grandmother, embraced by all the children. Faith went on to say Miss Gertrude would sit outside on sunny days. Adorned in one of her flowery dresses, she warmly greeted one and all and gave the children hand-crafted woollies. *Who would ever have imagined? The sinister hoods and black dresses were gone, old things passing away like a brooding storm.*

In spite of the cold, the journey was pleasant as she entertained herself with memories and taking in all the renovations. To her dismay, the grocer was hemmed in between two new buildings: a bank and a town hall. In front of the latter was a splendid monument of Cedric. The remnants of the pier came into focus, just as much a memorial to Cedric as the monument.

And then the Wayfarer Inn. An extension had been constructed replacing the old livery, a line of new cottages extending north toward the estuary. A new sign hung over the entrance. She found it peculiar that a *No Vacancy* sign was posted so late in the year. Glancing in the window, the tables were filled with animated guests.

A large painting of Pinky greeted her in the lobby. *Remarkable. Dear Mr. Pinky had finally received his claim to fame.* It was signed *R. Thomson* to the bottom right. Then, upon the beam, she saw the archives. Many marks had been added since her departure. *Which one was hers?*

The tavern had changed. White tablecloths and tasteful crockery adorned the tables, with a youthful staff tending to the guests. She slowly made her way through the maze of seated patrons, searching for Pinky, finally seeing him sitting in solitude in the shadows of a remote corner. Though aged, how could she not recognize him? A crutch was leaning against the wall, a tell-tale sign that his good leg and cane could no longer carry him along.

Pinky noticed the young woman weaving her way around the tables. She was quite different from the rest. Yet, there was something familiar in that tall, rather attractive figure with cropped auburn hair. Then, a broad smile, *'Tis Ad'line.* Struggling to his feet, there was a heart-felt embrace.

Standing apart, the smiles reflected. On closer scrutiny, she clearly saw the added years. More crow's feet were extending from the corners of his eyes with deeply etched lines traversing the well-traveled face, a scraggly crown of white hair framing the features. There was still that piercing insight in his one good eye. Though, missing a beat, she knew his hobbling days were not over. For nothing could keep him down as he would never succumb to the whims of old age.

Though not a striking beauty, she was well-tempered, and the added years had done her good. Her subtle features complemented that inner beauty which he held so dear. And those lucid green eyes still told the story. For a moment, he entertained the thought that, if a younger man, strapped with strength and sinew, he would have pursued such a woman.

Their reunion contained far more than could be contained within the visit. On and on they went, filling in many of the details within those vacuous years. In time, the diners departed, the staff cleared the tables and went their way, leaving them in the luxury of solitude that was once so familiar.

The conversation invariably turned to Cedric. Like an old scribe, Pinky was the only remaining soul who could give firsthand accounts of all the shipwrecks. He spoke of that last brutal storm and the sinking of the *HMS Wellington,* the precious little girl whom Cedric had brought to shore, and how he had found the wee lass lifeless on the beach, Cedric's footprints around her and trailing off into the surf. Pinky drifted... recollecting when he still had his bounce and vigor, how he had made his way to the end of the pier on pleasant afternoons and basked in the sun with ol' Cedie boy. There were many a wintry eve when Cedric would come to the tavern, always to be greeted with a large bowl of mutton stew. *Was me bes' cust'mer.* Throughout the evenings, they would continue their conversation, similar to what he and Ketch had in years past. However, whenever a storm was *a'com'n,* he would head for the door and give a soft whimper...

Pinky then mentioned that the new owners kept him on the payroll and had given him room and board. *B'nev'lent, 'ey 'ees.* More or less, his only duty was to make his presence known, going among the guests and occasionally pulling up a chair to tell a tale or two or share some of the finer nuances of his recipe. Just recently, he had been placed in a new light, fancying him to be the official tour guide of the Wayfarer Inn. As coincidence would have it, he was giving his first tour on the morrow. That was why the house was full, *Ta 'ear ol' Pinky.* Broadening his grin, he mentioned that the painting in the lobby was *'imself* though it went without saying.

The time was right to share something he had kept close to the hilt all these years. Leaning in... It was not long after she had left for Ireland. The hour was late, and the tavern was closing. Cedric was by his side, keeping him company. Two cantankerous drunkards, fishermen who had docked in the cove for the night, were lingering at a table. Having had too much to drink, they became boisterous. *Not scallywags. Rogues 'ey was.* Pinky confronted them, saying it was late and the tavern was closing. One of them staggered to his feet. Puffing out his chest, he sneered, *What 're yer goin' ta do 'bout it, ya ol' goat?*

Pinky held his ground, standing toe to toe, Cedric watching every move. The man then pulled out a knife and held it to Pinky's throat. Hissing, he sneered, *Goin' ta cut yer from ear to ear!* It was a large kukri knife used by the Gurkhas. *Cedric rose an' stood by me side, growl'n an' bare'n 'is teeth.* He then leaped at the man and clenched his wrist in his jaws, the knife sliding across the floor. *'Ee would 'ave done me in fer sure if it twer'n't fer ol' Cedie boy.* He kept hold of his wrist until *'ah called 'im off.* The other man rose and urged his friend to back off, nudging him toward the door. Huffing and puffing, they staggered out into the night. When all had calmed down, Pinky returned to his chair, he and Cedric humorously talking about it until late in the evening. He then said he could have taken them both on in the old days. Pinky became pensive... silent for a long moment. Something was weighing on his heart. Finally, he told her he had put a notch on that beam the next day. It was etched to the side of the others, next to *Mus Gertie's. Fer as sure as 'ah be talk'n to yer, ol' Cedie boy saved me life.*

Adaline had to leave. Before departing, she said, "My dear Mr. Chesslewick, I have often thought how the name fits you quite well. That is if you polish yourself up a bit. Most assuredly, Pinky is not your *nom du plume,* for I have never seen you with a quill in hand. So, we will assume that Cecil Chesslewick is your christened title. If ever there was such a thing."

She embraced him once more. *So different from Roger.* Pinky watched her leave. Taking hold of his crutch, he made his way to the door. The sky was heavy with winter clouds and the beach barren, yet the sea air always held its vitality.

....

Chapter 98

Notches to Tales

T he initial tour commenced on a dreary morn. Though late in the season, it surpassed the owners' highest expectations. It was advertised in London weeklies as "Tales & Tours of Sir Cedric." The rooms were full, with the livery stable housing some of the finest carriages throughout London.

Donned in their fashionable best, guests descended the stairs in the morning and filled the tables. The honorable Mr. Percival also made his presence known (making sure to wear his button spats). The hearth was ablaze as guests sipped their tea and ate crumpets, waiting for the arrival of their legendary tour guide. In time, Pinky, the crutch bracing one side, hobbled into position near the hearth. Though as present-able as could be expected, clipped and snipped, no varnish would ever polish him over. Straight out of the days of yore, his battered uniform looked more like an old Union Jack after the Battle of Waterloo, and the patch and stump, along with that imperceptible smile, invariably set one's mind to wander. As authentic as his clothes, Pinky was a far extremity of the social graces. His appearance alone was worth the price of admission.

There was a prolonged silence as he continued to greet his audience with that smile, offering them time to absorb him from top to bottom. Knowing his hour had come, he then puffed out his chest. For no one could tell a tale like Pinky. His voice was coarse but resonant. Society's best found the accent most peculiar, evincing a mix of every dialect throughout the Isles. Amidst this quandary, they simply smiled and bobbed their heads like buoys upon the sea, giving the impression that they understood his every jot and title. Even with a dire lack of comprehension, his presence alone was more than enough to entertain them.

Letting out the line, he began with the first shipwreck and the arrival of Cedric. Abbreviating the tales, he went on to tell the name of each vessel that had sunk and those rescued. Though quite peculiar and rather dramatic, he remained an anchor of truth, not wandering with his own imaginings. He then requested them to rise, put on their coats, and follow him onto the beach. Pausing in front of his portrait, Pinky poised himself like old King George, allowing them ample time to admire it. Moving on, he stopped by the beam. Pointing to the rows of notches, he remunerated each account. There were twenty-four marks in all–four rows of five, the last four to one side. Focusing on the isolated marks, he mentioned that Miss Gertrude had been saved during the blizzard of '40. The next was that of Captain Hawkins and the lifeboats (the *condensed notch*). Third was the *wee lass* rescued from the *HMS Wellington,* the last to be rescued by Cedric. And then the final mark... more adrift than the others. Leaning on his crutch and studying it, he muttered it had been etched in undue season, carved the night Cedric saved his life. Pinky drifted into silence and led them out the door.

A strong wind awaited them. The women immediately struggled to hold their broad-rimmed hats in place as they headed toward the beach. Pinky directed their attention to the remnants of the pier, *ol' Cedie boy's post*, noting that it had been destroyed in the same storm in which 'ee *ne'er returned.* Their attention was directed across the channel to the sandbanks where skeletal bowsprits and tilted masts still marked the tales. Following their guide up the beach, they all but stumbled over flotsam embedded in the sand, half-hidden treasures, each with its story to tell. Crutch and all, Pinky was heartier than the best of them. Pushing northward along the shoreline, he stopped where he and Jarvis had found many a shipwrecked soul soaked to the bone, Cedric faithfully by their side. Their guide pointed out how far Cedric had to swim from the pier to a shipwreck and the long struggle to bring survivors to shore. Planting his crutch in the sand and facing the wind, he looked north, showing where the Thames clashed with the sea.

The hour carried a penetrating cold; the assembly of Londoners huddled together like sheared sheep. The ladies, shivering and with soppy toes and grit in their stockings, were ready to retreat. The advertisement in the weeklies failed to mention to bring along appropriate attire. Pinky trudged back to the Inn with his followers in tow, humorously thinking of Napoleon's entourage retreating from Moscow during that brutal winter.

The hearth was stoked, and a robust fire awaited them. The pleasant staff immediately tended to the guests, helping them with their attire and serving hot toddies. Pinky, none the worse from wear and with a healthy blush, waited with that ever-present smile as they were primped and pampered.

There was one more story to tell–that of Captain Sumpter and the lovely Miss Rachel, which Pinky would now thoroughly expound upon. Though the tale of one shipwreck was as fascinating as the next, the sinking of the *HMS Ballantyne* always held a special place in his heart. He began by telling of the fateful battle in Kabul, recollecting the slaughter of an entire British attachment. That is, save for a young lieutenant. As destiny would have it, he would also be the only survivor of a fatal shipwreck off the coast and rescued by Cedric. He now gave his mind the liberty to wander with a romantic touch, telling of the damsel who painted his portrait. She was none other than the renowned Miss Rachel Thomson, whom they remembered from her illustrations in the *London Illustrated Times*. The same lovely artist did the drawings over the mantel during her younger years when living in Sheppey. As fate would have it, the officer was stranded in the village for several days.

Unbeknownst to anyone, the young couple fell in love, though ne'er a word was ever spoken, for it was a love silently deeply embedded within their hearts. Unfortunately, he was shipped to Afghanistan with another British attachment and killed in battle. After many years of painting in London, the renowned Miss Thomson has returned to Sheppey, her studio just over the hills. Pinky let it settle in. For, do we not all cherish tales of chivalry and love long lost?

Not to be contained, he began telling of the Battle of Salamanca. Sipping their toddies, they could all but hear the trumpets blowing and the sound of charging horses. Coarsely pouring out the drama, he concluded with the moment when, with one canon shot, he lost an eye and leg along with his dearly beloved horse. The wind had picked up outside. However, the patrons, coddled and comforted, remained enthralled.

Pinky went on to say how Cedric and Ketch always had a way of speaking to him–eye to eye. Many an afternoon ol' Cedie boy would come in from the pier and rest by the hearth. Then, on that final day, when the storm was bearing down hard, he gave that look and a soft whimper. Pinky knew that age had taken their toll on Cedric, and he no longer had the strength of his younger days. Yet, he realized *ol' Cedie boy* could not be contained. Following him to the door, he released him and, buttoning up, followed him to the pier. A heavy rain was falling, the sky sinister as Pinky watched Cedric struggle across the planks, waves crashing against it with all their fury. Always stalwart, he settled at the end of the pier. And then, "Me sees ah ship." It was leaning heavily to the lee side, its sails shredded. Cedric stood, focused and ready. "Raised me fist an' saluted 'im, one ol' soldier to 'nother." His words were broken. "Las' time ev'r laid me eye on 'im." When the storm had ebbed, Pinky made his way up the beach and found a little girl lying lifeless on the sand, Cedric's footprints all around her and trailing into the sea... Her flesh was soft. There was still life in her body. "Raised 'er up an' me an' Jarvis carried 'er to the Inn."

Could it have been the aftermath of the cold or the tally of his tales? For, there was ne'er a dry eye in the house and only the sound of the wind and sniffles. In the wake of this tender moment, Pinky passed his battered cap 'round. Purses opened, and hands reached into pockets. Soon, the clinking sound of pounds and crowns filled it to the brim. For when all was said and done, who could not help but love ol' Pinky and the tales he told?

....

Chapter 99

"'Tis good 'nough fer me."

Early morning, the sky and sea still merged in darkness. All the guests had departed the day before, and the tavern lay still, save for the hearth and the flicker of lanterns. Having a pot of tea, Pinky waited for the first light of day. Bertie's Bible was once again by his side.

He reflected on the tour and all the prestigious people who came to hear him. Yet it was but a side note in his life, nothing more than a cap full of coins and a tear or two. Looking out into the dark, he was lost in thought. In retrospect, the world had given him a path compacted with adventures during those youthful years. And he knew full well–peg leg, patch, and all–that any path he chose would have had its vitality. Though, at this present hour, he questioned it all. For life had become an empty pail, as bleak as the sea outside his window.

There was one incident that he could not shake off... something peculiar... and out of step with his rhyme and reason. Why had he made his way to the altar on that rainy morn? Was it the deep sorrow over the loss of Bertie and Cedric? Little Mus Winkie being taken away? Or just the vulnerability of age and the lonely road we all must travel? He had an uncanny feeling that something had nudged him to the altar, one of those rare incidents too strange to put into words. During that moment, bent and hobbled, he found hope, a glimmer of light entering

342

the darkness of his soul. Just as mysterious was that it was now begin-ning to make sense.

Light gently spanned the horizon, pale blues, and lavenders spreading upon the morning sky. The lone eastern star, the last to float into the depths of a fading night, seemed to carry a special meaning. Pinky looked down at the Bible and tapped his fingers on the table. Never having a propensity for reading, he found it especially rigid and uninviting. If truth be told, he could tell just as tall a tale as that of a floating ark sailing upon the stormy seas with every kind of critter or a seafaring man finding himself in the belly of a whale for three days. He gave the Bible a long look and respectfully pushed it aside.

His thoughts settled on Napoleon. Pinky considered it an honor to have fought against him. He remembered what the professor had said that evening about the emperor being alone in exile and beginning to read the Bible. After much consideration, Bonaparte concluded that Jesus Christ was the greatest man who ever lived. Again tapping his fingers... Putting on a pair of battered wire-rimmed glasses, he finally opened Bertie's Bible and, turning to the first page, began to read: *In the beginning, God created the heaven and the earth. And the earth was without form and void, and darkness was upon the face of the deep. And the Spirit of God moved upon the face of the waters. And God said, let there be light, and there was light.* Pinky looked out the window as a new day ascended above the channel. Nodding his head, he mused, "'Tis true. An' if 'twer good 'nough fer Bertie, 'tis good 'nough fer me."

....

"Now, in a frail craft upon the storm-tossed flood, doth this my life draw nigh to the port we all must go."

Michelangelo

....

Chapter 100

𝕿𝖍𝖊𝖓 𝕿𝖍𝖊𝖗𝖊 𝖂𝖆𝖘 𝕺𝖓𝖊...

T hough Roger lived a long life, surpassing the good pastor, Mildred, Jarvis, Bertie, Agnes, and even Gertrude, he would not outlive Pinky. In the winter of 1866, the professor, withered and gaunt, lay upon his bed breathing his last. And so, the question arises: *Where does this journey lead after death?* The cottage was silent; the moment drew nigh… Adaline held his hand, Roger no longer struggling with such physical gestures. With his last fading breath, he opened his eyes and whispered, "God..."

Roger Osborne was laid to rest in the church cemetery. Adaline stood by his grave as Pastor Thomas spoke a few words of hope. As good fortune would have it, he had bequeathed everything to his young protégé. Roger's cottage was now hers and everything therein: the window by the sea, the desk, and a good sum of money. Adaline Brennan had a place to call home and financial liberty for the first time.

She also inherited his wealth of pens and quills. Sorting through the collection, she was especially fond of a contemporary steel-pointed rosewood pen. Dipping it into an inkwell, she practiced several lines of verse. *A true pearl.* And she had his library with its assortment of well-chosen literature to now peruse at her leisure. Within the orderly rows was an old Bible, heavy and quite large. While thumbing through its pages one morning, she noticed he had placed notations in the borders. Some were dated. Ironically, it seemed as if the dates were marked after their meeting in the tavern. *Let's see, twenty years ago...?* There was a scribbled note to the side of a verse at the end of Romans that especially caught her eye: *O the depth of the riches both of the wisdom and knowledge of God! How unsearchable are his judgments and his ways past finding out!* To the side was penned, *1843/Adaline.* She then recollected how she had enthusiastically spoken to him about the rich treasures of God. *How remarkable. That a young, uneducated girl could have influenced such a brilliant mind!* Looking out the window, it was another windswept day, the gulls flying recklessly over the whitecaps as the cold seeped through the window pane.

The hours passed pleasantly at Roger's desk. Crowned in solitude and the pristine silence, she finally had the luxury to go through the volumes of manuscripts cluttered around his desk and the reams piled on the floor. Page after page revealed his mastery of the English language and his unique perspective on life. The deeper she delved, the more she realized it should be shared with mankind. *How curious, never publishing a book. Was he writing just for the sake of writing?* As she went through the stacks, not a page was carelessly passed by. One might consider it tedious and overwhelming, but it was a treasure to her. And then it appeared–a pile of papers titled *Cedric*!

She devoured the manuscript throughout the day, marveling at how Roger had brought Cedric to life. The heroics were all well documented, including the names of the vessels and survivors. Everything was written with a touch of prose and personal insight. Then, a chapter titled *The Shipwreck of the Libertine*. Sitting back, she took her time, cherishing his words about a young Irish girl who had been stranded in the village.

To her dismay, the last chapter was the sinking of the *Prince George*. *Dated 1850–several years after her departure.* The final pages were illegible, the lines crimped. Searching through the stack, then another. *Nothing. Had his pen been retired for these many years?* A classic masterpiece with no ending. *Who really knew the stories within each shipwreck after the Prince George?* And then Adaline had her epiphany. *Pinky!* She remembered that day he had shown her those marks upon the beam and vividly shared with her each tale.

During those dreary days of winter, Adaline made her way north to sit at the feet of the great sage. Though the storms had ebbed in recent years, the bitter cold remained. All lay still, as if frozen, save for the smoke emanating from the chimneys. Head down, she continued north, fending against the wind.

After three scores and ten years, Pinky's good leg finally gave way, the crutch barely able to keep him stable. There would be occasions, though, when he struggled to the door to breathe in the fresh air.

It took little persuasion from his endearing friend for him to open the scrolls and delve into those final notches. Awkwardly making his way to the beam, Adaline pulled up a chair for him. There seemed to be an inexplicable joy as he slowly backed into those years, sharing the depths within each story. It was all there, vividly captured in his mind. She marveled at how he brought them to remembrance with his back to the notches. All the while, she filled page after page and kept on writing. Adaline continued to visit him throughout the winter and early spring days.

With a wealth of information, Miss Adaline Brennan was ready to bring the story of Cedric to its conclusion. At times, she wondered if Roger knew this all along. Though of different thought and style and honed within their varied worlds, she was now confident in penning her own words, threading them into the final chapters.

Picking up the rosewood pen, she dipped it into a well of ink and commenced, the gulls sailing over a placid sea and carrying their note of encouragement.

....

"And, departing, leave behind us,
Footprints on the sands of time;
Footprints, that perhaps another,
Sailing o'er life's solemn main,
A forlorn and shipwrecked brother,
Seeing, shall take heart again."
Henry Wadsworth Longfellow

Epilogue

![decorative flourish]

L et's return to the painting, *Bob, a Distinguished Member of the Humane Society*. It was completed in 1831 by the renowned English artist Sir Edwin Landseer. As you know, Bob was a Newfoundland dog, and, truth be told, he did indeed survive a shipwreck, spending the remainder of his years on a dock in a small village by the Thames River. Bob would go on to rescue twenty-three souls from other shipwrecks and became an honorary member of the village's humane society.

Bob had since passed away when Landseer was commissioned to do the painting. Not having an image to go by, the artist selected another Newfoundland as his model. The markings may not be true to form, but the brushstrokes are masterful, and the viewer all but delves into the heart of this remarkable creature. What was Landseer thinking when he did this painting? After all, artists spend countless hours of solitude behind an easel. Did we truly begin to have a sense for this remarkable dog as he brought him to life, musing upon his heroics? Like the artist, the viewer's soul is given the liberty to wander in this painting. For art has its tendency to offer incomplete statements and, in our own unique way, we begin filling in the blanks. Thus, a picture becomes part of our creative process. And is this not part of the beauty of art?

Sir Edwin Landseer lived during the Victorian era. He was a favorite of Queen Victoria, doing numerous portrayals of her animals within her court. He was knighted in 1850 (not with a hug but a sword). The painting *Bob, a Distinguished Member of the Humane Society,* still hangs in the Tate Museum.

As with a brush and paint, pen and words also give the reader an opportunity to imagine and wander; whether brushed or penned, there is invariably a fine line separating reality from our imaginings. The tale of *Cedric* has been woven within threads of fact and then proceeds with the writer's whims. Such a journey oft makes for a pleasant venture indeed. May your thoughts meander upon a good path. Follow the flight of the gulls.

Barry Stebbing and his wife live on a farm in North Carolina. A teacher, artist, and writer, he graduated from Salisbury University and did graduate painting studies in Tuscany. He enjoys morning campfires, journaling, chess, and hiking. For more information about the author visit: www. howgreatthouart.com

ISBN: 978-1-66288-916-5
How Great Thou ART Publications
P.O. Box 48 McFarlan, NC 28102
www.howgreatthouart.com

Printed in the USA
CPSIA information can be obtained
at www.ICGtesting.com
LVHW010726140124
768654LV00014B/818